Massacre at Point of Rocks

Doug Hocking

Buckland Abbey, L.L.C.

ISBN: 978-0-9907619-0-7
LCCN: 2013934623

To Marion Rutherford Hocking who, haunted by her scholarly ancestors, pushed me to write.

To Debbie who put up with it all.

And to Nosman Vigil, Jicarilla Apache artist, who painted the warrior on the cover and who despite all odds, never stopped trying.

And to Roque, Peregrino Rojo and San Miguel.

"Long ago it happened at Point of Rocks at that very place . . ."

Traditional Jicarilla Apache beginning to a story based in history

Chapter 1

Going West on the Santa Fe Trail

The affair ended in blood and icy death for Indian and white alike. How strange that chance meetings and hasty words of no more weight than seeds of *chamisa* dusting the fall breeze should bring so many to calamity. Bad acts and actors abounded. Small things, done by people meaning well enough, led to disaster for everyone, but through it all, a boy grew and moved toward manhood.

He was tall for his age and broad shouldered, nearly a man and working his first real job. Insulated by school and native intelligence, he used his wits to escape the lessons apprenticed boys and laborers learned early working with men. Possessing the body of an adult he had not yet fully matured as many younger than he had already done. Still expecting men to be the bold, perfect heroes in his books, he was disappointed by the imperfections of real men. The

West was the land of his heroes. He would find a man to look up to on the Frontier. He was called Danny Trelawney, or more often by the men of the slow moving caravan, *Danito*. They trudged, their wagons four abreast, through dust and sweat following the long, dry road to Santa Fe, which stood in imagination and dreams a gleaming citadel of wealth and exotic sight, sounds, and smells. Santa Fe was where men made their fortunes. Danito thought of it as the home of Kit Carson and a place where folks met wild Indians.

He walked behind an ox team, whip in hand and cracking it now and then above a beast's back as warning to keep moving. He was lucky to have this job occasioned by a man's demise. The sickness was a mystery to those in the caravan. Fortunately, it took no one else, but death on the trail was all too common. The men who ran the *ramuda*, the horse and mule herd, were all New Mexicans, so the boy wouldn't fit there. The cooks were Cajuns and Quebec French speaking a language few but they could understand. The boy replaced the one who had died walking beside an ox team.

"I used to sit and listen for hours to the mariner's stories of their travels and of the clever trading they had done in foreign ports," Danny said to the man driving oxen to his right across the wagon-tongue. His voice hinted of having breathed New England air. "Greenport, Out East, on Long Island, was a small port, but still mariners came from all over. They escaped the import duties that way."

"Aye," responded the bearded man, Danny's friend and mentor to the trail, "like we do by running mule trains into Taos. No Santa Fe officials in Taos."

"Ever since the Mexican War," he went on, "I've wanted to come West and trade with Indians. I read the Pathfinder's books and wanted to see where Kit Carson lived. Mr. Carson seems so much larger than life, so brave, a real hero."

The bearded man, dressed in a motley mix of heavy cotton and buckskin, spluttered, spitting dust, "Pathfinder? You mean Fremont? His didn't find no paths. Went the way ever'body did, but he wroted about it. Tha's all. Talk less boy, and you'll eat less dust."

Danito didn't take this well meant advice and continued his monologue. "My mother died long ago, and my father passed on this last winter. My brother was kind and shared a small inheritance with me. It was enough to buy an outfit with something left to purchase a few trade goods. I left knowing I might never see my brother again. I headed West."

He was quiet for a while. They trudged across the plains day on day, walking beside tall Conestoga wagons packed with trade-goods to the bows that supported the greyed canvas covers. Danny searched a veiled horizon where the green ocean of grass met the blue sea of sky in a haze of rusty dust.

Then Danny broke the brief silence, again. "I can't wait 'til we get to Santa Fe. Do you think I might really meet Kit Carson?"

"We'll be there soon enough, boy," said Joe Cassidy who'd taught Danny bull-whackin.' "One day you'll look up and the Shining Mountains will be there, a real horizon." He smiled through the bird's nest that surrounded his mouth. It was stained at the corner with tobacco juice. His straw hat, worn low shading his deep-set eyes, was a begrimed mural of hard work and harder travel, unraveling from long use.

Danny cracked his long whip in air above the lead ox's back to hurry him along. "That's right, boy," Joe applauded.

"Never let the whip touch him. The pop is enough. Now hush and eat less sand."

Nights and mornings Joe willingly taught Danny Trelawney about oxen, mules, and wagons. Conestoga wagons had high sides made higher by rail extensions.

"Built high and tight," he said. "High at stern and prow like a ship and narrower at the bottom than the top. Makes fer easier crossin' of streams. We packs 'em all the way to the top and covers 'em with canvas. There's no room to sit ner sleep. Every bit of space is worth money."

They slept under the wagons, and when the rain blew, they were cold and wet. Danny choked on dust and the smell of mules, oxen, and their waste. He walked through the powder and stink of wagons and animals ahead of his.

"Joe," he asked, "why do we travel four abreast and all bunched up like this? If we spread out or even travel in a line, there wouldn't be so much dust and stink to wade through." His mouth was dry as salt, and his teeth were full of grit.

"You'll know, boy," said the teamster, "soon as we see some Injuns. Look on the bright side; eatin' sand don't make you fat." He spat a wad of something brown that could have been tobacco juice or mud.

Morning began before daylight in early July on the broad plains. Danny gulped a cup of coffee, swallowed some stale bread, and then hitched his team to the tall wagon. Shortly word came to move out, and the wagons set out four abreast while the *ramuda*, the herd of spare animals, followed behind eating dust. Danny tried to start a conversation, but this early Joe was having none of it and pretended not to hear. In the twilight, voices drifted through the dust cursing and cajoling teams in Cajun and Quebec French. At mid-morning, the caravan halted in square formation as the order came down to unhitch the teams and bring them to safety among the wagons.

"Are we going to be attacked?" asked Danny.

"Not likely," replied Joe. "Most likely practice, but the Skimmer doesn't tell 'til it's done to keep us sharp."

Traveling four-abreast, it was relatively simple to bring the caravan into a square, giving the train an instant defensive formation against Indians and Texas raiders. Rifles were always close at hand as they traveled, and Danny, as he'd been taught, checked his before taking breakfast during the hour-long halt to rest the teams.

At breakfast, Danny asked Joe, "There isn't really danger from Texans, is there?"

"Hard to say with them Texians," said Joe. "They haven't raided since the war, but they claim New Mexico is theirs all the way to the Rio Grandy, that Santy Anna give it to them at San Jacinto. They figure they got the right to collect taxes and tariffs, to git their proper share o' the Santa Fe trade."

Irrepressible, the boy went on. "Do the Indians really ride in circles around the wagon train while we shoot at them? Seems pretty silly to me. They say it's because they're showing off their bravery instead of attacking like normal people."

When Danny paused for breath, Joe cut in. "Not silly a'tall. They're hopin' for a bunch o' tenderfeets who kain't hit a movin' target. Once the tenderfeets fire off all their guns, the Injuns move in whilst they're reloadin.' Smart, danged smart if you ast me."

A mountain man traveled with the caravan as scout,

guide, and advisor to Captain F.X. Aubry, known widely as the Skimmer of the Plains. Danny thought the mountain man looked ancient, though Tom Trask was not above fifty years of age. His beard was gray. The sun-cured leather of cheeks, forehead, and around his eyes made him look older. Danny thought Tom Trask looked more like an Indian than anyone he in his limited experience had ever seen. Tom wore moccasins and fringed buckskin adorned with broad strips of beadwork. Though the skins were caked with dirt and grease of many long miles, the fancy adornment marked him among the tribes and other men of the mountains as a man to be respected, one of wealth and position, or at least one having a very industrious squaw, which suggested wealth and position in any event.

Trask spent his time out ahead of the train searching for good grass and water. A caravan too close ahead might have used up both, forcing the wagon train to veer off the route in search of other supplies. Much of the way they followed the Arkansas River, but there were many small and not so small diversions. Tom also watched for Indians and for buffalo, which if encountered in large numbers, might attract Indians but also would mean fresh meat for a few meals. On the Southern Plains, bison were seldom so thick as to force the train to diverge from its course. And Texas pirates, it had been a few years since they'd attacked a wagon train, but they might show up at any time with official papers indicating they were to collect Texas taxes. Water and grass were Trask's greatest concerns. Vagaries of weather could leave water holes barren and grass brown.

Tom Trask had met Daniel Trelawney in Independence, Missouri, where the Santa Fe Trail began. The boy went there seeking passage west in the spring of 1849.

"Sir," he had said walking up to the mountain man on the street. His outlandish dress was a beacon to a young man headed west. "You look like you might know the way to the Shining Mountains. I want to travel to Santa Fe."

Someone would soon capture the idea in the words of a song. "I see by your outfit that you are a cowboy . . ." It was the age of muscle power for both man and beast. Men's muscles grew into the work. Sailors had bulging forearms from pulling ropes, cowboys were lean, and blacksmiths had powerful shoulders. Likewise, a man with only one suit of clothes, or at best two, protected his clothing and wore accoutrements suited to his trade: leather aprons, long or short, chaps to fend off *chaparral*, or sleeve garters to protect cuffs from ink. One really could tell by a man's outfit the line of work he pursued. Trousers with riveted pockets would soon come into vogue with prospectors in California, but word of the wealth that could be picked up off the ground was just arriving in the east.

Trask, with his pale blue, sun-squinted eyes, had looked the boy up and down. "Now ain't you a sight? But I guess you'll do. You're in luck. My friend Captain Aubry is puttin' together a caravan and needs bullwhackers. Ever whacked a bull, boy?" He cocked his head to one side quizzically. "More likely he'll put you to doing doin' odd jobs about the camp, but we need someone for thet, too."

"Why no, sir," Danny replied, having no idea what Trask was talking about.

"Not to worry. You're young, and you can learn. Don't call me sir. Name's Tom. And we don't take on passengers. Everyone who travels with us has to work. You can work, kain't you?"

"Yes, sir, um, Tom, I can. I'm Danny Trelawney," he said, beginning a friendship that would endure, despite the inequality of master and pupil.

Danny accepted the mountain man as teacher. Teachers didn't have to be heroes or heroic. Trask was the scout. It never occurred to Danny that Tom Trask was one of those giants he'd read about, one of those mountain men and trailblazers who'd braved mountains, Indians, grizzlies and unknown land to open the West for others, like Fremont, to follow. It didn't occur to him to measure Tom against the gage used for heroes.

"You haven't got any guns or a knife yet, Danito?" Tom asked. When the boy shook his head, Trask said, "Come with me, and we'll get you set up. You've got money, haven't you? You said you wanted to pay for passage."

At the gunsmith's shop, Tom showed Danito a rifle. "This here's a Hawken," he said. "In the mountains when we say a thing is 'hawken,' means it's the best of its kind. This is the rifle you need. Uses percussion caps, not flint. They're more reliable, and you don't have to fret the weather as much.

"You got enough money?" he continued, and the boy nodded. "Get you a pair of Colt's revolvers. They fire six shots each. In a fight with Indians, you ain't got time to reload the rifle. You'll need those shots.

"And a good Green River knife," Tom went on. "It's your best tool and most reliable friend. Keep it on you always."

Danito bought them all with the money from his small inheritance. His brother had converted Danny's share of the family business to cash, although this conversion would mean tough times for the company until sales made up the difference. Danito didn't dare tell Tom he already had a knife. A smith had made it for him, huge and sharp with knuckle-guarded grip. "Just like the one Jim Bowie carried," the smith had said. Danny Trelawney lacked the courage to wear it in public as yet.

"Danito," Tom continued, "you'll need a possibles bag. Like the knife, you'll keep it with you always. Keep your bullets, caps, and tools in it, everything you need to shoot and survive." Rifle, knife, possibles bag, powder flask, and Colts were part of the outfit Tom always wore; Danny never saw him without them.

Later that day, Tom introduced Danito to Captain Francis Xavier Aubry who hired Danny as a laborer. Aubry, known as FX to his friends, was in charge of the wagon train. Riding his fine horse out in front of the caravan, he darted back and forth attending problems. Captain Aubry would lead them across the plains to Santa Fe, making and enforcing decisions that would affect the lives of everyone in the caravan. Aubry, in turn, introduced Danny to Joe Cassidy, a teamster who would teach him about wagons and introduce him to the ways of mules and oxen.

"The Conestoga is a work of beauty, boy," Joe taught. "Built tight of aged oak. That's important. Green wood shrinks and cracks and falls apart. On'y a shame, mos' stays in Mexico and never comes back. The Mexicans treasure the wood and wheels—ain't got no tools nor iron to make they's own, and we don't have more than a few wagons to drag back. Mostly the return trip is herds of mules, a few Rio Grandy blankets and hides, and money."

"I've heard of Missouri mules, sir," interjected Danny.

"Missoura!" the teamster snorted. "Missoura mules is native to Mexico." Then he continued. "And those little wagons," he pointed, "are Dearborns. They're not much more than a board-floor with four wheels. Merchants like 'em 'cause of that spring-seat. They ride. You 'n' me'll walk mos' the way. The fancy canvas cover makes 'em look like a box on wheels. They're tough enough. Seen 'em hold up to things ought to tear them apart."

As they neared the *ramuda*, Joe started a lesson about the animals. "Mule is faster than an ox, but an ox can pull a much heavier load." He liked to talk in camp, around the fire, while out hunting, but he didn't like to open his mouth while walking along with a team of oxen in dust so thick you'd put knots on your head running into it. He made a good teacher for the boy who learned fast in any event. Joe was a better choice for Danny than others might have been. Most working men don't talk about their work; they demonstrated and the apprentice observed. They lacked the words and the understanding of how to use them to describe difficult tasks. So the apprentice worked at cleanup and observed, and learning took years. The teamster taught the boy in much the way he'd learned from his tutors, but he also taught lessons that could only be observed, much of it over the doubletree hitched to a team of mules, watching the boy from the far side of a wagon.

"A singletree hitches to a horse collar. It rides behind the animal," Joe taught, "where it can be hooked to a doubletree with another animal or to a wagon tongue." During the day, Danny watched Joe across the doubletree where he walked on the far side of the wagon plying his skillful whip. "Oxbow works much the same, on'y it ties two beasts together.

Singletree and oxbow let the animal pull with his shoulders where he's most powerful. Wait 'til you get to New Mexico and see oxes hooked to the tongue tied by their horns. Pulls their head back. and they draw the load with their neck and can't pull half as much."

They walked beside their teams across short-grass prairie to the Council Grove and then turned south and struck out for the Arkansas River, following it west across land growing ever drier. The river supplied their need for water as long as the caravan followed its course. In places, the trail was deeply marked with the ruts of passing wagons. In others, the signs of passage were faint.

"Joe, why is it some places there's deep ruts from the wagons and others there's no sign at all?" Danny asked.

"The trail is miles wide," Joe said. "Captains travel where the grass is good and not yet eaten by the caravans ahead if they can. But some places they has to come in close to get pas' one obstacle or another."

They camped early in the evening letting the stock graze. Many evenings when dark came, the teamsters brought the animals inside the square of wagons.

"Critter's gotta eat or they gits weak," said Joe. "Graze 'em all night when we kin. But when there's Injuns near, gotta bring 'em in. Makes it harder for Injuns to steal. Not that they likes mules and oxes very much. They likes horses. Steal 'em to ride. Hickory Apache even steal 'em to eat."

"Hickory Apache? Who are they?" the boy asked. "They sound tough. Do they eat hickory nuts or are they just hard as hickory wood?"

Passing by, Captain Aubry overheard and said in his soft, French-muted voice, "He means Jicarilla Apache.

J-I-C-A-R-I-L-L-A is how the Mexicans spell it, but they pronounce it like hickory." Smiling, he moved on.

"Tha's right," said Joe who Danny suspected couldn't spell in English or Spanish. "They's plains Apache, lives in tepees and hunts buffalo. We'll see 'em e'rywhere from Point of Rocks to Taos."

Antelope and buffalo made an appearance as the train moved west. The buffalo were in small herds of not more than 100 animals.

"The big herds you've heard about are farther west," Tom told the boy, "and further north. There's Indians all around them big herds. Even so, we have to start being careful. We'll put out our fires at dusk and sit facing out into the dark. Look into a fire, and you won't see nothin' in the night for hours.

"Seems all the tribes follow the big herds," the mountain man continued. "Jicarilla Apache, Arapaho, Comanche, even the Utahs come down from their Shining Mountains to hunt. The captain plans to go south over the Cimarron Cutoff, I think, so we won't get far into the buffalo plains of the Cheyenne. The Cheyenne are a prissy lot, fussy as women and showy in their dress. They trade at Bent's on the Mountain Branch of the Trail, a big adobe that looks like a castle. Fort William is run by William Bent who's married to a Cheyenne woman."

These were things that quickened Trask's blood. Usually he didn't string so many words together. Danny thought he might have a Cheyenne woman up at "Bent's Big Lodge," as Tom and Joe sometimes called it. Bent's wife, Danny learned, refused to live in the fort. She kept a tepee outside.

"Might be more comfortable that way," Trask commented.

"Tom," said Danny, "I've heard of Northern and Southern Cheyenne. What's the difference?"

Tom thought a moment. "In 1832 or '33 when Bent built his big lodge, he invited a band of Cheyenne to come south to the Arkansas to trade with him. They became the Southern Cheyenne. While their northern cousins still wear elk and buffalo hide, the southerners are partial to cotton and wool, in nice bright colors. Arapaho are Cheyenne, too. I've heard their stories. They broke away a bit further back."

Since the first day out, Joe Cassidy had been taking Danny out at end of day to practice shooting. Powder and shot cost money. Many of those who went west could not afford to practice. Danny was fortunate in having his inheritance, besides which both he and Joe deemed this an important part of his education.

"Boy," said Joe, "Never-ever cap yer rifle first. Always last. Same goes for yer pistol. If the hammer fell whilst you were loadin', you'd lose somethin' sure. Pro'ly yer head. Turn yer flask upside down with yer finger over the top of the spout, then open the gate with yer thumb. Close the gate. You've captured the right load of powder. Now pour it 'to the muzzle. Fetch a patch and ball and lay it over the muzzle, pushin' the ball in it, and ram it down the barrel. Lift her up and half-cock the hammer fittin' a cap on the nipple. Yer ready to fire."

He taught the boy to aim and squeeze the trigger and, if in a hurry, to bring the moving sites across the target, squeezing off a shot as it passed over the target.

"Aim at somethin' small," taught Joe, "not at the whole animal. Aim where the heart is. That way you won't miss. Aim at a spot the size of a dollar. Keep it small."

The teamster taught Danny to walk until he could almost see over the top of a hill and then to crawl the rest of the way so as not to expose himself, skylining Joe called it.

"Always see wa's on the fer side befer it sees you," said Joe. "Whether it's animal or Injun, you want to see it first so you can get a shot off first or run like hell."

One day Tom Trask rode into camp with the announcement there were buffalo ahead. A hunting party that included the boy was formed. Together, they moved out to the last hill before where Tom had seen the animals, dismounted, and staked their horses and mules. They edged up the hill. Danny's eyes grew large. Before him below the hill were the great shaggy bison, called buffalo by Westerners, the first he'd ever seen. About 30 of the beasts grazed quietly in the valley beyond.

"Squat here," said Tom quietly indicating a place on the hilltop. Danny sat. "We'll each fire a shot. Me first."

Tom fired and a buffalo slumped forward onto the ground. Nothing else happened. The next hunter in line fired, and another buffalo fell. Finally, it was Danny's turn. He was nervous and excited, but he had been taught well and managed to control himself. His shot hit true.

"That's enough," pronounced Tom. The buffalo ran as the hunters approached. Tom took Danny to the buffalo the mountain man had felled. "I'll show you how to butcher him."

Tom dismembered a foreleg and set it aside. He then reached into the creature's mouth and cut out its tongue, setting it on the grass beside the leg. Next, he made a cut all along the buffalo's back from head to tail.

"Give me a hand here," he said and the pair proceeded

to pull the bloody hide down from the hump to the ground. "This here behind the head is the bass," said Trask. "Good eatin' but you got to boil it." He handed the fatty ball to Danny. "And this is the fleece," he went on peeling fatty meat from the ribs. "Nice and tender, juicy and sweet."

He picked up the foreleg and struck the hump ribs where they protruded upward from the back. "Hump ribs," said Trask, "also very good."

Making a cut he reached into the body cavity and produced the liver. Trask bit into it, blood dripping from liver, mouth, and hands, and with his knife cut free the piece in his mouth.

"Your turn," Trask mumbled through the gob of liver. "Try it with a little gunpowder for flavoring, if you like."

Danny did as directed although he'd never learned to eat raw meat. Blood dripped from his chin.

Trask grinned. "Best while it's still hot." Trask pondered something for a moment and then said, "You'll do, Danny, you'll do. We'll make a mountain man of you yet, despite yourself."

In camp at night, they cooked, ate, and talked. Captain Aubry always sat on bags of beans, flour, or anything else that put him up high, sometimes throwing his saddle over a bag and sitting on it.

Danny whispered to Joe, "I can't see how the Captain would be comfortable like that after riding all day."

"Captain loves his saddle," said Joe. "Don't you, FX?" FX was what his friends and trusted employees called the captain.

"Why, Danito," said Tom, "they call FX *Skimmer of the Plains*."

"That's right!" Joe pressed on warming to the story. "He's a hero. Las' year he rode from Santa Fe to Independence, that's 950 miles, boy, in five days. Ate and slept in the saddle. Neva stopped a minute 'cept to change hosses.'"

"Never took any rest," the mountain man picked up the tale. "He rode three horses to death. He had 'em staked all along the trail. At one place, he found the hostler scalped and the horses stole by Indians, but he didn't stop. Kept riding 'til the horse died under him. Stripped off the saddle and bridle and ran twenty miles to the next place a horse was waitin'."

"You shoulda seed him," said teamster Joe. "When he got to Independence, couldn't talk, couldn't stand. We had to lif' him down off'n the hoss and carry him inside. There was blood all over the saddle. Yup, he surely loves his saddle."

"Why'd you do it, Captain Aubry?" Danny asked.

Aubry smiled. He was a small, handsome man, almost a foot shorter than Danny, a dapper dresser in the Mexican style. He wore a black on black embroidered vest over a white shirt with a red cummerbund that Danny had learned concealed a knife and pistol. His trousers had silver *conchos* made from Mexican dollars up the outer seam buttoned down to the knee and open below to reveal rawhide *botas* that, like chaps, protected his shin. In the New Mexican style, his feet were clad with moccasins. About his hips was strapped a belted holster carrying a Colt .44. During the heat of the day, a broad-brimmed straw hat with a flat crown covered his head. His eyes could stare right through a man. He had to have real determination and will to get much larger men to do his bidding.

Captain Aubry seemed to consider his answer. "Well, I

done it in nine days a few months before that and figured out how to do it in five and a half. I said so, and a fella bet me $1,000 I couldn't. I was pretty sure I could, and I couldn't let him insult me like that."

"But five days!" Danny exploded.

"Five and a half," Aubry corrected. "I was pretty drunk," he continued, "and I wanted to get to Independence before the hangover set in. Almost made it, too."

The group chuckled, and Danny thought about how a sense of humor and a fair and even hand were part of Captain Aubry's makeup. Most leaders were tall and could intimidate their men. Aubry had to rely on other talents. Danny noticed how Captain Aubry cultivated his reputation and legend. That helped, too, the boy thought.

Even told these stories, it never occurred to Danny that Captain Aubry was a giant, well known to all those who traveled the Santa Fe Trail. He'd pioneered new cutoffs and new trails to California and, of course, set speed records for the trip back to Missouri. To Danny, Aubry didn't look like a hero, a man opening the frontier West. He was just a man good at his job. He wasn't the kind of hero that appeared in books.

"Captain's famous," said grizzled mountaineer Tom Trask, "for leading caravan's, too. He moves fast and safe."

"What about you, Daniel?" asked Captain Aubry. "What brought you west?"

"My family set me up for a scholar," the boy replied. "I spent a lot of time in school, reading books, avoiding work, but I really didn't have the aptitude for it. I didn't care for digging out tiny, niggling details. I love solving problems, but once I find the solution, I lose interest. I wanted action and adventure, not moldy tomes of forgotten lore.

"It was bad times. Last winter a fever came into the Greenport harbor with the fleet. It took my father. My mother died when I was very young. Without my father's income I couldn't continue in school. My brother asked me to help run the family business. Father left us his ship's chandler's store. Even with both of us working, we didn't do so well as father had."

"What's a candler?" asked Joe. "You make candles?"

"A chandler," Danny replied, "supplies ships with most of their needs for sea. I had no wish to spend my life endlessly counting brass fittings and lengths of rope, haggling over casks of salt meat. My brother kindly paid me for my share of the inheritance.

"Reading about the Mexican War got me interested in New Mexico. I read about the Santa Fe trade in *Commerce of the Prairies* and then discovered the Pathfinder's books. I wanted to go where John Fremont and his scout, Kit Carson, had been."

"I hunted beaver with Kit for a season," murmured Tom. "He's good people."

"Really? What's he like?" the boy asked.

Aubry cut in. "He's big, Danny, broad-shouldered, and hard-muscled as stone. He's got a voice booms like thunder and piercing eyes can look right through you. But mostly he's big, tall as a tree."

Joe and Tom were looking away, hiding something. They looked fit to burst. Captain Aubry didn't say anything more. Danny looked at him sitting in his saddle, one of the great captains, famous across the west.

"The saddle suits him," Danny thought. "He's no bigger than a jockey, but put him up on a horse and men follow him all the same. He isn't a big, broad-shouldered man that men are forced to respect, like Kit Carson."

Kit Carson was one of the heroes of the Mexican War. A great deal had been written about him, and Danny Trelawney had gathered in all he could find and borrow. Some of what he read bordered on the fantastic describing an American Odysseus. Kit Carson was a member of a pantheon that included Davy Crockett, Jim Bowie, and Hawkeye of the Leatherstocking Tales. Some of the stories were obvious exaggerations, but others like those of Pathfinder John Charles Fremont claimed to be relaying the truth.

"Tomorrow," announced Captain Aubry, "we ford the river."

They would be taking the Cimarron Cutoff across the dry *Llano Estacado*, the Staked Plains. The Mountain Branch was difficult for wagons and less used. Those who weren't headed for Bent's Fort avoided it. Upon a time, before the American invasion, traders went by pack mule to Taos to avoid paying Santa Fe's customs, just as those who went to Santa Fe were avoiding Mexican customs. Mexican customs duty was as high as $500 per wagon. That was in local Mexican dollars, which were worth only a fifth of an American dollar, but it was a lot of money. Still, it was a lot less than the government in Mexico City collected at the ports. Distant, remote Santa Fe ignored Mexico City.

"The cutoff is a risk, Danito," Tom told the boy. "There've been rumors of Comanches raiding down that way. The Staked Plains are dry, and the grass is poor, but it will save us a few hundred miles and some time if we have a little luck."

The Arkansas was shallow and bottom firm. In a few

hours, the entire caravan had crossed without loss of any kind.

"We'll need some luck," put in Aubry. "The California gold seekers, the ones they're calling Forty-niners, have got no discipline at all. Usually, I know how recently a caravan has passed, and I can guess how long the grass has had to come up again. We captains time the caravans' departures from Independence allowing for the grass. But these gold hunters! They take off whenever the notion strikes. We'll find their bones along the trail. They don't know how to find water or grass."

"We wait for the summer rains as it is," said Tom. "They make the grass come up and feed it so it keeps coming back, but it still needs time to grow. Need the rain to fill the waterholes."

"Tom, why do they call them Staked Plains?" Danny asked.

"There's not many trees, rocks, and hills a man can recognize," the mountain man replied. "Some folks say there's nothing on the *llano*, that it's just flat as a flapjack, an' easy to get lost. The Old Spaniards used to bring stakes and pound them in the ground every mile so's they could find their ways home agin."

"Just like Hansel and Gretel leaving a trail of bread crumbs," said Danny. The others looked at him quizzically. "But what's a yah-no?"

"*Llano*," said the mountain man, "is Mexican for plains."

"At the other end," said Aubry, "you'll see the cliffs rise up like the walls of a stockade where the Llano Estacado comes to an end. Estacado also means stakes driven in the ground like a stockade."

"Anyway," said Tom, "it ain't worth puzzelin' over too much. That's what they're called, and they're big and flat and dry with here and there a hidden canyon. And hidin' in the canyon more Comanche and Kiowa than you can count."

The caravan crossed the Arkansas without loss near Choteau's Island. A few days march beyond, they made the first dry camp. Danny found no stakes on the staked plains. The *llano*, as he was learning to call it, was barren of trees and firewood.

"How will we make a fire tonight?" Danny asked Joe when they stopped late that evening. The captain continued the march longer each day knowing they must reach water soon.

"Well, Danny," replied Joe, "You're going to have to gather us some buffalo wood. See those squat round things growing on the ground? Gather in a bunch and mind that they're nice 'n dry."

"You mean the things that look like cow pies?"

"Aye, that's buffalo wood," replied Joe.

"Doesn't look like wood to me," Danny appealed. "Looks like something a buffalo might have deposited."

"Aye, they did at thet," said the teamster, "but it burns well 'nuff."

"And you want me to pick them up?" Danny asked incredulously.

"Aye, you being the yonker 'mongst us, the task falls to you," Joe replied.

Danny did as he was bidden and gathered a pile of chips. Soon they had a fire going and food cooking.

"A word of warning, Danny," said the teamster. "Sit away fum the smoke. Yer food will taste the better for it, and yer eyes won't water so much. The smoke doesn't smell too bad as long as y're not directly downwind."

"That's for truth," added Tom Trask as he approached the fire. "There's no firewood to be found on these dry southern plains. Chips add a special flavor to the meat. A child from the mountains and bayous grows to yearn for it."

"Mountain men have strange tastes," mumbled the boy.

"Ai?" queried Tom.

"Buffalo hump, bass, beaver tail, boudins, fleece, buffalo tongue, raw liver," the boy muttered as the others laughed at his distaste for fatty foods and innards.

Danny, Trask, and Joe went out to hunt one fierce July day hoping for some fresh meat to fill empty pots and bellies. Not much more than a mile ahead of the wagon train, they looked over the top of a hill. Below them four Indians had a man staked to the ground. Two other white men lay nearby, apparently dead. Three saddled horses and four Indian ponies stood nearby. The Indians had a small fire of buffalo wood burning. The man on the ground screamed as one of them shoveled coals onto his belly. Trask motioned them back to where they couldn't be seen or heard.

"We've got to rescue him," insisted Danny.

"No, we don't," said Trask with finality.

"Comanche." Joe nodded. Screams drifted over the hill.

"They'll spot our wagons when they're done," said Joe. "The caravan is headed right toward them."

"We've got to do something," said Danny. "Maybe fire from a distance and put him out of his misery." Trask and Joe looked at him oddly.

"That'd git the Injuns attention fer sure," said Joe. Turning to Trask he said, "They'll see our wagons an' dust an' run back to their tribe."

"Yup," nodded Trask. "We'll crawl to the top, bringing the stock with us, fire once, and then mount and charge amongst the heathen. Check your weapons."

They crawled up, and at Trask's signal, he and Joe fired, felling two Indians. Danny couldn't bring himself to fire on a man. Trask flew into his saddle and six-guns blazing rushed after the remaining, very surprised Indians. Joe was right behind also blazing away. In moments the remaining Comanches lay on the ground.

Joe and Trask began to scalp their victims as Danny approached slowly leading his horse, dejected at his failure, yet somehow pleased that he hadn't had to kill.

A Comanche, covered in blood, but still very much alive, leapt suddenly to a horse and charged directly toward Danny.

"Danny, fell him!" yelled Trask. "I've fired my last shot."

The Comanche flew passed Danny nearly tumbling him. The boy spun about and fired hitting the Indian behind the head, killing him instantly.

Danny looked at his victim, and his stomach began to heave. With little to eat that day, his retching was only bile bitter in his mouth.

Trask placed his hand on Danny's back. "It had to be done. He'd have alerted his tribe, and they'd have fallen on the caravan."

"I know," he said. "I know. What about the man staked to the ground?"

"He's dead," said Joe.

"It still don't seem right," said Danny. "We didn't even do it to save that man on the ground. We fired without warning..."

"Would you rather it was us lyin' dead than them?" asked the mountain man.

"If we given 'em warnin'," said Joe, "they'd sure 'nuf tried to kill usn."

"No," replied the boy, "but now scalping them. . . It's barbaric. I've read about it, but I never thought it would seem this terrible. This feels like brutal murder."

"Look at me, boy," ordered Trask. "They'd already killed Americans. If they'd had the chance, they'd have killed us, too. If they'd got the chance to warn their tribe, they might all have fallen on the caravan."

"But taking trophies," Danny replied. "It feels like we're exulting in murder!"

"It's a warnin' to their people," said Trask. "If they attack Americans, they will be dealt with harshly. It raises the cost of an attack on us to where it isn't worth it to the Indian. That keeps us safe.

"The Indian in his talk reckons his tribe 'the people' as if everyone else wasn't" Trask continued. "He's apt to attack anyone that isn't people. They ain't human. Other tribes, Mexicans, or whites don't count for much. But us Americans ain't much better. Lot of us don't think Indians are human. I do, but I've lived with 'em a spell. We given them plenty of cause to dislike us. We've been pushin' them off the land and killin' 'em for hundreds of years.

"Comanche are *muy malo*, bad," he went on. "They been fightin' Texians for a lot of years. An' Texians are the worst white men there is. They attack travelers like us an' Mexicans. All the same to them. The Texians are pushin' the Comanche out this way. Been a lot of nasty fights an' dirty tricks on both sides. Comanche aren't happy with anything that wears white skin. They're dangerous We got no choice but to kill them afore they kill us. There. . . I've said my piece. It's enough."

Danny nodded but pondered things he'd once thought heroic but no longer felt bold and brave. Together they returned to the wagon train, Danny sadder, less full of questions, and somehow older.

Crossing Llano Estacado was dry and dusty. Increased traffic along the trail had used up the already poor grass. Water was scarce, but Tom found them enough to keep the caravan going.

"Here we are, boy," said Joe as they settled into camp for the evening. "Come to Point of Rocks 'n' a good fresh spring. N' a good thing, too. My ox team barely made it the las' mile. Used up, they are, tired, worn out."

"My team, too, Joe," Danny replied. "I think they all are. Not enough grass; barely enough water. Their ribs are showin'." He set out to gather "wood" for the fire, topped a low rise facing west. Danny halted suddenly, stared off in the distance, and then turned and ran toward camp.

Joe stirred and jumped to his feet as the boy ran toward him, reaching for his rifle. Tom Trask, too, turned toward the young man who now lean, and hard, bounded across the *llano* with the grace of an antelope. The long journey had worn the boy-fat from him leaving muscle in its place.

"Joe, Tom," he called as he neared camp. They cocked their rifles, concerned at the occasion for the excitement. "The blue haze on the horizon . . . is that the Shining Mountains?"

The men relaxed. Tom said, "Aye lad, the Shining Mountains, the Stonies. We're close now."

They talked that night. Danny, though still learning,

had fewer questions, choosing to watch and listen more than ask. His interest in stories of the mountain men and Indians and the strange land ahead was undiminished. Discovering that Tom knew Mr. Carson and had spent time with him, Danny prodded Tom for information. Kit Carson aroused something special in the young man. He was exceptional in Danny's view. John Fremont, the Pathfinder, wrote about the new lands in the West and the new trails over the Rocky Mountains. Fremont made himself and his trusted guide, Kit Carson, famous.

"Out in the Mojave country," the mountain man related, "a band of digger Indians made off with most of our stock. We was in bad straights, but nobody except'n Kit an' his friend, Boggs, wanted to go after 'em. Them two pursued the critters for a day and a half before they caught up. Straight away, Kit and Boggs attacked. There was a hundred Indians in that band. Didn't affright Kit none. Kilt a bunch an' recovert most of the stock, too. Another chile might ha' thunk the Indians was too many. Not Kit. Carson, he acted 'cause it was the right thing to do."

Danny might have doubted Tom, thought this another tall tale, but he'd read the same story in Fremont's book. He had doubted Fremont, too, when he first read the story, but here were men who knew Kit Carson and clearly they believed.

"He's a giant among men," grinned Captain Aubry, "big, powerful, broad-shouldered, towers a head taller than normal, and totally fearless."

It wasn't difficult for Danny to imagine a man so brave, so big, so tall, and as powerful as Captain Aubry described. The men who claimed the new continent must be giants.

There were wonders and dangers that ordinary men would be unable to face. The Pathfinder had written as much.

"Out here, Danny," Aubry explained, "there's no law or sheriff to rely on. A man is on his own and has to take care of things himself. In a land without police or army, your show of strength alone keeps thieves and Indians at bay."

Another thirsty, dusty day went by. The shimmering mountains drew closer.

"That's the *Sangre de Cristo*, boy," said Joe. "Means blood of Christ. Ought to see them mountains from Santa Fe at sunset and you'd see why."

Danny noticed something else, Indians. They appeared as if from nowhere beside the trail.

"Joe," he called, "we have company."

Orders came from ahead. The caravan halted and unhitched stock from front and sides, bringing the oxen and mules in among the wagons where they would be protected.

"Hickories," said Joe. "Means basket or chocolate cup or some such. Depends on who you talk to. They're Apaches, boy. This group will be *Llaneros*, which means plains band. They live out here. There is another band called *Ollero*, water jug. The Ollero live over between Abiquiu and Taos. They're tough fighters and mean. You don't want to get caught by them for sure." He spat tobacco juice into the dust.

Joe was talking up a bee swarm as he checked and rechecked his weapons. He might have been nervous. Danny checked his weapons, too. He could see about twenty warriors. From what Tom had taught him, Danny thought that might mean there were a hundred more, out of sight.

The teamster kept talking. "See the one in the red jacket? That'll be *Saco Colorado*, means red jacket. So the one who seems to be in charge must be *Lobo Blanco*, White Wolf. See the big one that tries to stay near *Lobo*? I heard about him. They call him *Acha*, means hatchet. They say he's about subtle as an axe."

The Jicarilla were armed with lances, bows, and rifles which they brandished overhead. menacingly. Danny'd heard stories about Apaches, good fighters and nasty. Travelers didn't want to be captured by Apaches.

"How many do you think, Joe?" Danny called.

"No tellin'. We're in Hickory country."

Trask rode by. "We can't count on any support," he said. "Nearest Army post is Las Vegas, days ahead. Even if they have a patrol out, it will be too small to be much use. Stay nice and polite. Don't fire unless you're told. We don't want a war. There might be hundreds of them out there, out of sight, waiting."

"Forty wagons in our train, one teamster to a wagon," Joe said. "And a few hostlers as well. Fifty of us against God knows how many of them."

Danny felt rising panic in his chest. Joe, rested a hand on his arm. It was good to know another fighter was near.

Tom and Captain Aubry rode out to talk to the Jicarillas. Both sides gestured and signed in the Plains Indian style. Danny heard a few words of Spanish. Some sort of agreement was reached. Captain FX Aubry and the mountain man returned and had the teamsters hitch up again. They continued their march toward Ocaté and camped for the night.

"Tom, what did those Indians want?" Danny asked after camp was set.

"The toll, Danny, the toll," the mountaineer answered. "We gave them an ox and some cloth and beads. It compensates them for the game we kill and run off. Seems fair to me."

Wagon Mound appeared in the distance, looking like a covered wagon pulled by an ox-team. The Mountain Branch of the trail and the Cimarron Cutoff came back together there near water and good grass. Captain Aubry thought it best to graze and rest the stock on good pasture and thus planned to camp for a couple of days before continuing on to Santa Fe still a hundred miles ahead. Part of the way the caravan would be climbing up through Apache Pass.

The captain approached Dan. "Isn't it about time you met your hero?" asked Aubry smiling between his mustache and goatee. The young man straightened from staking down a tent as Aubry continued. "To the north along the Mountain Branch a small settlement is growing around the Rayado and Cimarron creeks. I hear Kit Carson is staying there."

"What's Mr. Carson like?" Danny asked Captain Aubry as he had almost every day since they'd left Independence three weeks before.

"Oh, he's about six foot four, broad at the shoulders as an ox bow, narrow at the hip, all leather, bone and sinew with cold, piercing, blue eyes, squinted to slits by the sun. He dresses in buckskin decorated with fringe and beadwork, carries a knife big as a pirate's cutlass, a tomahawk like a double bladed axe, a Hawken rifle, and two of Colt's six-shot pistols. He wears a coonskin cap. At least I think it's a cap. I'm not sure Kit ever stopped to skin that coon, just told it to sit still. His jaw is chiseled out of granite. He's got a big, thundering voice; men obey when he speaks and obey from the first word. But it's the eyes you notice first. When he turns them on you, you know that unless you're careful, it's your death you're looking at. Many and many is the Indian he's killed and maybe some white men, too. He's the bravest and the strongest and the biggest and the fastest man you ever saw anywhere. There's none other like him."

Captain Aubry had told the same tale about Kit Carson every time Danny asked. The boy believed it, having read and reread the books about the travels of John Fremont. Kit had guided the Pathfinder through all kinds of danger. Fremont chose Carson because the mountain men told him there was none better anywhere in their ranks. Danny had learned about Mr. Carson through more than the Fremont books. Word of mouth had spread back to Missouri with the mountain men and from there to Orient Point at the eastern tip of Long Island near where his home, Greenport, lay. Stories were told over campfires every night on the trail to Santa Fe. Kit Carson was a giant busy building the nation.

"Get your mule, Danny. Kit lives near here. He has a rancho on the Rayado."

"Carson ain't so special as all that." The speaker was a big man in the greasy buckskins of a trapper. Danny had noticed him coming into camp with some others. Bearded, he wore a wide-brimmed felt hat with a feather tucked in the band, a long-fringed shirt and pantaloons, and moccasins on his feet. A big knife and a tomahawk were tucked into his belt.

"There's others that can track as well and fight Indians even better," the big man said. "There's them what's done more, but got less credit. They didn't have no fancy friends to write them up in books."

Aubry turned. "Hello, Leroux. Still got your hair, I see, or did something crawl up under your hat to die? Let the boy have his hero. There's plenty who know your work is good."

"Better than good. Best. I can out track, out trap, outride, and kill Indians faster than Carson," the big man said and stalked off.

"Danny, you just met one of Kit's friends. For all the bluster, they respect each other. Antoine Leroux hasn't made it into books, and he's a little touchy about being passed over. He is good. Maybe as good as Carson."

"But he's smaller," Danny replied, "and his voice doesn't quite thunder."

Aubry smiled. Then, as if responding to some private joke, laughed out loud. They mounted and rode north.

"You know, Danny," said Aubry, "it isn't size or speed or courage that makes Carson great. He's the most trustworthy man I've ever met. If he says he'll do something, he'll do it or die trying. So far, he hasn't died. If he feels an obligation, he will live up to it. That's part of what makes him a real life hero."

Chapter 2

The Rancho on the Rayado

The Rayado tumbles out of the *Sangre de Cristo* crisp, cold and pure. Danny and Captain Aubry rode upstream amid hillsides forested with towering ponderosa along bottoms deep with grass. The wind hissed through pine needles carrying with it the tang of the forest.

Soon they came to a jumble of scattered buildings. A corral penned several healthy-looking mules.

"Fine riding stock," said Aubry. "Kit and a lot of mountain men prefer mules to horses. They're less temperamental, more sure footed, and harder to hurt."

Chickens and goats wandered about. Danny studied the layout of Kit's rancho, guessing the purposes of each building. There seemed to be a slaughterhouse, a smokehouse, a barn, and a blacksmith shop. All were small and built from *adobe,* mud brick. A very modest home with two wings looking in on a central court stood amid the outbuildings. The house had a few small—about eight by ten inches—glass windows and larger window openings without glazing that could be covered by wooden shutters.

Danny looked at the windows, a puzzled expression on his face. "Why would anyone leave a window opening without glazing?" he pondered aloud.

"Glass is rare in New Mexico," said Aubry. "It isn't manufactured anywhere in the territory and has to be brought from the States in wagons like ours.

"See those shutters," continued Captain Aubry, "the ones where the design is cut all the way through?"

The wooden shutters bore crosses cut right through in decoration. Their placement seemed odd to Danny and the decorative holes made no sense.

"That'll cause a draft," the young man scoffed. If he'd been born on the frontier, he might have understood sooner.

"They're firing ports," Aubry said. "Kit aims to defend his house if need be. Most houses here don't have windows at all. If Indians attack, they close the door and hide, blind to the theft of anything left outside. Mostly the Mexicans are too poor to own guns, and their government discourages it anyway. They have lances and bows and arrows. So if Indians come raiding, they huddle inside and hope they'll go away soon. They build wall to wall in plazas, hoping their numbers will discourage raiders."

Danny hadn't seen a Mexican town as yet. *Las Vegas*, the meadows, a village surrounded by good grazing, miles to the south, was the closest town. There had been no permanent towns along the trail since the caravan departed Independence, Missouri, only a few scattered trading posts close to the Missouri River. These were among the first buildings Danny saw in New Mexico. Made of mud, their construction was very different from anything he'd seen before. Kit's house had a wooden door, but there were other houses outside of which Mexican women busied themselves grinding corn. These houses had only blankets hung in the doorways and no windows. Danny imagined them dark, cold, and smelly.

"If they cower from Indians," Danny asked incredulously, "why don't they build solid doors?"

Aubry looked at the boy. "They lack the metal for sawmills, and have no lumber other than that which they reclaim by tearing down the wagons we leave behind."

"There are no privies!" exclaimed the young man.

"There's no lumber to waste," replied the captain. "You wouldn't build a brick privy, would you?" Danny shook his head. "Nor do they waste adobe on temporary structures."

Danny looked the scene over again trying to see passed his prejudices as he'd learned to do with the new and different sorts of men he'd been exposed to on the trail. He'd learned to like many of them and to see beyond habits, like chewing tobacco, that he'd been brought up to despise. He'd learned to look past dirty clothes, long hair, and tattoos. His parents had been adamant that only low-classed, drunken sailors got tattooed. Danny looked around and thought a while.

"It's pretty obvious to me that someone," he finally concluded, "that someone here is very industrious and intends to provide a wide range of services to travelers, even if he was building with mud."

"Kit's prepared to offer a whole village worth of services," the captain replied, "but I'll bet you don't see how carefully the buildings are placed so they don't provide cover to anyone attacking the house."

"They're made of mud!" Danny protested. "How can civilized people live in mud houses?" Like most Americans he was used to structures of frame and brick.

"You're reacting like the Missouri Volunteers in '46," Aubry said, shaking his head. "I thought you had more brains. Missouri Volunteers heard stories of the lucrative Santa Fe trade, but when they got there, instead of streets paved with gold, they found houses of *adobe*. It's adobe, by the way, not mud. They promptly rechristened Santa Fe 'Mud Town.' Even the mountain men thought the Missourians dull-witted, dirty, and ignorant."

Other early travelers shared the Ozark hillbillies' disdain. Few buildings anywhere in the territory were over one story. Lower walls had to be massive to support taller structures.

"The Volunteers saw people hurling balls of mud at their *casas*," Aubry went on. "Missourians thought that was right funny. They even offered to help. What they didn't know was that's how Mexicans make repairs. They throw mud where the building is eroding; it works very well.

"Give it some time, Danny," Aubry went on. "You'll learn to see the beauty in adobe and the practicality. It absorbs bullets and even cannon balls, instead of splintering to harm folks inside. It absorbs heat, too, and releases it real slow. Build up a fire in an adobe *horno*, a fireplace, and it will radiate heat all night. *Casas* are warm in the winter and cool in the summer. They gather heat in the day and release it at night."

"That sounds wrong," Danny said.

"It takes a longtime for the sun to heat the adobe walls. By the time the heat is starting to come through, it's evening," the captain replied.

"Another thing, Danny," said Aubry picking up the lesson again. "For the people of New Mexico, adobe was both a necessity and common sense. One of the reasons our trade works so well is because Mexico City doesn't want to let the outlying provinces have tools or any way to manufacture things. *Nuevo Mexicanos* have almost no metal tools, and for the same reason, they lack the means to make glass for windows.

"That's why they don't use wood for furniture," Aubry explained. "They sit on adobe *bancos*, benches. Only the *ricos*, the wealthy, have tables and chairs. There isn't much hardwood in these mountains. Pine and cottonwood are all they've got. Those are softwoods, so they have to be cut to larger dimensions than hardwood. What furniture you see will be large and heavy looking, made of thick boards.

"Everything else is made of adobe," he concluded, "furnishings, seating, fireplaces and ovens, and even cabinets. They call them *nichos,* and they're cut into the wall."

Danny had an active mind, open to new ideas. That came from listening to the tales of sailors about the strange lands they had visited. However, he carried, too, the prejudices of Easterners who thought themselves better than most people, including other Americans. Nonetheless, his mind was open to the new, and he could learn.

"See that square form?" Captain Aubry asked. Danny nodded as Aubry continued, "It will hold ten adobe blocks for forming and drying. *Mexicanos* mix clay with sand and wool, if they can afford it, other fibers, like straw, if they can't. The wet blocks are set out in wooden molds, like the one you're looking at, to dry. So you see? It's not mud. It's a special mix of things that make it last. When they dry the blocks are mortared together with mud."

Danny began to see beauty in *adobe casas*, cool in summer, warm in winter. Their earthen *hornos*, fireplaces, radiated heat from the bricks themselves. Rounded at the corners, built from the earth they stand on, they merged in color and form with the landscape. *Vigas*, roof beams, protruded the length of a forearm near the top of the wall. Beams, garlanded with colorful *chilis* set to dry, make the *pueblo*, the village, seem perpetually decorated for celebration. *Casas* smell of earth, pine *vigas*, cedar bark, *piñon* fires, *chili*, onion and spice. Adobe was smooth and warm to the touch.

They rode up as far as a large beehive-shaped, adobe object, big as a dove cote, that stood in front of the house. The captain gave Danny a sign. They did not dismount.

"Stand fast, Danny. They've heard us ride up. Let's give them a chance to look us over and get ready for us." So they sat for some minutes studying the rancho while Captain Aubry explained about adobes and *hornos* and other mysteries of an ancient land new to the young man.

"Once, I saw them bake a whole turkey," Aubry went on," in an *horno* like this one. Best turkey I ever ate. They build a big fire inside and let it burn to ash. Then they scraped out the ash, put in loaves of bread or whatever they wanted to bake, and sealed it up. The heat in the blocks does the cooking."

Two women came out of the house and looked the riders over. Both were surprisingly well dressed. The taller of the two was small with fine soft features and kind, brown eyes.

"She's beautiful," Danny said under his breath. Aubry looked at him. "I can't imagine a woman more beautiful. There's a waft of lilac in the air about her. I may fall in love."

She had none of the edge of hardness one sometimes sees in Spanish ladies. The woman his loving gaze embraced was very young.

"She can't be more than sixteen or seventeen," Danny whispered.

"Perhaps too old for you," said the captain. "She's already seen twenty and more. And you've got competition. Daniel Trelawney," he said indicating his young friend, "this is Josepha, Kit's wife."

Danny soon realized the other was a girl of no more than twelve.

"And this," said Captain Aubry doffing his hat, "is Kit's niece, Teresina, Little Teresa."

To Danny's eyes, the pair, aunt and niece, could have been sisters.

"*Señor Francisco! Tio Pancho*," the younger girl cried, obviously delighted to see Aubry. She called Captain Aubry "Mr. Aubry" and in the same breath "Uncle Frank," her *Tio Pancho*. She continued in Spanish which Danny could not as yet understand, but Mr. Aubry soon signaled him to dismount. They were welcome. Tio Pancho got hugs and Danny smiles.

"*Mi esposo no es aqui*," reported Josepha. Kit was not at home but was expected soon.

They unsaddled their mules, and after drying them with handfuls of grass, hobbled them and turned them loose to graze. *Tio Pancho* soon produced gifts for the ladies from his saddle bags: ribbons, silk handkerchiefs, sticks of cinnamon, raisins, small sacks of coffee beans, and sugar. Josepha Carson and the girl invited the travelers into their home and soon had coffee brewing. Teresina, the young girl, ground the coffee beans in a small mill, checking the drawer and grinding again until they were fine enough to suit her. Neither lady spoke English, so Danny was forced to communicate by signs, smiles, and through Captain Aubry.

Aubry spoke to Danny. "They're not sisters. *No es hermana.*" The ladies giggled. "Teresina is Charles Bent's daughter. Her uncle, William, runs Bent's Fort, or Fort William as some call it, on the Mountain Branch of the trail. Her mother is Josepha's elder sister, Ignacia. Charles Bent was the first American governor of New Mexico. He was murdered in '47 in Taos while saving Ignacia, Teresina, and Josepha from a mob."

"Wow!" said Danny. "That had to be traumatic for both of them, especially Teresina watching her father get murdered."

"It was," Aubry continued. "They were saved by Padre Martinez who hid them and others in his *hacienda.*"

"I thought," Danny pondered, "you told me he had started the uprising."

Aubry nodded. "Padre Martinez got the Taos Indians all stirred up about losing their religious rights to the Protestant *gavachos*, which is to say in an uncomplimentary way gringos or *Norte Americanos*. Really he was more concerned about losing his influence with the government. He was the very priest who married Kit to Josepha. Once stirred up, the Indians got drunk, turned mean, and the people of Taos joined them. They followed Governor Bent to Kit's house and shot him full of arrows. The ladies escaped through the wall into the next house while Bent, mortally wounded, fended off the mob. Kit was away with Fremont in California and didn't know about any of this until months later."

Teresina and Josepha bustled about making dinner and pouring more coffee. Teresina smiled and winked at Danny each time she passed while her aunt would stop and exchange a few words with Aubry making sure her guests were taken care of properly. Conversation was ackward as Danny didn't speak Spanish, so she allowed them to speak together. Captain Aubry had much to say as he knew he would be parting from Danny soon, if not today, then in Santa Fe, and Danny had much to learn.

"Josepha is from Taos," Aubry went on. "These people are proud. Her family name is Jaramillo. They're one of the old families. They talk like they've been here since 1540 when Coronado arrived.

"I read somewhere," Danny interjected, "that in 1680, the Pueblo Indians . . ."

"Yes," said Aubry, "the ones who live in adobe villages."

Danny nodded excited at knowing something his captain was talking about. "They rose up and drove the Spanish out. New Spanish settlers started to arrive around 1700."

Aubry laughed quietly. "That's why I'm telling you, Danny. Don't ever tell a Jaramillo or a Valdez that he or she isn't a direct descendant of the Conquistadors. Their language is different from the Mexicans. They believe they preserve the old language of Spain in all her glory."

At the mention of conquistadors, Josepha turned to Abury, one eyebrow shooting up as she said something in Spanish.

Aubry translated. "She's telling you that she is

a descendant of Coronado's *tenente,* lieutenant, Juan Jaramillo."

Danny smiled and nodded indicating that he too thought this important. He liked his new acquaintances and wanted to understand their lives.

He respected Captain Aubry and liked hearing about history and culture from him. Danny felt like he was back at school. He was comfortable in that long accustomed role. Aubry's precise speech and slight French accent made him seem an educated gentleman that Danny could respect. Schoolmasterish, Danny thought, even is he is dressed like a Mexican grandee, but not the kind of giant who tamed the west and opened new trails, not the kind of hero Danny was searching for. Somehow Danny overlooked everything Aubry had done, new trails he'd located and records he'd set riding from Santa Fe. Aubry was scarcely bigger than a jockey.

Inside Kit's home and out of the sun and wind for the first time in months, Danny inhaled the scent of fresh coffee. Content, he leaned back and turned his eyes to the ceiling. Great peeled logs, *vigas,* were set atop the walls to support the roof. *Latillas,* smaller tree limbs, were laid atop the *vigas* in a herringbone pattern. *Viga* and *latilla* formed the ceiling. The effect was quite pleasant.

Two rooms were sleeping chambers. Another, a very long room, served as a kitchen and *sala,* or living room. This room was festooned with *ristras* of *chilis,* onions, and garlic. Dried herbs, pots, pans, and other cooking equipment hung from the *vigas.* A rifle hung over the window with a powder horn and "possibles bag," probably containing lead bullets, percussion caps, and tools. Adobes had been laid to form a *banco*, a place to sit, on either side of the *horno*. It was a comfortable room.

The walls had been treated with a white plaster making the rooms appear brighter than they might otherwise have been. The floors were made of mud mixed with oxblood. This made them hard, reddish, and as glossy as if they'd been lacquered. Nichos had been cut into the wall a few inches deep. Some had wooden doors making them into fine cupboards. One was open displaying a *bulto,* a wooden carving, of *San Francisco*, St. Francis, patron saint of New Mexico, a kind of family shrine.

A parapet lined the edge of the roof which was used as additional workspace where food could be dried away from animals. *Canales,* water spouts, pierced the parapet and moved water outward away from the walls. The walls had been plastered with a specially prepared mud to make them smooth. If the rains begin to wash them away, they were repaired with more mud in the dry autumn.

Hearing the rattle of horse's hooves in the yard, the women ran out the door to greet Kit. Aubry, glancing through the cross in the shutters, saw something and jerked him back. "Stay low, Danny, don't show yourself. Always look before you run to greet visitors."

Danny peered through the shutter and saw a party of Indians on ponies.

"Jicarillas," hissed Aubry. "See how their buckskins are trimmed with beads in white and shades of blue? Sure sign. That big one is *Acha*, I think. Kit says he's about as subtle as an axe. He's big and powerful and has more followers than brains. He and his friends are probably the ones who have been making trouble along the trail."

The women who'd run out planning to greet Kit were in the yard with the Jicarillas.

"How do these women survive out here when he's gone?" Danny asked.

"The ladies are tough. But it's more than that. The Indians respect Kit because he treats them fair. He gives them livestock and feeds them when they come by. They know he'll retaliate if they take anything he doesn't choose to give. They fear his reputation."

There were seven Jicarillas, all young. The biggest one was well over six feet and muscular throughout. He was fast for such a big man. Leaping from his pony, he towered over tiny Josepha demanding, "*Mas frijoles, mas tortillas, mas carne!*" Bring us beans, bread and meat.

Another smaller man who smiled almost constantly approached Josepha and said softly, "*Por favor. Hambriento. Un bondad,*" which in poor Spanish means please, we're hungry. Give us a kindness.

Josepha nodded yes, signed them to sit and wait and turned to enter the house. A slovenly, smallish man sprang up between her and the house. The men hidden in her house saw Josepha's nose wrinkle at his stench. "*Aguardiente! Mas!*" This was a call for alcohol, lots of alcohol. Food Josepha would gladly give, but not alcohol. That was trouble.

"No!" she stamped her foot, and stepping around him, continued into the house. She signed to her Anglo visitors to stay low. She could handle the Jicarilla. She told Teresina to make coffee with lots of sugar and to heat some *tortillas*. A flame was built up under pots that had been heating by the fire. Josepha and Teresina dragged the table and chairs outside.

Once the women had the Jicarillas seated, they started them on sweetened coffee. Josepha brought around a pot of stew made with beef, onions, green *chilis*, and garlic; Teresina followed with a pot of *refritos*, refried beans. Acha, the big one, stroked her arm. Teresina pulled away as if stung, dropping her pot. An arm flashed across the table grasping the pot before it hit the ground.

"*Acentellado*," whispered Aubry, "like a flash of lightning. He's even faster than I'd heard. I think the one on the end wearing white is *Peregrino Rojo*, Chief Vicente's son. Rojo's name means the Red Pilgrim. Vicente is an Ollero, who stays in the mountains further west. Wonder what Rojo's doing with this bunch of *Llaneros*, plains people?"

Danny saw a man of medium height and build dressed in loose fitting white cotton with a red sash and headband. His moccasins came to the knee and had a fringe around the top. The others were dressed in buckskin. Aubry whispered, "Rojo dresses more like a Western Apache or Pueblo than a Jicarilla."

Acha was gripping Teresina's arm. "*Cuanto es? Tres caballo.*" How much, he asked, and offered three horses. The others signed and helped with words. They were all laughing, eating, and enjoying themselves immensely.

"That devil Acha wants to buy Teresina to marry her. He's offering three horses," whispered Aubry.

Teresina pulled away. Josepha ordered, "*Teresina, mas tortillas. Pronto.*" More bread, quick. Crying, the girl ran toward the house to hoots of laughter from the Apaches.

The smallest Jicarilla, a man bent and dirty, scuttled to intercept her. "*Teresina, cinco caballo, muy bueno*," he said entering his own mock offer of five horses. His speech came with difficulty. Danny concluded that the small man had problems of both head and body, and he thought he saw cruelty there in the man's eyes. In cruelty it seemed, as Danny viewed the interaction of the Apaches, the small man captured the approval he craved from companions who otherwise despised him. Life in the open wandering Indian camps demanded physical as well as mental prowess. Its lack was something to be loathed and feared, a punishment from the gods.

Someone, maybe Rojo, called out, "*Pinacate, no!*" Pinacate spun as if stung by the name. The girl escaped to the house.

"They call the little one *Pinacate,* meaning stink bug," snickered Aubry. "It implies he's stupid and smelly."

Returning with the *tortillas* Teresina tried to avoid Acha, but he called out, "*Cinco caballo!*" Five horses. He grabbed her thin arms again and pulled her to him.

The smiling Jicarilla said something to Stink Bug that angered him. It might have been, "Knock it off. Can't you see the little girl is crying?" But Danny had no way of knowing. Peregrino Rojo added something, and suddenly Acha's joke, if it ever had been one, was serious. "*Cinco caballo!*"

Acha turned to Josepha and held up a finger. "*Cinco caballo.*" He opened his hand to display five fingers. He pointed to his head and then to a spot in the yard. He called to his friends, and they proceeded to the spot. They made a small fire and began checking over their weapons. The one called *Acentellado* took out a tube of what appeared to be lead and then cut off its end with his knife, finally putting it in his mouth and chewing it into shape. When it looked good to the Indian, he loaded the lead into his rifle as a bullet.

This loading and checking of weapons was a clear threat. Acha cut off pieces of lead and then chewed them into shape as bullets. This apparently was not uncommon among the Jicarilla. Danny glanced at Aubry who showed no surprise. That seemed confirmation that this behavior was normal and not some crude display of power.

Josepha hustled Teresina into the house and barred the door.

"It appears that five horses is the final bid for the girl, and Josepha has been given some time to think it over along with the consequences," Aubry grinned. "This *casa* will be a hard spot to take. Fortunately, they don't know about us. There are three rooms to defend and only two of us to do it." Josepha got down a rifle. "Well, three then. I'd heard women liked weddings. Guess she's feeling too young to serve as the mother of the bride."

Danny looked through the cross cut in the shutters at the Jicarilla. The deadly earnest of his situation sunk home as he recognized the importance of the aiming slits for rifles that covered the doors and grounds quite well. Kit's house was a small fortress. Bedrooms at the ends were slightly longer than the center room was wide so that a small shuttered opening covered the door and front. Shutters looking toward the front from these rooms were close enough at hand that one man could cover both openings. To the sides and back, the land fell away steeply toward the creek, making an approach on those sides difficult for an attacker. There were openings that could be monitored. The outbuildings were spaced so they wouldn't offer cover to attackers. The four hunkered down and watched the Apache make bullets.

Danny wished for a hero. He was sure something heroic

could be done to chase the Indians off. A true western legend would confront them boldly and challenge that big Acha to single combat. Since he was just a little man, Captain Aubry wasn't up to such feats.

Acha had a beautiful rifle. A Hawken, Danny thought or something very much like one. It was a fine weapon, unlike the much less expensive fusils traded to Indians. His followers were not so well armed, having bows, spears, fusils, and trade guns of low quality. Soon they began to sing. Danny thought it eerie, and the hair rose on the back of his neck.

Danny and the captain checked their loads. Aubry and the young man each had Colt .36 caliber revolving pistols. They capped the sixth cylinder of each which was usually left uncapped for safety. Josepha had a similar weapon, a Remington .44 caliber revolver. Each had a rifle and Josepha got down two shotguns and a Spanish weapon of great age and dubious utility. It had a matchlock, something Danny hadn't seen before. It used a burning cord or match in place of the spark of flint or the snap of a percussion cap. With a wide muzzle, it was no longer than a musketoon. Josepha first poured in powder and then dumped broken glass and scraps of metal down the muzzle. Danny thought that combination might make an interesting surprise for whoever got too close.

They braced furniture against doors and made as ready as could be. The western bedroom would be their redoubt, a last place of refuge and retreat, and the men directed Teresina to wait there. Josepha took the *sala*, the long living room, while Aubry and Danny went to opposite ends of the house. They watched and listened.

The Apache were singing as they waited.

Josepha stood in front of the carving of *San Francisco* and crossed herself. Then she knelt and mumbled a prayer.

"Mr. Aubry, you believe in God?" Danny asked.

"Reckon so, Danny, but I'm not plannin' to meet Him anytime soon. Call me FX and say a prayer for me, would you?"

"Sure thing, Captain, uh FX. Suppose it matters the way we pray or the way she does?"

"If He did all the things they say to save us, Danny, do you really think it will matter to Him?"

"FX, you suppose those Jicarillas pray?"

"What do you suppose all that singing is about, Dan?"

"Do you suppose God looks on their prayers same as ours?"

Aubry thought for a moment then said, "You're prayin' that we keep our scalps. They're asking if they can have them. Let's hope God makes a distinction in the quality and sincerity of our requests. All the people I've met have similar rules for how they treat their kin and tribe. It's how we treat strangers that we differ on. Some folks figure that strangers are there to be robbed and scalped. The God you share with Josepha had a different plan. He told us about a Samaritan that helped strangers.

"Enough theology," said the captain. "Cock your rifle, Dan. The Jicarillas are stirring up. When I tell you to fire, shoot near one of them, then reload fast. We don't want to kill anyone yet. They're trying to intimidate the women. If the risk gets higher, they may back off. If we kill one, they'll want revenge."

The Apaches rose, spread out and approached the house.

Josepha stuck her weapon through a shutter, "*Halto!*"

The others stopped well short of the house. Only Acha came on.

"*Cinco caballo o muerte!*" Roughly: accept five horses or die.

"No!" Her reply came crisp and clear. That single word ended negotiations. They backed off.

But soon they came on again, crawling, dashing from cover to cover, not that Kit had left much of it. The Jicarilla were exposed through almost all of their approach. They fired the first shots. One would fire while a second came on. It was hard to find a target. Wood splintered from the shutter above Danny's head. Bullets impacted the adobe walls with a dull thwack.

"Josepha, Danny, fire, *fuego,*" shouted Aubry. "Don't worry about a target. Make them think about it."

The three defenders fired. The Apaches withdrew again and huddled. They hadn't expected this many guns. Ache would have to talk this over with his followers and convince them the prize was worth the risk. Was it a trap? The Indians seemed to be paranoid about traps, and Danny said as much as the defenders reloaded, sweated, and waited. And waited.

In the yard, the Jicarillas were getting ready to attack. They scattered out far to the flanks of the house hoping to find blind spots there so that any targets they might offer were well separated, forcing defenders to sweep a wide field with their rifles. The Indians approached using every bit of the very little cover Kit had left to their best advantage.

"Here they come," Danny yelled.

Suddenly the Jicarillas rose from cover and gestured up canyon. Danny looked through the shuttered window he had guarded. "Captain Aubry, there's a cloud of dust coming this way with horses and riders in it! Looks like a whole troop of cavalry."

"*Milagro. Es Cristobal, mi corazón!*" cried Josepha. She was saying: It's a miracle. It's Christopher, my darling!

The Jicarillas were running for their horses. Only Peregrino Rojo stood fast. He turned over the table and knelt on the side away from the house, his rifle pointed toward the approaching riders. He signaled Acha and his followers that he was their rear guard. Acha and his band galloped off across the plain.

Danny charged out the door trying to outflank Rojo who calmly rose from behind the table. The boy took aim. Still unaware of him, the Jicarilla set his gun against the table. Two riders appeared from the dust.

Rojo waved to them, "Hey, Kit. Thought you'd never get here."

A rider pulled up between Rojo and Danny. He was a large man, tall, with bulging muscles rippling under expensive but trail worn Spanish clothes. His clothes were black, pants belled to fit over tooled boots with *conchos* sewn to the seam. His white shirt was frilled, though now very dusty. His embroidered vest had dark blue piping. His mustache would have been the pride of any pirate. He topped the whole with a large sombrero making him tower well over six feet.

"Mr. Carson, I am so pleased to meet you," said Danny pumping his hand.

"*Que?*" said the rider, "I am Roque Vigil. Pleased to meet you, too, *hombre.*"

"Danny," called Captain Aubry, "Come meet your hero!"

The other horse had carried a small man, not over five foot four, though square built and thick through the shoulders. There was power there and endurance. He was dressed in moccasins and fringed buckskins and wore a Mexican style hat, wide brimmed and made of straw. His eyes, though quick and alert, were soft not piercing.

He said softly, "Danny, is it? Pleased to meet you."

Dumbstruck, Danny shook his hand. This was not the Kit Carson he was expecting. He looked askance at Aubry. "Captain, are you making sport of me?"

Aubry shook his head that he was not.

"Pleased to meet you, sir," Danny Trelawney finally managed to stammer. Off to his side, Aubry was laughing. Disappointment and the urge to kill someone flickered across Danny's face as he realized his friends had been making sport of him for some time. He suppressed the rage that only the young can feel, realizing that they have been the brunt of an adult joke.

"Call me Kit."

Regaining his composure a little, Danny said, "Uh, yes sir, Mr. Carson, Kit, sir. . ."

Trying to soften the blow, Aubry allowed that, "Kit looks big to me," making a joke of his own diminutive stature and small frame barely topping five foot two, one hundred pounds.

Like Kit, Aubry stood tall in legend and tale. Danny was not the first to confront a man who "was not the kind of Kit Carson he was expecting." The boy struggled with his feelings. Western men told tall tales about their adventures. Perhaps the stories about Kit Carson were no more than tall tales and wild exaggerations. Having been fooled and, as he thought, made a fool of, Danny was disinclined to accept easily this new Carson as the one in his imagination. It seemed an insignificance that Carson was considerably smaller than Danny had been told, but it tore at the fabric of his world. If Kit Carson was not the powerful, gimlet-eyed giant of legend, what else was not true?

There was a class of men Danny considered to be "the bad guys." He had known a few, and they always seem to aver that there was no difference between themselves and the good guys. Everyone was corrupt, they seemed to say. There are no heroes, only normal men with underhanded motives who projected an image. Behind the image, stripped of the legend, men are just men, none better than any other. Danny was seeking heroes not contradictions. He wanted his heroes to be perfect, and bigger than life.

Teresina and Josepha bounded from the house and engulfed Kit in hugs.

"*Chepita*," said Kit opening his arms.

"That's his name for her," FX confided. "They're really newlyweds. They were married in '43, six years ago when she was only fifteen, but Kit has been away so much, he's only spent a few months with her. Lieutenant Fremont told Kit his duty called, and his country needed him, so Kit followed on expedition after expedition. Fremont made Kit Carson famous, but he and Josepha have yet to have a child of their own. Before coming to Rayado, they had not lived together more than a few weeks at a time. This sojourn at Rayado is their honeymoon."

Danny realized that they had all forgotten about the dangerous Apache in their midst, Peregrino Rojo, Acha's rear guard, who stood behind a table.

Dismounting, Roque addressed Rojo. "*Hola*, Rojo, how you been? *Que paso, amigo?*"

To Danny's surprise, Rojo stepped out from behind his table. "Thank you, *Señor* Gi-di, for getting me away from my cousins. Acha is a great fool. He's gonna get somebody killed."

Danny was amazed. He had thought Indians spoke in broken English. Rojo's speech showed only traces of an accent, perhaps Spanish, but something else as well. The boy caught on quickly that Gi-di was the name Jicarilla used for Kit Carson.

Rojo continued, "Acha!" The Indian shook his head. "That *hombre* been up and down the trail demanding gifts. He's wants white man's trinkets, much as white men want gold. He stopped some California loco gold seekers. They wouldn't make him presents. So he beat them, stripped them naked, and burned their kit. He left them to walk to Santa Fe. Maybe they didn't live. They didn't look too tough."

Rojo paused for breath and went on obviously upset. "He's gonna bring the Army down on Jicarillas. I wish he'd make out he was Comanche or Ute. He wants everybody to know how tough the Jicarillas are."

Trelawney had heard Indians were taciturn. Rojo did not seem cold and aloof.

Danny whispered to Roque, "Where'd he learn English?"

"He stays around the settlements Taos, Santa Fe, and Chimayo and around the Pueblos. He even made a trip to St. Louis and back with wagon master Aubry. That's why they call him *Peregrino*, the pilgrim; he's always on the move looking for something he lost, I think. He speaks good Spanish, too. *Señor* Kit says his English is good like people from St. Louis. Talks a lot for an *Indio*, too."

Livestock cared for and table righted, Josepha seated the five men in the yard by lantern light. There they were: the mountain man, the captain of wagon trains, a *gavacho* new from the east, a wild Apache, and a Spaniard for so Roque insisted he was, his ancestors having come directly from Spain long ago clad in armor.

Josepha and Teresina served coffee and *enchiladas*. Josepha cooked corn *tortillas*, a round flat bread, in a little oil until they were soft and then dipped them in hot enchilada sauce made from red *chili* peppers.

"I love *enchiladas*," said Captain Aubry, continuing to serve as Danny's teacher. "Mrs. Carson serves them out layer on layer with cheese or meat between the layers and sometimes with a fried egg on top. You may find it a little spicy on your Eastern tongue, but once you get used to it, there is nothing better in the world.

"Green *chilis* ripen to red," he continued, "so the red are a little sweeter. How hot *chilis* are depends on the type of *chili*; generally, the smaller the *chili*, the hotter it is. Big *chilis* are usually mild."

Dipping the *tortillas* in sauce, Josepha then laid them on a plate and sprinkled them with grated cheese and chopped onions. Teresina topped a stack of three with a fried egg and served it at the table.

After dinner, the men smoked their clay pipes and talked about their plans. Captain Aubry was bound for Santa Fe and trade. He hoped to get back to Independence in time to bring out one more train before winter.

"I should make it back in mid-October before the snow flies," he said.

"I think I'll head down to the Pueblos and see if I can

find me a fat girl," said Rojo. "I've been practicing with my flute and the Pueblo girls like it."

"You should look for a skinny girl," volunteered Roque. "At the Pueblos that would be more challenge."

"Don't need challenge. I'll need something to keep me warm next winter."

"What about you, Danny?" asked Kit.

Danny had been lost in thought about his own future. This little, soft spoken Kit Carson was not the hero he'd expected. He was deeply disappointed and uncertain what to do next. Maybe, Danny thought, he should stay in the Santa Fe Trade returning to St. Louis with Captain Aubry. If there were no heroes, at least he'd be rich.

Kit's question roused him. "I had a little money," said the boy, "and bought a few things on Mr. Aubry's advice. I thought I'd like to trade with the Indians."

"*Go Jii Ya.*" The men looked at Rojo. "*Go Jii Ya,* big Jicarilla ceremonial. Maybe six weeks from now. All Jicarilla will gather in the *Piedre Lumbre* up beyond Abiquiu. Olleros, Llaneros, all the *N'deh.*"

"*Piedre Lumbre,*" said Roque, "means the rocks on fire. It is a most beautiful place, *muy linda.* The rocks are red, gold, and white. It is like being surrounded by fire."

"Trading with *cimarrones,* wild Indians, will get you more profit than trading at the Pueblos," mused Kit. "You go where other traders haven't been, and the prices will be better. It's not too far, a few days ride, and along the way you can trade for things that will be worth more there. Go Jii Ya might be what you want."

The words were mumbled shyly. Kit seemed embarrassed at having presumed to give a near stranger advice even if the advice contained an implied offer of assistance. Among friends, Roque Vigil, Peregrino Rojo, and Francis Aubry, Kit had momentarily relaxed his usual reserve. He was very conscious of being a man from the backwoods with little education and unable to read and write. Instead of elaborating on his scheme, he waxed into silence.

Danny liked the man dispite his disappointment. Kit Carson just didn't seem to be what the stories said, not just the legends, the stories that seemed to be true as well.

"*Cristobal*, you promised Josepha, no more long trips," admonished Roque locking eyes with Kit. "When you gonna tell her?"

"When I get back," quipped Kit. "This is a short trip. She'll hardly notice I've gone."

Danny almost laughed aloud. The quip was funny, but it was funnier still to think of a hero who had to worry about getting his wife's permission for an adventure.

"Danny," said Captain Aubry, "I expect you'll want to stay here." Kit nodded his assent. "That won't be a problem with me. I'll be selling some goods to Barclay at Mora and can get by with one less teamster. I'll leave your pay at the Mercure Brothers store in Santa Fe along with your goods."

"Yes, sir, I'd like that," Danny said surprising himself. Even if Kit Carson didn't match the legend, it would be a chance to trade with Indians and he was starting to like the real Mr. Carson.

"You must trade well, Danny," said Rojo. "The Jicarilla are great traders since the mountains were young hills."

"I'll do okay," Danny said thinking himself the great trader already. "New Yorkers like me traded the whole island of Manhatten from the Indians for $24 in beads and trinkets."

"So the *N'deh* have heard," replied Rojo. "But the whites did not know the land belonged to another tribe and it was the whites who did not make a good trade. The *N'deh* trade in turquoise, obsidian, salt, buffalo robes, meat and brain-tanned buckskin."

"Where do they get these things?" asked Danny.

Rojo took the question as an accusation that his people weren't clever enough to gather property for trade. He answered prejudices that Danny did not voice. "Only White people are so foolish to think that *N'deh*, Jicarilla, don't know how to farm or trade. They think us children who only hunt and gather."

Danny was puzzled. "I was told your people lived in tepees and roamed the plains hunting buffalo and eating wild plant food."

Rojo glared at the boy. "The gringo looks at a piece of ground and says, 'Oh, such rich soil; I can farm here.' So he farms and grows three times what he can eat, but there is no one to trade with so what he doesn't eat rots."

"That's not fair," protested Danny. "Mr. Carson has made a good farm here even if he's far from a town where he can trade!"

Rojo spoke again. "*Señor* Gi-di has chosen his ground well. He grows mules and horses, hay, cattle, and sheep. When the travelers come, they will arrive hungry and tired, and he will have what they need, providing it before they reach anyone else. He is a good trader.

"Before the Mexicans came," Rojo continued, "the Pueblos would live in a place until the game got scarce and their trash dumps got high around them. Then they would move to a new place. Always they need more meat, more skins and salt and things not of their land. *N'deh* would provide these. Now the Mexicans say, 'You must stay here, in this village, on the land you own. You cannot move.' So the Pueblo hunt all the game until it is scarce and they hunger for meat and the filth builds up around their houses. Then sickness comes. Do you think the People, the *N'deh*, would want this? No, Jicarillas will travel freely, hunt and have bellies full of meat, sleep under warm buffalo robes, in clean comfortable tepees. We would not live as these poor people do."

Danny was surprised. He thought living in houses, owning land and growing food was the good life, the way everyone wanted to live if they knew how.

"I was told," Danny said, "that the Comanche keep you from hunting."

"It is true. Comanche have come to the *llano* and make it difficult for *N'deh*. They are more numerous than the People. Hunting buffalo now has great risk. Jicarilla are now poor. Does this mean we should give up our good life so we can work hard and be poor as farmers living in poverty surrounded by filth?"

Danny was taken aback, surprised at Rojo's speech. It gave him much to think about. He sensed Rojo was trying to be helpful and liked him for it.

Rojo, seeing the white boy silent, worried that he had given offense.

"Among my people," Rojo said, "I could not speak so. We are careful not to offend one another. But I have learned whites speak more freely."

"It's okay," said Danny. "I'm thinking about what you said."

Rojo nodded. "My people are not afraid of silence as you whites are."

"Rojo has a very clear understanding of the economics of New Mexico," said Captain Aubry. "I've never found him to be in error."

That night they struck a deal. Danny would stay with Kit and help him with the ranch until time for *Go Jii Ya,* and Kit would prepare Danny for trading and travel in the wild. He would even go along to *Go jii ya* and show the boy the way.

Danny sought the captain alone, outside, away from the others. "I don't get it, Captain," said Danny. "You told me Kit Carson was a huge man and with big booming voice and piercing eyes. He's none of those things. Small, shy, and humble, I don't see how he could have done all the things Fremont said he did, let alone the things stories attribute to him. I'm very disappointed. This man looks pretty ordinary. He doesn't seem like any kind of a hero."

The captain looked at him. "Give it a season, Danny. Perhaps you'll learn in time. Watch him. Observe. He's a giant in his way and a great man."

"I sure don't see it," grumbled the boy.

In the morning, Danny awoke to the sound of a flute and found Peregrino Rojo lying on his back against the side of the house, knees bent, flute pointed toward the sky playing for Teresina who smiled and fussed about helping make breakfast.

Rojo stopped playing and called him over to display a large earring hammered from a Mexican dollar. "I picked this up in Taos, and I want to hang it in my ear."

"Nice," Danny allowed.

"Teresina is heating up one of her aunt's needles," continued Rojo, "but she's afraid she won't be able to push it through."

"I don't think that's how it's done," Trelawney mused.

"Would you help?" the Indian asked.

Teresina returned with a needle heated to red hot and held in a cloth. "*Abuja*," she said smiling so pretty she stunned Danny's heart and judgment.

Danny pushed the red hot *Abuja* through Rojo's earlobe in one quick thrust. He had heard that Indians were stoic and did not scream in pain. Rojo must have been the exception. The Jicarilla's yell brought Kit and Roque running and laughing when they understood the cause. That scream may have given rise to rumors that Kit had captured and tortured Rojo before he escaped. Perhaps Acha's companions were still close by and heard the scream. With Rayado Canyon behind them to build an echo and the open plains before them with nothing to break it up, they might have heard that scream from ten or fifteen miles away. Despite incredible volume of his scream this, Danny later thought it more likely Rojo had started the tale himself to explain his miraculous escape or to impress some girl.

Rojo rode off that morning up the Rayado toward Taos and, as he told his Rayado friends, toward his "destiny." Rojo was already Danny's friend. His earring glinted in the morning light. Before he went, Danny observed him stealing a kiss from young Teresina. Then and there Danny decided he would learn to play the flute.

That evening after a long day of work and an early dinner, Danny's training began. "Show me your weapons, Dan," Kit said quietly.

Kit inspected them closely, trying the lock, the firing mechanism, on rifle and pistol, feeling for balance. He appraised the big knife carefully also checking its balance and weight but saying nothing. It was hard for Danny to tell if he approved or not.

"You've got a good rifle. Rifling will make the ball spin and fly true. You can hit targets at 400 yards. Take care of it. Keep it clean and don't let it foul," Kit told him.

Instructing Danny to kneel, Kit silently showed him ways to brace and support the rifle to keep the barrel steady while aiming. Supported against the stones of the well, Kit had the boy fire a few shots at a target over 300 yards away. After each shot, they adjusted the sights a little for the extended range.

Thus did Danny's apprenticeship begin. The boy was drawn to the man, but not sure why. Kit Carson was not the sort of hero Danny had imagined and he was anxious to be off searching for a real hero. Nonetheless, he accepted the friendship and training offered. He had been promised Indian trade and that had to be worth something.

"Now, show me how fast you can load and fire," Kit said.

Danny was slow, so Kit demonstrated some tricks to speed the process.

"Patch and rammer are good for long-range accuracy," Kit taught, "but in a fight, you'll need to be able to fire faster at shorter ranges. Forget the patch, and you won't need the rammer. The ball doesn't need to grip the rifling so tightly for short ranges. Once the charge is in, drop the ball on the muzzle, and stamp the butt on the ground. That will seat the ball well enough."

Kit had Danny repeat this process until he could get off four rounds in a minute.

Kit showed Danny his rifle. "It was built by Benjamin Mills of Kentucky. He calls it a Plains Rifle. It's a bit shorter than your Hawken, making it easier to reload in a hurry. The caliber is a little larger for taking down big game like buffalo."

Danny admired this work of art, which though now worn by many years in the mountains, had obviously been well cared for.

Kit, who was always one to give credit to others, said, "Lieutenant Fremont's generosity on our first expedition made it possible for me to buy this.

"Men get excited in a fight," Kit continued, "and they miss easy shots. In a fight, or hunting, calm comes over me, and I'm a better shot than I am in target shooting. I want you to try relaxing and letting instinct guide your shots. Don't try to force anything."

Danny tried relaxing instead of tensing and his shooting improved. Instinct played a part as well. Wind, temperature and how finely ground the powder was all played a part in the strike of the round. There were too many factors to calculate them all, but the human brain has a wonderful faculty for guessing and estimating, and, when all else fails, just knowing.

Kit was not one who talked a lot. He kept to short statements when he talked at all. He demonstrated whenever possible, showing without saying anything, expecting Danny to observe and learn. It was a new kind of learning for Danny who was used to books and lectures. Although, while he was on the trail, Joe had eased him into this new kind of learning.

Schoolmasters are full of words and know how to manipulate them. Men who work with their hands lack all the fancy words to put into speech all that they know. It is easier and more accurate to show, less confusing.

Danny gleaned many lessons from Kit. Most of them weren't verbal. He'd simply adjust what Danny was doing or show him. He limited himself to very few words, seeming almost shy. He was truly kind and soft spoken.

After a few days, they switched to working with revolvers.

In those days, there weren't yet brass cartridges that could be loaded through the breech or back end of the weapon. The six-shooter took time to reload. The cartridge was "assembled" as a man loaded. The pistol would be half-cocked so the cylinder could be freely rotated. The cylinder was about 2-1/2 inches long with six open holes at the front to accept powder and ball and six nipples at the rear. With the barrel pointed up, the cylinder was rotated and black powder poured into each opening. He then topped the first cylinder with a ball and drove it home with a lever under the barrel. This was slow work, but necessary. When all this was done, a tiny percussion cap had to be seated on each nipple. Caps might fall off as the weapon was fired. They were supposed to 'blossom' and fall free when fired, but they could fall into and jam the mechanism.

Again Kit gave advice and instruction. "Danny, count the cylinders in your head as you load, and teach your fingers their tasks so they can do them fast without thought from you. Push the balls home with your thumb if you can. That lever under the barrel is slow in a fight.

"Teach your fingers to work fast with caps. They're small

and get tricky when you're hurried or under fire. Now, if you have time, grease the front of the cylinder with any grease at hand. A little black powder sometimes gets alongside the ball. Flame leaks out the front of the cylinder where it meets the barrel when you fire. The flame can ignite this excess powder. Then two or more cylinders fire at once. That can be embarrassing and leave you with an empty pistol at the wrong time."

"Don't put the cap on the last cylinder until you need it. Let the hammer rest on that one. If you leave the hammer on a cap and bump the pistol against something or drop it, it's sure to go off."

Roque quipped, "If you keep the pistol in your waist band, and it goes off accidentally, you probably won't have too many children, maybe."

Kit smiled. "Roque, show him how to shoot."

"*Bueno, Cristobal.* The *pistole* should be like your *mano*, your hand. Point with it like you point your finger. It's good for close targets. If the targets are far away, use your rifle. The muzzle will kick up when you fire so practice bringing the muzzle down to the target and squeeze the trigger as you cross the target. Don't jerk it. Try that."

Danny fired off six rounds at a target they'd set up twenty paces away.

"*Bueno.* Now reload quick as you can and do it again," said Roque.

In the closing dark, long flames shot from the muzzle. The lessons weren't given all at once but a little at a time with little speech and much demonstration.

As the men walked toward the house, Kit told Danny, "Carry two pistols. Twelve shots are better than six. If you're firing from a horse on the run, you can't aim. The horse moves, you move, the target moves. Get up close until you're almost touching, then fire."

As dark closed, in they settled down to smoke and talk. Danny watched as Roque built a *cigarrillo*, rolling a corn husk around his tobacco. Over at the *cochina*, the kitchen, Josepha was making a *cigarrillo* as well. Danny was shocked when she lit the thing. Where he came from ladies didn't smoke. He said nothing since no one else seemed mindful of this breech of morals. Kit pulled out and packed a pipe so short the bowl was close to his nose.

Cajun teamsters had talked Danny into a clay pipe with a stem so long he had to stretch out his arm to reach the bowl.

"Eet is good," one teamster had told Danny. "Eet makes zee smoke much coolair, no."

As he lit it the first time with the Cajuns, one said, "*Laissez les bons temps rouler.*"

"*Oui, oui,*" chorused the others. "Let the good times roll!" They laughed and slapped his back.

As Danny packed his pipe, Roque coughed. Danny tought the Mexican was surpressing a smile. He looked to Kit who also smiled.

"The short stem don't break so easy. And it keeps my nose warm."

Although Kit was shy of talking about his adventures, Roque liked to tell "stories of long ago" and stories about *brujos*, witches. The ladies loved them. Roque told them of an old man who was *loco,* crazy:

> There was a *viejo*, an old man, Don Quintana
> de *la Manga* from far away, down near Socorro

perhaps. This *viejo* loved the conquistadors because they were bold and brave and went into fights heavily outnumbered. He knew all their virtues and knew they were good Christians come to take the land from devils and idolaters. *Viejo* thought about them all the time. Disgusted with his own times, which he considered degenerate and lorded over by corrupt politicians, Don Quintana wanted to be like the conquistadors to share their virtue and their glory. Don Quintana wrote poems about the conquistadors. He became obsessed.

One day he was polishing an old cuirass and helmet left him by his ancestors when it came to him that he, Don Quintana, was a conquistador. He donned the armor, grabbed his sword, and hurried outside to mount his mighty steed, a donkey called *Acamorrado,* drowsy. He had with him his father's lance and cowhide shield. Perhaps his brain had broken a little bit.

Roque told his tale in Spanish for the ladies who sat enthralled, and then he and Kit translated it for Danny, who noticed that Kit's eyes glowed childlike as he listened. Roque went on:

So, Don Quintana set out to rid the world of evil. All around him he could see men who do not keep their oaths, who did not worship God as they should, who lied and cheated and stole. They were disgraceful, not like the conquistadors who lived by a knightly code.

As he went on his adventures, he was followed by his friend and neighbor, Nacho Sanchez. The don told him, "Nacho you will be my squire."

"What's a squire?"

"A squire serves a period as servant to the conquistador, cooking his meals and helping him with his armor and tending him when he is wounded. In return, the conquistador teaches the squire the arts of warfare, the uses of weapons, and the moral code of a conquistador. When the time is right, the conquistador will dub his squire a knight and raise him to that high plateau of being."

"*Bueno*," said Nacho.

They rode on for half a day until they met an old man in a hooded robe. The old man said, "*Hola*, traveler, whither do you go?"

"I am off to do great deeds and right injustice wherever I find it," replied the don.

"*Bueno*. If you give me some money, I will tell you a story," said the hooded traveler.

"I have taken a vow of poverty and don't have much," says the don.

"How much do you have?"

"Only two pesos."

"It is enough. Give it to me." The don did, and the old one told him. "Never be deceived. Charge in and attack evil no matter what."

"That's all?"

"That's all."

Later the don and Nacho spied a slave caravan returning from the Navajo country with women and children slaves.

"Ho, Nacho, Navajo raiders taking our people to captivity in their land!"

"Master," for that is what the don told Nacho to call him, "I think you are deceived."

"The *Viejo* told me not to be deceived." And with that he was gone, charging down the hill on his donkey with great ferocity, chasing the slavers with his small lance, hitting them with the side of his sword. His attack was so unexpected that he soon scattered the slavers, and the captive Navajo in turn escaped returning to their own country.

"Nacho, we have won a great victory!"

"Master, I don't know. We could be in big trouble if these *vatos* report you or even if they catch up to you. We better ride fast."

"Nonsense. I must stop and say a prayer and dedicate this victory to San Pedro."

"Why San Pedro?" asked Nacho.

"The *viejo*."

"The old man? You mean the one who took all your money?"

"*Si*, he was San Pedro."

Danny wasn't sure he understood these Mexican stories of Roque's. The moral seemed to be: "Trust strange old travelers and give them all your money receiving in return strange advice which you should follow." The strange traveler was always St. Peter or some other saint.

Roque taught Danny about knives.

"Let me see your knife," the Mexican said one day.

Danny pulled it out and started to hand it to him, butt first. Startled, Roque jumped back and fell to the ground, landing on his rear. He and Kit started laughing.

"Where did you get such a thing, *Amigo*? It is too large. That is no knife. It is a headsman's axe."

Danny looked puzzled. "I had it made. It's a Bowie knife, like Colonel Bowie carried in his fights and died with at the Alamo."

"Met Bowie once," said Kit. "Guess it was before he had that big knife made."

Roque continued his instruction. "It's too heavy to fight with. You want something light so you can flick in and out. Threaten your opponent's face and eyes. Then move away. When your knife is high like that, your belly is open. So flick and move. Make small cuts. Maybe he will drop his knife if you cut his hand. A cut to the shoulder might slow his arm. With such a big knife, you could never move fast enough.

"Here, I show you." They practiced, using slivers of wood for knives.

"This is okay for practice," said Roque later, "or for a duel maybe, but in a real fight you want something in your other hand, like maybe a tomahawk. Flick at his eyes, distract him, then smash the back of his head with your 'hawk."

They practiced this, too, and fighting with bare hands. Roque did not teach boxing with formal rules. Rather he taught free-style, anything goes, battling that keeps one alive. The roads in New Mexico in 1849 held many dangers. One might be challenged by Indians or thieves.

Danny worked hard at his lessons despite feeling like he was just killing time waiting to get his chance to trade with the Indians. No frontier heroes passed his way, just common folk. He carried his guns, knife and tomahawk with him everywhere as he was taught. It never occurred to him that he was doing this because danger lurked just over the horizon, which at Rayado seemed so far away. He never sensed that he was surrounded by *Indios cimarrones*, wild Indians, and Mexican *banditos*. The nearest help was in Las Vegas or Taos more than a day's ride away. Just living here beyond civilization was an act of courage. Kit's reputation held chaos at bay.

Danny scanned the horizon searching for giants.

Chapter 3

The Camp on the Llano

They were camped on *piñon* and juniper shrouded hills near Pecos, the greatest of all Pueblos for hundreds of years going back before memory. *N'deh*, the Jicarilla, came each year to this portal from the *llano*, the plains, to the Rio Grande, great river heartland of New Mexico. Since long before the elders' grandfathers' grandfathers' time, they had come. Once there was a great village here where a pass connected the *llano* and the *rio*. Crumbling walls abandoned, the last remnant of Pecos people had long since departed to live with their kin at Jemez. Once there had been great trade. The Llanero Jicarilla brought finely wrought baskets, salt, dried buffalo meat, and hides that they traded for pottery, corn, beans, squash, cloth, and turquoise jewelry. All of the river people depended on these Plains Apache for the meat they brought. It might have been an old habit that brought the

Llanero Jicarilla to Pecos in 1849. Like the Pecos village, the trade they once knew was now gone, stolen by *gavacho*—American—and Comanche, making Jicarillas and the Pecos people obsolete. They might have come here because Pecos was on the trail to Santa Fe, and there was some slim hope of trade.

No one knew how long the Jicarilla Apache had been coming to Pecos. Some say they were named for a nearby mountain that looked to the Spanish like an upturned chocolate cup. Others say the name referred to the fine baskets they made. The tribe was divided into two parts: the Llanero lived on the plains, the *llano*, and hunted buffalo, while the Ollero lived in the mountains along the Rio Grande and Chama. They farmed and made pots, *ollas* in Spanish, in addition to hunting and gathering.

Family camps were scattered across the hills like wildflowers in a mountain meadow. At each camp, a handful of tepees were occupied by the family of a senior woman with her husband, her daughters, and their husbands. At one camp there was much activity. Women worked under a brush arbor around a fire pit preparing food for everyone. They wore skirts of deerskin with bead decorated deerskin ponchos over their shoulders. A black belt, wide as two hands held side by side and decorated with *conchos,* decorative disks of silver hammered from coins, girded each woman's middle. Nearby a central tepee faced east. A girl emerged from this tepee, ran east, south, and west around the camp, and then reentered the tepee. The gathering was in her honor. It was the fourth day since nature had declared her a woman, and her family had gathered to assist her in the transition and to teach her control of the power that was now hers. If she paid attention and completed the ceremony properly, she would have health and long life.

Elsewhere, tepee sides were rolled up to admit the warm late summer breeze. Dogs ran unchecked about the camp. Scavengers who kept the camp clean and were sentinels, warning it of approaching strangers, they belonged to no one, but followed one family or another. Around the encampment, horses grazed. Children ran and played, happy to see their cousins again after long separation. The younger ones were completely naked and the dogs ran among them protecting them from rattlesnakes, wolves, and coyotes. Here and there a flute could be heard as a young man courted a girl he hadn't seen in many months. Men lounged, gambled, and contended at games of skill and prowess. One group wrestled.

Stripped to the waist, two young men faced each other, one perpetually smiling. He was called *Sonrisado*, the smiler. In a flash, the other charged. The opponent was the one the Mexicans called *Acentellado*, a flash of lightning. The Smiler held his ground, then suddenly stepped aside, grabbing Acentellado's arm as he flashed by, and pulling him off balance. The Flash recovered by spinning about and grappling with Sonrisado. The Smiler stepped back suddenly, stumbling. With lightning speed, Acentellado leaned into Sonrisado to push him to the ground. This action forced Acentellado into an awkward position.Too late, the Flash found the Smiler had stepped away again. Acentellado wrenched himself backward, but the Smiler was on him, using the Flash's own momentum to push him backward while hooking a heel behind his ankle. The Smiler's opponent fell hard in the dust.

There were cheers and groans from the crowd. The betting had been heavy on these two. The Flash was very fast and strong, the Smiler subtle. It was a good match. Bits of flint, some arrows, turquoise, shell, and *conchos* changed hands to settle the bets.

Two older men looked on. The smaller of the two, a man of medium height with long, iron gray braids, his back still straight and firm against advancing age, was speaking: "Subtlety is important. He does well."

"But speed and muscle work even better," the taller one replied. "Watch how Acha does."

A young man rose from the crowd of wrestlers and stood with his head and buffalo-shoulders towering above the others. He was Acha, the Hatchet, and subtle as an axe. From the cheer that went up, it was apparent that at least some of the crowd considered him their leader and champion.

"Ah," said *Saco Colorado,* Red Jacket, the smaller of the two elders, "your protégé. I understand he wants to wed your daughter, *Abuja.* A clever woman like the Needle, who is always sharp and to the point, should appreciate his subtlety."

This statement was more pointed and direct than was usual for Saco Colorado. He was concerned with the future of the tribe, and this discussion of young wrestlers was a political discussion of the merits of direct action over a more measured course. Acha figured prominently in this discussion of tribal politics because the old chief felt he was taking risks that were dangerous for the Jicarilla. Acha and his friends were what in other times and places might have been called highwaymen. The younger chief quietly condoned their behavior. Travelers on the Santa Fe Trail expected to pay the Indians a 'toll' for passing through their lands as long as it wasn't too much or too often. Acha was testing the limit in both directions. The two chiefs were careful not to press issues too directly with each other in fear of giving offense. On the *llano*, hazarded by the numerous Comanche, they needed each other, needed to keep the band together. This unity could only be accomplished cooperatively. Not only each chief but also each man had a right to make his own decisions and go his own way. Only when committed to a war party were the rights of the individual submerged in the group; only then could one leader expect to be followed without question.

"He is strong and has many horses and as much wealth as any of us," replied *Lobo Blanco,* White Wolf, the taller of the two, a man in early middle age at the height of his physical power. "The young men follow him."

Acha handed a fine rifle decorated with brass tacks to the man beside him in the crowd of wrestlers and then stripped off his deerskin shirt.

Saco Colorado continued, "He seems to have traded for a new rifle, and his friends appear to be rich in cloth and ribbon. Even Pinacate, the dull-witted Stink Bug, has been in favor with the young girls, making them gifts of ribbon and beads. How do you suppose they came by such wealth?"

"Perhaps they have been to Taos."

"Perhaps."

A beefy opponent, who looked powerful, but was smaller, rose to challenge Acha. He charged. Acha stood his ground unconcerned. Head down, the beefy one struck Acha in the middle. Unmoved, Acha bent and grasped him around the waist, and then straightening. Acha raised him from the ground feet up, head down, and threw him into the dust. Dazed, the smaller man rose to his knees.

"Such subtlety," applauded Red Jacket. "In Taos, the *Nakaiyeh,* the Spanish, say the long trail to the home of the *Mangani,* the Yankees, has been very dangerous this year." The Santa Fe Trail led to the land of the *Mangani.*

"The *Mangani* are few," said Lobo Blanco, "and their homeland far away. They did not always come."

Acentellado, the flash of lightning, rose to confront Acha. He feinted left, withdrew, then flashed to Acha's flank, and assaulted an unprotected shoulder. Acha barely stumbled and then spun, but Acentellado had moved beyond his grasp. The fast one circled and struck low at Acha's knees. Great paws grasped air where he had been. The knees remained unmoved. Acentellado began to glisten, but he did not slow. One lightning attack and withdrawal followed another with little effect.

The crowd was on its feet roaring with delight. Seldom did a fight continue so long. Speed was matched against brutish strength and only slightly less speed. The crowd sucked its collective breath. As Acentellado flashed to the attack, the other fighter whirled to grab him, catching only the air where he had been. The crowd roared with delight. Sweat dripped from Acentellado, the smaller fighter. He spied an opening, closed on a flank. Acentellado grasped Acha's waist to spin him to the ground. He grunted and strained as Acha stood like a tree. Acha's countering arm swung back and down. With crash of thunder he grasped the Lightning Flash and hauled him aloft. With a crashing jolt Acha hurled the Lightning Flash to the sand. Once Acentellado was caught, brute power and weight was more than a match for speed.

The crowd hushed fearing the young man's death. Acentellado rose slowly, shaken and, by the rules, beaten. He had been thrown to the ground. Acentellado staggered away unwilling to nurse his hurts in public.

Flexing his muscles, Acha showed his power. So far he had not exerted himself.

"Who is next?" he called out. "I'm just getting started!"

He strutted around the circle, glaring into the eyes of potential combatants, daring them to test themselves against him. He intimidated many with his display. Even bold fighters backed away disliking Acha for shaming them.

"*N'deh* are swift. Comanche and Kiowa are powerful," retorted Lobo Blanco seemingly unaware that flashing speed had just been defeated by brute force. "We will move fast and keep our enemies off balance staying beyond their grasp."

"Look at your young hero," said Saco Colorado point his lip at Acha. Jicarilla consider it impolite to point with a finger. "See! Like the Slayer of Monsters, the first of our People. His brute strength has overcome speed."

"*Zapato Negro,*" called the crowd bringing forth another champion to face Acha. His moccasins were beaded with a black background instead of the usual white, thus the name they called him, Black Moccasin. He was a medium-sized man, well muscled and quick.

Zapato did not charge Acha as the previous fighters had done. He first feinted left to see how Acha would respond. He dived right, rolling onto his side and shoulder, and then from behind, he kicked Acha's calf with both feet, dropping Acha to his knees. Acha recovered, spinning to face Zapato as he came back to his feet.

Zapato danced around Acha, staying just out of reach.

He feigned a strike and then withdrew, forcing a violent response from Acha who roared his displeasure. The crowd cheered, happy to see Acha frustrated for a change. He might be their champion, but he was overbearing. Zapato feinted low as if to grab Acha's ankle. Acha followed, gulping air as Zapato straightened to his full height. As Acha rose, Zapato grasped him about the shoulders and held Acha's head to his stomach. Acha rose as if the additional weight weren't there, leaving Zapato nowhere to go but up and over. Zapato flipped in midair landing on his feet and spinning to face Acha. As Acha turned fully erect, Zapato dove between his legs, kicking the backs of both knees as he landed. Acha went to his knees as Zapato scrambled to turn and rise. Before Zapato could follow up his advantage, Acha rose, sweating with the effort of overreacting to feigned as well as real moves. Now Acha was angry, and the anger added to his exertion. The crowd cheered wildly. "This one knows how to fight," judged Saco Colorado. "Zapato Negro is showing us the way." Indeed, although swift and muscular, Zapato fought with his head as much as his body.

The bout continued with Zapato repeating his tricks and feints, but now Acha was anticipating them. Zapato, despite feints and rolling dives, was using less energy than Acha whose moves were broad, powerful, and wide. Acha was tiring. If Zapato continued without a mistake, the bout would be his.

Zapato Negro faked left and started to roll to his right shoulder. Acha anticipated the move and had Zapato about the waist and spinning like a discus thrower. Lifting and using Zapato's momentum, Acha cast Zapato off in a lift that went over his head. Zapato wheeled through the air and landed hard without grace. He was done.

The wrestlers broke up and went on to other pursuits and games. A horse race was arranged and was soon underway. In the main tepee, the singing that would bring a young girl a long and prosperous life continued. Saco Colorado and Lobo Blanco moved on, their issue undecided and the elder, understanding how the application of wit, skill and speed had lost to brute force, feared for the future of the tribe while the younger missed the point.

The tribe would either need a buffalo hunt or a livestock raid against the Mexicans, the *Nakaiyeh*, along the *Sangre de Cristo*. They would need to raid along the Santa Fe Trail, as well. Saco Colorado knew that both courses held danger.

The chiefs returned to their conversation.

"The *Mangani* did not always come," said Lobo Blanco. "Perhaps one day they will come no more, especially if they find the long trail too dangerous. They are not a numerous people. Perhaps that is why they have learned to fight well. As for the *Nakaiyeh*, the Mexicans, what do they know? They are an ignorant, timid people who dwell in smelly houses of mud. Armed with bow and spear, they run from Apache."

"Perhaps it is as you say," replied Saco Colorado. "Perhaps." The old chief did not wish to give offense by directly disputing Lobo Blanco's claims, but he worried about the strength of the *Mangani*. "The *Nakaiyeh* say there were big battles far to the south in which *Mangani*, far from their homeland, defeated many *Nakaiyeh*."

"Every trail is dangerous to the *Nakaiyeh*," Lobo Blanco evaded. "They fear shadows."

"Some trails are dangerous for Jicarilla," Red Jacket needled.

"How are we to live then?" asked Lobo Blanco

rhetorically. "Many more travelers have come along that trail this year, more than last, more than ever before. It has been so since the *Mangani* soldiers have come, but this year is worse with the undisciplined ones traveling to the big water far where the sun sets. The *Mangani* traders kill and scatter the game along the trail. They bring new trade goods and leave little for Jicarilla to trade in the *Nakaiyeh pueblos*. If we cannot hunt and cannot trade, are we to starve? Are the Jicarilla to be little men of no substance?"

"We could hunt buffalo as we have always done," answered Saco Colorado.

"That's a dangerous trail for Jicarilla," said Chief White Wolf. "Wet Foot, Kiowa Apache, and the Comanche are on the buffalo *llano* in great numbers."

"I do not wish to face Wet Foot who dwell in caves and wear the paws of bears to maul their enemies. Wet Foot are our most hated enemy even if they do speak the language of *N'deh*, the Jicarilla," replied Saco. "I would face them rather than starve so I might walk as a man. I would even face the ant-numerous Comanche. Perhaps if we gather our cousins, the Olleros, with us and move swiftly, we can kill the buffalo without having to fight our enemies."

"Perhaps," the old chief muttered to himself, "if our brethren of the White clans, the Olleros, will come over the mountains and hunt buffalo with us, we may have some strength for the dangers of the *llano*. We must ask them at Go jii ya."

Acha went in search of Abuja, Lobo Blanco's daughter. He found her on the edge of the encampment preparing her horse for a ride. Her hair was long, black, and lustrous. Her slim figure was covered by a skirt fringed to her knees and a cape in white, brain-tanned deerskin decorated in beads of white and light blue with dark blue for contrast. Leggings, just visible through the fringe below her knees, covered her limbs preserving her modestly when she rode. Between skirt and cape she wore a black belt, broader than a hand, decorated in silver conchos. Suspended in a beaded case from this belt was a long, thin Spanish dagger she called her *abuja*, needle. The year before, a Mexican buffalo hunter had insulted her and she had scarred him deeply across the face. She would have killed him if she had not been stopped. She shook back her hair.

"I love it when you do that," Acha greeted her. "It is like a fine mare shaking back its mane."

"I know where you can find a good mare," Abuja retorted, black eyes flashing, "but it isn't here."

"I have offered your father twenty ponies for you." Acha tried to mollify her.

"Horses again? Perhaps you should marry one. Do you think I come so cheap?"

"It is a very good offer, more than I would give for any other," Acha stammered.

"Perhaps you should take another then," Abuja needled, "and save yourself some horses."

"But I want you," he protested trying to sway her.

"Perhaps you should have asked me first. Have you played the flute or violin for me?" queried Abuja. Like all women, Jicarilla maids liked to have love songs played and sung to them. The fiddle and flute were associated with courting rather than medicine.

"You know I can't play. I am strong in war and raiding," replied the robust brave.

"Then ride away to war and let those who can play court me," Abuja answered. Hiking her skirt, she swung up onto her horse she rode away, leaving him in the dust.

She rode far out of sight of the camp to the clear, cold water of the Pecos River. Abuja stopped and dismounted. The Apache were modest and fastidious about their camps, traveling a mile and more each morning to do their toilet. At the river, she found a secluded spot and, stripping off her garments, began to bathe herself in the river using mashed yucca root as soap.

Above her on the hillside, two Mexican hunters spotted her horse and with stealth began to search for its rider. They concealed themselves where they could watch her bathing.

"Ah, I know this one," whispered a hunter with a jagged scar on his face. "I have seen her before. She is good to look at, no? She will bring a good price in Santa Fe. See, the smoke from the camp is far to the east. When she starts to wash her hair, let's grab her."

The other nodded his assent. They were dressed much alike, ill-shaven with long, greasy hair under straw sombreros. They wore tattered moccasins, greasy *botas*—leggings— broad, red sashes about their waists, and dirty, loose-fitting, white cotton shirts. Their shoulders were covered with boldly colored *serapes* also well worn and dirty. They carried well used and ill-treated flintlock rifles. Each carried two knives, one of which was so large as to be almost a small sword.

As Abuja bent, hair over her head, face almost to the water rubbing in the yucca suds, the two men loomed over her. Sounds of the river and splashing water distracted the maiden while the long hair hanging over her face blinded her. Thus, the hunters were able to take her unawares. Abuja struggled, adding four, fresh, bleeding welts to the one's face, but she was a girl, and they were strong men. They wrapped her kicking and biting, a piece of someone's ear in her teeth, in a blanket and bound it round with a lariat until she could barely move. Then they tossed her across her horse's back and tied her down. This would make it hard to breathe and take some of the fight out of her.

The one with the bleeding ear was ready to take his revenge once she was securely tied down, but the man with the bleeding face stopped him.

"Two things, *amigo*," he said. "If we bruise her, she will bring less in Santa Fe. If we do not leave now, her family might catch us." They started out for Santa Fe, heading west away from the Jicarillas at the best pace they could manage.

A scout from a ten-man patrol returning on the trail from Santa Fe to Las Vegas on the plains saw the dust raised by the approaching horses. From an artillery company stationed at Las Vegas, the patrol was acting as infantry away from their big guns. A portion of the company was mounted on horses, and this patrol was using most of them. On foot or horseback they were expected to keep up with the elite dragoons, who were trained to fight both from horseback and on the ground as infantry.

The scout reported to his leader. "Lieutenant Burnside, there are two riders approaching up the trail coming fast leading a third horse."

Ambrose Burnside was tall with a high forehead. He wore a cap of blue, with a shiny leather bill and high mushroom-shaped crown. His epaulets of rank were pinned to a cotton duck shell jacket that came to his waist and was worn over a blue flannel shirt. He wore tan cotton duck trousers with a red stripe down the side, indicating he was a "Red Leg," an artilleryman. His feet and shins were covered by tall black leather boots that came to his knee. Saber and Colt revolver completed his uniform.

"Sergeant Swartout, let's find a bend and spread the men out east from there along one side of the trail," ordered Burnside. "You and I with the interpreter will wait to the west of the bend and surprise these riders. If they balk, the men can scoop them up."

Burnside's men wore cotton duck trousers and plaid cotton shirts, an odd collection of boots, along with broad-brimmed felt hats, some with an ostrich feather. The regulation uniform was ill-suited to summer wear in the warm Southwest and soon wore out in the field. So the men supplied themselves and, except for their weapons, didn't much resemble soldiers. They carried muskets in .69 caliber and short artillery swords. A few had "horse pistols" in .69 caliber, pistols too large for a man to carry on his hip and so holstered to the saddle.

The Mexicans rounded the bend and came face to face with Lieutenant Burnside and Sergeant Swartout, with their revolvers drawn, and the interpreter. Seven "red legs" emerged from hiding along the road behind the Mexicans. Through his interpreter Lieutenant Burnside inquired as to the Mexicans' haste and cargo.

Walking up to the trailing horse, Swartout pulled back the blanket to reveal Abuja's face. She spat in his.

"Sir! Lieutenant Burnside, I think I know this woman. They call her Abuja, the Needle. She's the daughter of Lobo Blanco, the Jicarilla leader," called Swartout. He was tall, over six feet, though slender, in his late twenties, tough, and in bad need of a shave.

"Where did you get her?" Burnside demanded of the Mexicans. Turning to Swartout, "Get her down from there, Sergeant."

"We found her running *en pelota*, naked like that and thought somebody bad must be chasing her," said the scar-faced Mexican, still bleeding from his scratches. "We gave her that blanket and tried to help her."

"Then why is she bound like that?" continued Burnside.

"Oh, to hide her from her pursuers and because she is *muy cimarron y loco*, very wild and crazy. See what she did to my face when I gave her the blanket? We will take her to the priest in Santa Fe. He will know how to cast out her demons and return her to her people," said Scarface.

"Ask her what happened," Burnside told his interpreter who consulted with Abuja. Like many Jicarilla Apache she was conversant in Spanish.

"She says her people are near. These men took her captive while she was bathing in the stream. She heard them say they plan to sell her at the slave market."

Scarface interjected, "No, no. We only tried to help. We will take her to the priest."

Burnside's eyes were hard ice. "That's all right then. You were only trying to help. We'll take her off your hands and see that she comes to no harm before she is returned to her people. Since you are only trying to help her, we'll relieve you of the burden and the danger."

"No, no. We'll get her to the priest, very safe," Scar-face insisted.

Sergeant Swartout cocked his pistol. The click came loud and unexpected. "Well then, *amigos*, it's time you were running along. The lieutenant has told you how it will be. We are soldiers, he is an officer and them's his orders. We don't want to detain you further. *Adios*."

The Mexicans departed with many backward glances, quietly mumbling inspired curses. The terrors of hell might have been welcome had any of them come to pass.

"Well, sir," Sergeant Swartout inquired, "what will we do with her?"

"She'll be a hostage against her father's good behavior, I think. But first, let's get her something to wear and get her tied on a horse in an upright manner. We'll get her to Las Vegas and let Captain Judd decide," Burnside replied. "We'll want to pass the Jicarilla camp in the early dusk without being seen. Have the interpreter explain her new situation to her."

"You will be treated well while you are held a hostage," the interpreter explained to Abuja in Spanish she barely understood.

"What is hostage?" asked the Needle.

"You will be hostage to your father's good behavior and that of his people. You are safe as long as they behave well. If they rape and kill *Americanos*, you will be raped and killed. If they torture our people, you will be tortured. I think your father loves you and will want no harm to come to you, so he will act well and you will be treated well. Do you understand?" asked the interpreter.

"Yes."

Back in camp, Acha thought of himself as lovesick. He wanted Abuja. She was the most beautiful of the Jicarilla maidens, and he wanted to posses her. He would have her. No one had ever been able to keep anything from him. He was a war leader and soon, with her at his side, he would be a chief. Mounting his horse, he went in search of her. He did not find her but ran into a group of hunters returning with fresh game for the camp.

Lieutenant Burnside's small patrol passed the Jicarilla camp in the dusk unnoticed. A little further on, as often happens in the semi-dark, they found themselves among riders crossing their path. Before either side realized what was happening, the two parties were intermixed. Then they saw each other. Recognizing them as Jicarilla hunters returning to the camp, Abuja called out to them. There were shouts.

"No firing!" yelled Burnside. "Use your swords in self-defense only. We're too close to the camp and don't want shots to be heard. Follow me to Las Vegas!"

"You heard him, men," called Swartout. "Swords only. Fall in on the lieutenant. We ride hard for the north, for Las Vegas. Don't let the girl escape. Get her up near the lieutenant. Now ride."

In the dark, arrows flew. Burnside grunted. Swartout looked and saw an arrow protruding from the lieutenant's neck, fletching to one side, barb to the other. The lieutenant couldn't speak, but signaled that they should continue. The "red legs" were at a disadvantage and far from help. All the Jicarilla needed do was rouse the camp and then slow the artillerymen till help arrived.

Among the Jicarilla hunters, Acha was surprised and confused. A chill ran down his spine. He called to the others, "They are too many for us. We must break off and get help from camp." A chance was lost, and Abuja was whisked away to the soldiers' camp at Las Vegas.

The small party of Jicarilla hunters did not pursue the

mounted artillerymen and returned to camp. The soldiers continued their hard ride, alternately running and walking their horses. The lieutenant stayed in his saddle for more than an hour and then slumped.

Mercifully, Sergeant Swartout called a halt. Gently lowering the lieutenant from his horse, they cut the barb and fletching from the arrow to shorten it. They then wound a bandage around his neck to slow the bleeding. Nothing major seemed to have been cut, or Burnside would have been long dead. The Sergeant deemed it better to wait for a doctor to remove the stump of the arrow. Having done what they could, they tied the lieutenant's wrists to his saddle and his ankles to his stirrups. They still had a long ride ahead.

In the Jicarilla camp, Saco Colorado and Lobo Blanco sat on one side of a tepee watching two teams play the Moccasin Game. Four moccasins had been buried on either side of the fire pit. A blanket was raised in the middle, and the first team hid a stick in a moccasin. The blanket was lowered and on the other side Acha's friends, Sonrisado, Pinacate, and others, prepared to guess which moccasin contained the stick.

"I am owl. I can see through the dark," said Sonrisado.

Bets were made on his ability.

"The stick is there," he said pointing to a moccasin.

"Perhaps you are only a day bird, Sparrow," Zapato Negro told him from the other side. "The stick hides elsewhere." He laughed and the blanket was raised. This time Acha's friends hid the stick.

When the blanket was lowered, Zapato said, "I am mole and can see underground." More bets were made on the basis of how strong the mole spirit might be in Zapato who was about to guess the location of the hidden stick. All Jicarilla had powers drawn from various spirits. Which spirits supported them and how strongly at any given time were the basis for the gambling. "The stick is there!" he said pointing.

He was correct, and his partisans cheered and laughed.

There was a clatter of horses' hooves and shouts as fast moving riders approached the camp. A woman's wailing was heard from outside as a hunter rushed into the tepee.

"Lobo Blanco, Abuja is taken by the pony soldiers!"

For once, Acha was not eager to say anything.

Chapter 4

Taos

Achill was already in the high country air. Early September brought fall, if only gently so far. One fine, crisp morning, Danny and Roque saddled up two gentle mules for the ladies and two more spirited mules for Kit and Danny. Danny's trade goods and some that Kit had were loaded on a string of pack animals. Roque cut out and saddled a fine stallion that had been "gentled" to the saddle. It was a magnificent animal, black, with white stockings.

Kit kidded him. "Haven't I told you about horses and mules, Roque?"

"*Si*, Kit. Mules are better, you say; they are more gentle and friendly. They are smarter and more sure footed. If you cut them, the smell of their blood frightens the *Indios'* ponies. If you're hungry, they taste better. They can smell *Indios* coming."

"And *Indios* ain't so likely to lift your hair to steal a mule," smiled Kit, "'ceptin' some Patches who count mule a great delicacy."

"But I am so handsome on such a fine beast, no? All the *senoritas* will flock to me!" said Roque.

The men bid farewell to Tom Boggs and his wife, Rumalda, the eldest sister of Teresina. Tom was Kit's partner and longtime friend. Tom figured prominently in many of the stories about Kit, at least, in those that were true. He would watch the rancho while Kit was away.

As they rode, Danny and Roque talked.

Danny asked, "I've been told the names of many Jicarilla, including those who raided Kit's rancho. It seems to me that they all sound like Spanish names. Why is that? Don't they have Apache names?"

"Si, " replied Roque, "they do. When you have seen their little children, you will notice that they don't start to speak until they are nine or ten-years-old. This is because their language is so difficult that no one can speak it except Kit and other Jicarilla, but it takes them a long time to learn." He smiled at his wit. "We can't pronounce their names, and they don't like to tell them. They are afraid it will give us power over them. They come into the towns to trade so we know them, and we give them nicknames that seem appropriate. Some have lived with our families for a time and have taken the family's name for their own, or, at least, people think it is their name."

Kit overheard the conversation and added, "Even among themselves, they go by nicknames."

"Si, si, " said Roque. "That is why their names often seem funny to us and appropriate to them." Josepha and

Teresina were eager to get over the mountain to Taos where they would visit relatives while the men were away. The five rode west following the Rayado Creek up its canyon to the heights of the *Sangre de Cristo* and entered the Moreno Valley where they camped for the night, enveloped in the sharp tang of pine and earthy smells of their stock. These smells were soon joined by *piñon* smoke and the aroma of Josepha's cooking.

Danny and Roque prepared camp, the sting of high mountain air turning their cheeks rosy. Suddenly Kit turned to the east transfixed. He bent and grabbed a handful of dust and tossed it in the air as he reveled in the show of light over the peaks. The setting sun caught the high peaks in fiery red light made brighter by darkness already abroad in the valley beyond. The mountain itself gave up a reddish mist, like flames dancing over peaks on the horizon. Kit was chanting a prayer in a language neither Spanish nor English.

Finishing he turned and whispered to Danny, "Angel fire. Can you see that and not know God rules? Look there."

The long red rays of the setting sun striking mist or ice crystals formed a reddish flaming band along the ridge in the east. Some call this angel fire "alpenglow." It is like cold fire blazing among the trees on the ridge. Danny Trelawney had never seen it before and thought the display awe inspiring. He, too, whispered a prayer, while the women knelt in prayer.

"Do you suppose God minds they say Catholic prayers?" Danny wondered aloud. "I was taught that Romanism was full of superstition and evil."

"Would any God who claims to love men reject a prayer from angels such as these?" Kit replied.

They passed the night peacefully, hardly daring to break

the silence of God's own cathedral. In the morning, their journey continued down the other side of the mountain, and they arrived near Taos in the late afternoon. Below them rolled a sea of grass enclosed on three sides by *Sangre de Cristo* Mountains. Taos stood on a spit of land, a sheltered harbor in a great grass bay.

"Over there, Danito," Roque pointed to the mouth of the bay ten miles away, "is the Rio Grande Gorge, thousands of feet deep, with cliffs all the way to the bottom. You can't cross it unless you go to Ranchos de Taos and follow the River Road many miles south. Or you could go way up north to Arroyo Hondo, where mountain men distill Taos Lightning."

Taos was in the high country on a plain surrounded by mountains. Isolated by these mountains, the town was accessed by high passes and steep, narrow trails beside the river.

"The road divides at Ranchos de Taos," continued Roque, "The rougher road descends into the Rio Grande Gorge and follows the river as far as Santa Cruz before climbing to Santa Fe. The mountain road goes up the canyon back into the *Sangre de Cristo* through the villages of Picuris, Trampas, and Truchas before dropping down to Chimayo.

"See the church there in the plaza Ranchos de Taos?" Roque pointed. "It is dedicated to San Francisco de Asís. *Es muy bonito, no?*"

"It is very pretty, yes," replied Danito who was rapidly acquiring New Mexico Spanish, a language of strange meanings and exceptional idioms and mysterious to all other Spanish-speakers. In the distance to the south, Danito saw a church with two bell towers and massive, flying buttresses of adobe. As Roque said, "Very handsome," or as Danny reminded himself, very handsome from a distance. As they drew closer, he could see that it was adobe and his old prejudices rebelled.

"It looks good from a distance, Roque," he protested, "but it's made of mud. And it has no windows. Can this be a proper house of God? At home churches have stained-glass windows and are made of the best materials."

"When Bishop Zubiria visited in 1830, our first visit by a bishop is 80 years, he was of like mind with you," Roque scowled. "He ordered all of our *bultos*, *retablos* and *santos* removed as too ugly for a church, too ugly for God. But they were made with love and devotion to Him, and when the bishop departed, Padre Martinez put them back. How can anything made with love of God be too ugly for Him?

"The church ignored us for a very long time," Roque went on. "New Mexico belonged to the Franciscan missionaries and had no bishop. All of the priests were governed by the Order. They were friars, monks, come to convert the Indians and only "visited" our churches. I learned the church and its history from Padre Martinez. When the Mexican government in distant Mexico City kicked out the Spanish Franciscans, he was the only priest left. The bishop is far away in Monterey, Danito."

"Can't you ask for priests to be sent?" Danny asked.

Roque continued his account. "They do not want to come. We are a poor people, and priests do not like to come far to a poor parish where their life will be hard. Padre Martinez, he trains new, local men for the priesthood. Now there are almost 20 priests between Taos and El Paso."

"Tom Boggs told me something the other day," said

Danny. "He criticized the people because so few are married, suggesting they were immoral and given to vice. Is this why? Because there are so few priests?"

Roque scowled again, his anger growing. "The Yankees bring this criticism often, that we are immoral. Our women smoke and drink and gamble, they say. Even our priests gamble and on Sunday, too, they say. And the priests charge too much, making the people poor and priest-ridden, they say. It is custom for the priests, who get few tithes, to charge high fees to perform the rites. Nobody is married in church. Only *ricos* can afford it. Better to save money for last rites."

"But that's simony!" protested Danny. "It's immoral to charge for religious rites. The Reformation tried to correct such evils. Christ didn't charge for salvation. It's wrong to make money from church offices and ceremonies."

Roque fumed.

"Josepha and I are married," stated Kit trying to ease a conversation that had become tense. "I'm no *rico*." He looked fondly over his shoulder at his Chepita riding a little behind the men and chatting with her niece.

Roque was well versed in affairs of the church. He understood why it wasn't simony, was just the local custom, practical and a relief to the poor who were beyond being burdened by the tithe. The few *ricos* ended up paying the most. When he was orphaned, Padre Martinez raised the boy in his home intending to prepare him for the priesthood, so Roque got as fine an education as any man in New Mexico. But Roque was too full of energy and sin for the priesthood and ran away, taking up with Kit as Josepha's guardian during the long years when the mountain man was away with Fremont. Still, Roque liked Danito, and he dreaded the day when the young man would learn about the *Penitentes*. They had done much good, but their way seemed outrageous even to Catholics, like Bishop Zubiria of Monterey. Roque decided he must explain, must help Danito understand that he was being narrow minded.

Taos was the first town Danny had seen in New Mexico. Cimarron and Rayado were no more than a few scattered ranchos while Taos had a plaza and three, widely scattered, churches: one in Ranchos de Taos, one at the Taos Indian Pueblo, *San Geronimo*, and one in Don Fernando de Taos near the plaza. It was the first town Danny had seen since leaving Missouri 950 miles behind him.

Set on a hill above the Taos River, the town was a castle, walls smooth and featureless without windows or doors, a bastion to repel enemies. A few turrets rose above the walls, second-story rooms, although they were rare. When building in adobe, the lower walls had to be very thick indeed to support an upper room. The tall, twin bell towers of a church stood outside the plaza away from the town. Mexican men congregated along the south, outer wall of the plaza.

"How indolent," said Danny. "Don't they have anything better to do than sit lazily soaking up the sun like a bunch of lizards smoking *cigarettos?*"

With an effort, Roque held his temper. He'd heard this all before, but more important, he knew that Danny, although he had grown up in narrow-minded, straight-laced New England, learned quickly from experience and was willing to set his preconceived notions aside. Roque gestured toward the seated men. "They sit where it is warm to talk and smoke and observe the traders as they come and go. They don't have much to trade and take no part; they just sit here, politicking amongst themselves.

"These men work hard on their farms and ranchos when there is need. They run herds of sheep and cows on communal grazing land in the mountains, farming with water from the *acequia madre*, the mother ditch, where water belongs to all. Their fields are watered in rotation. They work together very hard when there is work to be done, but they do not try to do better than their neighbors.

Roque continued sadly, "They share everything with their families. *Primos*, cousins, are everywhere. Working hard and doing better than your neighbors is the road to disaster. On communal land, if a man's sheep produce better than his neighbors, he must be stealing more than his share of grass or worse, stealing lambs. If his crops do better, there will be accusations of water theft. It will be said the man does not treat his family properly, that he does not share. He will be thought of as a bad man, and soon they will call him a *brujo*, a witch. And so, they sit in the sun and smoke and politick and try to advance in their neighbors' esteem." He shook his head. "Meanwhile, the *gavachos*, the Americans, amass fortunes."

Old communal habits die hard and inhibit individual initiative. In New Mexico, one got ahead, perhaps a little bit, with the consent of the neighbors by politicking. The men were excellent politicians. While they basked in the sun on the south side of the plaza smoking cigarettes, they were not being lazy; they were politicking. They did not lack ambition but knew its risks.

"There is more to it, Roque," said Kit. "The government in Mexico City didn't allow these people to have basic tools. It didn't want them to buy or sell outside the country. All manufactured goods were supposed to come from Mexico City. This kept the people poor."

"*Si*," responded Roque. "But even with the coming of the Yankees, they have little they can trade to buy things. *Taoseños* trade potatoes and beans with Chimayo for blankets, fruit, and *chilis*. Corn, potatoes and beans don't travel well across the plains. They don't have enough money to buy tools, and without tools, they can't make very much to trade.

"Under the Mexican government, only corrupt officials in Santa Fe and a few *ricos* in the *Abajo*, the land south of Santa Fe, garnered much from the Santa Fe trade. New Mexicans were too poor to buy very much. This came as a shock to many coming to the city for the first time. Goods passed through New Mexico affecting the people of the *Rio Arriba*, the high country north of Santa Fe very little. Santa Fe was a remote backdoor to Mexican trade where tariffs, though seemingly high, were much lower than in Mexican ports. Goods went deep into Mexico where people had the wealth to buy the things the *gavachos* brought. Americans now rule in Santa Fe. The old rules and tariffs are gone, but for New Mexicans in *Rio Arriba*, life changed little. The people of *Rio Arriba* still had no wealth and little to trade.

"In Taos, Anglo traders buy furs from mountain men," said Roque. "These mountain men are mostly *gavachos*, or French from St. Louis and Canada. Some are *Indios* from the States, but very few are Mexican. Strong Taos Lightning fuels the fur trade. This whiskey is traded all over the mountains to buy furs. It is distilled from local wheat by old mountain men at Arroyo Hondo. *Taoseños* have very little part in this."

Near to town, Mexican *carretas*, two-wheeled carts, drawn by oxen creaked by the travelers to the slow pad of the hooves of huge beasts. Great, heavy wheels four or five feet across and many inches thick squealed as wood ground on the wood of greaseless axles.

Responding to Danito's puzzled expression, Roque explained, "The wheels are made entirely of wood with no iron at all. See how the bed of the *carreta* is made of a few rough boards? The sides are branches tied together."

Danny noticed how the sides were peeled, and twisted branches stuck up at intervals looking very crude and even fragile through poor construction.

"We have no sawmill to make fine boards," Roque went on. "Wood is split with an axe. We lack iron for saws and iron to make carts and put tires on wheels as the Yankees do."

Carretas were ugly and crude, but not as ugly as the way oxen were hitched to the cross-trees which were bound directly to horns.

Kit noticed Danny looking. "It forces the animal to pull with its head back using the strength of its neck. It's uncomfortable for the ox. We use oxbows across the shoulders which let the animal push with its strength."

Between the weight and design of the *carreta* and manner of hitching, most of the advantage of the wheel was lost. *Carretas* were small compared to Yankee wagons.

The party stopped at the *casa Jaramillo*, home of Kit's in-laws. Its rooms were built in a square around a central courtyard. Josepha and her niece were greeted by family and taken inside while the men, less welcome, were left to tend their livestock. Chores taken care of, three men, Kit, Danny and Roque, set out to see Don Fernando de Taos. Roque, a native son, served as tour guide.

Walking through a long, narrow passage between

buildings, the three entered the plaza swathed in the smell of *chili*, garlic and onion, and the aroma of meat roasting and *piñon* smoke. After the clean smells of the pine forests, the odor of too many humans too close together was overwhelming. Danny thought it might be easy to close off the entrances, making the plaza a fort sealed to the outside world. *Casas,* with their own courtyards, adjoined each other around the plaza, showing only *zaguans*, gates large enough to admit a wagon, to the plaza. The rooms inside closest to the *zaguan* were merchants' offices and display rooms. Family lived further inside. Peddlers sat against walls of the plaza, their wares on blankets before them. Except for the *zaguans*, the plaza was as closed inside as out.

"There are no doors or windows," commented Danny.

"Glass is very expensive," Kit told him. "There is no mill to make it here. Any that you see came across the plains in a wagon. There are windows at my house. I got them for my Chepita. Doors need metal hinges and these, too, are very expensive."

"Look how the doors of the *zaguans* are hinged," said Roque. Danny saw that round wooden pegs extended from the corners of the doors into the adobe or the lintel.

"That must loosen up pretty fast," he reflected. Roque nodded.

"The plaza is for *fandango*, for parties," Roque said. "It is kept clear. If *Indios* attack, people bring their livestock here. See the bell tower? The bell is to warn of attacks and to call the people together."

Danny began to inspect the wares of the seated peddlers. He picked up a sconce to give it closer inspection. It was beautifully decorated with a pattern of tiny holes that would light up. He realized that it had been created from a tin can, hammered into shape and pierced repeatedly with a nail.

"That can probably came across the plains full of peaches," Kit said. "New Mexico is very poor in metal."

Taos bustled with activity. A surprising number of the buildings on the plaza were occupied by Anglo traders.

"All the men of business seem to be Americans," commented Danny.

"Kit, Roque," boomed a big man, "Good to see you. Who's this with you?"

The man was powerful and tall with a great drooping mustache. He wore black city clothes and knee-high riding boots. Bulges under his long coat suggested hidden knives and guns.

"Hello, Luke," said Kit. "Danny Trelawney, I'd like you to meet Lucien Maxwell. I know he looks like a pirate, but he's a man you can rely on and trust. He's never let down a friend. He used to be a mountain man. Now he just likes to own everything."

Liking the introduction, Luke beamed as he shook Danny's hand. Kit had already explained that the land grants Lucien owned stretched from the *Sangre de Cristo* across the Llano Estacado and that Maxwell was his benefactor who helped Kit to buy the land at Cimarron.

"William Bent's in town, Kit," Luke said before departing. "He's pretty upset with St. Vrain. They say he blew up Fort William rather than let St. Vrain sell it from under him to the army. Stop by the *hacienda*, *amigo*. Bring your friends."

"There are a lot of mountain men here," Roque said, "as well as other people connected to the fur trade."

"They revel on Taos Lightning and *fandango*," said Kit, "and they live with women who are not their wives as Padre Martinez reminds everyone on Sundays." He scowled at this last indictment. "He doesn't like Americans, especially William Bent. Didn't like his brother, Governor Charles neither, and now Charles is murdered."

"Kit," said Roque softly, "the padre speaks against immorality and against those who encourage the *Indios* to drink and steal for their own profit. During the uprising, he protected many people."

Kit was not mollified. "Charles Bent was my friend and a good trader. He treated Mexicans and Indians well. That old priest is a devil!"

Roque changed the subject. "The mountain men like it here because Taos is far from Santa Fe. There are fewer rules to break and no one to enforce them. Indians and mountain men come here to trade. They are not bothered by government."

After Kit turned them in through the *zaguan*, the front gate, of Bent, St. Vrain. and Company. Ceran St. Vrain spotted them and hurried over.

"Kit, I'm glad you're here," he said, hardly noticing Roque or Danny. He was another powerfully built man, clearly one who had come here from the mountains, though well dressed in the city clothes of a merchant. His broad, jowly face had a sad, bulldog look, but his eyes were intelligent. He spoke with a French accent. "William's here. You'll want to see him. He's gone crazy. He's blown up the fort! They say he's gunning for me. I might have to kill him first in self-defense. I don't want to do it. He's been my partner for 20 years."

It sounded like he wanted Kit's protection.

Kit introduced them to Ceran.

Roque whispered to Danny while St. Vrain and Kit talked, "William Bent is St. Vrain's business partner and the proprietor of Fort William, Bent's Fort, on the Arkansas River. William lost his younger brother George last year to illness. George ran the store here until he died. His elder brother, Charles, was murdered in the Uprising of '47. William likes the Plains and the Cheyenne. He seldom comes to Taos."

"Kit, you've got to help me," St. Vrain pleaded. "I think he's going to kill me."

"No promises," Kit said. "I'll do what I can. What did you do to make him so angry?"

"Nothing," swore St. Vrain. "I talked to the army about selling the fort to them, but the price was much too low. The Indian trade is down. Too much competition since this became the United States. We should sell it. He thinks I went behind him."

"Did you?" asked Kit.

"I talked to the army," St. Vrain said, "but I would have taken any offer to him before I accepted. He's my partner. I think someone from the army must have gone by the fort and said something."

Kit nodded.

"But he's really angry, Kit." St. Vrain continued. "They say he blew up the fort. He must be killing mad. I'll have to shoot him first."

"'They' say a lot of things that aren't so," said Kit softly.

"You know how he gets." pleaded St. Vrain. "He's killed men before for doing him wrong. He burned out those traders who tried to build a post above him on the Arkansas."

"I'll tell him you didn't try to cheat him," said Kit.

They stepped back out into the sunlight from the dark interior of the store almost bumping into a stocky man in buckskin. He was different from many Danny had seen. His buckskin was clean and white, beautifully adorned with beads and tufts of fur. He wasn't a dandy, too tough for that, but he came close. Of medium build and height, he was only slightly taller than Kit. His eyes were deep, brooding, and intense. Anger boiled close to the surface, but he held it in check.

"Kit," the man said obviously pleased. "Am I glad to see you."

"William," Kit replied, "It's good to see you, too." Kit introduced Danny and Roque to William Bent, Teresina's uncle. "Let's find a place to sit and talk over some coffee."

They found a *cantina* with a new *portal,* a covered porch, where tables were set up in the open. *Portales* were becoming more common in 1849, an idea the Americans brought with them. Once seated, Bent launched into his narrative.

"The fur trade is dead, Kit," he said. "Dead as can be, gone beaver. Even trade in buffalo robes has no more profit in it. Since the States took over New Mexico, there's just too much competition. It's not like the glory days. Hardly need the fort anymore."

Kit nodded.

"Ceran told you I blew up the fort, didn't he?" Teresina's uncle continued. "I didn't. I heard the story. Someone passin' at a distance saw smoke. I burned a few things I couldn't take with me. Thought 'bout burnin' the whole thing; make it useless to the army. Did Ceran tell you why I did some destruction? Bet he told you I was crazy and coming to blow him up next. Good! He ought to think that. Did he tell you what he did?

William continued without waiting. "Ceran tried to sell it to the army without telling me. Price was way too low. He'd have given me my share, I'm sure. He's honest, but he knew I'd object to the price.

"The Army would have used it to control Cheyenne," Bent continued. "That idea lacked appeal, not at the price they offered. I didn't need it anymore so I moved out. It's Ceran's conscience makes him think I'm coming for him. Let him worry."

"How'd you know he'd tried to sell?" Kit asked.

"This brevet captain came by with a patrol, makin' noise and talkin' big. Told me the price and that the deal was almost done. He'd be back soon to evict me he said. Mr. St. Vrain was gonna sell it right out from under me and leave me with nothin' but a tepee and some beads." Bent was fuming.

"And you believed him?" Kit asked.

"Didn't seem quite right," William said, slowing to think. "That cap'n was intent on makin' hisself look important, but Ceran shouldn't have been negotiating."

"Probably not," said Kit quietly. "Of course, he's here where the army is, and they approached him."

Bent thought for a minute. Kit was silent.

"Aw, well," said Bent after reflection, "I didn't really want to kill Ceran anyway. Guess I'll go see him now and patch things up."

"He wants to make things right," said Kit.

"Guess I'll head on over to the store," said Bent.

"Don't enter too sudden-like," said Roque. "You

wouldn't want to surprise a man who thinks you've come to kill him."

"Where are you staying, William?" Kit asked.

"Moved into a tepee with my wife, Owl Woman, and her people. It's comfortable enough. I like the Cheyenne."

"I'll go with you to see Ceran," said Kit. Bent nodded.

It appeared the tour was over. These old friends were apt to talk all night about times-that-were.

"Let's go, Danito," said Roque. "I'll show you the pueblo. It's only a league away."

Pueblo gets used two ways. It means a village, but it's also used to refer to Indians who live in villages and to these Indian towns as well. The Taos pueblo, the original, Indian city was about two miles distant.

Along the way, they were accosted by a Jicarilla.

"Roque, I recognize him." Danny gasped. "He is the one Rojo called Pinacate, the Stink Bug."

Up close, Danny could see that Pinacate had a deformity of the spine that made his walk twisted and scuttling like a bug. His speech was slurred, and he was very slow of thought, stupid. The foul odor that emanated from him was uncommon in Indians.

"It must have been hard for this one as a child," said Roque, "surrounded by Jicarilla who value physical strength and agility above all else. He must have been teased until he developed his own cruel streak. I think he will torture unmercifully anything over which he has power."

With signs and broken Spanish, Pinacate tried to tell the pair he wanted a letter.

"Do you know what he wants?" Danny asked Roque.

"*Si*, Danito, I understand," said Roque. "*Indios*

sometimes carry a letter from a *gavacho* saying they are "good Indians" and well behaved. Such a letter might come from an Indian agent or from a traveler they have met and helped. It helps them get a little work with travelers or a handout. The trader might not let him in the store without it for fear he'll steal things."

Danny nodded. "After what he did with Teresina, he wants a letter from me? He's got some cheek."

"He takes you for a stranger," said Roque, "new to the country. He thinks you are a fool who can be intimidated because you do not know the right thing to do. You can be sure Acha put him up to this."

Already annoyed with this creature that had so frightened little Teresina, Danny was now doubly insensed at being taken for a bumpkin to be toyed with and intimidated. He thought of Acha who had demanded a child as his bride and saw a way to turn the tables, to make Acha's little band the fools. Pinacate might not recognize Danny, but Danny had seen the Stink Bug and his friends at their worst.

"Okay, Roque, I understand. Let me make him a Certificate of Good Conduct. We'll provide Acha with a little surprise." He wrote:

Certificate of Good Conduct

Hail, know all ye by these presents that the subject Pinacate, meaning Stink Bug, a Jicarilla, is a good Indian. He will not steal more than he can carry, nor will he take anything that is securely fastened down or attached to anything heavier than he can lift.

He is known to be lazy and indolent. A fair day's labor might be gotten out of him in a month provided one supervises him intently to the exclusion of all other tasks. Avoid him and all his clan, sort, and tribe at all costs.

Signed, Daniel Trelawney
September 9, 1849

Danny signed with a flourish and then read the letter back to Roque who said, "*Bueno, amigo,* this letter will be *estupendo! Muy bonito.*"

Smiling, he handed the note, with bow and flourish, to Pinacate who scuttled away highly pleased to take it to his little band of friends.

Pueblo of Taos came as a surprise. There were no doors. *Indios* came and went by ladders set in smoke holes. The pueblo was like seeing mountains in miniature. Smooth adobe sides went up and up to five stories. Taos pueblo was miniature only when compared to the mountains. It consisted of two large apartment buildings rising in steps, like foothills joining mountains. The two were separated by the Taos River, a small stream. Danny had passed through New York City, then the largest town in the States, on his way west and these apartment houses were bigger than anything he saw there. A newspaper writer claimed they were the largest dwellings in North America.

"Roque, these are huge!" Danny exclaimed.

"*Si, muy grande, no?*" he smiled. "They have two churches dedicated to *San Geronimo,* St. Jerome."

He showed Danny one that lay in ruins.

"What happened here?" Danny asked.

"When General Kearney brought the army to New Mexico in 1846, he named Charles Bent, Teresina's father, governor, and then he left for California. The Uprising of 1847 started and ended here at the pueblo. The *Indios* rose up and then Mexicans all over *Rio Arriba*. They were told that the *gavachos* would tax them and take away their religion. They fought a battle at *Santa Cruz de la Cañada* and retreated to this church. The mountain men and the Army were angry and did not accept sanctuary.

"They fired a cannon at the church," Roque went on, "but it had little effect. Finally, the cannon made a small hole, and through it they tossed in torches starting a fire. People ran out to escape the flames. Mountain men pursued them and killed more than one hundred. I survived."

"You were a rebel?"

"Si," he said, "I was. We were told lies. I know the Yankees better now. I am a patriot. I have a new country." He paused and then said, "We should be heading back to town."

Along the way, they passed the Church of Our Lady of Guadalupe. *San Geronimo* was for the pueblo, this church for the town. "Once there were only two priests in the *Rio Arriba*," said Roque, "one at this church and one in Santa Fe. Now there are more, but still not enough. The Taos priest must serve many scattered churches. In the small villages there are only the *Penitentes*."

"Who?" asked Danny, but Roque went silent.

Josepha Carson spotted the men and insisted on showing her Danito the church.

Roque translated for them. "This is where Kit was baptized a Catholic, and this is where they were married when Taos was still part of Mexico. She is very proud of that since so few get married in church. It's too expensive. Most of the mountain men, who could afford it, never marry their wives. It shows Kit's love and respect for her and for her family. It was a big day for Josepha. Her *Cristobal* did this for her."

Josepha separated from them to talk happily with a black-robed priest. He scowled in the direction of the two men. Deep set, dark eyes glared from under his cowl. The priest had presence and projected his authority even from across the church. Beside him Danny noticed Roque shivering.

"*Amigo*," said Danny, beginning to mix in convenient Spanish words, "what is wrong?"

"The black robe is Padre Martinez," Roque shuddered. "After my parents died, I was raised in his household, raised to be a priest. I ran away. He is very angry with me and may cause me some evil. I don't think he is a *brujo*, but who knows. Kit doesn't like him either, not anymore. He married Kit to Josepha, but that was before the Uprising. The padre was outspoken against the Americans, especially against Charles Bent. Kit blames him for Bent's murder.

"Black Robe roused up the *Indios* first. He got them very angry with lies about Yankees stopping their religion. I think," continued Roque, "he only worried he had lost his authority in civil government. The *Indios* killed many people, mutilating bodies and carrying their heads around on lances. A lot of Anglos and Josepha's brother were killed. Martinez caused this. The *Indios* were joined by the *paisanos*, the local Mexicans.

"They went to Bent's house." There may have been a tear in Roque's eye. "He was Kit's brother-in-law, a man who had long dwelt in Taos and who was respected by all. Kit was away, but Josepha and her sister Teresa, Charles' wife and Teresina were there with Bent. The mob shot arrows in him as he protected the women with his body. Finally, the women escaped through the wall into the next house. Bent plugged the hole with his body so the mob couldn't follow. Bent was killed and mutilated. The *Indios* scalped him."

Roque paused a moment before continuing. "When Padre Martinez saw the violence he had roused, I think it frightened him. Once the women were out of Bent's *casa*, Padre Martinez helped Josepha and Teresa escape to his rancho. There Padre Martinez protected them until the troops came.

"One hundred and fifty *paisanos* and *Indios* died in the fighting," Roque said. "Later fifteen more rebel leaders were hung. But not the Padre! He wasn't hung, and he roused them to rebellion. Why wasn't he hung? Some say he helped the troops with information. *Traidor!*" Roque spat in the dust. "Let's get out of here. It stinks bad, no?"

They stayed that night with Josepha's family, the Jaramillos. The homecoming for *Josephita,* as her family called her, and Teresina was warm and happy. The reception for Kit and the new *gavacho* was cooler and very formal.

The people of the *Rio Arriba*, the area north of Santa Fe, were closely related, descending from a few hundred original settlers. At times, Kit said they all seemed to be cousins. The *gavachos* were not family, and there was some uncertainty in how to relate to them. It was obvious that the Jaramillos were a little uncomfortable and trying not to show it. A guitar was produced from somewhere and a relative sang painfully sad love songs. At intervals, he'd pick up the beat and the ladies would dance and twirl. The food was good. They ate it rolled in *tortillas*, using the *tortillas* as spoons.

Chapter 5

The High Road to Santa Fe

In the morning Kit, Roque, and Danny bid *adios* to friends and family in Taos and set out on the road for Ranchos de Taos to the south where the roads to Santa Fe divided. There they turned away from the river, ascending the canyon to the mountains. Coming to Picuris about dark, they camped outside town. The valley at Picuris was grassy, well watered, and yielded good crops, a place of beauty. From there the stream ran down to *Embudo*, the Funnel, on the Rio Grande. The Picuris Pueblo people had lived there since they emerged from *sipapu*, a hole in the earth that led to an older earth below. They were related to the people at Taos. Despite laws about Indian lands, Mexican settlers had encroached on the pueblo.

The next day, the three men rode up over a mountain spur, through ponderosa pine forest, and down into the green, fertile valley at Trampas, a village built around a defensive plaza. A fine adobe church with twin bell towers stood on the south of the plaza. The towers were connected by a *mirador,* a recessed balcony.

Roque showed Danito the choir loft.

"They don't have a priest," said Roque, "but one visits sometimes from Taos or Santa Cruz." They entered the church. "Here, look up at the underside of the choir loft."

The wood of the ceiling was burned with twenty or more fantastic symbols: a compass rose, a medieval coat of arms, a flower, a vine. "They are brands that represent families who built the church."

Outside a crowd was gathering at the far reaches of the plaza. They stared at Kit, mounted on his mule and holding the lead line to the pack animals in his hand. The villagers looked hostile. They did not smile and held farm implements menacingly.

Roque said, "We should go. They don't look friendly. They are *genizaros*, Christianized *Indios cimarrones*, wild Indians. This river makes a pass in the mountains. Comanche use it to raid along the Rio. Forty years ago, the Spanish government gave the *genizaros* this land. It was theirs if they defended *Rio Arriba* from the Comanche. The governor gave them only one gun. The people asked for more, but the government told them, 'Build a strong plaza for defense.' But they didn't give them any more guns. They think they are tough guys to fight the Comanche. Mostly, they don't like anybody. If we looked weak, they might rob us."

Roque smiled and waved to the villagers. Kit and Danny followed his lead as they rode on. Then he spotted someone among the villagers and rode over to him. Roque dismounted and the two embraced. He led the man over to where his friends had halted their mounts and sat waiting.

"This is *mi amigo* Pablo," Roque introduced them. "He comes to Taos all the time with meat, cheese, and wool from his *churros*, his sheep."

Not speaking any English, Pablo nodded and smiled. Roque had friends everywhere it seemed to Danny. The young man soon learned that his Mexican friend was nervous, perhaps with good reason, of any village where he had neither *amigos* nor *primos*, cousins.

"If Pablo is here, you'll be safe here next time you come," said Roque.

Roque arranged for a noonday meal of *tortillas* and *frijoles* with *chili rojo*, the red *chili*. The villagers, now friendly, gathered round them as they ate.

Bidding *adios* to Pablo, the trio rode out and up a mountain spur into pine forest. The land sloped toward the west down to the Great Rio, and upward on the right to jagged peaks that seemed close enough to touch. Here and there, they rode through a gap where land rose on both sides and down into handsomely watered valleys.

"I'm surprised there are no villages in these valleys," opined Danny.

"The elevation is too high," replied Roque, "making the growing season too short for crops. See how the mountains have snow. It is September, and it has lasted all summer."

"And too many Indians," said Kit, "Jicarilla, Ute, and Comanche."

"They steal the sheep and cows," added Roque.

Far downhill, miles away, Danny saw that the country gave way to sandy wasteland, and beyond the river rose into the cliffs of the Parajito Plateau dominated by the cloud-capped, brooding Jemez Mountains. The land varied from ice and clammy cold to hot, arid waste, but together Danny thought the effect pleasing, even beautiful. It was unlike the eternally green landscape of his Greenport home on the great sandbar called Long Island where green sea lapped at a green shore. This land was different. Its harsh extremes exposed beauty of a different kind and made its meadows and dark forests all the more beautiful. Even the stark cliffs held a wonderful beauty like frozen fire.

Raised with the incessant lapping of the sea and the cries of waterfowl and crowded people, Danny found the quiet of the mountains and desert pleasant. The wind had different tones for passing through fir forest and barren desert, but it rustled softly in both on calm late summer days. They rode on until the sun stood a hand's breadth above the horizon.

The trail passed through a break in a rocky outcropping that ran as far as they could see to either side. Gimlet-eyed, Kit spotted something far off the trail. He signaled, and the young men rode with him to the spot he pointed out on the ground. There was another notch through the rocks like the one the main trail ran through, only smaller. The earth was beaten down and round pellets the size of quail eggs were scattered about. Kit dismounted and picked one up, breaking it with his fingers.

"Fresh. Still moist. Some last night. Some this morning," Kit indicated.

He pointed again this time at a print about three inches long, like two tear drops side by side curving inward at the top.

"Elk," he said.

Kit led them back to the trail, the High Road. They climbed up through the notch and then worked their way downhill along the spur until they were well out of sight of the trail. Hobbling their mules, which would allow their mounts to move and feed but not wander far, they took their rifles and headed back uphill toward where they had seen signs of the elk. Along the way, Kit indicated that they should roll in the thick forest litter.

Not sure he'd understood correctly, Danny looked puzzled at this non-verbal instruction from Kit.

Roque looked at him. "It's to cover our scent. Now cut a few small limbs to disguise yourself. Poke them into your collar, your hair, so you can look like a walking bush."

The breeze was moving gently up from the warm valley toward the peaks. Kit led them to the high side of the break in the rocky outcrop, upwind of it, and located a place of concealment among the rocks only a few yards above the elk trail.

As dusk fell, Kit indicated that they were to remain silent and still. He signed that they would take their elk in order, each firing at a different one, his shot to be the signal to fire. The trio waited for the elk to come down to the valley to feed and drink from the stream.

After sunset, with only a little glow left in the western sky, they saw the elk coming, a bull elk and a small herd of cows. They waited in the dusk for the elk to pass by barely daring to breathe, hoping themselves well concealed and scent and sound blown away from the wary animals. When all but four cows had passed, Kit fired. An eye-blink after his shot, Roque's and Danny's rifles cracked in unison. Three cows fell, hit in vital spots at close range.

With Danny following Kit's silent lead and instructions, they began the butchering, saving the liver from the innards for dinner. Only after this task was completed did they recover their hobbled mules and transport the carcasses to a spot well away from the offal where they would camp for the night.

"Bears," Kit explained with a single word, as was his way.

The offal would draw them as would the smell of fresh meat. They hung the carcasses high in trees near their camp, but not in it, and then cooked elk liver, seasoning it with bile, salt, and the *chili* peppers Danny had started to like.

Feeling good about life in general, Roque favored them with another of his stories.

A boy was sent away by his parents to work for a *rico*. The boy, José, worked for many years. *Rico* only paid a few coins. On his way home, José ran into an old man in ragged clothes.

"*Chico*," said the *viejo*, "I will give you good advice if you give me all your money." Jose' gave the man his money.

The *viejo* told him, "Marry an ugly girl."

José continued on home. His parents beat him for his foolishness in giving away his money. They sent him back to work for *rico* again. After years of work, José started for home with a little money.

José met the same *viejo* who had taken his money before. The old man asked for José's money in exchange for good advice, and José again gave the ancient one, the *viejo*, his money. *El viejo* told José, "If you come to a dangerous river, swim across without hesitating."

Of course, his parents beat José again for losing his money. They sent him back to the *rico* again to work for small wages. After many years, José returned with his meager earnings. On the way home, he met the same *viejo* as before.

Once more, the *viejo* promised good advice and took José's money. As soon as he had the money, the *viejo* said, "Beat your head against a rock."

José, afraid to go home, wandered about. He came to a dangerous river and swam across. On the far side, there were some rocks. José accidentally knocked his head against one dislodging it. Where the rock had been, he discovered a small cave full of treasure hidden by *banditos*. He took the treasure, bought a farm, and married an ugly girl.

And he lived happily ever after," said Roque, "because…"

In unison, Kit and Danny finished for him, "Because the old man was San Pablo."

Roque was crestfallen that they had guessed his surprise ending. He recovered his smile quickly though when his *amigo*, Danito, asked, "What I don't get is how come he married an ugly girl?"

Danny thought he might have chosen the ugly bride because St. Peter told him to, which would make as much sense as the rest of the story.

But Roque surprised him, "Oh, the ugly wife was so grateful she never fooled around and always cooked and cleaned and took good care of José his whole life." To illustrate, Roque sang a song about pretty girls, their jealous husbands, and having to depart hastily out the window *en pelota*, in the pelt, that is, naked.

Kit stood and looked thoughtfully up and down the valley spread below us in the light of the rising moon. "In the Blackfoot country, I camped in a valley so big, it took eight hours for your echo to come back. When you were ready to bed down, you'd holler, 'Get up!' and the echo would come back around in time to wake you for breakfast. Don't know if it will work here. You want to try, Danito?"

Danny was surprised. Kit seldom spoke at such length, but when he was relaxed, around good friends, his sense of humor emerged. They tried for an echo. The echo did not arrive in time for breakfast. Maybe the land was too vast.

As he bedded down that night, still sure his echo would wake him in the morning, Danny thought about the kind, humorous, gentle man he was coming to know as Kit. Try as he might, Danny Trelawney couldn't reconcile this man with the heroic giant of legend and stories or with the mighty frontiersman Fremont had described. Danny, and Roque for that matter, looked up to him like a father, but the stories made him out so much more.

One story chimed with the ring of truth. It told of a Rendezvous, the annual gathering where trappers traded furs for supplies and whiskey. The best beaver pelts were only available in winter when the fur was thick. Adventurers who wintered, often alone, hunting beaver in the Shining Mountains were known as mountain men. In summer, hundreds of them gathered at a prearranged rendezvous to meet with traders. Indians came, too. During Rendezvous, they kept truce. The trappers held contests of skill and strength, shooting, wrestling, tomahawk and knife throwing, and drinking. Fights were common among the hard drinking mountain men. Kit did not stand out as a winner of these wild contests, but rather as a man the others had selected to lead them.

A big French-Canadian named Shunar went about the Rendezvous encampment beating up anyone who displeased him. He berated the American trappers calling them "little children" and claiming all Americans were cowards.

"I can beat the little American children with a switch," he said. "I shall cut one. These Americans are nothing but babies."

When Shunar offered physical insult to an Arapaho woman, a friend of Carson's, the outrage was too much for Kit. He hurried back to his campsite where he fetched his horse and pistol.

Shunar and Kit charged at each other until their horses met nose to nose.

"I have no quarrel with you, Carson," cried Shunar, but as he spoke, he raised his rifle and aimed it at Kit's heart. Kit fired his pistol, breaking Shunar's arm and spoiling his aim. The story, recorded by a missionary bound to Oregon to teach the Indians, didn't say if Shunar died, but the tales of the mountain men don't include him after that day.

On the mountain trail, Danny found a moment to ask Kit about the Shunar fight.

All he would say was, "Can't tolerate a bully or anybody talking bad about my country."

Daybreak snaked over the *Sangre de Cristo* a little at a time skirting peaks and slithering down valleys. Kit arose first, greeting the sun with a song in some Indian language and a pinch of pollen. Danny watched.

Kit noticed the observation. "I got a beef with priests, not God," he said. "My father died when I was young, so I didn't get religion from him. The way women like my mother pray is different from a man's way. I look to my own way and thank God every morning that I'm alive."

They finished the butchering, wrapping the meat tight in the elk hides, and not taking any extra weight with them.

"We'll trade the meat and elk hide in Chimayo," Kit indicated as they rode out through the pine forest.

Toward dusk they approached *Truchas*, a village placed high on a mountain spur to guard against the Comanches. The name meant Trout in Spanish, though Danny couldn't discern why any more than he could figure how the nearby river, called *Quemado*, could be burned. The adobe plaza stood like a castle at the end of its spur. Ranchos were scattered around the plateau. Far to the west across the Rio Grande, the sun was setting over the Jemez Mountain. The land fell away sharply on three sides toward the plain of the Rio Grande and rose behind them to the high, jagged peaks now bathed in crimson light, *Sangre de Cristo*, the blood of Christ.

They made camp in a hollow some distance from the town. A windowless, abandoned building standing between them and the plaza blocked their fire from easy observation.

Roque told them, "These are not good people. They're

tough guys who'll rob anyone they think is weaker. They don't like strangers. We should stay outside town."

"What do they consider weak?" Danny asked.

"Don't worry too much, Danito," replied Roque grinning. "They only got one gun, just like the Trampas."

With the mules cared for and tethered and a small fire started, Danny set out to gather more firewood against the high country chill of approaching fall. Returning, he stumbled in the dusk having lost sight of camp and fire. In the increasing dark, he retraced his steps and found a hollow much like their campsite, but with no one in sight and no fire evident. It was then he heard behind him a low harmonious moaning and rhythmic slapping. Turning he saw in the light of the rising moon a skeleton with long hair and a bow and arrow, being pulled in a two-wheeled cart by faceless, hooded, stooped creatures in long robes. The axles squealed seldom allowing the wheel to turn. Instead, they skidded along their path. The cart was pursued, so Danny thought, by demons naked to the waist flaying themselves with whips. Some of the demons moved awkwardly as they had cactus pads bound tightly to their naked bodies. The young man verged on frightened flight as a *pito*, a flute, shrilled notes from Hell.

A whippoorwill called from the slope below him. Startled Danny turned and beheld two disembodied faces behind a bush. He stifled a cry, fearing to be found out by the fiends, and then realized Kit and Roque were motioning him to get down. He dropped and slowly crawled to them.

"*Penitentes*," hissed Kit.

"The building with no windows must be their *morada*, their church," whispered Roque. "There aren't enough priests. None come up here, so they make their own church. *Doña Sebastiana*, Death, she is their *santo*. They don't like people to watch them."

Kit, Danny, and Rogue watched as the *Penitentes* lit a ring of fires, *farolitos* Roque called them, illuminating their ceremony in dim flicker. Writhing in this hellish glow, they beat each other with whips scratching bodies with cactus and thorns till they bled from arms, legs, faces, and backs. Through it all, they intoned a rhythmic, nasal chant. They fashioned a wooden cross and pushing a wreath of thorns onto an acolyte's head before they tied him to it. They raised him aloft securely footing his tree. The march continued round this horror as they chanted a new hymn. The cadenced scourge flayed on.

"They take on the wounds of *Cristo*." Roque awed himself to silence for some minutes and then said, "I think they'll cut him down before he dies. They must have had bad crops or something. This is their sacrifice. Padre Martinez is their leader. He told me about them."

Covered by the sound of their singing, the travelers moved away, down toward the valley.

Kit asked Danny and Roque, "If your God came to relieve your suffering, why would you do that to yourself?"

The young men didn't answer. Danny couldn't, and Roque was in conflict between all he'd been taught about God's love and the spectacle he had just observed. Repelled and afraid of detection, they continued their descent in the dark. They kept going for hours, letting the concentration of walking down a mountain slope in the dark clear their minds of what they had seen, stumbling but not stopping, exhausted but willing themselves away from the horror. They finally stopped and made camp in an unknown quarter.

Danny woke to the sun rising over the peaks as Kit offered his morning prayers. Breaking camp, they found themselves near Cordova.

"Cordova is a place of skilled *santeros*," Roque told them. "They carve *bultos* and *santos,* statues of saints*, muy linda* and create *retablos*, the painted boards you see in church showing the holy stories."

Instead of going down the verdant hillside into the village, they continued down the long mountain spur that started near Truchas and led to the *Plaza del Cerro*, the courtyard on the hill, the largest of Chimayo's pueblos.

Two streams come together at Chimayo, the Quemado, which they had been following albeit on the spur far above, and the *Rio Santa Cruz*, River of the Holy Cross. They looked down on patchwork fertile fields running across the lush valley floor. From the height they traced a valley that extended for miles west to *Santa Cruz de la Cañada*, the Holy Cross of the Canyon, near the Rio Grande, but was only a mile or so wide, ending abruptly at sandy hills so barren that even rocks didn't want to grow on them. It was the garden spot of New Mexico whose *paisanos*, while not *ricos* by any means, were a people whose opinions had to reckoned with by the powerful at their peril. Chimayo had risen in revolt in 1837 and again in 1847.

"Chimayo has rich farms," Roque said. "*Acequias*, irrigation ditches, draw water from the rivers. *Chimayosos* raise the best *chilis* in the world," Roque went on with growing appetite. "*Largo y dulce*, long and sweet or small and *muy caliente*, very hot." He held his hands a foot apart to demonstrate and then held up thumb and forefinger to show the size of the smaller, hot *chilis*.

Scattered ranchos dotted a patchwork valley where fields competed in color and texture. Like the water in the *acequias*, the meadows were held as commons where everyone's sheep and horses could graze. It was the most prosperous village Danny had yet seen. Its wealth came from more than fertile soil and plentiful water. It also came from its weavers.

Roque explained, "*Chimayosos* weave fine Rio Grande blankets from wool that comes down from Truchas and Trampas. These blankets are so tight they shed water and *muy bonito*, so beautiful, the traders from St. Louis want them. This is what we have come to trade for our elk meat and skins. We can sell these fine blankets to the Jicarilla, in Taos or Santa Fe, at a profit everywhere."

Plaza del Cerro nestled at the base of the mountains near where the road reached the valley floor and the rivers came together at the southern end of the Mountain Road from Taos. In late morning, as the travelers arrived, the *pueblo's* large plaza bustled with activity.

Roque pointed. "Two roads lead on from here. One leads up the steep valley wall and south through desert to Santa Fe. The other leads west to Santa Cruz at the mouth of the canyon near where the river reaches the Rio Grande. It follows the river and climbs up to Santa Fe beyond San Ildefanso."

The fortified plaza was built around an interior rectangle fifty yards across by one hundred yards wide, larger than the plaza in Taos. The outer walls were windowless and doorless. Everything faced in toward the plaza except the beehive *hornos* for baking bread near the entrance.

Roque, continuing to act as guide, happily showed

Danny around as Kit quietly followed. "There are only two narrow openings there between the houses. They lead into the plaza and are easily blocked. They fear the *Indios* even here, especially the Apache and Comanche. See the bell atop that house? It is to ring if the *Indios* raid nearby. Over there, near the western entrance, is a *torreon*, a little tower, their last place of defense."

The circular two-story tower, a redoubt, was Chimayo's last resort. For a century and a half, they had defended themselves with bows and spears. Fortunately, the Indians came not to kill and burn or to drive the people out as the Pueblos had done in 1680, but to take cattle, sheep, and captives.

"Pedro, *amigo*," Roque called out to a roguish figure as he and Danny entered the plaza. "*Que paso?*"

As Roque waved to Pedro, Danny wondered if Pedro was *amigo* or *primo*. Both lists of Roque's friends and of his cousins were lengthy. He had already learned that Roque hesitated to venture where he had no *primos* and thought about what this singular behavior might mean. He had observed that strangers were feared and wondered if it might be that in a land and in villages isolated by mountain and desert, the rare stranger was a harbinger of trouble, someone cast out by his own people. But there was something else. The people of the villages intermarried across the *Rio Arriba*. What could it mean, Danny pondered, when a village was so isolated from others that there were no *primos*, no cousins? There was something dark here.

Pedro Ramirez's face lit up on seeing Roque and Kit. A man a little taller than average, of medium build, he had dark flashing eyes that shone with quick intelligence. His handlebar mustache was wider than his face, Pedro dressed like his countrymen in woolen clothing with a *serape* about his shoulders, although his were cleaner and newer than most and he wore tooled boots instead of sandals or moccasins. His dark face, hooded eyes, and impish smile told the world he was a born rogue and happy to be so.

Introduced by Roque, Danny asked, "Are you one of the famous Chimayo weavers?"

"No, I am not a weaver, but I work with them," Pedro replied. "I trade their blankets in Santa Fe with the St. Louis traders, so I learn their English. And buy wool for the weavers in Truchas. I have a fast horse and outrun the *banditos* everywhere.

"See these Rio Grande blankets?" Pedro went on, pointing at fine work hung in the plaza. "They are very high quality woven wool, handmade on looms, not felted like your Saint Louis Pendletons."

To people in New Mexico St. Louis and Independence, Missouri, were "the States," America.

"These are our designs," Pedro said. "We call these "steps," those "mountains," those "clouds," and zig-zags have no name."

The patterns were geometric in bold, bright colors. Some patterns resembled geometrical flowers and the compass rose, the pattern of eight points on the face of a compass. Mexicans folded and looped these blankets over their shoulders to make the *serapes*.

"They are very warm in winter and at night, even when wet. We prize them highly and so do those who might buy them from us. I think we might trade all of your elk meat for one blanket," Pedro finished.

Behind him, Kit shook his head no and smiled. He and Roque had warned Danny that he would have to haggle.

"I'll have to think on that, Pedro," Danny said. "Have you seen the chemical dyes I brought? Red, black, blue, turquoise, yellow, and green."

Danny watched Pedro's eyes. At the mention of dyes, his pupils enlarged slightly while he remained otherwise pokerfaced. *Chimayosos* needed the dyes to make their blankets, and they weren't readily available except in Santa Fe where the price was high. Kit had explained that *Chimayosos* would want the elk meat but would be desperate for the dye.

The haggling continued for some time. Wisely, Danny offered a small bargain on the dye while insisting that the deal must also include the elk meat and hide at slightly inflated prices. In the end, both sides were pleased. Pedro bought scissors, black velvet, and a revolver for himself.

"Come back tonight," Pedro welcomed them as they finished the trade. "Tonight is *fandango,* a party; we celebrate the feast of San Tomas. Lots of food and dancing."

Roque accepted the invitation and then said to Kit and Danny, "Our business is done. Now for pleasure. You must come with me to see the sights. We will go to the *Santuario*. It is very famous. Pilgrims come from all over *Rio Arriba* and even the *Burqueños* from Albuquerque walk to Chimayo at Easter. We must go and see this *milagro*, this miracle. I have never been only heard about it."

"I'll stay here at the plaza and watch our goods," said Kit, his mood darkening slightly. "I've seen the *Santuario* before."

"I must go to help prepare," enthused Pedro, "but I will

see you here at dusk. We will have food and *fandango.* You'll dance the *cuna* and the *baile, no?*"

Roque marched Danny to the north, following the road to Santa Fe. "There," he pointed to a large, well-built rancho up against the hillside, "is the Rancho Jaramillo, home of Josepha's grandparents."

A little farther on, they waded the Santa Cruz River and stood before a chapel of two bell towers and a connecting *mirador.* Inside, *vigas* resting in finely worked corbels, called *zapatas,* supported the ceiling. The wood was old and black. A brilliant altar screen painted in vibrant colors filled the other end of the chapel.

After kneeling and crossing himself and encouraging Danny to do the same, Roque led him to a little room beside the altar. People knelt taking pure, white clay from a round hole in the floor about the size of a pumpkin.

"What is this?" Danny asked.

"It is *tierra bendita,* the blessed earth. It cures us if we are crippled," said Roque. "Take some. Mix it with your food tonight. It is the cure. If you have faith, it will cure anything that cripples you." He pointed around the room, which was filled with abandoned crutches and canes. "Everyone knows about the clay in Chimayo. They even come here from the *Rio Abajo,* as far as Socorro. When they leave, they can walk, no? So they leave their crutches behind."

"Clay, Roque?" puzzled Danny.

"*San Salvador*, the Holy Savior, used clay to cure the blind," continued Roque Vigil. "It only takes a little clay and a lot of *santa fe*, faith. At Easter, thousands make pilgrimage to be here when the sun rises Easter morning. They walk all night from Santa Fe and even Albuquerque carrying candles."

Standing in the doorway between chapel and anteroom Roque turned and gestured toward the crutches, canes, and other items left by pilgrims. He must have noticed something out of the corner of his eye, for he suddenly turned and faced the altar in the chapel. He froze, horror stricken, his eyes fixed on the altar screen.

"Roque, what's wrong?" demanded Danny. "You look like you've seen a ghost!"

"There, on the altar screen," stammered Roque, "*Madre de Dios*, there are symbols. I recognize them from Padre Martinez teaching. They are Penitente signs. *Vamonos*, let's go."

Outside in the afternoon sunlight, Danny observed a hooded figure, face pale as a skull, emerging from the *Santuario* coming toward them. Roque saw it too and suddenly grasped his friend's arm hurrying him away.

"That looked like Padre Martinez," Danny said.

Roque nodded. "The priests are all his former students. He has power everywhere in the *Rio Arriba*, and he leads the *Penitentes* who are strong here in Chimayo. Their symbols cover the altar."

"It looked like he was approaching us," Danny shuddered. "What could he want?" Cold fingers crept up Danny's spine, but he could get no further explanation from Roque. There were many strange and wonderful things in New Mexico and some quite terrifying.

They returned to the plaza as the sun was setting. Gay *farolitos*, small bonfires, lit their way to the baile.

"Come, eat," Pedro greeted them. His clothes were brushed and he wore a clean shirt. Only *ricos*, the wealthy, had more than one set of clothes. This was true of *Americanos*, too. A man owned the clothes he stood in and perhaps a heavy coat, a clean shirt and a change of underwear and socks, or perhaps not, if the trail had been hard on him.

The whole town seemed to have assembled in the crowded plaza. On blankets near the *casas*, food was spread in serving bowls containing stews of pork, venison, lamb, and beef, all cooked with *chili*. Tables were found only in the homes of the *ricos*. Danny was invited to sample a salad, *salsa*, made with nothing but *chili* and seasoned salt, onion, and garlic. He was offered beans stewed with *chili* and *refritos*, refried beans, cooked, mashed, and fried in lard. There were no spoons, forks, or dinner plates. *Tortillas*, warm from being cooked, were used as plate and spoon. Danny ate *posole* made from hominy with *chili* and pork from a bowl using a *tortilla* as his spoon. Most things could be wrapped in a *tortilla*, held in the hand, and eaten without the need for utensils. Soups and some of the stews, were served in bowls with folded *tortillas* used in place of fork or spoon.

Men and women alike were dressed in their best, or at least cleanest, clothes. The women wore dark, ruffled skirts without bustles, thus revealing their natural shape and their ankles. Above the skirt was a *chamisa*, a loose white blouse that exposed much of the bosom and upper arms. A *rebozo*, a shawl of bright colors, was worn about the shoulders and tucked under the arms. Men and women wore moccasins on their feet. Unlike New England, both sexes smoked tobacco and participated in games of chance. A young woman produced corn husks and tobacco from within the folds of her skirt and made a *cigarrillo* and blew billows of smoke toward Danny.

Danny, raised in a middle class family, self-conscious about its status in a town full of lowly sailors who drank, smoked, and got tattoos, was appalled, reeling from scenes he'd been taught existed only in Hell and sailors' dives. It was outrageous. The women not only wore no gloves, but also they exposed their ankles, shoulders, arms, and most of their breasts and they smoked, gambled, and drank in the company of men. And they danced, raising the dust of the plaza until combined with flames and fumes of *farolitos*, it seemed he'd entered some smoking inferno. The food and liquor burned lips, tongue, and throat so that thirst could not be quenched. The past few days flooded back in memory: flayed skin, blood, a crucified man in Truchas, people afraid of travelers in Trampas, and witch-ridden people frightened of *brujos* in Taos. He stumbled about as they offered him food and drink in the kindest way.

The men were attired in pantaloons split from ankle to thigh and adorned with *conchos*. They wore white shirts and wrapped a red sash about the waist to hold up their pantaloons. Tied at the knee and covering shin and calf was a kind of legging. Some wore Rio Grande blankets folded over their shoulders. Those who could afford it had short jackets heavily embroidered and looking much like vests but with sleeves and more silver *conchos*. They also carried knives and a short sword. Men and women alike laughed, sang, smoked, ate, gambled, and danced with abandon in a way that would never be seen in New England.

A pretty girl grasped Danny's arm, and they danced the *Cuna*, the Cradle, to the music of guitars, fiddles, and rattles. To form the *Cuna,* the man approached his partner and put his arms about her waist, and she did likewise. They come together at the hip to close the bottom of the cradle below with shoulders back keeping the top open. Danny circled the floor with his smiling partner, rocking the cradle and doing a kind of waltz. They spun about, heads thrown back, locked together below the waist in a manner shocking to the New England bred. If this was Hell, Danny was beginning to enjoy it.

"Get out there, boy," whooped Kit. "You need the exercise."

"But Kit, there are so many foods to try," protested Danny, "how do I know which is the last course?"

"When you've had enough!" laughed Kit.

Roque and Kit laughed at Danny's awkward efforts though he experienced no lack for willing partners. Although Danny's Spanish was still as awkward as his dancing, one young lady seemed to pay him exceptional attention, batting her eyelashes and playing with her fan. She chattered in words too fast for the young man to follow and insisted on dancing again and again. Finally, she pulled him away from the party into the dark, away from the circle of light. It might be wrong in New England but here he became a willing follower.

As they were about to exit the plaza, Roque and Pedro intervened.

"*Señor Danito Trelano, mi amigo,* I would like to introduce you to *mi prima,* my most esteemed cousin Sebriana," Roque said of the woman who held Danny's hand. He winked. "They call her *Doña Loca.*"

Doña Loca smiled and batted her eyelashes. Danny knew enough Spanish to realize he was holding hands with Madame Madcap.

Roque continued, "I think she might be too old for you. She is already nineteen and has outlived two husbands. Of course, people say they died smiling and had to have closed caskets at their funerals because the priest was embarrassed."

The thought of the two dead husbands, smiling or not, chilled Danny's ardor. The boy from New England was uncertain of local customs and did not want to use Roque's kinswoman lightly, though she seemed willing enough. He wasn't sure he was ready to be husband number three, although she looked mighty inviting. Thus headed off, Doña Loca had no choice but to lead her Danito, as she'd begun calling him, back to the party for another dance, leaving Danito to fantasize about what might have been.

In the plaza, the crowd cleared the way for a man, slender and graceful as an elf and very popular with the young ladies. His clothes were a little neater, cleaner, and fancier than the others. He laughed and smiled and danced, and the ladies loved him. Some of the married women insisted he dance with them to the apparent displeasure of their husbands who let it pass as soon as their wives were safely returned.

Pedro saw Danny watching and grinned. "His name is Miguel, but we call him *San Miguel*, the Archangel Michael. The ladies think him an angel." It was clear San Miguel enjoyed the ladies' attention and they in turn enjoyed that Miguel enjoyed it. The ladies had the angel's devotion.

The crowd parted to allow a young lady to step forth. She took San Miguel by the hand and led him willingly to the dance floor. They were enthralled, the crowd hushing to watch as two angels spun about. Danny thought San Miguel's partner had come from paradise, flying too close to the ground. The prettiest girl in Chimayo, she was dressed in the finest clothes. Among graceful ladies, she stood forth for her grace. Together they whirled about the floor laughing while the others clapped time.

"Maria," breathed Pedro as he watched this sweet angel dance with San Miguel. Pedro too, was smitten by her beauty and grace.

As the dancers stopped to catch their breaths, a man emerged out of the darkness, the crowd cringing and parting before him. By the other's deference and his demeanor, Danny understood without being told that this was a man of importance, a *rico*, a *don*. His shirt was white and shone like silk, his vest embroidered black on black. The *conchos* on his velvet pantaloons glinted like fire. He stood a head taller than the others and carried himself as if he were king of the realm. Long strides brought the "dark king" to San Miguel and his short sword flashed up under Miguel's chin, forcing the Archangel to the tips of his toes.

"Don Carlos," breathed Pedro indicating the dark king. "He thinks Maria is his, but she thinks otherwise. He's used to having his way. His father has a big rancho, and Don Carlos has ruined many girls. He would not hesitate to kill if it suited him. Who could stop him?"

"*Miguelito*," said Don Carlos, "didn't I tell you to stay away from Maria? Perhaps it's time I sent you back to heaven."

Watching this display, Danny understood *angel*, *paraíso*, and *muerte*. He got the sense of what was being said and understood that no one here would lift a hand to stop Don Carlos in his rage. He had that much power, and these people had that little.

Pedro confirmed Danny's feelings, "If he kills Miguel now, no one will even say a word. I would like to kill Don Carlos myself, but he has too many thugs to protect him."

Unexpectedly Kit, who appeared to be drunk, bumped into Don Carlos knocking him away from Miguel.

Don Carlos stormed at Kit. "Stupid, clumsy pig of a *gavacho*. Wait until I have finished with San Miguel, and I will teach you a lesson, too, one that your whole rude, clumsy race needs to learn." Don Carlos flashed his blade at Kit menacingly.

He might have intended Kit an injury, but Kit staggered, continuing to push Don Carlos farther away from San Miguel. Kit said, "I'm sorry, friend. Come have a drink with me. No one wants any unpleasantness. I'm a stranger here. Let the boy go for my sake and the sake of the party."

One arm around Don Carlos's shoulder and the other at his waist, Kit led him back to where Roque, Pedro, Sebriana, and Danny stood. Only when Kit drew near did they see that he held his cocked revolver jammed deeply into Carlos's belly. There it was hidden from the eyes of the revelers deep amongst the folds of Don Carlos's clothes.

"Get this man a drink!" Kit called to Danny in English. In a hushed undertone meant for one pair of ears only, Kit hissed, "I am Kit Carson. If anything bad happens to San Miguel because I have interfered, I will come back and cut your heart out. Do you understand?"

Don Carlos nodded.

"Good. Then we will have our drink, and you will walk away with your pride intact."

After Don Carlos slipped away, Kit turned to Danny, "I can't tolerate a bully. I shouldn't interfere, but I can't stomach a bully especially one who insults my country."

Danny saw the wrath in Kit's eyes was barely under control, like a half-broken bronco on the brink of tossing its rider. Kit's rage was something new for Danny in a man he knew as self-effacing, gentle, and soft-spoken. Danny wondered what had roused this beast. Perhaps the bully angered Kit who was small and might have suffered as a child. Patriotism entered into it, but there was more, much more. Danny felt he saw in Kit a deep-seated sense of duty and obligation that would not let him rest in the face of injustice. In any event, Danny was proud of Kit and thought the affair neatly played.

"Carlos will not forget," said Roque. "He has gone to find his *lambes*, his lackeys. There will be trouble."

Kit nodded, but he waited until three a.m. to ease his friends away from the party and to separate Danny from the soft grasp of Doña Loca. She'd clung to him all evening and into the wee hours, but his friends kept Danny from slipping away into the night with her. The young man's nerves and morals were badly frayed as they packed up in the dark.

"Pedro, you take care, *amigo*," said Kit. "You know Carlos will try to interfere with us. Tell him you heard us say we were headed to Santa Fe and Albuquerque to trade, going over the desert road to Nambe. *Hasta la vista*."

"I won't tell him too easy," grinned Pedro, "so he'll believe."

"Don't let him hurt you," said Kit. "It's not worth it."

They rode south on the road to Santa Fe in the dark, entering the ford of the Santa Cruz River. Walking their mules in the water down the river to hide their trail, they found a convenient place to leave the water, and then, riding hard, they took the road west to *Santa Cruz de la Cañada*. The trio passed the pueblo around sunup and continued on north and west to the Indian Pueblo San Juan on the Rio Grande beside the River Road. There they forded the great, but shallow, river and soon after the Rio Chama as well.

They followed the valley of the Rio Chama northwest as the canyon narrowed around them until they were riding up a fertile valley about a mile wide.

"We'll be near Abiquiu at dusk," said Roque. "It's not a good place to stop for the night. We should camp outside town."

"What makes it a bad place?" Danny asked.

"*Brujos y brujas*, witches," replied Roque.

"Danny," interrupted Kit, "*genizaros* here have a bad reputation."

Danny looked at him. "I think I understand what you and Roque have tried to teach me. The people have very little market for their crops and very little incentive to work hard. If they do make money, the wealthy among them are apt to steal it since there is not an honest court to curb their power. They water crops on a communal ditch and run livestock on communal land. If one man's herd increases, what can be the explanation? How did it happen? He must be stealing from the community. He must have power. He must be a witch."

"But in Abiquiu it's different." Roque came back. "They had real trials before a judge and the Inquisition. These people sold their souls to the devil and poisoned their priests. Many were accused of witchcraft, and many of those confessed. Those convicted were burned at the stake. It's a bad place to be after dark. They can turn into owls and coyotes. They hold a special *fandango* where they dance *en pelota con Diablo*." Roque couldn't bring himself to say "naked with the devil" in English.

"And it is the last Mexican town on the Rio Chama," continued Kit after the interruption.

Roque continued, "Beyond Abiquiu there is only

cimarron, wild *Indios* and wild country. Besides, the people from Abiquiu let the Apache, Navajo, and Utes trade in their town. The *Indios* trade goods and slaves, Mexican people they have taken from other Mexican towns."

"I can't imagine why the people of Abiquiu are unpopular," finished Kit with a grin.

"Yes, but they can turn into coyotes with glowing red eyes to spy on the people in the night. They have owls to spy for them. *Es verdad*, they hold *bailes* where they prance around *en pelota*, without any clothes, and dance *con El Diablo*. They are very evil," finished Roque undaunted.

The three friends camped along the river well away from the town.

Chapter 6

Go Jii Ya

From the Rio Grande to Abiquiu, the valley of the Chama is a mile wide and bordered by dark cliffs. At Abiquiu, the cliffs burst into flaming red, white, and yellow and closed in on the river. The trio followed the Chama through a wall of frozen fire, their horses' hoof beats echoing off the canyon walls now little more than arm's length away.

Danny spoke in wonder. "These rocks. . . I have never seen anything like it before. They are bright yellow, red and white. They really do look like they are on fire."

Kit turned in his saddle. "Danny, we're passing through a gate. Mexican civilization stopped back there. After this, it's the country of wild Indians, bears, and deer."

"How far like that?" Danny asked nervous at the closeness of the passage.

"Five or six miles," Roque replied. "Then this Red Wall Canyon opens out a little, and we can get up on the *Llano del Vado*, the Plain of the Ford."

Danny shuddered. "I'd sure hate to get trapped down here."

The narrow gorge echoed the clop-clop-clop and ringing of iron-shod horses walking on stone and their splashing as they wound through the gurgling stream. The wind was still, unable to find the narrow canyon mouth, and the smell of horse sweat and moss gathered close around them.

"It's a bad place for an ambush or flash flood," Roque agreed. "Still it's the best way north."

"*Amigo*, wait till you see such pretty country," continued Roque with rising cheerfulness as he thought about the land beyond the narrow passage. "Ahead is *Piedre Lumbre*, the rocks on fire. It's *muy linda*, very pretty. You forget about *oso*, the bear, and *Indios*."

Danny guessed this canyon might be why the Mexicans hadn't settled farther north. It was a narrow gateway in a wall of rock standing between civilization and the *cimarron*, the wilds. They continued for several miles. Where several canyons converged, the travelers found an easy slope on the east and emerged into a grassy plain surrounded by fantastic cliffs.

"*Piedre Lumbre*," Roque repeated. "The rocks are on fire."

That was how they appeared. Vibrant red, topped by white and leaping yellow-orange, the rocks were pleated and resembled flickering flames. The Jicarilla camped on the low rolling hills of the plain, scattered in clusters of three and four tepees around a brush arbor called a *ramada*.

"One tepee in each group belongs to an older woman," Roque explained. "She lives with her husband and unmarried children. The remaining tepees in each group belong to her married daughters."

Under the ramada, the women were busy cooking a variety of stews and other dishes. The travelers were enveloped in the aroma of meat boiling and roasting over *piñon* fires. Anyone who came into camp had to be fed, for such was the custom. This meal was truly a feast.

The tang of horses everywhere on the air mixed with the smell of the dust they raised. Some were hobbled; others were fenced in by rope corrals. Young boys tended to them, moving the livestock often to fresh grass. The girls worked with their mothers, grinding food on stone *matates* and gathering firewood while the boys lazed about, lords of the horse herds.

One smell was missing. Although hundreds of people were gathered here, this camp that smelled of cooking meat, *piñon* smoke, horses, and mountain air did not stink of the privy as Mexican and Yankee towns did.

In the middle of the camp, was a flattened area perhaps a half a mile long, like a roadway or racetrack. To one side of it was a circular dance floor, surrounded by shelters set up by traders. People from the Pueblos were there with corn, *piki* bread, thin and flaky, and decorated pots. Others traded woven cotton sashes and kirtles. Still others offered *tortillas* and *masa,* cornmeal dough. For formal occasions, the Apache still wore beaded buckskin decorated with *conchos* and tiny bells, but for other uses, those who could afford it had started wearing cotton and wool. Woven Rio Grande and felted Hudson's Bay blankets were replacing buffalo robes.

Danny, Kit, and Roque unpacked their mules and rubbed them down before giving them a little corn. Then they erected a simple canvas shelter on the edge of the dance floor.

"One of us," said Roque, "will have to stay with our goods all the time. They might "wander" around without us. We've got to make sure they sit still. I don't think we'll get much sleep this close to the dance floor. The *Indios* sing and dance all night. Maybe we sleep in daytime, no?" Kit arranged with some young boys to care for their mules in exchange for ribbons, beads and brass tacks. They led the stock away to grass.

Looking around, Roque, as always, saw someone he knew. He strode off, hastening toward a strange little man. Although this man was close to average height, he seemed much smaller, clad as he was in a strange collection of Indian and Spanish clothing, all of it worn and dirty. On his feet were beaded moccasins, and he wore *botas*, chaps that covered the shin, under woolen trousers, whose outer seams blazed with large *conchos*. His broad belt boasted a large silver buckle in an intricate woven vine design and supported a revolver and knife. His upper body was covered by a fringed and beaded buckskin shirt. A silk top hat dyed green decorated with a band of silver *conchos* sat atop his head. Suntan and wrinkles concealed his age, which could have been anything from fifty to ninety. He smelled of whiskey.

Roque grabbed him and hugged him, lifting him off the ground.

"Let go of me, you *loco* greaser! You might break a rib. What's the matter with you? You don't like the ladies anymore? You been drinkin'? What did I tell you about demon rum?" The strange man sputtered in obvious pleasure.

"Danito, I want you to meet *Rodado Verde*, the Green Vagabond,*"* Roque said as Danny approached.

Danny started to extend his hand and then saw that Rodado Verde had drawn his revolver and was holding it out toward him. There was no way Danny would be able to draw his in time. He knew he was about to die and didn't know why. This strange little drunk was going to kill him. The pistol in *Rodado Verde*'s hand reversed and came toward Danny butt first.

"Mr. Carson doesn't like me to have the revolver around him when I been drinkin'. Would you hold it for me?" asked the Green Vagabond. "Pleased to meet you and top o' the morning to you, Danno. Call me Verde; everyone else does."

"I've never heard any other name for him," Roque said.

Given Verde's love of the gratuitous insult and guiding principle of never saying anything if he didn't have something nasty to say, he was probably hiding under this name. He might have been from Ireland and on the run from English justice, but it was hard to tell. They probably had him scheduled to hang for insulting their Queen, Danny mused.

"Maybe he don't got no other name," smirked Roque. "He's bound to be wanted for something somewhere. He likes to stir up trouble almost as much as he likes to drink."

For all that, Danny thought he sensed real affection in the way Verde said "greaser" or called an Indian "blanket-ass." He treated both fairly with his insults. Danny could understand why Roque liked the little man.

"Why, boy, there isn't a scrap of *la plata* about you anyplace nor any turquoise, neither. How are you going to look like a prosperous trader to these Indians if you don't wear some silver? Let me make you something."

From this statement, Danny concluded that the Green Vagabond was a traveling silversmith by trade.

There was constant activity all around the travelers and their new friend. People cooked and visited from camp to camp. They ate, romanced, sang, and drummed. Part of each day was focused on two brush corrals, one bearing a white flag, the other a red one, at opposite ends of the racetrack from each other. Most of the adult males gathered in one or the other for a couple of hours on the day they arrived. The drum sounded, and they assembled within.

"They call those their *kivas,* Danno. They're up there making magic and gettin' purified for the big ceremony on the last day," Verde informed Danny on one of his visits to their shelter. "The red flag is Olleros, and white is Llaneros."

Danny looked at him quizzically. "I thought that *kivas* were the underground rooms the Pueblo peoples use for their ceremonies. Roque told me that they're like churches, but that only men can attend and are like men's clubs where they meet to talk and sleep."

"So they are, too," Verde replied, "but Jicarilla *kivas* are corrals above ground, but they serve a similar purpose. Men go there to prepare for ceremonials."

Two horses pulled up in front of Danny's "trading post."

"*Peregrino Rojo*, it's good to see you again, *amigo,*" called Roque. "Who's that with you?"

Rojo had been among the raiders at Kit's rancho on the Rayado a few weeks before but had proved a friend. The second horse carried a comely girl dressed in a cotton shirt and leggings with red piping in the manner of the Pueblo Indians. The leggings were so large and heavily padded that her toes barely stuck out from under them. Her hair was wound up close to the sides of her head in large butterfly buns indicating, as Danny had learned, that she was unwed.

"Roque, Danito, this is my fat Pueblo girl who will keep me warm this winter. I'll be back to buy her some presents," Rojo announced. The girl smiled shyly unwilling to meet their eyes.

"She don't look so fat to me," said Roque.

"Plump in all the right places, Roque," Rojo smiled. *"Hasta!"* They rode off.

Activity had stopped in the Llanero *kiva*, and the men had started to circulate through the camp again.

Danny was surprised, though he shouldn't have been, to see other Jicarilla whom he had encountered before. He thought hostile Indians were outlaws who wouldn't appear in a friendly encampment. Any sense he'd had of being safe here among friends departed. Paranoia took firm hold of him. Anyone here might be a killer out for white blood.

Suddenly fearful, Danny pointed and said, "Look there, Kit, Roque, those are the ones who came to your house in Rayado."

He pointed at to two men nearby. Unlike Rojo, these braves had fled as Kit and Roque arrived. "The big one is called Acha and the little misshapen one Pinacate," Danny said. They were joined by others.

"Don't point, Danito," Kit said gently. "The Jicarilla think it very impolite."

"Si," added Roque, "they will think you are a *brujo* or something, giving them the evil-eye. These people point with their lower lip."

Acha's band stopped by Verde's shelter where the silversmith was heating and pounding on an object with hammer and finer tools. An animated conversation began about silver and its high cost. Danny understood the repeated word *plata*. The discussion was conducted in Spanish and English on one side and broken Spanish and Jicarilla on the other. The three friends were close enough to hear most of it as their voices grew louder.

"I hear Kit Carson run you off. You're sure enough scared of him. You insulted his lady, and he'll be looking to get even. I hear you wet your breechcloth," teased Verde.

They heard Acha reply, "Acha very brave. No scared. Beat him up, little man, little Gi-di."

Then from Verde, "Gi-di is here. Come on!" Gi-di was the name the Jicarilla called Kit. Verde marched toward Danny's tent trading post with Acha and entourage following. Acha's face showed red under the brown and the veins in his neck were throbbing.

"He wants to wrestle you, Kit," said Verde smiling.

"No, thanks." Kit had taken off his weapons and set them aside as he sat down in the shelter.

"He says, 'No, thanks,' Acha, *no, gracias*," Verde told the brave.

Acha slapped the small Green Vagabond with the force of a thrown hammer so hard he flew several feet before hitting the ground. Kit despised bullies. He rose in one motion and came out of the shelter while Verde slowly got to his feet, shaking out the bees buzzing in his head.

Acha charged head down, arms extended. At the last instant, Kit sidestepped and tripped him. Acha fell on his face. By the rules, that should have been the end as Acha's body had touched the ground, but he leapt to his feet spinning and charged again. Rules didn't seem to matter when your opponent isn't one of the *N'deh*, the Jicarilla.

Kit stooped over, and as Acha impacted with him Kit's shoulder caught the big Jicarilla in the middle. Kit rose up to his full height, letting Acha's momentum carry him up into the air. He flipped and went sailing over Kit landing with an audible thump on the ground that raised a cloud of dust. Shaken, he rose and charged again, obviously beyond rational thought.

Kit swayed to one side and extended his arm catching Acha across the throat. Acha's head stopped, but his lower body kept going until he was parallel with the ground. Then he fell. He rose gasping for air, shaking his head, his mouth and nose bleeding. Kit backed away from him.

Arms extended, Acha approached warily, hoping to grasp Kit. Kit moved suddenly, grasping Acha's arm with both of his, twisting his body, and hooking his knee behind Acha's. Acha fell with Kit still bracing his wrist in one hand and forcing Acha's elbow the wrong way with the other. Acha screamed in pain.

"Enough?" asked Kit.

"Enough," whimpered Acha. He and his friends departed sullenly.

"Well done, Kit," smiled Verde.

Danny was impressed with the small man's victory over the huge warrior. He, Roque and Verde all patted the victor's back and congratulated him. Kit had made it look easy not even breaking sweat.

"No, not well done," Kit shook his head. "That's trouble later on. I made it look too easy. I humiliated him. He'll be back."

Thus, a troublesome victory was won. Kit had given Danny something to think about, a piece of wisdom to chew on.

All afternoon women came by to inspect their wares. On the advice of Kit and Frank Aubry, Danny had brought beaver traps, knives, iron pots, a few rifles, Rio Grande blankets, ribbons in various colors with the majority being red and white, beads of white, light blue and dark blue and a few red beads, small bells, small circular mirrors, gunpowder, lead bars, percussion caps and a few other items. The women would inspect and choose as shopping seemed to be below the dignity of the men who stood aside and waited. Then, when the women were out of sight, the men came in and haggled for what their wives and girlfriends had selected.

Danny took in the skins of fox, marten and beaver, as well as fine, brain-tanned elk, deer and buffalo. Kit advised him to accept colorful feathers and buffalo horns as well as their skulls which could be traded to the Pueblo Indians. The same applied to semiprecious stones and crystals. He accepted their finely woven baskets, the finest he had ever seen. A few Indians had coins and he took these as well.

Roque advised Danito, "Take stones that can be polished. Apache don't attach much value to them, but jewelers will in the settlements. Jicarilla don't see much value in coins. You treat them like they aren't worth much, too."

Danny listened carefully to his friends' advice on what things might be worth in other places.

"Brain-tanned skins that are worth little to *Indios* will be worth a lot in Taos," Kit explained.

"So will those baskets," Roque chimed in. "Don't feel bad if the prices you're charging seem high. If they could get things for less, they would. There's got to be enough in it for you, Danito, to make you want to take the risks and spend the time again. If your profit wasn't high, you wouldn't come all this way."

On the advice of his friends, Danito tried to make 200 percent profit on things brought from Missouri and 50 percent on things acquired in New Mexico. He'd brought them a long way at great personal risk and had a half year of his labor invested in them. Red beads sold for less than he'd paid for them. The Jicarilla had apparently acquired a lot of them somewhere. That was part of the risk.

As daylight faded, the trio and Verde wandered about the camp in pairs, or threesomes when Rojo or Rodado Verde joined them for a while. One of the travelers, Kit, Roque, or Danito, always remained at their shelter to watch their goods. In each of the camps where they stopped, the women forced food on them until they could eat no more, but they continued to eat anyway, fearful of giving offense. The Olleros, with white flags hung from the poles of their tepees, seemed a little more prosperous than their Llanero cousins. And the Ollero food seemed tastier, flavored with onions, *chilis*, and vegetables. In the camps of the Llaneros, where red flags flew, there was more meat. A surprising amount of it was mutton. Strange, Danny thought, for a people who didn't herd sheep.

"Wealth that walks is a temptation," said Kit enigmatically when Danny pointed this out. He didn't say more, just smiled.

Rojo was more helpful. "You want to steal pumpkins from Pueblo *Indios*? How many can you carry? You want to steal sheep from a Mexican? How many sheep can you drive? If you need food, which will you take? If Jicarilla could make pumpkins walk, we'd steal them more often."

As dusk fell, they heard the sound of flutes and fiddles here and there about the encampment as young men courted their ladies. A group of four slightly chubby men in their late twenties or early thirties began beating a drum in unison nearby and singing. One sang a line, the two others repeated it, and they'd join on the chorus together.

Rojo translated:

> Pretty woman I see you grinding corn.
> You are sweating.
> I would make you sweat.
> I would make you sweat like my horse.
> I would make you sweat like my horse.
>
> Pretty woman I see you grinding corn.
> You are sweating.
> I would make you sweat.
> I would ride you without a saddle.
> I would ride you without a saddle.
>
> Pretty woman I see you grinding corn.
> You are sweating.
> I would make you sweat.
> I would ride you all night.
> I would ride you all night.

At least, that was Rojo's translation. He had a strange sense of humor. Then again, the song was written by committee, and the committee didn't seem to be attracting any ladies.

There was drinking. Taos Lightning was mixed with fruit juices and water. The most common drink was *tizwin*, a kind of beer made from fresh corn, which old women brewed in big pots.

Young boys gathered wood, and at the direction of gray-haired old men built it into a bonfire. A group of older men began playing a drum and chanting. Men and women in a long line danced with arms linked over each other's shoulders, moving forward and back in time to the music. Next, the beat and tenor of the chant changed to a "girl-dance."

"The young, unmarried women select partners," Roque told Danny. "If you are picked, you dance with her under her blanket as she holds it over your heads."

"If you dance with a girl," said Kit, "you must make her a gift afterward. As a trader you will be expected to be generous, as generous as their mothers were with food."

"But not too generous, Danito. You might find yourself married in the morning," warned Roque with a laugh.

Offering gifts of ribbon, beads, bells, and round mirrors made the girls happy and made Danny Trelawney a popular dance partner. Sitting to rest a while, he noticed Rodado Verde in his green hat swaying on his feet. Verde was addressing a small group of enthralled Jicarillas swaying as badly as he. They nodded and murmured assent as he spoke.

Roque helped with translation although Danny was beginning to understand a little Spanish. The lecture went on for an hour or more. Verde's theme went something like this:

> Alcohol is the devil's brew. It takes away a man's manhood and leaves him weak. God put the demon rum on earth to be brewed by the English and Spanish so the Irish and Jicarillas wouldn't rule the world. He wants us to cast it off and take our rightful place in charge of everything. We must swear off the

evil this very night. And then Jicarillas and
the Irish can pick up their crowns of silver
and be kings of the earth.

Periodically he paused to sip from his bottle and fortify
himself in the effort. Danny noticed the group again much
later in the evening sitting with arms about one another Verde
in the middle —kings of the earth, all snoring contentedly.

The dancing and singing went on most of the night.
Sometime after midnight during a girl-dance, Roque
disappeared and wasn't seen again until just before noon the
next day. Toward dawn, Danny fell asleep and slept late into
the morning. That seemed to be the pattern for everyone.

"Get up, boyo," grumbled Verde nudging Danny with
his moccasin. "You got any soap? One of them blanket-asses
had fleas."

Shortly after noon, two long processions wended their
way through the great camp. Leading in the front were the
respective flags of the clans, red for the Llanero procession
and white for the Olleros. The flags were followed by four
drummers carrying a great drum that they beat as they
chanted calling out the foot racers. These were followed by
drummers carrying drums made of black pottery. Behind
them came mounted men, their best horses gaily decorated
for the occasion, also singing and calling out challenges.
More joined as they passed the family camps. It was two
grand parades. As they played, the Olleros proceeded to
march and sing as they headed in column for the kiva of
the Llaneros. Before long, the Llaneros emerged and began
singing their own songs, which were different from those of
the Olleros, a counter-parade. Out of sight of the main camp

and at opposing poles, the processions halted and all grew quiet as the young men raced against each other to determine if they would be chosen to run in the following day's great race between clans. The elders selected the runners and determined the order in which they would run.

In the afternoon, Rojo came by their shelter with a man of medium build, well proportioned, and athletic with long black braids. He was in his mid-forties and well dressed in beaded and fringed buckskins, all very clean. One look in his eyes, and Danny knew this man was very intelligent and a leader.

"This is Vicenti, my father," said Rojo.

Danny rose and offered his hand. Chief Vicenti took it with a smile, letting Danny know he knew something of gringo ways. Kit rose, and they embraced warmly. Danny suspected from the tilt of the chief's head and the way his eyes moved that Vicenti could speak Spanish and probably some English. However, his father always let Rojo translate. Danny thought this an interesting ploy, a way to gather information without being observed.

Vicenti was one of the chiefs of the Olleros, the mountain people, who were associated with the moon, vegetable foods, and the color white. They lived west of the Rio Grande and farmed a little in their peculiar way. They would plant a field and then move away to gather plant foods and to hunt, returning in the fall to harvest the crop. They were keen traders and always had something to bring to the Mexican towns. In those days, they had a lot of dealings with the Moache Utahs, or Utes. Both Jicarilla and Utah took trade goods to Abiquiu and Taos. Vicenti was the youngest chief and a man greatly respected among the Ollero. He had come to talk to Kit, whom he called Gi-di.

"Gi-di, the game in our land grows scarce," Vicenti informed Kit. "The gringos trade where we once traded. Comanche occupy the buffalo plains. They have many more people than the *N'deh*. The people will be hungry this winter. The Llanero, I fear, will win the race again this year, and the world will remain imbalanced. The Llanero will take the moon's plants, but the people will be short of meat as we Olleros have not beaten the sun's people in too long to gain his animals."

"Vicenti," said Kit, "I hunted beaver until they were almost gone, and there was no value in their pelts. Then I worked for William Bent bringing meat to his fort on the Arkansas River where he trades with Jicarilla, Cheyenne, and Utah. When I had need of more for my family than Bent would give me, I scouted trails for Fremont. Now I farm and raise some animals at Rayado near the long trail from Missouri. There I sell what I grow and raise to travelers. I would not give advice to the Jicarilla. They know best how to be *N'deh*. I can only say times have changed for me and for all. We seek new ways."

Danny was surprised at this long speech from Kit but soon realized that it was necessary. Kit was speaking indirectly, talking of things that seemed only personal of little consequence. He was providing advice, laying it out where the chief could pick it up and examine it without being told what to do and how to proceed.

More people began to return from the kivas and races, and the men moved about the camp. Two men came and joined Vicenti talking to Kit. Rojo whispered to Danny that they were Chacon and *Huero Mundo*.

Chacon was a big man with long braids shot through

with gray, probably in his sixties but still powerful and athletic. He was the most respected and well known of the Ollero chiefs. He had very broad shoulders and narrow hips with a belly that was beginning to paunch. His eyes showed deep intelligence. This man was a thinker as well as a man of action. *Huero Mundo's* name meant "the blondest guy in the world;" however, he had black hair and dark skin. He didn't look blond to Danny. Later Danny learned that this was some sort of pun on *huevo*, egg, which sounds similar to ears attuned to *Rio Arriba* Spanish and indicates someone ballsy or brave. He was younger than Chacon, in his fifties, Danny guessed. He had a small, slender frame, but wiry and tough like jerky left in the sun too long. His arms were scarred, and he moved as if parts of his body were stiff. His eyes were hooded and dark. Between them, his nose stood out like a tomahawk. He wore a necklace of huge bear claws.

Rojo noticed Danny staring at four parallel scars on Huero Mundo's face. "*Shik'isn shash*, brother bear, did that to him," whispered Rojo. "Mundo dodged, and the claws barely touched him, or the blow would have taken his head off. He attacked the bear with only lance and knife. It is a famous story among us."

"Black bear?" Danny whispered back.

"Grizzly. See the claws."

It was no wonder Mundo was considered a great war leader. Brave men feared approaching a grizzly with only a rifle. The rifle allowed them to attack from beyond the reach of the bear, even if it provided only one shot and could misfire. If the bear didn't die instantly, the hunter was unlikely to have time to reload. A single blow from the huge bear could snap a limb or a neck, and the claws could open a man's bowels. Approaching a grizzly with lance and knife alone gave the bear all the advantages. The hunter had two knives, the bear ten and much stronger arms to wield them. The hunter would have to strike many times, the bear but once.

"*Cristobal*, Gi-di, have you heard news from the plains travelers? Have the buffalo come south?" Chacon asked Kit in Spanish.

"It has been cold in the north and the rains have been good on the *llano*," Kit replied. "The buffalo have come far south in great numbers."

"Come, Gi-di, walk with us," Chacon invited as Vicenti signaled his son that he would not be needed. The four of them walked off away from camp.

As an old woman approached them, Roque suddenly jumped to his feet.

"*Doña Luna, como esta?*" Roque embraced her. He continued in Spanish, which she spoke quite well.

Danny did his best to follow their conversation.

"Meet my *amiga*, Danito," Roque said turning to him. "This lady saved my life. I cut my leg with an axe, and it infected. I had fever, but she cured me. I was sure I would die or lose the leg."

"A great pleasure, Doña Luna," Danny bowed and she smiled.

"*Tiéná'áí Izdzánii*, Moon Woman, is one of our great medicine women, a famous healer. She gathers plants in secret places and knows when and where to get them," said Rojo pleased with his relative. "She has great power."

Danny saw before him an ancient woman of good humor standing barely five foot tall. Time had wrinkled her skin but not bent her. She had a wonderful warm smile. Her clothing was eccentric, made of bits and pieces of this and that and festooned with pouches strung from shoulder and waist that held her special herbs. She came close and looked up into Danny's eyes.

Danny hadn't completely understood. Rojo had really said, "Great Power is with her." Power was an animate thing that dwelt in nature. Rocks, trees, wind and animals all had their own Power. There was Power in perception as well. One who could sense the enemy approaching had Enemy Power. Power was like a god or gods. Power had its own will and could depart from a man or woman if they did not behave appropriately to nuture Power.

"I think I need to purge him," she said looking somber.

"Not the purge," Roque and Rojo intoned together with dread.

Danny looked shocked, and she cackled, "Not this time, young man. Maybe next time."

Roque and Rojo laughed at her joke.

Rojo told Danny, "She has great wisdom. Go to her if you wish to understand anything about the customs of the Jicarilla. She will help you."

They bid her farewell.

"Let me show you around, Dan," Rojo suggested.

"It's okay, Danito, I'll watch our goods," said Roque.

Among those with things to sell around the dance floor. they found Rojo's "fat Pueblo girl" making *piki* bread. She ground hominy into a thin paste, which she poured onto a flat stone she had heated over the fire. A few moments later, she lifted it off, wafer thin and already cooked. She placed this one with others of its kind and rolled them into small bundles, which she bound with strings of cornhusk.

Nearby sat a woman surrounded by marvelous baskets tightly woven in shapes ranging from almost flat platters to gourd-shaped bottles nearly three feet high. Some displayed running deer and fine fat turkeys. Others were decorated with geometric designs, diamonds, stepped clouds, lightning bolts, and more. These were of the highest quality, woven so tightly they could hold water.

The woman continued her work stripping sumac withes with her teeth. She bundled the inner withe with others of its kind to form the base of a coil. These coils were stitched or sewn together with the sumac bark using the colored bark of other plants to create patterns. The rim of each basket was stitched in a herringbone design that added strength and beauty.

"Danny, this is *Guust Cha'du*, our best weaver of baskets," said Rojo. She looked up and smiled. She was a woman about fifty, neatly dressed, well built, and still slender. Danny bought a number of her baskets, confident he would be able to trade them on the way back to Rayado.

Rojo translated as she told him, "Look. See? In each basket, there is an opening. It is a place that is blank without design. It leads from center all the way to rim."

Danny looked. Her work was so clever, it was difficult to pick out the opening in some of the baskets, but it was always there. It was easiest to see in baskets where a band of color ran all the way around the rim or interior, a single stitch of uncolored sumac.

"Yes, I see it."

"It is a portal for my spirit to escape from the basket, otherwise, I might be trapped within," she informed the young men. "If my spirit were trapped, it would be difficult for me to sell, or even give away, my baskets. I would be unable to part with them."

"Do all Jicarilla practice this philosophy?" Danny asked Rojo.

Rojo nodded. "It carries over into everything we do."

The Llanero kiva finished its work, and Rojo pointed out José Largo, a tall, thin man, Saco Colorado and Lobo Blanco who was followed closely by someone Danny had seen before—Acha.

An elderly man was admonishing some children who were teasing a snake.

Rojo interpreted. "He tells them, 'Do not touch the snake, or it will paralyze you. If you touch the snake, you will be crippled. Leave it alone. It is a messenger of the rain gods.' He goes on to tell them, 'Do not eat or even touch fish. They are cousin to the snake.' We call the old man *Shitaá Piishíí*, Father Nighthawk. Tonight we will come back and listen to him tell stories to the children."

After dark enclosed the camp, Rojo and Danny returned and found the storyteller with a group of enraptured children. He began:

> In recent times in Turkey Valley in that very place, there were a people who lived in the Turkey Valley and Long Canyon and Willow Creek. They lived in houses on top of the mesas, built underground like the Pueblo kivas, and in the crags, too, but in the cliff-houses, they mostly stored corn. Farmers and hunters, they made pottery and beautiful baskets as well.
>
> They raided the Pueblos on the river and

so made enemies of them. Because of this, they built towers so they could see enemies approaching at great distance. The towers also gave them a place from which to fight if they were attacked. In some places, they made the whole top of the hill a fort to hide in.

A great drought came, and ancestors of the Pueblos had difficulty. In the high country, the people I speak of did not have so much trouble as the high country gets more rain. On the river, they did not have so much trouble because they made ditches to carry water. They moved down closer to the river. But far away in the west near Sleeping Ute Mountain, those people had real trouble, and they had to leave their homes. They came a few at a time to join their brothers on the river.

Some of them came through Turkey Valley and turned south. They were the ancestors of the Jemez, and at first, there were only a few. They did not know how to farm this country, and their crops did poorly at first. The people from Turkey Valley, seeing the Jemez few and weak, began to take advantage of small parties of Jemez. They robbed them and killed some of them and kept others for slaves. All the time they pretended to be friendly to the Jemez, inviting them into their villages and then surprising them. It was a bad thing to do.

The Turkey Valley people thought them few and weak, but they were wrong. There were many more Jemez coming from Sleeping Ute Mountain.

The Jemez learned of the bad way the Turkey Valley people treated strangers and travelers, and they made a plan. They would enter the villages of the Turkey Valley people as friends in many, many small groups everywhere at once. At a signal, they would surprise these people and kill them.

The Jemez did this all in the course of a few days. They surprised the villagers, killed them, and left their bodies unburied on the hillside. Then they burned their towers and houses. Some people they took captive, and their descendents eventually also became Jemez. Very few escaped.

Those who escaped from death and slavery wandered around their country hiding from the Jemez. Afraid to build houses, afraid to farm, their lives were very bad. Then new people came into the area, the *N'deh*. They took these people in and the former Turkey Valley people became *N'deh*. That is why the *N'deh* can say their ancestors have always been here and that is why some *N'deh* can make fine baskets and pottery. It is also why some *N'deh* make farms. And lastly, that is why of all the Pueblos, the *N'deh* can claim to have cousins among the Jemez only.

Danny learned later that how Father Nighthawk started a story indicated whether he considered it recent history or a legend. "Long ago it happened… in that very place" was like saying "once upon a time." The stories were real for him, even though they were about a different age. If he said, "In recent times," he was reciting history. The children were supposed to make associations with hills, mountains, rocks, groves of trees, berry patches, streams, and valleys. These were places they had been and knew well, and the story would become real for them. A story might tell about a taboo that had been broken and of the horrible consequences that followed. Merely mentioning the name of the place was enough to remind them to think about their own behavior and get them to consider whether they had been violating the same taboo or something akin to it. It was a way to admonish without directly criticizing.

"This way," said Rojo, "we do not have to scold our children or yell at them the way the *Nakaiyeh*, the Mexicans, do. We make them think. We do not make them angry."

"Father Nighthawk, tell us another story. Tell us about Coyote," cried the children. Father Nighthawk started his tale.

> Long ago it happened at Red Rocks Go Up in a Line to White Cliffs in that very place, when the fourth world was still new, the holy people walked the earth. The animals could still talk then. They were like people. Most walked upright on two legs like a man. Each was the progenitor of his race. He was all the things his race would be, and he had all the Power his race would always have. Coyote

was always coyote, and he caused much trouble and brought much chaos. Wanting the Power that others had rather than being content with his own, Coyote was always trying to trick people and to take what was theirs. Usually his schemes all came to no good. One time, though, Coyote got the better of Wildcat. This is how it happened.

One day Coyote took a long stick and attached a piece of red cloth to it. He went marching around and singing until he got to the Prairie Dog town. Then he marched in circles up and down through the town singing. Finally, he called out in a loud voice, "Now you must all come and gather around, and we will sing and dance." And the Prairie Dogs all came out and gathered around Coyote.

Coyote said to them, "You must hurry back to your homes and block up the doors tightly. We don't want anyone to get in and rob you while we are dancing and celebrating." The Prairie Dogs hurried back to their homes and blocked the doors, and then they ran back to where Coyote was singing and dancing and began to dance with him. Up and down, they went, round and round, in and out through the Prairie Dog town. The littlest one came last, for he was crippled and couldn't dance very well.

Coyote began to sing, "Let the big Prairie Dogs approach me, let them come. Let the little Prairie Dogs approach me, too; let them come." Coyote held a rock in his hand, and he kept this hand behind him where the Prairie Dogs couldn't see it. As Prairie Dogs approached Coyote, one at a time, Coyote hit them in the head with the rock he was hiding, and they fell down dead, one at a time. Some of them cried out, and the other Prairie Dogs became alarmed. But Coyote calmed the remaining Prairie Dogs, "They are just overcome with exhaustion, joy, and celebration. There is nothing to worry about." The Prairie Dogs believed him. They kept dancing right up to Coyote. Coyote killed a great many Prairie Dogs at that time.

The littlest Prairie Dog came limping up from behind the other dancers and behind Coyote. Seeing the rock in Coyote's hand, he cried out, "Coyote has a rock in his hand. He is killing us." The Prairie Dogs panicked. They began to run every which way. They wanted to dive into their homes and be safe, but they couldn't! Before the dance, they had blocked up their doors as Coyote had instructed. They couldn't get in. Coyote killed a great many more Prairie Dogs, including Littlest Prairie Dog. But some Prairie Dogs got away.

Coyote took the Prairie Dog bodies down by a stream and built a big fire. When the fire burned down to ashes, Coyote opened the Prairie Dogs up and buried them in the ashes with only their tails sticking out. He put Littlest Prairie Dog on the end with his tail sticking up out of the ashes. After all this work, Coyote was very tired, so he went and found some shade and lay down to take a nap.

While Coyote was napping, Wildcat came along, drawn by the smell of roasting meat. He circled the ashes a couple of times swishing his long tail and sniffing with his long snout. It smelled good. Seeing the row of tails sticking up from the ashes, he pulled on the biggest one. Out came a big Prairie Dog completely roasted, and Wildcat ate it. It was good…"

"But Father Nighthawk," interrupted one of the children, "Wildcat has a short tail and a scrunched up face."

"Is it so? Go get me a wildcat right now and show me, or sit down and listen to my story," said the elder. The child was silent. Nighthawk continued his tale.

Wildcat continued to pull out Prairie Dogs, and he ate them until he was full. The only thing he didn't eat was the tails. When he couldn't eat any more, he hung the rest in a tree, all except Littlest Prairie Dog, who was too small to be bothered with. Wildcat left him in the ashes. Then he arranged the tails in a row sticking up from the ashes just as they had been before. Being very full of roasted meat, he wandered a little ways off and went to sleep.

Coyote woke up looking forward to his meal. He went to the ashes and pulled out Littlest Prairie Dog. "This is too small to bother with," he said, and he tossed the little Prairie Dog away. He pulled on another tail and only the tail came out. "Oh, I have cooked the tail right off," Coyote said. So he pulled on another tail, and it came out just a tail. He pulled on another and another, and all the tails came off. "Oh, these are very well cooked," Coyote said. He went a got a stick to dig in the ashes and poked around, but he couldn't find any Prairie Dogs.

"Oh no," said Coyote, "I have cooked them all to ashes and burned them up to nothing! Where is that little one I tossed away?" He looked around for the little Prairie Dog, but he couldn't find it. In the stream, Coyote saw the reflection of the Prairie Dogs that Wildcat had hung in the tree. He reached into the stream and tried to get them, but he couldn't grab them, so he waited until the stream cleared and he could see clearly again. Then Coyote pounced on the reflection of the Prairie Dogs in the stream. He missed them. He jumped in the stream again. Every time he saw the reflections, he jumped in the stream. Finally, Coyote was very tired and lay on his back panting.

While on his back panting, he looked up in the tree, and he saw five perfectly roasted

Prairie Dogs hanging where Wildcat had left them. He was so hungry, he jumped up and ate one bones and all. Then he had another and another. After a while Coyote thought, "This is very strange. I only threw away one Prairie Dog. Why are there five hanging here? I think someone has been here."

Coyote went looking for signs. Finding the tracks of Wildcat, he followed them to where Wildcat was still sleeping. Coyote was very skilled as a thief. He was so skilled that he stole Wildcat's rectum without waking Wildcat. He took the rectum and put it on a stick and roasted it in the ashes until it was perfectly done.

Coyote then took the perfectly cooked rectum back to Wildcat. He awakened Wildcat by pushing hard on Wildcat's long snout scrunching it up all flat. Coyote said, "Cousin, I have cooked you some meat. Here take it and eat." He gave Wildcat the perfectly cooked rectum to eat. Wildcat took it and ate greedily.

When Wildcat had eaten about half of the rectum, Coyote laughed and called out, "Ha, ha, look Wildcat is eating his own rectum!"

Wildcat became very excited at this, and he tried to push the rectum back in where it belonged. He got so excited that he pushed in most of his long tail with it. That is why when you see Wildcat today, he has a short tail with a tip burned black, and his face is scrunched up and flat. Now we call him Bobcat when we see him, for his face and tail are bobbed and shorter than they once were."

They left the storyteller and found their beds for the night.

On the last day, the men gathered at their kivas. Two elders came out and cleared people off a racetrack that had been set up running east and west and about a half a mile long, brushing it with eagle feathers as they jogged to purify the ground. In the kivas, the singers made sand drawings of a hummingbird, a sandhill crane, an eagle, and other fast birds. They adorned the runners in the colors of their clan, red ochre or white clay, and attached the feathers and down of fast birds to purify them. Once the track had been cleared, the relay teams emerged from their kivas and lined up behind their banners now suspended from poles three times a man's height. Following their banners, the teams danced down the length of the course toward each other and then past each other, until the teams were lined up outside each other's kivas. They danced down the track again with half of each team remaining behind.

Because Rojo was in the race, Danny looked around for Doña Luna, Moon Woman, to explain the ceremony to him.

Finding her he asked, "Mother, can you assist me?"

The women and children and old folks lined up along the sides of the track many mounted on horses. The elders worked the track with their aspen fronds keeping the people back and the track clear of any bad influence. "Certainly not. I can't purge you at a time like this. They are racing," she cried out, eliciting smirks and laughs from people in the crowd.

"It is well, Doña Luna. May I ask some questions?"

"Ask."

Danny asked her to explain the significance of the race.

"A longtime ago there was too much food of both kinds, both meat and vegetables," Moon Woman began. "It was all mixed up and didn't come in season. The sun and moon decided that it must be divided. So the moon said, 'I'll bet my vegetables against you in a race.' And the Sun said, 'I will bet my animals.' So they ran a race. The Moon won the bet and for the next year, Moon and his people hunted, and game was plentiful. The next year Sun won and he and his people were able to find plentiful vegetable foods. In this way, the world stayed in balance and the people were fed.

"The race is run to ensure that there will be plenty of food of both kinds for the people and to see which kind of food should dominate in the coming year. The Ollero represent the Moon and the Llanero the Sun. That is why white is the color of the Ollero and red the color of the Llanero. If the Llanero win this race, animal food from the Sun will predominate for the next year. And if the Ollero win, plant food from the Moon will predominate. In this way, we ensure a plentiful and balanced food supply."

Four elderly men came out and ran the length of the racetrack to clear it for the runners. Then the race began. The people on the sidelines cheered for their runners, two runners who started from the end nearest the Llanero kiva. As they reached the end of the track, elders designated the next runners. The Llaneros took an early lead and soon were a lap, Doña Luna called it a season, ahead. Then a runner stumbled, and before long, the Ollero caught up and then were a season ahead. Danny saw a runner go by that he had seen before.

"I've seen that runner before!" he said to the old woman. "Do they run more than once?"

"Sometimes," she said, "If the elders tell them to, they run again. Sometimes they run three and four times. The teams are of unequal size. They will run until one team or the other is two seasons ahead. Then the slow side will concede defeat."

The crowd cheered. The elders waved their aspen fronds and told the other team's runners to "slow down" and "take it easy." They batted at their own runners from behind to urge them to go faster. The Llanero pulled into the lead again, and then the Ollero were ahead by a season. Then it was a season and a half and finally two seasons. The Llanero had lost. The Sun had lost and game would be plentiful. Only a successful fall hunt of the combined tribes out on the Llano Estacado could make it so. Kit had said the buffalo were plentiful this year and had come far south.

It was the turn of the youngsters, the boys too young to run. They were adorned in the manner of their older brothers and were told that no matter how much clay and ochre and bird feather itched, they must not scratch. They mustn't remove anything until the sun had gone down. They ran as a group and not in relays while the elders and their elder brothers prepared the final phase of the ceremony.

To the beat of drums and led from their kivas by their clan banners, the men half-stepped down the track toward each other. Coming even, the two teams backed up 30 paces and then approached again, once, twice, three times. On the third approach, they halted and began to throw things at each other. Danny saw ears of corn, *chili* pods, and jerked meat go high into the air to be caught by runners of the opposing team. Women rushed out onto the track, and they too caught the thrown gifts. Everyone laughed and was joyful. For the Jicarilla, it was the happiest time of the year.

Soon there was dancing in the plaza, and off to one side the men organized an impromptu rodeo displaying their skill with horses. Drums beat, and the people sang and danced. They drank as well, for the ceremonial was over, and they knew game would be plentiful. The world was in balance, and all was right. The dancing, drinking, drumming, and singing continued through the night.

That night there was a council of all the chiefs. Chief Vicenti came over with Rojo to talk to Kit afterwards.

"The race decided it," Kit told Roque and Danito. "The whole tribe is headed from here out onto the plains to hunt buffalo."

It was a brief statement from Kit that left Danny wondering. Roque explained. "They're taking everyone, the whole tribe, as protection against the Comanche. The Comanche are pushed west by the Texans onto Jicarilla hunting grounds. The Jicarilla are a small tribe. You've seen them all here, only about eight hundred. The Comanche are numerous, however. There are many thousands of them. It is a risk for the Jicarilla. Still, they will have to kill a lot of buffalo to feed themselves for the winter. And the omens are good. The Moon won the race, and the Sun has lost his animals."

When Rojo and Chief Vicenti were about to depart having delivered this message, they heard an owl hoot near the camp.

Rojo shivered. "It is a bad omen. When Owl hoots, someone will die."

In the darkest part of the night, long before dawn, Kit's moccasined toe nudged Danny awake. "Start packing," said Kit. "We're leaving." Roque was already packing.

Chapter 7

The River Road to Taos

There may have been something to Rojo's omen. The three travelers got a later start than Kit had intended. Trading had gone well, but the goods taken in trade were bulky and hard to pack. The sun was well up before they entered Red Wall Canyon. The clopping of mules' hooves returned ghostly echoes off canyon walls far too close for comfort. The smell of sage, horse, and men too long unbathed blended with the smell of fear and rotting vegetation and hung close about them. Only Kit seemed calm. For the others saddle-chafing was aggravated by constant turning to look behind combined with cramped legs tense from riding unrested from too much dancing. Eight hundred of the wildest Indians in North America were behind them. Both Danny and Roque sensed that Kit's call for an early departure without goodbyes meant the mountain man smelled trouble.

"Danny, this is a natural place for an ambush," said Kit quietly. "All advantage lies with those springing the trap."

Rojo had warned the trio about Acha's growing anger. He was convinced Acha would try something as soon as the truce of *Go Jii Ya* was over. Red Wall Canyon would be just the place.

"Look, Danito," Roque intoned, for once somber in tone. "In the *cañon*, there is nowhere we can go except up or downstream. It is impossible to go *a la carga*, charging, up the walls to where attackers lurk. Weapons fired from the cañon rim will be deadly. If they block our path, we will have no choice but to fight."

Roque scanned the road ahead while Kit scanned the canyon rim. Danny watched their back trail, the hairs of his neck standing on end while the spot between his shoulder blades twitched awaiting an arrow. Tense necks and eyes soon began to ache with the effort of watching. Soon galloping horses' hooves sounded behind them.

"Kit, there's something coming up behind us. Moving fast!" Danny called.

Their rifles were held at the ready, for they expected long-range fire from above. Danny pulled the hammer of his to full cock and then rested his rifle across the pommel of his saddle, ready for come what may. Kit circled back and joined him in the trail. They drew revolvers. A fight on horseback, or muleback, would be at close range. They would wait until they could almost touch an enemy before firing. There was no way to aim on a bouncing horse.

The sound of approaching hooves grew louder. Kit, pulling in tight to the canyon wall motioned Danny to move out toward the middle to distract the oncoming riders and draw their attention. This would buy Kit critical moments to make the first shots.

Danny recalled Roque's lessons on fighting with guns.

"Danito, imagine two parties of five men lined up," Roque had said. "They are sharpshooters and never miss, no? Both sides fire at the same moment. Both sides die. Now imagine one group is a little quicker and gets off the first shot. The group that fires first will live to tell about the fight. That's why an ambush is so effective. They fire first.

"Not everybody is a sharpshooter. If you have more shooters, you kill more of your enemy sooner. The side with the most shooters doesn't lose as many men."

The two young men were counting on Kit's skill as a sharpshooter and warrior, there was none better. Given the chance, they'd fire first. With a little luck, the approaching riders might pass by Kit before they noticed him. Then he'd be firing on them from behind, causing confusion. Of course, if there were more than a handful, Kit would be cut off and beyond aid.

"If they can't tell where fire is coming from," Kit had taught, "that leads to panic. It's hard to defend against."

In Red Wall Canyon, they prepared for a fight.

Kit whispered, "If the road is blocked ahead, and there are shooters on the cliffs above, going back the way we've come might be our only choice. We'll have to clear a path."

Danny nodded, knowing he meant they'd have to kill whoever was behind them.

Around a bend in the canyon came one rider leading two pack mules.

"Ahoy, the riders. Mind if I join you?" queried Rodado Verde, tipping his green top hat with a grin.

He had a knack for showing up when trouble was brewing. That could have been because he liked to brew it. But there was substance to Verde. He was a man who would stand with his friends in a fight even if he'd started it.

They didn't get jumped in Red Wall Canyon—not until after they'd left it.

An arrow flew past Danny's face as they emerged from the canyon into the valley near Abiquiu. A second thunked into the pack of the mule ahead of him.

Four riders careened towards them from the left. Danny noticed ponies tethered off to the right and on looking closer saw Apaches scaling the canyon walls now behind the four traders.

"That," Danny thought, "is where the arrows came from. Good, we are almost out of their range." It appeared to him that they had sprung the trap before it was ready and might be just beyond its grasp.

"With me," yelled Roque from the lead. "*A la carga!*" He spurred his big stallion toward the riders. They were at least as surprised as the four friends where.

"Charge!" cried Verde delighted.

Away they went, crashing into and among the riders and disrupting them. Roque's big horse knocked one pony rider and his mount to the ground. He knocked another rider sprawling.

Kit meanwhile had ridden after the tethered ponies and scattered them.

Pursuit was not immediate. They had surprised the Apache as they formed their ambush. Roque led them to the nearest rancho, and from there they rode to the next, knowing that pursuers would hesitate to come near buildings for fear of being fired on from within. After a couple of miles, they rested their mounts briefly near one of the ranchos.

Except for Roque, they were on mules, and mules, especially loaded pack mules, are slower than ponies. Resting the mules gave them a slight edge. They would be able to sprint if the Apache grew close, but the Jicarilla on jaded ponies would not. It also allowed Acha and his companions time to catch up. Kit calculated the risk, and he held them near the rancho.

Danny could see among their pursuers Jicarillas they had come to know. Acha led them, and Pinacate was with them, together with Sonrisado, Acentellado, and Zapato Negro. Danny counted about fifteen in all.

"I count fifteen," he said.

"Them's good odds," cheered Verde. "Let's stand and fight!"

Dusk was approaching. This would be a bad night to camp in the open. They were still about two miles from Abiquiu plaza. The stock weren't breathing as hard as they had been. Between his knees, Danny could feel his mule beginning to relax.

"Abiquiu," Kit said. Roque nodded. They left the rancho going full out. The mules were rested. Acha's ponies had run three miles to catch up. They were winded.

One other thing saved them. The effective range for bow and arrow and pistol on horseback is about the same. They'd have to be able to smell each other's breath before they fired if they hoped to hit anything. The traders had six-shot revolvers and could fire a lot faster than the Apache. They kept their distance, the leaders holding back until slower ponies caught up. If they took them, it would be all together or not at all. The Apache fought to win, and winning meant minimizing losses. They were not showy Cheyenne Dog Soldiers out to display their bravery at the cost of losing the battle. They were skilled fighters and brave, but not foolish.

The four traders hadn't killed any of their number, so the Jicarilla weren't out to revenge a murder. They wanted to rob and humiliate the mountain man and his friends so Acha could prove himself better than Kit. While a contfrontation could easily get deadly, their willingness to risk death was lower than it might otherwise have been.

Kit organized them. Roque took the lead on the pack train and rode in the front on the left. Verde took the lead on the right. Danny trailed left, and Kit right. Thus, the pack animals were in the middle where the Apaches would have to go through one of the four friends to get the stock being led. Stealing the trader's wealth might be enough to assuage Acha's anger, but being robbed was not an option the four riders were in favor of as long as there was an alternative.

Periodically, two or three of them pushed their ponies ahead of the pack and split going left and right on either side of Kit or Danny. Their intent was to get them to raise a pistol toward one side leaving the other undefended. The Indian rider on the undefended side would close in and try to dispatch the man whose pistol was pointed the wrong way. It didn't work, but it could have.

Kit called out to Danny, "Worry about the riders on your left. Let me cover your right!"

Danny had no choice but to trust him for flank protection.

Roque led them away to the right and up a side canyon and then up a steep trail onto a river bench. The plaza was surrounded on two sides by the canyon walls. The third was a steep drop to the Rio Chama. On the fourth, alongside the trail they'd come up, was the church. Doors and shutters slammed all over the village.

"The church!" directed Kit.

At first, Danny thought Kit meant to take their animals into the churchyard or even into the church. The churchyard was a profusion of jumbled crosses as the Mexicans bury their dead on top of and among each other willy-nilly. Bones from previous burials formed part of the fill for the new grave. The churchyard was about ten yards on a side, and surrounded by a thick adobe wall about four feet high.

The church was massively constructed with a *mirador*, a recessed balcony, and heavy doors. Windows for light were high up near the roof, close to thirty feet from the floor. People stood or knelt for services, for there were no pews.

As they barged in, the priest bustled toward them demanding that they leave. Roque, in turn, demanded sanctuary, and the priest, dubious, subsided in his protests.

As Kit directed, they brought the packs and saddles inside after tethering the animals along the churchyard wall on the far side from the trail and feeding them grain from their packs. Kit foraged the plaza picking things from the ground. He strung pot shards (broken pieces of pottery), broken glass, bits of metal and even some bones together with sinew and thread. These he attached to plants and tree and grass in such a way that anyone approaching and touching the thread would cause the bits of broken stuff to knock together and make a sound.

"Two on watch, two sleeping," he instructed. "One guard will hunker down in the *rincon*, inside corner, of the wall on the side opposite the mules. Get deep in shadow and be sure you can see the stock. When it's time to change shift, come back into the church along the wall so you don't give the position away. The other guard will be in the *mirador*."

They built a fire and cooked on the church floor, which was dirt, so they did no harm. Tired from early rising and recent exertions, they slept early.

Sometime after midnight, Danny had the watch. The night crept up on him. The excitement of the chase and unfamiliar spices combined to make him jumpy. He was sure he saw and heard the heavy wings of an owl in the night hunting over the churchyard. Owl flight is silent, but Rojo's forecast that an owl hoot presaged death played on his mind 'til even the silent owl could be heard. He also heard sounds from up canyon, chanting or singing. Red eyes glowed from the dark. Shivering with mountain cold and fear, he thought about what Roque had said about the *brujos y brujas*, witches, in this place. As he sat among their jumbled crosses, he wondered how peacefully those resting below him slept.

More practical than Danny, Kit had said, "We need to protect the stock and our goods from the locals as much as the Apaches."

Tucked into a *rincon* of the churchyard wall in deep shadow he waited, quaking, although the night was not cold. He looked and listened, his mind providing him with more entertainment than the night alone offered. All Danny's senses were alert; his hair stood on end. Odd, icy drafts reached him, touching one side of his face or body, but not the other, stroking him gently like a lover's hand. The air shimmered and moved. At times, it seemed he saw the stock through clear water touched by a light breeze. Danny was terrified and would have run, but he did not want to fail Kit and his friends. It wasn't courage like Kit's that held Danny in place.

"I will not run," Danny told himself, a stubborn streak rising to the fore. Fear did not hold the young man in place, nor did cold-blooded courage. He simply did not want to fail Kit.

Danny's Hawken was cradled in his arms, a pistol tucked into his waistband. There was no moon, it having set early in the evening. The stock snorted and stamped. Then Danny thought he heard two shards of broken glass tinkle behind him beyond the wall. Turning silently, he looked toward the top of the wall behind his head. A foot slowly came over the top, followed by a leg, a body scarce inches behind. As a face started to cross the top of the wall, Danny swung the barrel of his Hawken across his body as hard as he could and struck the face dead center.

There was a grunt. Body, leg, and foot disappeared back over the wall, and he heard the sound of running feet on the trail. The sounds made were minimal, but in seconds, Kit was at Danny's side signaling the young man to watch, and then Kit crept to the gate and left the churchyard, crawling rapidly. Slow minutes passed before he returned, careful to let Danny know it was he before he entered.

"It's clear," he whispered and took the watch while Danny went into the church to sleep.

They weren't bothered again. In the morning, they found blood on the wall.

Verde cackled to the amusement of Kit and Roque. "Them Jicarillas gonna call you Breaker of Noses."

Danny never saw the people of Abiquiu. They continued to shun the four travelers as they breakfasted and packed their stock.

"Ain't you got no friends here, Roque? Or maybe a *primo*, cousin, or two?" giggled Verde. "What's wrong? You got something against witches?"

Roque scowled. "Watch out, or they get you with the *ojo malo*, the evil eye, Rodado Verde." The last was said loud enough and distinctly enough for anyone in the plaza to hear. If they wanted to curse Verde, the witches of Abiquiu now had a name to work with.

As they emerged into the valley of the Chama, Kit said, "I don't think they'll bother us again, at least not among the settlements. But keep an eye out for a watcher at the ford of the Rio Grande by San Juan. Don Carlos may have set the watch for us."

Sure enough, they watched a rider gallop away as they crossed the ford at San Juan. Kit signaled that they should dismount.

"Here's our situation." Kit drew in the sand with a stick. "We're here at San Juan Pueblo."

Roque explained to Danny what was already obvious to the others. "To get back to Taos, there are three ways we could go. One road runs along the river north to Embudo, which is a very narrow place between river and mountain, a good spot for an ambush. Another you've been on. It leads southeast to *Santa Cruz de la Cañada* and the narrow Santa Cruz Valley. The last leads south to Santa Clara Pueblo on the west side of the river near the mouth of the Santa Cruz. A dozen miles south of there on the east bank is San Ildefanso, and a few miles east away from the river is Pojoaque Pueblo. There one road leads to Santa Fe and the other to Nambe Pueblo, across the hill, back to Chimayo. It would take most of two days to get to Chimayo that way.

"What will Don Carlos do?" finished Kit.

Roque ventured, "In the old days, he would have had us arrested and our goods confiscated. We'd have fought him in court where he had influence, and we'd have lost. He may try to have us arrested, but I think all it will cost us is time, and he might get away with our goods. But who would he find to back him, brave enough and official enough to try to arrest us?

"He might gather his men," Roque went on, "we being few, and confront us with arms, or he might try an ambush, but I think it is most likely he will try to halt us and negotiate making us pay him for the insult he has suffered. His people have few guns and are poorly trained with them. He will not want a fight."

Kit nodded. "Unless he has us in a tight corner." He didn't need to finish the thought. If Don Carlos had them in a box, he would try to kill Kit.

"He'll have people watchin' the roads," said Verde. "That English lord'll know which way we go as soon as we leave this spot."

The others looked askance at him and then realized that any bad man, especially a rich one, was English to Verde.

Roque thought for a moment. "Embudo would be dangerous for us. There are not many people near there and not much room for us to maneuver." Kit nodded. "He has strength at Santa Cruz and will feel confident there. Going to San Ildefanso and Nambe only delays things and gives him a day to lay a trap near Chimayo. The shortest route is to Santa Cruz. It gives him the least time to prepare."

"I think I'll go to Santa Cruz," said Kit, "while all of you go to Embudo."

"And miss the fight," protested Verde.

"We stand with you, Kit," Danny said, feeling bold after the terrors of the night. This at least was an enemy he'd be able to see.

Kit looked at them. "He wants me, not you."

"You did right at the *fandango*," said Roque. "We all stand with you against him."

Reluctantly, Kit nodded, unwilling that his friends should face danger for him. He said, "Then, I think Danny and I should go ahead with all the pack animals toward Santa Cruz and Chimayo. But first, Roque, you and Verde head up the River Road a ways while we wait here. Perhaps that will distract him. You can catch up to us later."

"He may think we've split up," said Roque. "That will make him more likely to attack."

"Oh good, a fight!" Verde grinned.

And so they parted company at the river. Roque and Verde went north along the River Road toward Taos until they were out of sight while Danny and Kit rode southeast toward Santa Cruz. If Don Carlos's men were watching, they'd see two dust trails going in opposite directions.

The high *sierras* were a shimmering blue backdrop before them, nearer rose a brown wasteland of dusty, barren hills. Between the hills and the river were grasslands irrigated in places close to the great river. Near Santa Cruz, the *acequia madre*, the mother ditch, fed water to the soil creating a verdant band of farms. *Santa Cruz del la Cañada* was located 200 yards north of the *Rio Santa Cruz* at the base of the barren hills where the river emerged from its canyon to the lowlands of the Rio Grande. Santa Cruz's little plaza and big church sat on a low hill that consisted of the washed-down walls of Santa Cruzes past reduced to dust and pot shards, probably an Indian town before the Spanish came. The mountain road passed under the walls of the town, near the river where plowed fields, orchards, pastures, and giant cottonwood trees crowded the valley floor.

Two years before during the Taos Uprising, 1,500 rebels had waited on the hill behind the town for the troops coming from Santa Fe to quell the rebellion. The reasons they chose this spot at the mouth of the canyon were obvious to any military observer. This place was where the Mountain Road joined the River Road from Santa Fe to Taos. It looked like a proper fortress on a hill, but the flanks weren't as secure as they first appeared. The Taos rebels of 1847 were routed and retreated to the north.

As Danny and Kit came even with the side road to the plaza, Carlos's men rose from the rooftops armed with bows and arrows. Danny saw that some were armed with crude crossbows. He'd thought those were only used in ancient tales of knights in armor. Unfortunately, they looked deadly. In the plaza, Don Carlos sat smiling astride his horse, another elegantly dressed mounted figure at his side. Behind him, six mounted lancers waited.

"Danny, I've seen these fellows with the pointy sticks before. They can be deadly. They killed a lot of good men at San Pasqual. Don't try to face them on horseback. Get to cover and keep something between you and them," instructed Kit in hushed tones.

"*Don Cristobal*, a pleasure to see you again. See who I have with me? I have brought the *alcalde* to see you," blustered Don Carlos.

"Danny, I'm gonna try to keep this peacock talking

awhile," Kit whispered. "I don't want to give the *alcalde* a chance to say anything. He might tell me he's impounding our goods or something." Then he turned to the rider. "Well, Carlos, this is an impressive looking group you have here."

Kit nodded and smiled at the *alcalde*, an administrative official who was justice of the peace, mayor, magistrate, customs collector, and captain of the militia, all in one under Spanish and Mexican governments. American rule was only a few years old, and many *alcaldes* acted as if the old powers were still in force.

"That's *Don* Carlos!" came the frosty reply.

"Sure, Don Carlos, no offense, I'm sure," smiled Kit.

Feeling cornered, Danny looked behind them for Roque and Verde, hoping they'd catch up soon. It all depended on how far up the River Road they had gone. He thought that it'd be good to have them there increasing firepower, but even so being under the wall of Santa Cruz with armed men on top, they'd still be outnumbered and in trouble.

"Insolent dog! Come up here to speak to us, immediately," barked the *don*. "*Chico*, you can stop looking for your friends. My scouts saw them leave on the River Road."

"Well, we have all these mules to tend. Take me a few minutes to find a place to picket them," said Kit still smiling, but glancing back over his shoulder toward San Juan and help.

"Do you know who you are speaking to, dog?" growled Carlos.

"Name's Christopher Carson, by the way. Not dog. My friends call me Kit. You can call me *Señor* Carson."

Kit wasn't usually this rude to anyone. Danny was

starting to worry. He knew Kit hated bullies and was afraid he'd provoke Carlos into doing something stupid, afraid that Kit's temper would run away from him and let him foolishly challenge overwhelming odds. The bowmen on the roof were barely twenty feet away and could hardly miss. Danny wasn't looking forward to being chased by a lancer with a pointy stick.

"*Señor* Carson, then, do you know to whom you are speaking?" The veins in the *don's* neck bulged, his face turned red as a *chili ristra,* and the muscles in his neck expanded like a frog getting ready to croak. He seemed to think he was the biggest bullfrog in the pond.

Danny was even more certain Carlos would do something rash or perhaps even explode. Unfortunately, he and Kit were entirely too close to where it would happen.

"Why sure. You're Don Carlos, and he's the *alcalde,*" said Kit, still not moving to tether their mules.

"Come up here at once," spat Carlos, his eyes protruding from his head. He'd forgotten the *alcalde*. In a moment, he'd grab a pointy stick and come after Kit himself.

"Well, as kindly meant as I'm sure that invitation was, I'm feared we have to decline. It's getting late, and we've a long way to go yet. So *hasta luego*, Don Carlos." Kit urged his mule forward.

"Halt!" At that imperious command, Don Carlos's bowmen rose and drew back their bows. His crossbowmen took aim; they couldn't miss at this range. His lancers brought their points level with the travelers hearts. Danny saw death mounted on a pale horse about to ride his way. *Here it comes,* he told himself and started to draw his pistols, but Kit stopped him with a glance.

"Now, *don*, this is getting real tiring," said Kit pulling up his mule.

From up on the bluff behind the plaza a bugle blew. All heads turned.

"Hey, Kit!" called Roque. "We ran into some old friends from Taos and a patrol of dragoons. They wanted to see you, so I brought them here."

Something out of sight behind the bluff was raising a lot of dust. Danny estimated ten or fifteen riders at least to raise so much dust.

"Don Carlos," said Kit, "I would find it real friendly if your men would put down their bows and climb down off those roofs. And those boys with the pointy sticks can just drop them where they stand."

Bows and lances clattered to rooftop and ground. Kit had spoken in Spanish. They all understood and didn't wait for Don Carlos's order. The threat of dragoons and mountain men with rifles on the hill above them was enough to cow them into submission. Mountain men had made these men of Santa Cruz and Chimayo pay a fearsome price for the murder of Governor Bent in the 1847 Uprising. They hadn't forgotten the lesson.

Kit touched spurs to his mule's flanks. "*Adios*, Don Carlos," he said doffing his hat.

Sometime later Roque and Verde emerged from a side canyon onto the trail.

"Where are the others?" Danny Trelawney asked.

"What others?" asked Roque.

Verde produced a bugle. "Right here," he grinned, his wrinkled old face looking particularly evil.

Kit grinned back.

"Why didn't you tell me, Kit?" Danny asked. "I thought you and I were here alone."

"You were supposed to. I needed Don Carlos to see that expression on your face to convince him we were alone," Kit replied. "When Verde blew that bugle, the surprise was complete. He went from being sure that he held the overwhelming top hand to being outmaneuvered and outflanked. If you hadn't looked worried, he'd have been on his guard against some ruse and been 'specting visitors on his flanks or rear."

"Well, you convinced me," Danny griped. Verde and Roque were too pleased with themselves to notice.

Verde beat dust out of his shirt. "A man could choke to death saving your life for all the thanks he gets." He had been the one responsible for the dust cloud dragging brush behind his mule. They rode laughing into the dusk toward Chimayo and camped near the *Plaza del Cerro*.

In the morning, Pedro and San Miguel came by their camp. San Miguel's face bore a fresh scar that ran from forehead to chin where Don Carlos had cut him to ruin his looks.

"Miguel," said Danny, "you are wounded."

Miguel smiled. "No matter, the ladies fawn on me anyway. They say the scar makes me look more manly."

Pedro hadn't been hurt. The sly-devil could take care of himself. He would be almost impossible to find if he didn't want to be seen.

Still, it troubled Kit who blamed himself for bringing misfortune on them. Danny tried to remind him that Miguel was already in dire trouble with Don Carlos before Kit intervened, but his words had little effect. Something in Kit's character made him feel responsible for things over which he had no control. Anytime he'd meet a bully in any form, he'd go into a rage. He also felt responsible for people he hardly knew, sometimes for people he didn't know. He had a powerful sense of his duty to others.

Danny traded Jicarilla baskets, jerked meat, and brain-tanned doe skins for fine Rio Grande blankets. He took in *ristras* of Chimayo *chilis* reputed to be the best and most flavorful anywhere. Both the blankets and *chilis* would do well in Taos. Verde did a brisk business selling silver and turquoise jewelry. Danny's mound of goods was growing in volume and value; he was doing well, but he was beginning to wonder when and where he could exchange it all for cold, hard cash. It was beginning to look like he might have to go on trading and wandering forever.

Danny reviewed lessons Kit and Roque had taught him. What would be more valuable in Taos and Rayado than it was here? What would travelers coming off the Santa Fe Trail in Rayado want to buy? It wouldn't be skins and blankets or *ristras* of *chilis* or jerked meat. They'd buy the former in Santa Fe to take back to Missouri, and they'd have had enough of jerked meat by the time they got to Rayado. They might even have some to sell. They'd want onions, tomatoes, squash, apples, and bread for their own consumption, all the things they would have run out of on the trail. These items were bulky and wouldn't travel well over the mountains, nor would they keep. Danny would have to buy them in Taos, closer to his destination, not here. He'd get coin from the Santa Fe traders. Captain Aubry was due in soon with what was sure to be one of the last caravans of the season. Danny might have to store some of his goods and trade for fruit and vegetables in the spring.

The people at Taos were cash poor. The merchants might take some wares off his hands for cash, but the longer they would have to hold them before trading locally or selling to traders bound for Missouri, the less the demand would be and the lower the price would be. In their present economy, the value of items traded would always be higher in goods than their value in cash.

For some time, the economics of New Mexico had puzzled Danny. If New Mexico was cash poor, where was the money coming from to fuel the Santa Fe trade? Some goods, such as hides and Rio Grande blankets, did return to Missouri, but there was gold and silver coming from somewhere. New Mexico was not rich in gold mines.

Captain Aubry and Kit explained it to Danny.

Kit said, "The *Rio Arriba* and the *Rio Abajo* are like two different countries. In the *Abajo,* south of Santa Fe on the Rio Grande, are big ranchos where poor *peons* work for wealthy and powerful *ricos* who style themselves *dons.* They send hides down to Chihuahua and Saltillo much further south and get money in return. In the *Rio Arriba*, upriver from Santa Fe, you could almost say there are only the poor."

Aubry continued the story. "The real secret is that the Santa Fe trade isn't really with Santa Fe; it's with Chihuahua and Saltillo deep in northern Mexico. In Chihuahua, the Mexicans mine silver and gold. They have wealthy people to buy fine goods. Their government keeps these out of the country with high tariffs at the port cities so we sneak goods in through the back door. The rulers in Santa Fe under the Mexican government were corrupt and would take a cut and let goods enter the country. Once in country, the goods didn't get taxed again. The officials in Santa Fe were so distant from

Mexico City that they could get away with it. The border at El Paso del Norte is still remote from the capital and goods still enter Mexico."

The Santa Fe trade was really trade with Old Mexico like the Taos trade was trade with mountain men and Indians.

After a noon meal with friends, the four travelers headed up the long mountain ridge that led to Truchas and the high country. They stopped this time at Cordova and trekked down the hillside to the plaza. The little church held a fantastic array of carved saints. Sadly, doors slammed at their approach, and they felt eyes watching them from hidden perches.

"Roque, don't you have any *primos* here?" Danny quipped.

"No *primos*, but I've got one friend, a *santero*, a maker of carved saints," he responded without smiling.

After a short search, they found his friend. The greeting while friendly was not warm. *Nando* was nervous and kept looking over his shoulder. Danny traded for some of Nando's *santos* and *bultos,* which would sell in Taos, for the *santeros* of Cordova were famous.

"Let's get out of here," said Roque. "Cordova gives me the creeps. It's not a good place."

"It's almost nightfall. Does anyone want to camp near here?" asked Kit. No one did. "Then we'll ride as far as we can in the dark."

It was a miserable evening with the nip of the cold, high country autumn in the air. They stumbled on an uphill trek, difficult in the dark with an uncertain ghost driving them away from Cordova. What was wrong with this town? Neither Roque nor Kit could say, but they all felt it, even Verde who for a change was silent and withdrawn.

They made a cold camp without a fire sometime after midnight. Arising well past sunup, they skirted Truchas and pushed on past Trampas, camping among the pines in the pass above the town. They were all tired after their ride the night before and the long trek that day. Nonetheless, Kit suggested that they discharge and reload their weapons. Black powder is very quick to absorb water, and when it's wet, it's useless. Caps have to be loose or the user had trouble getting them off to reload because moisture can get in around them. Sometimes they even fell off, so it was good to check frequently.

One at a time, they fired and reloaded their weapons, aiming at this and that and betting on their ability to hit the target. Danny wasn't sure what it was that made Kit nervous enough to insist on doing target practice despite their exhaustion.

"Kit, are the Jicarillas headed for the *llano* to hunt buffalo?" Danny asked.

"They are."

"How will they get there? Will they pass through the towns?"

"Likely no one will see them," he responded. "They have passes and trails only they know about."

Tired and alone in the high mountains and despite Kit being ill at ease, they didn't set a watch.

Danny awoke with a start in the false dawn, sensing rather than seeing something huge lurking over him. The dark form was searching, searching for Danny! He felt around for his pistols and rifle, but in the inky dark and in his fear, he couldn't locate them. Something large made a shuffling noise near him. Certain that it was a grizzly, he sprang to his feet, drawing his huge knife from its scabbard. Moving with all the speed and force he could muster, he swung the big blade across his body, bringing it to guard position. *Clang!* He nearly dropped the knife. The impact was so severe, it numbed his arm. Danny heard a muffled grunt and a sound like a knife had dropped on the ground. The flat of his fast moving, heavy blade had connected with something in the dark. The lurking shape sped away into the gloom.

Beside him, Kit grappled with a form much larger than he. Locked wrist to wrist, each with tomahawk and knife, they fought to overbalance each other. Indians attacked this way, not bears, Danny realized. Behind Dan, Verde and Roque were rising. In the dark, no opponent had found them as yet.

Danny dove for ground seeking his pistols. Pulling them from under the saddle that had been his pillow, he aimed at the dark. Sensing movement on his right, he raised one pistol and fired. There was a bang and a roar and more bangs. Flames enveloped his hand, which stung of fire and shock. His pistol had chain-fired. His night vision was gone. In its place was a rosy glow. His ears rang. He sensed things scuttling in the dark, but afraid to hit a friend in his blindness, he dared not fire with his second weapon.

Beside him, he heard the thump of a hatchet cleaving a skull, taking a man's life. It was an awful thing. Danny was repulsed. He'd as soon not be near that sound again. Glad he was for his temporary blindness.

Moments later, Verde blew "charge" on his bugle. Unseen creatures scattered in the dark forest. Then Verde was thumping Danny on the back. "Way to go, boyo. You convinced 'em we had a whole army here with artillery and everything. You got to teach me that trick," he cackled evilly.

Roque was bent over Danny rifle in hand, "You okay, Danito?" There hadn't been time for Danny to come full upright since reaching for his pistols.

"Stings a mite," he replied.

"Did you forget to grease your cylinder?" Roque asked.

Danny nodded sheepishly. His pistol had chain-fired; one chamber had set off the others because the front of the cylinder wasn't greased. Only one bullet went down the barrel; the rest went around it. Powder that would have burned in the barrel ignited in each chamber but burned off at the front of the cylinder close to his hand. A bright cloud of burning powder and wildly flying bullets had enveloped the pistol.

Kit was kicking the corpse of the man he'd killed. It was one of the raiders from Kit's rancho, one of Acha's friends. Kit kicked him again before yanking his tomahawk out of the man's head and wiping it on the grass.

"When I was young, like you, Danny, I killed a lot of Indians. There was a kind of justice in it. They hurt us, we hurt them. They learned not to bother us. Sometimes we had to repeat the lesson." Kit spoke in a low voice. "Nowadays, I hate to take from a man what I can't give back. I stepped away from my pistols to answer nature and bumped into him. He was a clumsy fighter. I meant to wound him, but he got in the way. He tried to deflect my blow with his head." Kit gave him another kick.

"When I fought Acha," Kit continued, "I told you more trouble would come of it. Here it is. This settles nothing. Acha has led an unsuccessful raid. He has lost a man and gained nothing. He has to find success in war soon or lose the respect of his peers. This is even bigger trouble, but maybe not for us. He may have learned not to attack Kit Carson, but it's trouble for somebody. Others will die. I hate to be the cause of it."

"I guess Rojo was right, Roque," Danny said. His companions looked at him. "He said Acha would get someone killed. Now he has."

Verde doubled up with silent laughter. There were times, Danny reflected, that man was unfit for the company of humans.

Their livestock were unmolested. Acha had come after the travelers, not plunder, and had made a hash of finding them in the dark. In the full light of dawn, Danny found Acha's knife beside his bedroll.

"You did just right, Danny," said Kit. "You made their best fighter drop his knife."

They concluded that Danny had probably smacked Acha in the knuckles with the flat of his great, heavy knife blade. The sheer force of the blow had numbed Danny's arm. It was like hitting a rock full force with an axe handle.

Roque quipped, "It's better to be lucky than good, Danito."

"With luck like that, you must be Irish, boyo," laughed Verde.

They'd had less luck than it might seem. They hadn't posted a guard, but Kit had chosen them excellent ground for their camp. It was almost a fortress hidden among the boulders where the light of their tiny fire wouldn't show. Acha must have guessed their route. Danny thought it seemed unlikely Acha and his friends would have followed the four travelers up the Santa Cruz canyon. Firing their weapons the night before might have given them away. Careless as they were, it wasn't luck that saved them; it was Kit's skill.

Taos was still two days away. They rode through the high country, absorbed in its beauty, each lost in his own thoughts about what had happened. Kit insisted that this trip was so short that Josepha probably hadn't noticed he was gone. He must have been in a hurry, for they didn't stop to hunt elk even though they heard the bulls bugling on more than one occasion. The next night they posted a guard. They weren't molested, so perhaps, Danny thought, Acha was through with Kit and was out looking for an easier target. Conversation around the campfire was muted, and they killed the fire early.

"Roque," Danny asked before they put the fire out, "I've been in four scrapes with Indians, with Acha each time now that I think about it. None of them were what I expected. Don't we have an advantage in firepower over them?"

"You think your rifle has more firepower than the Indian with his bow?" asked Roque. "No, sometimes you have an advantage in range with your first shots, but you soon lose it. A good warrior will put a dozen arrows in the air while you're reloading. You can lie down to reload and fire, but it's slow. The smoke from your barrel gives your position away. You'll never see where the arrows came from."

"Up close," Kit added, "that pistol gives you an advantage. You can fire faster than he can draw bow."

"The real reason the Indians usually let us pass unmolested," chimed in Verde, "is that we're all traders at heart, us 'n' them. We ain't an army fightin' a war. We're all just trying to make a living. As long as we pass by and don't disrupt the game too much, the Indian lets us go. He expects some livestock as a price for using his land and for his loss of game. Long as we all act reasonable, there's not much point in spending lives."

The last night before they reached Taos, Roque and Verde turned in early. After the fire had died to glowing embers, Danny had the opportunity to talk to Kit alone.

"Kit, in the stories I've read and heard about you, you don't seem to mind killing Indians very much," I said.

"Don't believe everything you've read or hear. Some of those stories are no more than lies," he replied.

"Captain Fremont was your friend…"

"He was, and he tells a story that's true enough. I've changed some," continued Kit. "I ran away from an apprenticeship when I was fourteen. I've always been small. Men bigger than me would try to pick on Ole Kit. I learned early that if I retaliated fast and hard, they'd leave me alone and look for others to bother.

"When I came west to the Shining Mountains, the Indians would attack small parties and rob them. They stole our horses. The Blackfoot would kill us for being in their range. Retaliating fast and hard seemed natural to me. I learned not to let injuries pass. When I was a child, bullies picked on me because I was small. I didn't like it. Outnumbered by Indians, I learned to think of them as bullies.

"I don't like to give offense to any man. When I was younger, I didn't see where I was giving any to the Indian. Now I understand a little better. I understand how we disrupt his game and take the furs he might have traded. I'm not so sure we haven't given offense, so I'm not so sure I've a right to retaliate. Nowadays I try to get along.

"That's more words than I've said all at once in a longtime. You need to turn in. You've got next watch."

The setting sun showed Taos to its best advantage. It sat like a golden castle on its hill above the four travelers, the sun highlighting the warm yellow of the adobe. *Vigas* looked like arrow slits in battlements and second-story rooms like towers.

As they approached Kit's house, Josepha ran out to greet them, followed closely by her niece and a toddler. In the waning light, she took on an ethereal beauty unmatched outside the world of fairies. Kit swung down from his mule and took her into his arms. He'd only been gone for ten days, but any observer would have thought him a sea captain returning from a long voyage. His three friends sat on their mounts embarrassed and excluded, waiting for Kit and Josepha to remember the rest of the world. They were jealous of such happiness.

Finally, Kit and his wife separated. "*Cristobal*, my husband, I have something for you," she said, picking up the baby and presenting it to her husband.

"*Es milagro, Cristobal*," laughed Roque, "It's a miracle; you've only been gone ten days and your wife has made you a baby."

"Big 'un, too, she must have been real busy," piped Verde.

"Humph!" stamped Josepha, "He is Navajo. The slavers killed his mama and were going to sell him as a slave. So I bought him for us so that he can be raised as a child should be."

The child was plump and naked and very brown with long black hair. Kit looked doubtful. Then the child smiled at him, and the matter was settled. Kit smiled back.

Verde reached into one of his packs. "It's time for me to go, boyo."

"Can't you stay to dinner, *Señor* Verde?" asked Josepha. "We made plenty."

"*Doña* Josepha, *no, gracias*, but I thank you kindly. I can hear sinners over yonder drinking that Taos Lightning and the spirit has come upon me to go and preach to them about the evils of demon rum." Verde handed Danny an item from his pack. It was a *concho* only slightly smaller than a dinner plate set with turquoise. "I want you to have this, lad," the man known as the Green Vagabond said.

Danny took it admiring the work. Four stones were set near the edge with a figure in the middle. It looked like a man with a hunchback lying on his back playing a flute.

"It's a belt buckle I made for you. The turquoise stones represent the four directions. You'll see that figure in the middle carved on rocks all over the desert and mountains. The Hopi call him *Kokopelli.* That's a trader's pack on his back. He travels and trades just like you and plays the flute for the ladies just like our Rojo. I expect you'll learn in time," he grinned slyly.

"Verde, it's wonderful, but I can't begin to pay you for a thing like this," Danny said.

"It's a gift, boyo. I ain't had this much fun in ages." He waved and rode off toward the sound of singing.

Taos was a wide-open town with plenty of gambling, Taos Lightning to quench a thirst, and loose women to keep a man company. Danny would like to have spent a night celebrating with Rodado Verde and tasting some vice he'd never known before. Danny would have liked it if Kit had thought that it was out of respect that the young man stayed home playing with Teresina and the baby. That he stayed out of respect for Kit would only be partly true, mostly not. It was the look in Josepha's eyes that bound Danny to hearth and family for the night.

Kit had advised him well. Danny was able to sell for cash Jicarilla baskets, skins, hides and furs. The Rio Grande blankets, the *santos*, and *bultos* did well, too, though Danny had to put the word around and scout the town for buyers.

Danny began to plan for caravans coming off the trail. Aubry would arrive with the last one in about six weeks. He found a *gavacho*, a German by birth, who had set himself up as a baker. The "Dutchman" showed Danny how to bake an acceptable loaf in a beehive *horno*. Travelers would pay dearly for fresh bread, Danny thought. It was something they missed more than anything else on the trail. Danny bought some laying hens, for eggs would do well too. Fresh vegetables would also do well, but there were only a few of them he could count on to keep for six weeks. Danny ended up buying winter squash, squash with heavy shells that don't spoil if kept cool, onions, and potatoes, along with supplies for making bread. And he laid in a supply of Taos Lightning.

In Taos, there were rumors about Utes raiding along the Santa Fe Trail.

Their trip back over the *Sangre de Cristo* to Rayado was uneventful. Once home Danny helped Kit and Roque prepare for winter. There was haying to be done, a shed to be built, stock to be moved, and crops to be brought in. Their lives were busy, but Roque and Danny did find time to make a supply run over the mountains to Taos. They swore a pact of total silence concerning that trip, lest Josepha ever learn of their doings.

Chapter 8

The Aubry Caravan

"It's too dangerous!" protested Captain Aubry. "You don't want to be alone with your wife and child on the Llano Estacado. Anything could happen and help would be days away."

"Listen to reason, Frank," replied James White, a tall man in his early thirties. He was well dressed even if his clothing was now trail-soiled by the long trip from St. Louis on the Santa Fe Trail. White had the air of the businessman that he was. "Your stock is worn-out, and it doesn't look like there will be any good grass between here and Las Vegas. You're going to have to move slow and graze the stock well away from the main trail. It's October 18. The snows will fly soon. I don't want my wife and daughter to have to bear that out here on the Llano Estacado, the Staked Plains, where the wind comes straight down from Canada and the frozen north."

"It's true the grass is as bad as I've ever seen it," answered Francis X. Aubry. "The rains were good, and the grass is good away from the trail. It's all these Forty-niners on the trail headed for California. They've used it up." His small size was what made people think of a bantam rooster, small but aggressive, the cock of the walk. His jocky-size was also what had made it possible for him to ride from Santa Fe to Independence in only five and a half days the year before. Small he might be, but he was the best wagon master on the trail. This was his third trip to Santa Fe in 1849. "The Cimarron Cutoff is always dry with bad grass. Always. The grass will get better once we get to Point of Rocks nearer the mountains. By the time we get to Rayado, we'll be in excellent grass. The few of you going ahead alone isn't worth the risk."

"We've been on the trail for over a month now," griped White. "This is the slowest trip you've made this year. Let me take my wife, daughter, and a few men ahead to Santa Fe. I'll purchase fresh stock and bring it back to you. You're killing the stock we've got."

"We'll manage. We're safer together," insisted the diminutive wagon master.

"You said yourself we're beyond the Comanche country," the businessman continued. "So the road should be safe."

"Comanches," replied Aubry, "raid all the way to the Rio Grande when they've a mind to. We're entering Utah and Jicarilla country. They're a danger, too. Any of them would be glad to take your wife and sell her down to Mexico."

"The Comanche are the worst, and they're behind us," said White. "You said yourself, the Jicarilla aren't so numerous. We probably won't see any. Once we reach Cimarron and Rayado Creek, we'll be safe. I'll take enough men to fend off small parties of Apaches. And there's the Army to consider. They send out patrols along this part of the trail."

"Bah! That's no help," chided Aubry. "The Army is mostly camped along the Rio Grande trying to defend settlements from Navajos. They have neither enough men nor enough horses to do anything effective to protect you. Half of their force is infantry and can't do more than garrison towns."

"There's an Army camp at Las Vegas," argued White. "That's not far from Cimarron. We can travel much faster than your mules and oxen if we hitch up horses to two carriages."

"If you break an axle or have any kind of problem, you'll be completely on your own," Aubry pointed out reasonably.

"Your livestock is already in terrible shape," continued White.

"All right, you have a point. I'll send Calloway ahead to arrange for fresh stock," replied the wagon master.

"And we'll go with him," pronounced the businessman.

"Lord knows, I can't stop you," Aubry insisted, "but you know I tried. It's a bad idea."

"I'll take Juan and Carlos with me," concluded White, "and that German, Lawberger, wants to come. Bushman, my servant, will be with us. That gives us five rifles with two women to reload if needed. We'll take a few extra trade rifles and two Remington revolvers for each of the men."

On 18 October 1849, the little party led by White pulled ahead of Aubry's large caravan. In the first carriage were

James White, his wife Ann, their baby daughter Virginia, Ann's female slave, and a mulatto employee named Ben Bushman. The second carried William Calloway, an experienced wagon master, and Lawberger, a German thought to be stubborn and disagreeable by his traveling companions. All the men were armed. White's two Mexican employees, Juan and Carlos, followed driving the remounts and spare livestock.

"Keep a sharp eye, Bill. James, don't do anything stupid. Listen to Bill," called Aubry as they pulled away.

On the 20[th,] they passed a small party of forty-niners. One asked if he could join them, his mule being in better condition than the horses of his companions and able to move faster. They added him for the safety of one more rifle. They called the forty-niner "California" because he hadn't offered his name.

The night came cold bringing frost. They huddled near the fire after supper.

Ann White brought out a book while her servant cared for baby Virginia. "Mr. California, this should interest you. It's called *Kit Carson: Prince of the Gold Hunters* by Charles Averill. It's all about his exciting adventures going to California and how he discovered gold there."

The servant set Virginia in her little rocking chair where she rocked happily back and forth. The White family huddled about the fire entertaining their companions. Mrs. White, a cultured Victorian lady, thought it only right that she should do so. It was her obligation to set an example for the lower classes even though she was repulsed by some of the men who "still had the bark on" as her husband put it. They might have left civilization far behind, but she would bring it with her rather than succumb to brutality.

Her husband had told her, "I'm sure that there have been one or two white women in Santa Fe before you, but I don't know of any there now. Susan Magoffin went out three years ago but continued on south to Mexico. I think you'll be the first lady to set up housekeeping there. It'll be a challenge."

Ann White knew she had the fortitude to manage any challenge.

"Mr. Aubry said Carson's ranching over at Rayado now," interjected Calloway. "Saw him there in July. We'll pass right by there. Maybe you'll see him."

"Would you like me to read from the book?" asked Ann White.

By campfire light, she read to them from the dime novel she'd picked up in Independence. Dime novels weren't real literature, but these rough men seemed to enjoy them. In this stirring account, Kit Carson chased and slaughtered Indians, discovered huge amounts of gold, and rescued fainting maidens from merciless savages and Mexican *banditos*. All were impressed with Kit's exploits, except for Calloway who had met Kit. He thought the adventures overblown, but said nothing. He respected Kit.

Ann sighed, "Oh to be rescued by such a hero." James White looked jealous.

"Lawberger," said Calloway, "you help clean up the pots from dinner."

"Let the slaves do it or the Mex's," grumped Lawberger.

Calloway jumped to his feet ready to use his fists to enforce his authority.

James White intervened, "It's all right. Ben doesn't mind."

Calloway's eyes flashed, but he did nothing further.

Instead, he said, "Here are the watches for tonight. California," he said to the forty-niner, "You're first. I want you out among the stock always looking away from the fire. Lie down or sit still with something behind your back. Don't make yourself a target and keep your night vision. It will be cold, but you'll stay alive. Wake the next man and make sure he's up before you bed down."

"I heard Indians are afraid of ghosts and don't attack at night," objected California.

"*Ja*, that's right, I heard that, too," chimed Lawberger.

"They sure steal stock at night," growled wagon master Calloway. "I'll take the last shift before dawn. Wake me."

A coyote howled near camp, then another and another. Juan and Carlos looked terrified. "*Brujos*," they told James White, "witches." The Mexicans believed witches could turn themselves into coyotes with glowing red eyes and also into owls.

Toward midnight, Calloway awakened and found California slumped, rifle across his knees, asleep by the fire. No one was on watch. He kicked the forty-niner.

"I was cold," the would-be prospector whimpered.

Calloway woke White. "Your shift. Then see if you can get that German to cooperate."

In the morning, Calloway took White aside. "This is not going well. We have two idiots who don't want to listen to orders and two Mexicans scared of their own shadows at night. That leaves you, me, and Ben to carry the load."

"Juan and Carlos have stood beside me before," replied White. "They're brave enough."

"I'm sure standing beside you, they are brave enough. They use your backbone to stand. It's alone and at night, I worry about. They're right notional, taking strange ideas and fears from the dark. Or if they're startled. I'm not confident they'll react appropriately."

They made good time across the Llano Estacado covering twenty to twenty-five miles each day. Aubry's caravan lagged somewhere behind covering twelve to fifteen miles per day making camp early to let the stock graze longer. On previous trips, Aubry had averaged eighteen to twenty miles per day, but this trip was unusually slow. Used up grass was killing the stock. White's light carriages pulled by horses could go much faster than the plodding oxen or the mules pulling heavy wagons. Teamsters didn't like to use horses pulling heavy wagons because horses were delicate and easily injured, and they did not fare well on the native grasses. They would be the first animal to break down. White brought with him two complete teams for each carriage and alternated them, letting a team rest a day before it worked again. In the big caravan, there were smiths and wheelwrights. If anything broke for White's little party, there was very little they could do to fix it.

On October 21st, during his watch at around two a.m., Carlos discharged his rifle waking the entire party. White's baby daughter, Virginia cried, and Ann sobbed frightened for the safety of her child. Carlos was so traumatized, White and Calloway could make no sense of the boy's account of what had happened. Suspecting Indians raiding the stock, everyone stayed up until dawn armed and ready. In the morning, a search found only coyote tracks.

A cold wind started blowing down the plains from the north that day and stayed with them through the following days.

They got a late start on the 23rd because the watch did not wake them at the usual hour. Arising at sunup, Calloway found Lawberger who had gone on watch at 1 a.m. curled up sleeping by the fire. When he had finished his watch, he hadn't awakened anyone else. Calloway drew his revolver and would have shot Lawberger had White not intervened.

"Shoot him, exile him, or let me beat some sense into him," Calloway protested to White. "I don't care which. Without discipline, his like will get us all killed."

"Just a few more days," reasoned White.

"You, me, and Ben will pull the watches. We'll let the others drive while we try to get some sleep in the carriages and pray they don't do anything stupid in the daylight while our eyes are closed," concluded the wagon master.

October 24th dawned clear and cold with a brisk wind blowing down the plains from the north. They made good time all morning and crossed Palo Blanco Creek before noon. The forty-niner was driving the lead carriage and Lawberger the second, while the Mexicans herded the spare stock. Calloway and White were asleep. Looking up on the bank, California saw five mounted Indians, all smiling. One, a small, misshapen, dirty man, dismounted and approached. He handed a paper to California who had pulled out his rifle and had it across his lap. Lawberger jumped down from his carriage and came forward, his rifle raised.

The forty-niner opened the paper. "Hey, listen to this," he said and read the following:

Certificate of Good Conduct
Hail, know all ye by these presents that
the subject Pinacate, meaning Stink Bug, a

> *Jicarilla, is a good Indian. He will not steal more than he can carry nor will he take anything that is securely fastened down or attached to anything heavier than he can lift. He is known to be lazy and indolent. A fair day's labor might be gotten out of him in a month provided one supervises him intently to the exclusion of all other tasks. Avoid him and all his clan, sort and tribe at all costs.*

"How about the cheek of this Pinacate?" finished the forty-niner.

Pinacate rubbed his stomach and then pointed to his mouth indicating he would like something to eat.

"*Ja*, in my country we know how to fix beggars like this," replied Lawberger. He started toward Pinacate.

Awakened, Calloway saw what was happening and jumped from the carriage hastening toward the German. He was too late. Lawberger connected a boot to Pinacate's buttocks sending him stumbling as Calloway grabbed the German's collar and jerked him back off his feet. The forty-niner fired his rifle over the heads of the other Indians. Pinacate and the others departed in haste.

"See, this is how to get rid of beggars!" sputtered Lawberger.

"They're not so much beggars as asking for a toll to pass through their country unmolested," said Calloway. "Pull into one of those side canyons on the north to get us out of this wind. We'll make a fire to cook for our nooning."

"Ha," said the German as they ate their lunch. "All they had was bows and arrows. We could have killed them all easy."

"Yeah, we could have taken them easy if you hadn't interfered, Calloway," carped the forty-niner.

"Two things. One, this is their country, and they have friends all around," said William Calloway.

"Bill, we're only a day and a half from Cimarron. We'll be there tomorrow night," argued White. His daughter sat beside him rocking in her little chair.

"Two," continued Bill, "you ever seen an arrow kill? It ain't like a bullet. There's not so much shock. It kind of cuts its way into you. I've seen men who didn't even know they were hit. Unless you get hit in the heart or neck, you don't die right away. You bleed. Slowly. Usually, the arrow will incapacitate an arm or leg and sometimes your whole body and leave you a spectator. The Indians will put more arrows into you until you look like a porcupine. And you're still alive. Then they cut off your eyelids so you can watch and scalp you while you're still alive. Unless they're Apaches or Navajos. Then they just bash in your head with a big rock. Don't dismiss arrows. It's a bad way to go."

Lawberger and the forty-niner had gone pale while he spoke.

"That sounds awful, Mr. Calloway," protested stricken Mrs. White.

"Sorry, Mrs. White, I didn't mean for you to hear."

"Now that's the biggest Indian I've ever seen," gulped Ann White pointing over her husband's shoulder.

Walking toward them was a very large Indian accompanied by the small, misshapen man Lawberger had kicked. Ten more warriors sat their horses close behind. The big man was very upset and telling them something in broken Spanish.

"Acha," breathed Carlos.

"I've heard of Acha," said Calloway. "The name means "hatchet" and implies he acts without thinking. He's an up-and-coming Jicarilla war leader, and the stories say he isn't a deep thinker, but he's tough."

"I gather," guessed James White, "he's demanding reparations as well as a toll."

More Jicarillas—twenty or so—appeared above them on the lip of the small canyon. Lawberger and California, sweating and ashen, had their weapons raised. The two Mexicans stepped nearer to the fire to retrieve their rifles. Ann White held daughter Virginia tightly to protect her. Her servant huddled with them while Ben, the mulatto, stood in front with his rifle ready to protect the women.

"What should we give them?" asked James White, stepping closer to the carriage looking for something to offer.

"We usually give them food or livestock or trade goods—usually livestock," said Bill Calloway. "Group this big would need a couple of cows. Since we haven't got cows, we could offer them a team of horses. They aren't real particular eaters."

"Have my prime carriage horses eaten?" sputtered White.

"Jicarillas don't have any carriages, and these aren't riding stock," said the wagon master.

Acha became more animated, threatening with his tomahawk. Behind him, a horse reared. A grinning Jicarilla caught Lawberger's eye and eyes locked.

Startled, Lawberger thought he was being mocked.

"They are attacking," he screamed, raising his rifle and firing. The shot knocked the smiling Sonrisado from his horse.

California fired as well, his shot passing by the ear of a Jicarilla wearing black moccasins.

Like a flash of lightning, a Jicarilla charged, knocking Lawberger down, his lance pinning the German to the ground like a squirming bug. He would live long enough to regret his shot.

Acha split California's head with his tomahawk, the blade sinking far enough to cleave his nose.

An arrow took Juan through the neck severing the arteries. He was dead before he landed in the fire.

The women and baby screamed and cried.

Carlos bent to help his friend and arrows appeared in his arms, legs and back. He gasped and fell, alive but with no more fight.

Calloway turned to grasp his weapon as Pinacate grabbed his legs knocking him to the ground. With his knife, he neatly slashed Calloway's Achilles tendons. Stink Bug released the *Mangani,* white man, and watched him squirm toward his rifle. As Calloway crawled, arrows pierced one wrist, then the other.

"No, no," screamed James White. "Take anything you want, but leave us in peace. Spare the women and child." He gestured open-armed to show that it was all theirs for the taking. "Here take it. Take whatever you want."

Like the martyr Saint Sebastian, White sprouted more arrows than a porcupine has quills and yet still lived, calling piteously to his wife.

All of the men were down except Ben who stood rifle at the ready protecting the women. He had but one shot. Whoever approached the women would die. The mulatto stood as their bastion.

Acha now smiled and walked toward Ben. He held his tomahawk out to his side and then dropped it to show his peaceful intent. Ben raised the rifle. Acha shook his head, smiling. Ben could live. The women would go unmolested he seemed to be saying. Ben was uncertain.

"Stop right there!" Ben lunged toward Acha.

Still Acha came. The hand behind his back grasped a knife. With his other hand, nodding and smiling he grasped the barrel of Ben's rifle slowly pushing it out of line with his body. Ben never saw the knife that took him in the throat and ended his life.

Calloway, White, Carlos, and Lawberger still clung to life, but were rapidly dispatched, their heads battered in with merciful killing blows. Four Jicarilla grasped Lawberger's arms and legs, raising him from the ground—the lance still protruding from his belly—and tied him to the side of a carriage. Lawberger screamed. So did the women.

Lawberger had started the whole deadly affair by shooting the smiling Sonrisado. It was all so unnecessary. They had come to take only what was theirs by right. They meant no harm. Now the Smiler's cousins and tribesmen intended to exact a reckoning. Some might think the Apache cruel by nature. Any human might be equally as cruel in similar circumstances, given the same power over another being with no philosophy demanding restraint. They lived demanding lives surrounded by enemies, and life on the *llano* required strength. The best way to intimidate others was by demonstrating that strength. It is not surprising that the Jicarilla feared the night and the spirits of the dead.

Acha, the leader of this tiny band, knew neither wisdom nor restraint. He knew only power. Always one to push an advantage as far as he could, and much farther than was wise, called a new game. By turns, the Jicarilla shot arrows at Lawberger trying for non-killing shots, enjoying his fear and pain. Pinacate stepped to the side and planted one in the German's buttocks. This brought a cheer from the Jicarilla and a scream from Lawberger. They would see how close they could come to a vital spot without ending the German's life. A miss would be a kill. They were shooting at his ears when a miss through the left eye ended the game.

They did not touch the bodies. Apaches do not willingly touch the dead. Instead, they looted the camp, taking whatever they thought they could use and destroying the rest. They took rifles, pistols, knives, pots, and pans. Virginia's little rocking chair amused them, and they played with it for a while. They took the livestock, of course, but also the coins that White brought to make purchases in Santa Fe and the food and cooking equipment. They broke and ruined the rest, including the clothing from Ann White's trunks, which they cut apart and threw about the camp.

Lobo Blanco, the Llanero chief, rode up and surveyed the scene. He was upset, but he would not show it. They had come to hunt buffalo, not rob *Mangani*. He would not criticize Acha. Jicarilla did not directly criticize each other. They were even circumspect in how they disciplined children. Blanco's authority as chief did not come from election. It was a matter of who chose to follow him at any given time. If his gambles prospered, his authority could be very great, but it could disappear in a moment. It was based on what others perceived as his Power. Power was a mix of luck and magic. If he were successful, he had Power. If he were not successful, he was thought to have lost it or, more correctly, offended it. Power was drawn from the natural world from rocks, animals, mountains, and the air and would attach itself to a man. If he used it as Power thought proper, it grew in him. If he offended it, by doing other than what was proper, it departed.

Unlike the *Mangani*, Lobo Blanco would not shout and berate. He would accept the situation. As far as he could, he would draw from it the best outcome possible.

"Good. Take the women and child back to camp. Perhaps we can trade them. Take the one who has died" (he referred to Sonrisado) "far up this arroyo and collapse a bank over him to hide the body. With luck, the *Mangani* will think the Comanche have done this."

The Jicarilla do not like having a dead body around and disposed of it without ceremony. The evil spirit left behind might attack them. Neither would they say the name of the departed for fear of attracting the spirit. Had women been present, they might have washed the dead man's hair with yucca suds before the crude burial, but no more. All his worldly possessions might well join him in the grave, so there would be nothing to call his spirit back. As they carried Sonrisado's body up the arroyo, Acha slipped off his follower's fine, new moccasins.

Around him, warriors were recovering their arrows. Points made of sharpened bits of barrel-hoop did not break the way stone points did. They might be pushed through a body. The point was attached to a fore-shaft, which allowed the shaft and fletching to come loose and be recovered even when the point couldn't be saved. Soon they would ride out and continue their journey. Lobo Blanco would choose a new direction away from the buffalo plains and into hiding for a while. Later, he would lead then out onto *llano* far to the south of this debacle.

Ann White huddled near her Dearborn wagon, holding her sobbing child and mulatto servant, now nearly as white as Ann with fear. She closed her eyes so she didn't have to watch as the Indians stripped her deceased husband and companions of their worldy goods.

"At least they're not mutilating the bodies," she thought. Small consolation. Ann felt it the obligation of her class and position to set an example. Her husband was gone. She must lead and be strong for Virginia and the quivering maid.

Using the wagon for cover, she started edging her group away from the Apaches. Perhaps they could hide in an arroyo. They might go unnoticed. There were other travelers on the trail. If the three of them could hide, they might yet be rescued. She had purchased a dime novel about Kit Carson. He lived at Rayado, somewhere nearby. Her husband, she sobbed, had promised to introduce her.

If they could just hide for a little while, Ann thought, Mr. Carson himself might rescue them. She tried again to slip away with Virginia and her servant. Again she was intercepted.

She whispered to her maid, "We'll get away. Rescue isn't far off." The child was too young to understand.

The servant stopped her sobbing briefly and nodded. "They kilt Mr. Ben," she whispered through her tears.

The big, cruel young brave strode up to the women. He was their leader, Ann sensed. He barked an order and horses were brought. By signs the Indian indicated they should mount. Ann obliged mounting astraddle with her skirts hiked up to her waist exposing her limbs.

"Who cares if it's unladylike," she said aloud. These are only savages and wouldn't understand or care. Virginia was thrust roughly into her arms insurance against Ann trying to run her horse.

The maid had never ridden and ended up tied like a sack of grain, facedown, across a horse's back.

A few miles south and west, the entire Jicarilla tribe was on the move, headed toward the fall buffalo hunt. So many Jicarilla together would discourage the Comanche enemies from interfering. They were spread out over several miles with boys leading small herds of ponies and women mounted, dragging travois behind their horses. Their tepees and other worldly possessions were bound up with the tepee poles that formed the travois. Toddlers rode on top of the bundle while nursing children were bound in cradleboards on their mother's backs. Moving slowly, raising dust, they headed east from watering point to watering point, often near the Santa Fe Trail.

Now they would have to backtrack a little, Lobo Blanco thought, toward the Brakes of the Canadian River not very far distant to the west. The Brakes were a complex of deep canyons stretching for almost two hundred miles. The canyon of the Canadian was often over nine hundred feet deep. Numerous side canyons and dense vegetation made it a place where many could hide. They would be able to break up in small groups and come back together in the evening, concealing and dividing their trail and making it hard to follow. They could regain the buffalo plains further south.

Lobo Blanco had to get back to the tribe to tell what had happened. He needed to confer with Saco Colorado and José Largo and with the leaders of the Olleros, Vicenti, Chacon, and Huero Mundo. He had argued to come out to the plains. The responsibility for this disaster was his. Maybe there was another way, a way that wouldn't cost him influence.

"Acha, come speak with me," Lobo Blanco called. Acha came. "Acha, after I have ridden off, I want you to ride to the top of a hill to scout the plains alone. Ride back swiftly and tell the others that you have seen a large party of Comanche and that you must hurry and warn the tribe. Can you do this?"

"Yes, but why?" Acha asked.

"We need a reason for the tribe to turn back and go south," replied Lobo Blanco. "You have not killed *Nakaiyeh,* Mexicans. These are *Mangani.* I think their soldiers will pursue us for a while. We must take precautions, but there is no need for the Olleros to know you may have started a war. Keep the women and baby concealed for now. Even the Ollero should not know we have them."

Lobo Blanco and most of the warriors rode back toward the place where the women and children of the tribe were on the move driving the pony herd and dragging tepees. Risking Lobo's displeasure, Acha and his closest friends—Zapato Negro, Acentellado, Pinacate, and a few others—returned to where the bodies of the White party lay. . Pinacate was posted as lookout. Acha thrust his lance into the ground, hanging on it the moccasins he had taken from Sonrisado's body. This was Jicarilla custom. It said, "Jicarilla have done this; fear us." Acha was proud of being Jicarilla and wanted the world to know they were powerful warriors and this was their land.

Pinacate signaled and the group scattered to hiding places.

Approaching from the west were six eccentrically clad

and equipped individuals wearing broad, straw hats with low crowns turned up at the brim. The hats had seen better days in their grandfather's time. They wore jackets made of barely cured leather with the fur still on and turned inward for warmth, stitched together with large leather thongs. Their britches were of similar make open from thigh to ankle in the manner of chaps. Underneath the britches, they wore leggings of rawhide tied at the knee and sandals on their feet. To see them was to expect a bad smell of uncured hide and worse. The leather was stained with blood.

Equipped with knives, lance, and bow, they rode worn-out horses and led a string of burros. These poor New Mexico *ciboleros*, buffalo hunters, regarded as *cimarrones*, uncivilized wild men, by the *ricos* were brave enough in their fashion. They did what their neighbors dared not do and the neighbors despised them for it. Most were probably descended from Indians who at some point took Spanish names and started living in Spanish towns.

"*Madre de Dios!*" the eldest *cibolero* expostulated noticing the remains of the White camp. He searched the hills and canyon sides looking for the killers. Seeing nothing, he dismounted. "The killers have gone, I think."

"Papa, let us get away from here," said the youngest boy.

"No, my son, look at this clothing. It is valuable. Do you want to leave it here for the coyotes to eat? They have jewelry and coins in their pockets. Surely, the Virgin has shown mercy on her children this day to leave them such treasure. Help me, *chico*." The elder stripped off James White's shoes and pants. The others dismounted and began looking for anything valuable, though value for this group was a relative term. Everything that could be sold or used had value.

They stacked the shoes and clothing and made a small pile of coins and Ann White's jewelry. When they finished, the White party lay naked.

The boy was disgusted.

"We didn't kill them, *chico*; we just got lucky," intoned the father. "I will cut off their scalps so people know it was *Indios* who killed them and so they do not suspect us."

As the *cibolero* finished this gruesome task, Acha screamed his war cry from the hillside, instantly followed by the cries of his friends. Arrows flew and father and son went down. The other four *ciboleros*, seeing their companions so swiftly killed, mounted and rode for their lives back toward the settlements of New Mexico.

Pinacate, detailed to lead the horses of the women, now led them back to the noon camp where naked bodies lay scattered and bloody. Ann White glanced about in horror while the child in her arms cried. Tied across a horse's back Ann's maid did her best to scream but soon found her position made it difficult to breathe and fell silent.

"Thieving *Nakaiyeh*," spat Acha. "They are like coyotes stealing a mountain lion's kill." Scooping up the pile of coins and jewelry, he mounted.

"Wait here a little. I will look around," said Acha to his friends. He rode to the top of the hill, returning moments later at a gallop. "My friends, there are Comanche coming. It is a very large party. We must warn the others."

They rode out at a fast trot toward the southwest, leading the burros and horses of the Mexicans and the horses that carried women and child.

After while the young *cibolero* stirred. He held his ear to the ground but could no longer hear the beat of horse's hooves. Four arrows protruded from his body, but he was alive. He checked his father and wept. He then rose to his feet and stumbled west along the trail toward Point of Rocks some ten miles distant hoping to encounter other travelers. If not, he too would die.

The *cibolero* boy stumbled for a mile, then fell to his knees, and crawled for hours before collapsing in exhaustion. He passed out, awoke, got to his feet again, and continued. A little after dark he saw a campfire ahead. It gave him hope and he stumbled on.

A few miles away, Acha and his friends rode up to the Jicarilla migration and found Lobo Blanco sitting on his horse talking to Saco Colorado. Acha reported that a Comanche war party was headed west near Palo Blanco Creek.

"We must warn the others," announced Lobo Blanco.

"We should turn away from them back to where we can go unseen where the River Flows Below the Plain," said Saco Colorado, referring to the Canadian River.

"That would be well," said Lobo Blanco. "We can council tonight on what best to do, but for now we must turn away from them. Perhaps we can ambush the Comanche."

"We came to hunt, not to make war," replied Saco Colorado. With that, they directed Acha and his friends to find the other leaders and move toward their accustomed camping place at Piñons Grow in a Large Ring. The Jicarilla habitually divide up into small groups only to join together again at the appointed camping place. Scattering like quail made them difficult to follow.

In the late evening of October 24, the wounded *cibolero*

boy staggered into the camp of Hugh Smith, newly appointed Territorial Delegate to Congress. Smith was headed east with his escort to take his place among the legislators. The boy blurted out his story, and Smith's party patched him as best they could.

"In the morning we're headed back to Las Vegas with this boy to alert the troops," Smith informed his escort. "There's a white lady captive out there and the troops will have to respond."

Chapter 9

Responding to Outrage

On the night of October 24, 1849, council was held in the Jicarilla camp at Piñons Grow in a Large Ring. Vicenti, Saco Colorado, Lobo Blanco, Chacon, José Largo, and Huero Mundo sat inside a tepee around the fire discussing what they must do next. Women served them food as they talked.

"Acha has seen a large war party of Comanche headed in this direction. They occupy the part of the *llano* where we planned to hunt," reported muscular Lobo Blanco. A shrewd politician, Lobo had made his report and would now sit back and let the others decide.

The old man in the red jacket, Saco Colorado, spoke up. "I talked to Acha. He said there were as many as one hundred, but they are a large tribe. There are probably more of them nearby." They sat and thought for a while in silence. The

Apache was not troubled by silence as the *Mangani* were; they understood that one needed time to let his thoughts mature.

Athletic Vicenti, whose hair was still black, would like to have said, "This seems strange. Was Acha so close that he could both see they were Comanche and that they were a war party? It is strange they were so close, and no one else saw them. Acha also seems to have come into some new wealth, and he is concealing something." Instead, he said nothing. However, he thought Acha was acting much like Coyote. Something was not right. He would watch and listen. To make an accusation would have been very rude and dangerous, too.

This council was a true democracy. It operated by consensus. The members would confer until all agreed or there would be no decision. They would all agree, or the dissenting chiefs would take their people and go their own way. If the Comanche were close, and they would always be close to buffalo on the *llano*, it would be very dangerous to face them without the full strength of the tribe. The Jicarilla amounted to about eight hundred men, women and children, but only one hundred and fifty or so were warriors.

"We should ambush these Comanche and make them fear the Jicarilla," suggested Huero Mundo, stretching his arms that were stiff and scarred from battle with a bear. His nose was as sharp as a tomahawk, his eyes deep and hooded. It was difficult to know what went on in those depths, but none could doubt his courage.

Lobo Blanco nodded at the presumed wisdom of Huero Mundo's proposal. He would need Huero Mundo's support another time. It would be good to side with him now on a measure no one else would agree to.

The chiefs would not argue with Huero Mundo directly. They would let his proposal fall in silence. If time passed, and no one spoke in favor of the motion, one of the others would propose something else. Time passed. They lighted a pipe and passed it around, each blowing smoke to the four sacred directions. There would be no attack on the Comanche.

Powerful and large Chacon, respected for his intelligence and wisdom, spoke up. "The buffalo will pass by White Rock that Juts High from the Plain, that the Mexicans call Tucumcari Butte. We can go there to hunt."

The assembled chiefs murmured their assent. Heads nodded. There was consensus. They would go south and hunt the buffalo.

Wiry Huero Mundo spoke again. "If there is a chance the Comanche will pursue us, we should conceal our sign and act as if this were a war party. We should travel by separate trails tomorrow."

Again, the assembly murmured and nodded their assent.

Chacon suggested, "Let us meet again at Water Flows Inward under a Cottonwood Tree."

Again, they agreed, and the assembly broke up.

Vicenti found his son, Peregrino Rojo. "Son, go and watch Acha. Something is not right. He is up to something."

At the other side of the camp, Ann White lay bound next to her servant inside a tepee as they had been most of the night. There had been a few horrible hours, at least she thought it was hours, when men had come, untied her and done things she did not like to remember. When they were done, she was bound again while beside her the maid sobbed. A woman came before first light and untying her indicated she should step out of the lodge. Ann saw that the maid was taken by another woman. The Apache woman, using a length of firewood, beat Ann to indicate what she wanted done.

As soon as they were hidden from camp by terrain, the woman indicated Ann should do her business.

"Oh," said Ann, "you want me to make my toilet."

She did and found she'd been bleeding. Ann White tore a bit of material from her skirt. Pushed back toward camp, she dropped the bit of material over a branch. "Perhaps," she tought, "someone will find it and know where I've gone. Perhaps even Kit Carson."

In camp, she was given a bit of food. It was awful but she forced herself to eat. She must be strong for her child. "My child," she thought, "Where is Virginia?" Her eyes searched the camp and came to rest on the child held in the arms of a Jicarilla woman. Her daughter seemed safe for now. Ann would watch this woman and her child so she knew where they were when it came time to escape.

A grinning brave forced her to mount a pony. Her injuries hurt as she sat astraddle the horse and her limbs were exposed. She'd faced worse humiliation the night before and, not wishing to spend the day facedown across a horse's back, endured all.

The big brave, Acha, came running up. He seemed upset and concerned, constantly looking back over his shoulder. He snatched her suddenly from the pony and dragged her out of sight in the brush. Ann feared he had a sudden urge, but no. Something was up and when the danger passed, he let her go and indicated she would walk.

As camp broke up on the morning of October 25, Rojo rode to his father's side. "Father," Rojo said, "Acha is hiding a *Mangani* woman and her baby in the camp. I have seen her. She is his prisoner and slave. Not only this, but I know she was seen by two Pueblo hunters from Picuris who came to trade."

"*Mangani*, a white woman from St. Louis?" queried the chief. "Are you sure she is not *Nakaiyeh*, Mexican? Some are very light-skinned, I am told. Where would he get a Mangani?"

"I do not know," said Rojo, "but I am certain she is Mangani. He hides her and treats her very badly."

Chief Vicenti nodded. "I knew something was not right. I think we are not pursued by Comanche. I think we are running from something Acha has done. I think, too, that these Mangani are not like *Nakaiyeh*. They are men and will pursue us for taking their woman. I will talk to the Ollero leaders."

Miles away, west beyond the Canadian River near the Shining Mountains, Congressional Delegate Hugh Smith was angry. He had arrived at Barclay's Fort, New Mexico Territory, the day before, October 26, 1849, with a badly injured Mexican boy, a *cibolero*, buffalo hunter. The boy had been attacked by Jicarillas near Palo Blanco Creek on the 24th and had walked the ten miles to Point of Rocks where he found Smith. Arriving at Barclay's Fort, Smith had summoned Captain Henry Judd from Las Vegas twenty miles away. Judd had arrived at the *cantina* in the fort moments before.

Judd was of average height and build, saber and Colt on his hips, the latter covered by a flapped holster. He wore black boots now dusty, tan duck trousers with orange piping, and a shell coat of blue with more orange piping that identified him as an elite soldier, a dragoon, trained to fight as cavalry or foot soldier. A dragoon cap was tucked under his left arm. He was sometimes accused of lacking energy in pursuing Indian raiders. The dragoons were chronically short of men and horses, and the horses they had did not subsist well on western grasses. With saddle, weapons, equipment, and soldier, the dragoon horse had to carry nearly 300 pounds. They soon wore out. It was 1849. Men were deserting to the gold fields of California. In any event, Congress had not allocated enough men and horses to New Mexico to be effective against highly mobile Indians who held large herds of ponies bred to thrive on prairie grass.

Delegate Smith was an old Santa Fe trader used to dealing with obstinate and corrupt Mexican officials. With them, Smith had learned that bribed nonfeasance was the best one could hope for, given that the option was gross malfeasance with malice and greed. He was well dressed with top hat and black suit, both looking clean and pressed despite having been on the trail. Smith had learned to expect better from American officers when he went south to Chihuahua City with Colonel Doniphan in 1847. Doniphan had marched thousands of miles. His unit had no lines of supply or communication. In defense or attack, the colonel always faced forces much greater than his own, but he had never lost a battle. Delegate Smith expected action from the military, and he expected it now.

"You need to send a rescue party out after Mrs. White immediately," said Smith.

"I need orders from Santa Fe, from Colonel Munroe. I can't just abandon my post. I've sent a messenger. Besides we don't even know if she's still alive," replied Captain Judd calmly.

"That poor woman is suffering. God only knows what they're doing to her. I'll authorize the mission," argued Smith. Santa Fe traders were a close-knit group. Hugh Smith knew James White and had real concern for his wife. "Do you realize what the young bucks of that tribe are doing to her? Would a gentleman leave her out there?"

"Calm down, sir. I'm doing all that I can, and, I repeat, we don't know if she is still alive," spat Judd, who was an officer and a gentleman and didn't like the implication that he was anything less. Only Delegate Smith's rank restrained the officer from challenging him.

The door flew open. A tall man neatly dressed in knee-high boots and a tweed jacket strode in. Blessed with a long, jowly face like a hound dog, he looked perpetually sad.

"She's alive all right." The tall man spoke with an English accent. "Her body wasn't with the others."

"Barclay, it's good to see you," Hugh Smith greeted him. Judd nodded and bowed slightly. Alexander Barclay was an Englishman who had long been a *factor*, agent, for the Bent Brothers and St. Vrain at Fort William so recently destroyed. Years working as an Indian trader for William Bent had worn away fine English manners leaving a man almost as bark rough as a mountain man when the need arose. He started his own business and built a similar trading fort at Mora north of Las Vegas about 60 miles from Santa Fe. The Mexicans called the place, *La Junta*, the junction, though no one was certain if this name referred to the rejoining of the two branches of the Santa Fe Trail or to the union of Sapello and Mora Creeks.

"I passed by Palo Blanco Creek," Barclay told them. "The bodies are unburied. Wolves have worked on them. It's hideous. The lower half of James White's body was gone, eaten. Ann White's body wasn't there among the dead. This morning, I talked to Pueblo Indian hunters. They said she's alive. Just yesterday, they saw her in a Jicarilla camp. The Apaches plan to sell her."

"There, you see? Alive!" Smith looked at Captain Judd.

"How many Jicarilla in that camp?" asked the professional soldier.

"Hundreds," said Barclay. "The Pueblos thought the whole tribe was out there to hunt buffalo. To finish James off like that, with no casualties themselves, they must have had him desperately outnumbered. There must have been fifty or a hundred warriors. White's people were well armed and experienced. Captain Calloway was with him. "

The soldier considered. "I haven't enough men or horses to pursue them effectively. Lieutenant Burnside is injured and can't go out. He took a Jicarilla arrow through the throat. Most I can muster is twenty men. How can I pursue a hundred with that?"

"Indians have never stood and fought against soldiers," replied Barclay. "Jicarilla will sell Ann White to Mexican slavers. Delay much longer, and we'll have to look for her in a Monterrey bordello."

"I think there may be another problem," snarled Delegate Smith.

"There is," said Judd, circumventing the insult. "Lack of horses. I've only enough horses to mount the twenty. I don't have any remounts or pack animals. How can they pursue without remounts? The horses will be worn-out in two days."

Smith was beyond speech.

"There must be something," murmured Barclay. "Mrs. White is a lady. A bordello is no place for her. That life will kill her."

"I'm ordered to provide escort for the mail wagon in three days' time. I'll send out as heavy an escort as I can scrape together. Lieutenant Burnside captured Abuja, Lobo Blanco's daughter. We have her held hostage. I'll send her along. Maybe they can trade her for Mrs. White," suggested Judd.

"Perhaps that will work. May God have mercy on the poor woman in the meantime," replied Barclay. "I think the Jicarillas have headed south toward the Brakes of the Canadian River. They'll be difficult to find in the canyon country."

Hugh Smith stormed out.

"Let's hope Abuja wants to return to her people. She'll know how to find them," said Judd.

"It seems likely," Barclay agreed quietly.

"Delegate Smith can't really expect me to pursue them without orders and with just a handful of men," protested Judd. "We have no advantage in firepower. Each of them can put ten arrows in the air while my men reload. They have a pony herd and can mount a new horse each day. All we have are worn-out nags."

"You're lacking in everything a soldier needs," commented Barclay dryly. "Of course, Jicarillas are slowed by having their families along, and there's just a chance they'd like to protect their women and children from any kind of fight. It's not a group of raiders you'd be chasing."

"I'd better get back to Las Vegas and get the campaign started," said Judd.

Alexander Barclay said nothing. He ordered a drink, haunted by what he'd seen and what he suspected.

On October 29, Barclay's fort already behind him, Francis Xavier Aubry passed through Las Vegas riding hard. His caravan had reached Palo Blanco Creek and he had seen the carnage. Eastbound travelers had also told the tale. In the telling, a war party of Utes, the Jicarillas' constant ally, had joined the Apaches. Aubry's people had buried what was left of the bodies while Captain Aubry mounted a fast horse and headed for Santa Fe. He stopped at Las Vegas for a fresh mount.

Captain Judd found him resting while others moved his saddle to a new horse. "I take it you've heard?" he asked Aubry.

"Heard and seen," replied the wagon master known as Skimmer of the Plains. "We buried what was left." Aubry shuddered. "Is there any word on Ann White and her baby?"

"She was seen two days ago," reported the soldier. "Barclay told us Pueblo hunters had seen her alive in a Jicarilla camp near the Canadian River."

Aubry, mounted. "Then I'm off to Santa Fe to put up a thousand dollars reward. We'll buy her back if we have to. I think a company of mountain men will take the offer and find the Jicarillas for us," Aubry spurred his horse to a gallop. He'd kill horses getting to Santa Fe if he needed to.

On October 29, 1849, five days after the calamity at Palo Blanco Creek, Santa Fe began to respond to the news of Ann White's capture and the death of her husband. Messengers and partial information had begun to arrive two days prior. *La Villa Real de la Santa Fe de San Francisco de Asis*, the Royal City of the Holy Faith of Saint Francis of Assisi, Santa

Fe, was built at the foot of the western face of the *Sangre de Cristo* Mountains. Elevation was high, about 7,000 feet, but the sides of the canyon north and south rose higher still. The City of Holy Faith was built along both sides of the Santa Fe River. The Santa Fe Trail wound down into the canyon from the southeast. Taos Road went out on the north. Southwest of town, Cerrillos Road linked Santa Fe to the *Rio Abajo*, downriver.

The city was an aggregate of tiny fortresses built around a central plaza. On the east end by the mountains was an *adobe* church of little beauty. One elderly priest was all Santa Fe, for all her Holy Faith, could boast for the present. The religious establishment of New Mexico had long been under the control of Franciscan monks and not regular priests. They expected a monastic, almost military, obedience and discipline from their parishioners, especially government officials. Many governor's had been excommunicated. Ordinary priests would not have expected such unquestioning obedience. The discipline did not seem to extend as far as gambling, drinking, and other vices, which ran rampant in the town, and in which, it was rumored, the monks participated. After all, confession was held on Fridays. What else was forgiveness for? In 1849, the Spanish Franciscan monks had been gone for many years distrusted by newly independent Mexico, which drove them out. Secular priests were slow to replace them. No one wanted the poor, isolated parishes of New Mexico.

Around the plaza, were one and two story *adobe* buildings, each built around and facing its own inner plaza, an inward looking fortress. These structures were the homes and stores of merchants, the Santa Fe traders. A *zaguan*, a gate large enough to admit carriages and wagons, gave access to the street. Behind these bastions was another street of similar *casas* whose front rooms served as stores while lesser merchants dwelt beyond the inner courtyard. A few balconies and only occasionally a *portal*, a covered porch, or *zaguan* broke the blank *adobe* walls that faced the plaza. Away from the plaza, *casas* were more spread out. Farmed fields and scattered one-room homes appeared between little fortresses. On the south side, next to the Trail, one such bastion was called *La Fonda*, the inn. Across from the inn at the northern side of the plaza stood the Palace of the Governors with a long *portal* across its front. It was a large single-story building lacking in beauty and windows, a mud palace in a city of mud. Around the plaza, Mexicans and Indians squatted on blankets in front of the walls and in the *portales* displaying what they had brought to trade.

Above Santa Fe on the canyon rim north of town was Fort Marcy. Its guns kept Santa Fe covered, able to smash its buildings in the event of an uprising.

A haze of *piñon* smoke, mixing with the smells of onions and roasting *chilis*, privies, and the droppings of animals covered the town.

Two men, sharing drinks and cigars, sat in the *sala*, common room, of La Fonda. A few tables and chairs littered a room of low ceiling supported by heavy *vigas*. The floor was packed earth. Smoke hung heavy in the room, ascending from pipes, *cigarrillos* of tobacco and from the *piñon* fire in the corner lit against the late October chill. One man wore the long blue coat of a senior Army officer decorated with brass buttons and gold piping. The other was dressed in the black coat of a businessman. The former had a craggy face, scarred by smallpox, with a prominent Adam's apple and a bulbous, whiskey veined nose. His mustache drooped sickly. His forehead was high, his hair thin, long and greasy. His ears protruded like handles on an *olla*. His men said he was the ugliest man in the Army. No one had ever disputed the point. He was Colonel John Munroe, commander of all Army forces in New Mexico.

"We should take this heathen land," said the commander, "and give it back to Mexico. The weather's only got two seasons, bad and worse. The plants are full of stickers and thorns. There isn't a decent building in this whole country. It's all mud houses. The food will burn your mouth even when it's cold. What's more, there are Navajos, Apaches, Utahs, and more always running off with the livestock and the women. Heck, give it back to the Navajo." The colonel, having made his pronouncement, settled back in his chair and puffed his cigar.

Across from him, James S. Calhoun, the Indian agent for the area, grunted, puffed on his cigar, and ignored Munroe's diatribe.

"The Indians are your responsibility, Mr. Calhoun. You are the Indian agent. Can't you keep them under control?" Munroe asked.

"Washington doesn't give me much to work with, Colonel," Calhoun responded. The colonel's dislike for the territory of which he was military governor was an old tune, and he didn't take it personally. He knew about Munroe's dissatisfactions and knew they weren't aimed at him. The colonel's point was that no one could control the Indians with the resources available. He wished there were more he could do. "I've asked Garcia to come by."

"What can the Indian trader do?" queried the soldier.

"I've got a thousand dollars for him to use to buy Ann White back from the Jicarillas. That's more than they'll get anywhere else."

"They may not want to admit they took her in the first place," countered Munroe quietly.

"Best chance we've got," Calhoun insisted.

A man in Mexican garb entered and took off his broad brimmed straw hat. He searched the room, his eyes adjusting to the dim light. Spotting the Indian agent, he walked straight to Calhoun.

"You wished to see me, *Señor* Calhoun?" said the stranger.

"Colonel, I'd like you to meet Encarnación Garcia." Calhoun rose to shake Garcia's hand. "He trades with the Jicarilla."

"We've met," said Munroe, nodding to Garcia without rising.

"*Señor* Garcia, I have one thousand dollars from the government with which to buy Mrs. White and her daughter back from the Jicarillas. Can you find them?"

Garcia nodded.

"Do you think you can get them back?" queried the agent.

"Maybe." Garcia said and left.

"So what have you done to help the situation, Munroe?" asked Calhoun.

"I sent riders to Taos two days ago," replied the Colonel. "Major William Grier is authorized to take out his entire force of dragoons and to raise a company of fifty volunteers in Taos. That should net him a force of fighting mountain men and give him one hundred riders. In addition, there are four light artillery pieces he can take with him. Should make him a formidable force. I've told Judd to send out as many men as he can muster with the mail wagon. He's to take Lobo Blanco's daughter, Abuja, along and see if he can exchange her for Mrs. White and her daughter."

"Finding the Jicarilla will be the most difficult thing," Calhoun said.

In Las Vegas, on the evening of October 29, Captain Judd and Sergeant Phillip Swartout made final preparations for Swartout's escort of the mail wagon.

"You'll take two wagons, one for the mail and one for supplies," Judd instructed. "Put Abuja in with the supplies. Bind her when and if you feel necessary. I've given you all the remounts I can spare and all the men I can muster. It won't leave any but the sick and lame here. You've got twenty." Then he added, "Don't take any unnecessary chances."

"It's all chances, sir; we live with that." said Swartout.

The next day, in Taos, Brevet Major William Grier of the 1st Dragoons with the help of Captain José M. Valdez of the militia spent the day raising a company of volunteers. They were looking for former mountain men and Mexican *ciboleros*. These were men with skills at tracking and fighting. They recruited Dick Wooten, Jesus Silva, Robert Fisher, Tom Tobin, and Antoine Leroux. Leroux was to be chief scout. The *ciboleros*, buffalo hunters, knew the country they were going to be operating in.

Major Grier was a professional soldier of long standing. A good deal older than most captains, he was still waiting to be promoted formally to major, his brevet rank. Brevetted for bravery, he was paid as a captain but regarded as a major, the next higher rank. Tall and of medium build with gray mustache and hair, he was thought of as fatherly by his men. He was one of the most energetic officers in New Mexico, actively pursuing Indian raiders whenever occasion afforded. Dressed in a blue shell coat and black riding boots to his knees and wearing his dragoon cap with its mushroom shaped crown, saber and revolver at his side, he was making a speech to the men of Taos about the outrage the Jicarilla had committed and the need to rescue poor Mrs. White. He offered to buy Taos Lightning for every man brave enough to enlist for the period of operations.

José Valdez, a small man of quick intelligence and uncommon courage, followed Grier, appealing to *ciboleros* and *vaqueros*, cowboys, to join him in getting back at the despised Jicarillas.

The recruiting effort took longer than expected, and then they had to organize and equip the force. They didn't leave Taos until November 5, 1849.

In the evening of the same day, October 30, in Santa Fe in the common room at La Fonda, Colonel Munroe and Agent Calhoun sat at their usual table smoking and drinking after dinner.

Calhoun was holding forth on the problems of an Indian agent. "Usually there's no trouble along the Trail. If our people act reasonably, the Indians are pretty reasonable too. Our people need to travel in big enough groups and well armed so as not to pose a temptation. The Indians ask for compensation for the disruption and thinning of their game herds. That's reasonable. The traders know they're not being robbed when the tribes ask for some livestock. It's to replace what they've lost. They are not beggars and thieves. They're proud people.

"The problem comes when you get inexperienced fools traveling in small groups. When Indians show up, instead of being polite, these fools try to run them off or insult them or worst of all kill one. The Indian doesn't usually risk his life to steal or kill anyone, except in revenge."

Munroe nodded and grunted.

Calhoun continued, "When the game herds get really thinned out, you have problems. When Texans moving onto land east of here push the Comanche further west, the Comanches push Jicarillas and Utes off their regular hunting grounds. Then you have another problem. You have people starving. They need to make up the deficit somewhere. The cause isn't here in New Mexico. It's over in Texas. So, we have no control. All we get is the problem.

"The simplest thing and the least expensive would be to give the Indian agent enough money to see them fed. Instead, Congress sends infantry. Infantry! What are they going to do? Run after mounted warriors? And do you know why they send infantry? Because dragoons are too expensive." Calhoun snorted and spat on the dirt floor.

"Yup," said Munroe, "not near enough dragoons nor horses. And Congress still complains of the expense and wonders why we aren't doing our jobs. Give the whole place back to the Indians, I say."

"You send the dragoons out after raiders," Calhoun added, "but you're already days behind them. You kill horseflesh trying to catch up. The Indians don't mind. They'll ride their horses to death, eat them, and steal more. They outrun you and sit on a big old hill looking down at the dragoons, laughing up their beaded buckskin sleeves at you soldier boys."

"Yup," replied the colonel, "the dirty Indian bums. We ought to give the land back to the Mexicans instead."

Like the hard slap of the desert sun when you step out of the deep shade, a jockey-sized man entered La Fonda. Feeling his presence, the room hushed. He glanced about once and then strode to Colonel Munroe's table, a dust devil beating into a narrow canyon.

"So what's being done about it?" Francis X. Aubry demanded.

"Hello, Frank," said Calhoun rising.

Colonel Munroe rose and towered over Aubry. He had to stoop to meet Aubry's eyes. "Everything that can be done," he replied. Once they were all seated, Calhoun and the colonel explained the actions they had taken. "I've sent a man out," said Calhoun, "with one thousand government dollars to ransom her back."

"It's not enough," said the wagon master coolly. "What if he doesn't find them? I want Ann White and the baby back...unharmed." He looked into their eyes and knew they were telling the truth. They were doing all that limitations allowed.

"It's not enough," Aubry said again. "I'll put up another thousand dollars reward of my own to anyone who brings the two of them in safe and unharmed. I don't care if they buy them back, steal them, or kill the whole Jicarilla tribe to get them. A thousand ought to get the attention of some of our blood thirstiest, piratical, former mountain men. They'll know how to get her back."

Calhoun looked at him. "Aubry, you don't really want to start a war, do you?"

"Don't care. Want her back. She was my responsibility.

I let that headstrong James White do something I knew was wrong. Got him killed. Least I can do is get her back."

"A toast, gentlemen," pronounced the colonel, rising and raising his glass. "To the congenial locals, the mountain men, Mexicans, and Indians. May they kill each other off and save us the trouble and," nodding to Calhoun, "expense."

In the Jicarilla camp, Ann White tore another piece off her dress and hung it from a bush. She was cold, bruised and footsore. She was hungry. It was no use begging. Although she got the worst bits of food, she'd learned her captors were nearly as hungry as she. Ann was glad they'd stolen her mirror. She knew how bad she must look. Her daughter seemed happy and this was a blessing. Virginia played with the Jicarilla children and was well cared for.

Chapter 10

Disaster at Point of Rocks

On the morning of October 30, Sergeant Phillip Swartout prepared to ride out with a patrol of nineteen men and two wagons. Most of the men were young, barely out of their teens. Many were recent immigrants fleeing famine, war, and revolution in Ireland and Germany. Many of the rest were middle class boys with poor prospects at home seeking a new life in the West and graciously accepting the Army's offer of free transportation; some were simply seeking adventure. They wore a mixed bag of uniform parts, clothing they'd made from cotton duck, rugged cotton, and wool garments common on the frontier. On some, a blue Army shell jacket reached to a man's waist. Others wore fringed buckskin or jackets made from felted wool. Except for the red facings, trim, and ribbons adorning their clothing, a sign that they were artillerymen, they might have been outlaws who specialized in robbing laundries. Some even wore *botas*, a poor man's chaps, and rawhide shin protectors tied at the knee. Their mounts were equally mismatched, mules and horses of various colors, that their unit had gathered wherever they could find them. Lieutenant Burnside's artillery company was serving as infantry and had been given the important task of patrolling the Santa Fe Trail and carrying the mail. These activities required that the men be mounted. Only their weapons and Army issue tack seemed uniform.

Sergeant Swartout was tall, over six feet, though slender, and in his late twenties. He was dressed for the field in duck trousers and a broad brimmed felt hat to which he had pinned military insignia. He wore his blue shell jacket trimmed in red with a sergeant's red chevron. A capote, a cape-like overcoat made from a Pendleton blanket, was strapped to the back of his saddle. He had invested in boots that came all the way to his knee and that had a flap that lay over his knees when he was riding protecting his legs. He carried a cap and ball rifle and a Colt revolver. His artillery sword had been packed away.

Assembled on the parade ground at Las Vegas, the patrol was making final preparations to escort the mail wagon to the Cimarron River on the plains south of the Arkansas. This stream was not the Cimarron that flowed from the *Sangre de Cristo* near Rayado Creek. The Spanish only had a handful of river names, and these were repeated frequently to the chagrin of travelers. Not satisfied with the confusion, they also gave rivers multiple names. The Rio Grande was also the del Norte and the Rio Bravo. There was a Rio Colorado that rose in the Great Basin, but the Canadian River also bore this name on the plains. New Mexico boasted three *Rio Puercos*, filthy rivers. At the Cimarron, Swartout's patrol would be met by a patrol from Ft. Leavenworth that would escort the mail as far as Council Grove in Kansas.

Lieutenant Burnside staggered out from the hospital to see them off. "Wish I could go with you," he croaked. Burnside was healing slowly from the Jicarilla arrow that went through his throat the night Abuja was taken hostage. Abuja meant the needle in the language of the *Rio Arriba*; she was vicious with a knife.

Swartout saluted, "I know you do, sir."

His throat too painful to say more, Burnside gestured to where the sword should have hung and looked quizzically at the sergeant.

"In the wagon, sir. Too noisy," Swartout explained. Burnside nodded. They would carry musket and pistol. Each man had two shots before he had to reload. Some, like Swartout, had acquired a revolver that could fire five more times without reloading. Skirmishes were being fought at greater distances, and there were fewer occasions for sword and bayonet, especially when fighting Indians. They were lucky to have muskets. Dragoons were stuck with musketoons, a shortened version of the musket with less range. The ball was so loose in the musketoon that during a jarring horseback ride, if the muzzle was tilted downward, the ball could roll out.

The musket had an advantage over the bow in range but not by much. The Indian had an advantage in rate of fire and, if he recovered his arrows, seldom ran out of ammunition. Not so the soldier. When the paper cartridges in his ammunition pouch were gone, resupply could be a long time coming. The soldier was fortunate that the Indians weren't fighting a war; instead, they were raiding to acquire the means to live and seldom wanted to risk lives against an organized force.

Accompanying Sergeant Swartout was another noncommissioned officer, Sergeant Fernando Martinez who had been recruited in New Mexico a few years earlier. Swartout wasn't sure what to make of him yet or of the three other Mexican soldiers attached to his patrol. He remembered the Taos Uprising. Nevertheless, Nando, as he was called, seemed to be a good noncommissioned officer and a good sergeant, and the others good soldiers as well.

They weren't as troubling as the three Irishmen. All were recent immigrants and spoke English with heavy accents. The Army was a haven for the Irish coming without a penny from the Old Country. It was especially attractive to those who considered themselves to be of the Galloglass warrior caste and too good for honest work. In 1849, distrust still stalked the Territory. They were Catholic. In 1847, during the Mexican-American War, a group of several hundred Irish, who came to be known as the *San Patricios*, Saint Patricks, had deserted in Mexico. More than that, they had gone over to the other side and joined fellow Catholics in the Mexican army. It was one thing to desert, quite another to join the enemy. Those who didn't die in battle were executed when captured. Members of Sergeant Swartout's Irish contingent tended to keep to themselves. They were partial to Taos Lightning, the more the better whenever they could get it.

Balancing them were a few solid soldiers, also recent immigrants: a German—Eric Messerschmit, a Scot—Rob Dunn, and a Cornishman—Jack Pengelly. They had seen service in their native countries and came from strong military traditions. Of medium height and narrow at the hip with powerful shoulders and arms, they were fighters who could whip any man in the unit. They drank heavily and boxed each other for fun. A number of adventurers had joined the Army for the excitement and romance. Two were left—Davis and Stuart—both in their teens. The others had found Army life boring and routine. They disliked having to build their own *adobe* shelters and having to farm on the side to supplement rations. In 1849, many had deserted to the gold fields. The two youngsters had too much respect for their oaths of enlistment to depart. They were good lads and dependable but untried in a serious fight.

There were four civilians. Alberto Trujillo was a Mexican interpreter Swartout had worked with before. He knew Spanish and some of the Indian dialects. The scout, Jed Southerland, was a former mountain man who knew the trails and the Indians. Swartout could depend on Jed Southerland. The teamsters who drove the two wagons were loud, crude, dirty, and undisciplined. Flint and Evans would be trouble.

The remaining troopers were a mixed bag of bummers who'd failed in civilian life and alcoholics who'd failed at life. Failure in civilian life could come from many causes beginning with a lack of resources to make a start, laziness, or a lack of ambition, but failure in civilian life was not failure in the military. Some of the best soldiers were no good at being civilians. Many an alcoholic fought better drunk than most did sober, and if they could be kept sober, fought better still.

Guards escorted the Jicarilla prisoner, Abuja, to the

waiting wagon. Lifting her on board, teamster Evans caressed her posterior in an obvious and lascivious manner. Abuja rewarded him with a backward kick in the face that broke his nose. Blood spurted.

"Why, you!" he roared and started to climb into the wagon after her.

A powerful hand on each arm cancelled his move and sent him backward to land on his butt in the dust.

"Well, done, Private Dunn," said Pengelly to the owner of the other powerful hand.

"To be sure, Corporal Pengelly," nodded Dunn, smiling and saluting. "That's no way to treat a lady," he scolded looking down.

"Ah, laddie, yer nose is bleedin'," said Pengelly to the teamster. "Let me have a look at that." He tweaked the nose. "Pressure is the thing. Apply pressure to staunch the flow."

Abuja's eyes shot fire at one and all. She remained tense, prepared to defend herself, much more like a mountain lion than a deer. Both are beautiful. One is delicate, the other deadly. Both are graceful, but the cat's grace is full of power and menace.

"We're off to a fine start," the sergeant mumbled to Lieutenant Burnside who frowned. Indiscipline, even by civilians, could make life difficult for the sergeant on the trail, and it could prove deadly.

"Sergeant Swartout, we should not take her. It is too dangerous," said Sergeant Martinez. "She is Apache. She could cut our throats in our sleep. Her people will come to take her back. We are too few. They will kill us all."

"She's coming with us. We're going to exchange her back to her people," said Swartout. "That should make them happy."

"You do not know the Apache. Two things make them happy, killing and stealing," said Martinez.

"She's going. That's our orders," said Swartout with finality.

"Go over it again," Burnside croaked.

The sergeant understood this terse request. "First wagon, mail, half our food, four weeks worth, and ammunition, grain for the stock, two barrels of water," said Swartout. "Second wagon, the rest of the food, grain, and ammunition, tools to repair wagons, tack and weapons, axes and shovels, water and Abuja. Two teams of two mules for the wagons. One teamster and two guards will ride on each wagon, the rest of us on horse and mule. Two men will ride alongside each wagon all the time. The rest of us ride in double file one hundred yards ahead of the wagons. When we stop for meals or repairs or to sleep, four men will be on watch at all times."

Pleased, Burnside nodded.

At a signal from Swartout, they mounted and rode away north from the *adobe* huts that made up their cantonment, a military dwelling place, but not a fortification. They rode hard throughout that morning.

At noon, they met Captain Aubry's caravan on the trail coming from Point of Rocks. Swartout called a halt so they could talk.

Aubry's lieutenant, acting as wagon master in Aubry's absence, said, "It's disgusting. We had to beat vultures away from the bodies of Mr. White and his companions. It was clear coyotes had been eating them as well. We buried what was left. It wasn't much, and it was ugly.

"Despite the condition they were in," he continued, "we could still tell those demon Apaches had tortured them before they died."

"You're sure it was Apaches?" asked Sergeant Swartout.

"Sure thing. The dead were scalped. They were tortured," said the wagon master. "Them's sure signs it was Apache. And they stuck a lance in the ground and hung a pair of moccasins from it."

"Mr. Southerland," Swartout directed his question to the scout, "what do you think?"

"The scalping and the torture don't sound like Apaches," replied the scout, "but the lance with the moccasins, that is an old Jicarilla trick. Tells everybody they done it."

"Any sign of Mrs. White?" Philip Swartout asked.

"None. She and her baby were taken by the Apache," replied the wagon master. "That's what I've heard. We didn't find their bodies amongst the others. Who's the woman in your wagon?"

"Lobo Blanco's daughter," Southerland said. "We're gonna swap her for Mrs. White."

Swartout scowled. Soldiers don't share details of their mission with civilians. "After my men have eaten," he said, "we'll move on."

After the noon stop, the sergeant led his patrol east toward the killing ground. Behind them, the great caravan continued its four-abreast march to the west. The "red legs" made close to thirty-five miles that day and stopped at Santa Clara Spring. Artillerymen, even those detailed to act as infantry, wore a red piping down the outer seams of their trowsers and were known to other soldiers as red legs. With luck, they would reach Point of Rocks the next day. Sergeant Swartout set up his guard rotation while the men made camp. No tents were pitched, for the weather was dry. The men gathered at fires in squads of five. One in each squad was designated cook for dinner each night. This rotation of mess duties was one reason Army chow, which provided more meat than most civilian tables saw, was rated poor. Most men were poor cooks. As they settled in for the evening, Sergeant Martinez approached Swartout.

"We should bind her at night," said Martinez looking at Abuja.

"What do you think, Mr. Southerland?" asked Swartout.

"I don't see the need," replied the scout.

"Her people are near. She might warn them. She might slit our throats. She might run away," said Martinez.

"We'll have her sleep between me and Southerland," said Swartout. "If she tries anything, we'll know."

"She'll cut your throat," said the Mexican sergeant.

"I don't plan to loan her a knife," replied Phillip Swartout.

"*Filipe*, please, listen to reason," continued Martinez.

Swartout shook his head. Martinez meant well, but he, like many of his people, had an unreasoned fear of Apaches.

Swartout glanced toward the girl still seated in the rear wagon. Abuja wore the buckskin clothing common to her people. A long dress stretching from ankle to just beneath her breasts was secured with a broad belt decorated with silver *conchos*. A sort of buckskin poncho or short shirt decorated with intricate beading and elks' teeth covered her shoulders coming down to conceal part of her belt.

"Sergeant Martinez," Swartout said, "I don't intend to bind her."

A stir at the other end of the camp near one of the wagons drew Sergeant Swartout's attention. As Abuja was getting down, the teamster, Evans, grabbed her from behind, pushed a hand up under her leather poncho, and fondled a firm breast. He was strong, and though she struggled, she couldn't break his grip. The second teamster, Flint, stood guard. Messerschmit stood nearby showing little interest.

"What's the matter with you, Messerschmit? Don't you Germans protect a lady?" exclaimed Corporal Pengelly. This drew Flint's interest away from Evans and the struggling Jicarilla girl.

"Spoils of war. So we send her back to her people a little bruised. It's to be expected, no?" replied Messerschmit. Flint smiled having seen Pengelly's interference foiled.

Unseen, Dunn approached Evans, busy fondling Abuja, from behind and slammed his fists against the teamster's ears. Evans howled and released the girl. One ear bled, the eardrum probably broken. As Flint began to turn, Messerschmit felled him with a punch like the blow of an axe.

"Ja, but they wasn't his spoils." Messerschmit smiled.

The rest of the evening was without incident. Noticing that Abuja had grown sullen, Alberto Trujillo, the interpreter, went to her.

"Why do they drag me along in a wagon with these men?" demanded the Apache girl.

"We will trade you to your people for a white woman who has been taken captive," said Trujillo.

"What happened? How was she taken?" asked Abuja.

"Your people murdered the woman's husband and his companions. Jicarilla took her and her baby captive."

"You know this? You know it was Jicarillas?" pressed Abuja.

"They were seen," replied the translator. "Wagons we met at noon stopped at that place and the people buried the bodies. The teamsters said the dead had been tortured before they died. They saw no sign of the woman and girl. Some say Acha was the war leader; others say your father, Lobo Blanco. Pueblo hunters saw the woman and baby a few days ago in a Jicarilla camp."

"You told me I was hostage. They will do with me like my people do with this woman. Will they kill me now because her husband is dead?" Abuja asked.

"No, they want to trade you," replied Trujillo.

She shook her head unconvinced. "They will do things to me they think my people have done to her. These *Mangani* will torture me as the *N'deh* did to her husband. We go to see what they did to him. They will abuse me, torture me, and kill me," the *N'deh*, Jicarilla, girl said.

"No, they want to trade you for her," objected Trujillo.

"And if she is already dead? And if they think the *N'deh* have done things to her? Don't say no. It has already started," spat Abuja, "as you told me before it would. They have touched me as no man should. I will be brave. They will not hear an *N'deh* cry out or beg for her life."

Trujillo did not calm her. He did not want to, taking secret pleasure in seeing an Apache so frightened.

She sobbed quietly not wanting the *Nakaiyeh*, the hated Mexican, to see. She was ashamed of her fear and weakness. She promised herself she would not show fear, no matter what these enemies did to her.

The second night, October 31, they made camp near Point of Rocks where they would wait in hopes of making contact with Lobo Blanco's band of Llano Jicarilla Apache. Point of Rocks was a landmark and watering place where travelers on the Santa Fe Trail gathered, making it a place to garner news of Jicarilla from passersby. It was too late when they arrived for Sergeant Swartout to do much more than his original arrangements for the night. In the morning, he would send out riders to look for Apache and to intercept travelers. He passed the word to the handful of travelers he found at Point of Rocks that he had Abuja and was willing to trade her for an undamaged Mrs. White and her daughter.

Having done all he could, he looked around and noticed that Abuja was missing. "Where's Abuja?"

"I saw her head into the bushes a few minutes ago," replied Southerland, "to pee, I think."

"Where are the teamsters?"

Dunn, Messerschmit, and Pengelly, hearing that the teamsters had vanished, dashed off in the direction the Apache girl had gone. They found her in the ungentle embrace of the two teamsters who were alternately kissing and licking opposite sides of her face. One had a hand under her poncho caressing a breast and the other had reached up under her dress for darker realms.

"Gentlemen, they are all yours," Pengelly told Dunn and Messerschmit. "I'm going to escort the lady back to camp."

The teamsters rose slowly, Flint with a blackened eye swollen shut, Evans with both eyes black, though not as swollen, and a nose red and crooked from previous encounters with Abuja and the two soldiers. Released, Abuja jumped on Flint's back and raked her nails over both sides of his face. The welts bled as he screamed.

Pengelly grabbed her arm firmly. "Now, now miss. Let us take care of this." He nodded to his friends and escorted her away. Dunn and Messerschmit returned a few minutes later looking pleased. The teamsters returned much later and didn't join in dinner. Faint groans were heard coming from their direction.

Once in camp, Abuja sought Trujillo. Moments later, the interpreter reported to Sergeant Swartout. "Sergeant, she wants to go up on the rock to pray and look for signs of her people."

"I'll escort her," volunteered Southerland.

Swartout nodded his agreement. After dinner in the waning light, the scout and Abuja climbed the hill.

Atop the hill, Abuja began to sing mournfully, a prayer to the gods for strength and bravery. It was a song about her life and impending death. The song would die away and then start anew.

Southerland, recognizing her death song, took it as a sign the girl was frightened. And why shouldn't she be? Her people had killed gringos and taken a woman away to do God knows what with her. What revenge would the whites take on her? She'd already been attacked twice. Southerland let her sing. It might calm her.

The singing awakened the camp. The Irish demanded to know how they were expected to sleep with that banshee howling on the hilltop. The banshee was sure to come and take their souls. More than that, it was All Hallows' Eve, the *Samhain* of the Irish, and the dead were allowed out to wander the earth. This dreadful noise from the hilltop had the Irish frightened to the core in fear for their lives and souls.

"'Tis the *piskies* you boys need to worry about, lads," laughed Pengelly, referring to the impish little people of Cornwall. "She might be *piskie*-sent to lead you astray in the wilderness, too. That's what they do, you know. They come in the form of a beautiful maiden to lure travelers to their doom. If she starts leading us, let me know so I can start to worry.

"But if you start to hear knocking, lads, then you should worry, and let me know right away. For that would be the Tommy Knockers come to warn us that we're in danger. Now do go back to your fire and try to get some sleep. There be no banshee here. This is America. They don't allow them at all."

The Irish were not happy at being mocked over their fears.

"Sergeant Martinez," called Swartout. "Look after things here. I'm going up the hill to see what can be done."

Southerland saw Swartout as he approached, "It's her death song, Phil. Leave her be. It will probably calm her."

"She's scaring the hell out of everyone else. They're not getting much sleep," replied the sergeant.

Back in camp, the teamsters, Evans and Flint, were passing around bottles of Taos Lightning. The Irish and the drunks took it greedily. The Irish passed around stories about the terrors of *Samhain* until the entire group was disturbed by the sounds coming from above.

The Mexicans, except Martinez, took their share of the whiskey and, with it, a share of fear. Mexicans lived in terror of the chaos beyond the circle of firelight and the plowed field. Out there in the dark were Apaches, coyotes, and wolves that might be *brujos*, witches, traveling in disguise. Abuja, being Apache, might even now be calling down her people on them or worse. The Apache were in league with *el Diablo*, the devil. Jicarillas killed priests and never took mass. Apache were powerful *brujos*, the Mexicans told the others.

Even the youngsters, Stuart and Davis, felt compelled to join the group in taking a drink and shivering about the terrors beyond the firelight. Above them, the wailing continued. Before long, the soldiers became very rowdy and quite drunk. When they started singing, Swartout headed down the hill to investigate the new commotion.

As he approached his fire, the others took sight of him, and a delegation composed of the Irish and the two teamsters walked toward him. They were accompanied by two Mexicans and some of the drunks and bummers.

"She is a *bruja* calling demons," cried a terrified Mexican. "She is making evil magic, asking *Diablo* to help her against us."

Emboldened by alcohol Evans demanded, "You've got to shut that witch up. She's trying to call her people down on us!"

Cocking their weapons, Pengelly, Dunn, and Messerschmit stood up with their sergeant.

"I think the boy's a slow learner," Pengelly whispered to Dunn and Messerschmit.

"Give me the alcohol now!" ordered Swartout.

"You can't order us. We're civilians. That's personal property," sneered Flint.

Stuart and Davis, looking older than their years, stood to Sergeant Swartout's side. Martinez joined them, bolstering Swartout. Swartout didn't know if Martinez was standing with the side he thought would win or standing up for what he thought was right. At that moment, he didn't care. He did wonder how the drinking had gotten this far out of hand with Martinez in camp and presumably watching. Perhaps Martinez hesitated to correct *gavachos*, Americans.

"Nonetheless," replied Swartout. "Perhaps Captain Judd will see fit to compensate you when we get back to Las Vegas."

"Bah!" scowled Flint and Evans together.

"Sergeant, you've got to do something about that banshee howling," said O'Grady as the other Irish nodded. "She's calling up all the devils in hell on us, and I expect the Apache won't be far behind."

"First, we get rid of the alcohol. I get it right now or every man who's had a taste will land in the guardhouse," replied Sergeant Swartout.

A voice in the crowd called, "Let's settle Swartout's hash and head for California. We're not expected back, so they won't look for us for a while. We'll make it look like Apaches done it."

The crowd surged forward. The soldiers standing with Swartout raised their weapons.

"They wouldn't dare shoot us," called Flint. "They'd stand trial for murder."

Wanting reassurance, Dunn, Messerschmit, and the two boys looked at Swartout. They were loathe to kill their comrades; Pengelly didn't show any sign of hesitation.

"Hold it right there," came Southerland's voice from the dark. "I can fire thirteen times before I reload, and I'll take one of you with each shot. You won't be able to accuse me of anything. The shots will come from the dark, and you can't say who fired them."

The crowd sobered fast. The logic may have been strange, but they knew Southerland would kill them, and that he was a dead shot.

In one move, Swartout drew his pistol, stepped forward,

and stuck the muzzle in Flint's nose. "Evans! Collect the booze now and bring it to me, or I'll make a place for the evening breeze to pass through Flint's head, so help me God, I will!"

Evans flew to comply. The mutiny was over. The others melted rapidly away to their own fires. They did not want to be recognized, hoping they had been invisible in the dark. Sergeant Swartout had implied that if the firewater was turned in, the incident would be forgotten. They were eager to accept his amnesty.

"Thanks, Jed," Swartout said to Southerland. He nodded his gratitude to the others standing with him.

"No worries, Phil, but what are you going to do with Flint and Evans?" Southerland asked.

"Hope they've had enough," replied the sergeant. "Not much else I can do."

"They're slow learners. I'm off to fetch Abuja," said Jed. "Don't wait up." Dawn was not far off.

With the dawn on November 1, Swartout rose and saw to the needs of the camp. Stock needed to be watered and set to graze. Riders needed to be sent out in search of the Jicarilla. The men needed to be kept busy.

He called together his key men. "Sergeant Martinez, you're in charge of the camp. We're here for two days. Gather wood. Improve the site for comfort and defense."

"Yes, Sergeant," said Martinez pleased that he had the important task of making the camp defensible.

"Jed," Swartout continued looking at the scout, "take anyone you want and head out a day's ride and see if you can find sign of the Jicarilla. You're my best hope."

"I'll go alone. I can move faster," replied Jed. He got the nod.

"Corporal," the sergeant said to Pengelly, "send Dunn and Messerschmit. Have each take one of the Mexicans and one of the Irish. Have them ride out southeast and southwest off the trail and see if they can locate the Jicarilla, any sign of them or anyone who can take them word we want a trade. Send the kids, Davis and Stuart, along the Trail in opposite directions. Have them talk to everyone they see. That will leave you and me to look after the Indian princess. I think we can manage."

Abuja joined the others quietly at the breakfast fire. She ate with gusto, the terrors of the night seeming long gone. No longer a banshee, she was back to being the prettiest girl in the Jicarilla tribe. Calm, collected, and lovely she was again the Princess of the Llanero.

Soon breakfast was over, horses were saddled, and riders sent out. Sergeant Martinez oversaw the men working on the camp. From across the camp, Corporal Pengelly saw Abuja heading out to where the teamsters were moving their horses to grazing.

"That looks like trouble," he said to Swartout and headed toward her at a fast walk. Swartout followed. Noticing them, Martinez headed that way, too. From a distance, they could see her rubbing up against Evans and smiling at him.

Evans readily returned her attention. "Now you want it, squaw," he said with a grin as she drew close smiling. He pulled her in and started to reach up under her leather poncho.

She pulled his knife from its sheath and in a flash had cut his face to the bone. He pushed her away with a scream but not before she slashed his arm. The two sergeants and Pengelly ran toward the action. Abuja ran toward the other teamster and slashed his arm before he realized she had a knife.

She extended the knife in front of her challenging anyone to approach as she twisted from side to side. Few dared, none tried. Soon the whole camp had gathered.

"Put the knife down, Miss," Sergeant Swartout commanded gently. "We don't want to hurt you. Tell her, Trujillo."

Trujuillo tried without success.

"Liar!" beautiful Abuja screamed. "You told me what they would really do. Now they'll see what a Jicarilla can do."

She lunged toward a soldier who jumped away. The Apache girl menaced a second artilleryman, then whirled and jumped in amongst the stock, slashing the throat of a mule. Blood spurted, drenching her. The mule fell dead. She cut a deep groove in the back of a horse. It would be unable to take a saddle for weeks. She slashed the flank of another.

Sergeant Martinez raised his rifle.

"No! Be careful, Martinez, we want her alive," Swartout yelled. Martinez lowered his aim.

Abuja charged at a soldier, ripping a gash in the flank of a mule on the way. The man backed away. The men were circling again trying to get behind her. Flint and Evans backed away out of the fight. Abuja saw them and dashed in their direction, ripping a shallow gash across the abdomen of a soldier who tried to stop her. Flint and Evans stood transfixed, eyes wide in horror. The beautiful Apache girl was a Valkyrie come to waft them home. She was free of the ring of soldiers.

Martinez raised his weapon and fired. A pink cloud erupted where the Princess's head had been.

Pengelly looked down at her lovely, though headless, form. "Don't guess they'll give much in trade for her now."

Swartout bowed his head and said with feeling, "May heaven have mercy on Mrs. White and her child." And in a softer tone, he said, "The Jicarilla won't. Martinez, see she gets buried." Swartout didn't mention a burial detail. If Martinez understood, he was to dig the hole alone, that was okay with Swartout.

It was the first of November, 1849. Bitter cold, the day promised a long, hard winter. A light snow began to fall obscuring tracks and traces of what had occurred except where the fresh blood of man, beast, and maiden stained the snow crimson.

The riders returned at sundown the next day. They hadn't met with any success.

"Perhaps it's fortunate for Mrs. White. The Jicarilla don't know yet what has happened to Abuja," said Southerland.

"Yes, a real silver lining," replied Swartout glumly. "We move on with the mail in the morning. This place is cursed."

Chapter 11

Pursuit

On November 2, 1849, Encarnación Garcia arrived at Barclay's Fort. He had come over the mountain on the trail from Picuris. Before that, he had visited San Ildefanso and San Juan. The three Pueblos, he thought, were likely to have hunters returning from the plains. He hoped to find someone who could update him on the location of the Jicarilla, but he hadn't had much luck. Speaking to Alexander Barclay at Barclay's Fort on the banks of the Mora River where Indians went to trade, he learned that the Pueblo hunters Barclay had spoken to thought the Jicarilla were headed south along the Canadian. Garcia knew some of the places the Jicarilla camped along that river, so he headed east following Mora Creek which emptied into the larger stream. He'd need only a little luck to find them. Canada is *cañada* in Spanish and indicates a stream that makes its home in a canyon, in this case, one 900 feet deep with numerous tributary canyons. Garcia knew the entire population of New Mexico could disappear into its depths, and not be found all winter. If the Jicarilla did not want to be found, Garcia, though he was knowledgeable in Indian affairs, would not find them in the brakes of the Rio Cañada. Nonetheless, he was duty bound to try.

Still in Taos on November 4, it took Brevet Major William Grier longer than he had expected to raise a company of volunteers and equip them. Men they'd thought would volunteer disappeared out of Taos, headed to the plains on their own when word of Captain Aubry's offer of reward was heard; $1,000 was more than most earned in three years.

It also took longer than expected to get over the *Sangre de Cristo* from Taos to Cimarron. The Taos Volunteer's four-gun battery of six-pounder howitzers was not well suited to the mountain trail. On November 7, the major's little army finally approached Rayado where he hoped to enlist the aid of Kit Carson.

Major Grier had not been in New Mexico long, but already he had a reputation as an active and aggressive leader. He thought about his organization. Some of his volunteers had only sabers, no guns. That suited him fine. He was sure the affair would climax with a quick saber charge through an unsuspecting Indian village where he would swoop down and snatch up the maiden in distress and her child. Dragoons, like the major, thought of themselves as an elite kind of soldier, bigger than most and heirs to knights and cavaliers of old. They were the only cavalry the United States had at the time. No need to reload a saber at the gallop, the major mused.

Many of the *ciboleros,* Mexican buffalo hunters, he had recruited were armed with lances or bows. That would be all right, too. Men could fight without rifles and pistols. The battery would give him a range advantage over the Jicarilla and unmatchable firepower. It could scattered the Indians' pony herd and lay down a wall of steel to block their retreat. The rest of the forty volunteers were mountain men equipped with weapons of their own—Hawkin rifles, Colt revolvers and tomahawks—making each a mobile arsenal. Among the volunteers, he thought of them as his Forty Thieves, was a contingent of scouts, the very best mountain men in the area: Dick Wooten, Tom Tobin, Jesus Silva, and Robert Fisher. These were tough men of great experience. Their leader was Antoine Leroux who had gone west with Major William Henry Ashley in 1822. "Gone to the mountains with Ashley in '22," described the eldest and toughest mountain men. "Gone with Ashley" meant a mountain man was senior, experienced, respected and a survivor of incredible hardship. Leroux, who was reputed to be as good as Kit Carson, had guided Colonel Philip St. George Cooke to California during the late Mexican War. At the head of the volunteers was Captain José Valdez, who seemed to Major Grier cool and competent.

Major Grier had been able to come up with more than enough remounts for his entire party. He also brought a mule train for supplies, including grain to feed the horses. They would remain powerful and fast as long as the grain lasted.

Grier noted among the volunteers a strange little man in a green top hat, a pack peddler who made and sold silver and turquoise jewelry, *conchos,* and belt buckles. They called him Rodado Verde, the Green Vagabond, although he appeared to be Irish, not Mexican. He'd gotten a mixed group of Mexican *ciboleros* and mountain men drunk and convinced them all to volunteer. In an about face, he then got them all to take an oath never to drink again. Grier was amused and certainly couldn't complain too much about this volunteer.

Grier's troop of dragoons amounted to forty-two men, including, two competent leaders, lieutenants who had recently graduated from West Point like himself. His senior sergeant was a man named Cillian O'Malley, the only man in the unit who always had a uniform looking parade ground sharp. Grier didn't really trust such parade-ground button shining in an army where even the officers dressed like vagabonds in the field. Guidon and sabers were all that hinted this group of men was a military unit. Sergeant O'Malley claimed to be a crack shot with a musketoon. Grier had never seen anyone hit anything smaller than a barn with this bastard offspring of a musket. The weakness of the musketoon was why he relied heavily on the saber and on Samuel Colt's revolving wonder, the six-shooter. Training and discipline forged his men into dragoons. Every dragoon who ever forked a horse knew in his heart that he was the descendant of knights in armor. They rode for glory and to rescue maidens in distress. Grier sensed that O'Malley didn't respect the dragoons under him or trust them. He didn't like or trust O'Malley, and the men didn't seem to either.

Local New Mexican recruits accounted for a third Grier's troop of dragoons. They seemed steady enough, but Sergeant O'Malley appeared to have a prejudice against them. In fact, all the key positions in the unit seemed to be filled by Cillian O'Malley's Irish friends. Grier would soon rectify this apparent favoritism, but for now, he had what might become a problem. He had noted with interest that Rodado Verde didn't seem to have any respect for his fellow Irishman O'Malley. Strange, the major thought.

When Major Grier's force was finally ready to depart, Mrs. White and her infant daughter had been captives for weeks. Grier was paid as a captain but treated in all other respects as a major. Brevets were awarded for heroism in combat.

The days of September and October passed swiftly at Rayado. There was plenty of work for Roque, Kit, and Danny. They mowed and baled hay, rounded up livestock, moved the cattle from range to range when they'd thinned the grass, and cut firewood for the winter. They were happy in their companionable work until they received word late in October of the murder of James White and his companions. Kit had known White, and the news had visibly upset him. "Acha, it was bound to have been Acha," said Kit. "He's trying to build himself up as a war leader. We embarrassed him. I knew no good would come of that."

For days after hearing the news, Kit, usually happy in his work and the company of good companions, was depressed.

Danny Trelawney finally asked Roque, "What's bothering Kit?"

"He feels obligations to his fellow men that the rest of us don't usually feel," replied Roque. "It's part of what makes him great, no? He knows that our actions had a bad effect on Acha, so he feels responsible for the death of Mr. White."

"But we had no choice," Danny countered.

"I know, and probably so does Kit, but he feels responsible nonetheless," Roque allowed. "I've seen men so full of themselves, they claimed responsibility for all sorts of things good and bad. But with Kit, it is not like that. He is very humble. It is obligation he feels."

On November 7, in the early dusk of late fall, four riders approached Kit's ranch at Rayado. Danny immediately recognized Antoine Leroux among them, for they'd met in Aubry's camp. Tall, dark, and powerfully built, he seemed a little older than Kit, approaching fifty perhaps. He dressed in fringed and beaded buckskins and wore a wide brimmed felt hat sporting a beaded band and a feather. The other three were soldiers. Major Grier, the officer who led the group, tall with gray hair and mustache, was in his late thirties. The second officer was young and Mexican, not much older than Roque and Dan. The last man was a sergeant of medium height, heavyset, in his late thirties.

"Danito, look at this peacock," said Roque indicating the sergeant with his chin.

"That's the fanciest uniform I've ever seen on an enlisted soldier," Danny replied.

The peacock rode up to Roque and, without dismounting, demanded, "*Chico*, go fetch Kit Carson. Major Grier wants to see him."

"*Que?*" asked Roque.

"*Señor* Carson, *aqui muy pronto, chico!*" ordered the sergeant in broken Spanish.

Roque looked at him stupidly, "*Que?*"

The sergeant spluttered, "Go get him!" His face turned red.

Roque, Danny thought, wasn't going to take much more nonsense, though the sergeant seemed stupid enough to try pushing harder.

"I'll go get him," Danny volunteered and started off, hoping to avert trouble.

"Hold it," the sergeant called. "I told the Mex to go."

Kit's timely arrival probably saved the sergeant's life or at least, so Danny thought.

"Leroux, Capitan Valdez," Kit called, smiling warmly. "Good to see you both. Step down. and I'll have Josepha make sure we have enough dinner for you and your friends."

"Carson, Major Grier," the sergeant started to say, "wants to talk to…oomph…"

Roque's hand shot out and grabbed a wad of tunic above the sergeant's shiny belt buckle. With one arm, he lifted the sergeant down from his horse and set him on his feet.

With a bow, Roque smiled as if this were the most normal and polite thing in the world. "*Señor, Don Cristobal* has invited you to step down from your horse and have dinner with him."

Some men are frightened by casual displays of great strength. Sergeant Cillian O'Malley, for that's how he was introduced a moment later, was one of them. Danny was amused but worried Roque's actions might lead to trouble.

"I'm beginning to think like Kit," Danny mused, a little confused that he was beginning to think of distant consequences and the effect actions might have on others.

After dinner, Major Grier confronted Kit. He reviewed all that had happened to the White party and his plans for pursuit. "I need you as a scout, Mr. Carson," he said.

"Kit, please call me Kit," Carson replied.

"All right, Kit. We need your skills," the major continued.

"You've got Leroux as chief scout. You made a wise selection. He's as good as I am," demurred Kit.

Leroux beamed. "We can manage without him, sir."

"That's right," said O'Malley nervously. "We don't need them." Roque and the major both looked at him. Sergeant O'Malley said no more that evening.

"Mr. Leroux, I don't argue with your skills at all," said William Grier in an even tone. "They are well known to me, but it has been two weeks since the Jicarilla rode away from Palo Blanco Creek. We need all the help we can get."

"I live on Jicarilla land. They are my neighbors," said Kit. "We get along. They leave me in peace. I give them meals and a few of my livestock. I have no wish to hunt my neighbors or to upset the peace."

"Kit," argued the major, "the peace has already been upset. They've murdered James White and taken his wife and daughter. Who knows what they'll do to her?"

"I am at peace with the Jicarilla," said Kit quietly.

Danny thought Kit's comment sounded self-aggrandizing, but Kit wasn't like that. His relationship with the Indians was deeper and more profound. It was simply his statement of how things stood, a statement of fact.

"Mr. Carson," said the major, "I've heard tales of what these Apaches do to a white woman . . ."

O'Malley started to speak, probably of lurid and imaginative tales, Danny thought, but after a glance from Roque, O'Malley thought better of provoking the proud Spaniard.

"As I was saying," Grier said turning a cold eye on the sergeant, "the lady needs your help. I need your help."

Kit winced at Grier's words. Danny learned later that Kit, along with many people at the time, believed Jicarilla would make a captive woman a "casual lover." Anyone who cared to would be allowed to rape her. Kit had experience with Indians that few had. Although the Jicarilla denied their treatment of captives was ever cruel, Kit believed that the abuse was brutal and it worried him.

"I have responsibilities here. I have my own women to look after," Kit responded.

"If we keep the Jicarilla on the run, they won't have time to bother your rancho. You have a duty to your people and your country," Major Grier responded.

Those words struck home. Sucking smoke from his pipe, Kit was silent for a long time. He stirred the fire in the *horno* with a stick and watched the fire flare and die down again. Finally, he said, "All right, I'll go."

Kit turned to the two young men. "Danito, Roque, you stay here at the rancho," he said quietly. "You don't have to come."

"Where you go, *Don Cristobal*," said Roque, "I go. I will share your danger and hardship as I have promised."

"I too will go," said Danny, trying hard to sound as noble as Roque, but in reality, he was unwilling to miss out on the excitement and adventure.

"Josepha," Kit said to his wife later on, "I'd like it if you went to visit Lucien Maxwell's wife at Cimarron while we're gone. You'll be safe there while I'm away."

Josepha nodded. "*Bueno, mi espousa.* It will be as you wish. I understand."

Bruised, hungry and weary Ann White felt like she couldn't take another step. She kept going. She had to for the sake of Virginia and because she knew help would come, if not Kit Carson, some other hero would save her.

She heard a shrieking like a woman screaming far off.

The sound divided into multiple voices. Ann pictured a band of condemned souls in chains stumbling toward Hades. Before Acha dragged her away to a hidden spot, she made out three two-wheeled *carretas* drawn by oxen. The noise came from their ungreased axles. The men with the carts wore uncouth and outlandish costumes. These must be the Comancheros of whom she'd heard hideous tales. They carried white women away in trade to Mexico where they spent the rest of their lives as slaves in bordellos.

Held close to Acha, his hand on her mouth preventing a scream, she reached for and drew his knife. She cut him and he released his grip. She raised the knife to her neck imagining she would cut her own throat. She would take control ending the unspeakable things being done to her. Then she thought of her daughter and knew she must be strong for Virginia. She handed the blade back to Acha and he cuffed her for taking it and then motioned her to be quiet.

Across the camp, she saw her servant girl being dragged forward for inspection by the Comancheros who offered three blankets. The deal was finally settled for three blankets, a knife and a small cask of gunpowder. Ann never saw the girl again.

Late into the night of November 7, the Ollero Jicarillas held council at Water Flows Down on a Succession of Flat Rocks near the Canadian River, far to the south of Point of Rocks. The Ollero were traveling in company with their Llanero relatives as all of the Jicarilla had gathered from both sides of the mountains for a fall buffalo hunt. Together, they would have strength against the hated and powerful Comanche. They had been east of the Canadian and well out on the plains when the Llanero leaders suddenly insisted that they backtrack and take a course south through the brakes of the Canadian, a favorite Jicarilla hiding place. There were Comanche ahead, they said. Acha had seen them.

The tepee glowed like a Chinese lantern on the prairie pitched within a rolling sea of grass turning from green to winter brown. The Jicarilla occupied a hidden dell where oak, juniper, and *piñon* pine were the walls of their stockade. The wind did not harry the village but carried away camp smoke, leaving the air clear. The tribe had delved to the depths of the Canadian brakes and emerged onto an arm of land above. Their next camp would be down in the brakes. It was a good place to camp that pleased the *N'deh*, the people. Children played, dogs barked, and women worked and argued as they attended to chores of cooking, gathering firewood, and making clothing. Sitting around the fire within the tepee of Vicenti were broad-shouldered and powerful Chacon and wiry, fearless Huero Mundo. They were joined at the fire by the storyteller Nighthawk and shaman Moon Woman."The *N'deh* have stopped taking precautions against pursuit," said Huero Mundo. The others nodded. They knew.

"The Comanche are now far behind us," replied Chacon.

"I don't think we are pursued by Comanche," said Vicenti. "My son and others have seen a *Mangani* woman among our Llanero kinsmen."

"Where did she come from?" asked Chacon, clearly concerned.

"Many have seen her," said Vicenti. "I told my son to search along the trail behind us and see what was there. He found signs that a party of *Mangani* had been killed."

"That may not concern us," responded Chacon. "Who killed them?"

"Jicarilla killed them," Vicenti declared. "Rojo found a Llanero lance stuck in the ground and Sonrisado's moccasins hanging there. A woman's clothes were scattered around, but no woman's body lay dead."

There had been rumors. The Llanero talked too much, but it was Vicenti's story to tell, so Chacon would play along with the charade a few moments longer although he knew much of this matter already.

"I do not think the Comanche ever pursued us," Vicenti announced. There was an intake of breath all around the fire. They had all guessed at the truth behind his words, but contradicting the words of another chief was a harsh thing to say. The Jicarilla avoided saying such things among themselves. It was close to a declaration of war against Acha and Lobo Blanco. Among the Jicarilla, every man was his own king and could do as he thought best. Group effort was accomplished by common consent, which was achieved by being exceedingly polite among themselves. Only in war was it different. In that case, once a leader was chosen, his word was law until the war party returned to camp.

"Then why do we run?" asked Nighthawk.

"Acha has captured a Mangani woman and her baby. My son has seen her in their camp. The young men brag to him of having killed a party of Mangani near Palo Blanco Creek. They say the Mangani first insulted them, and then when they came back with more braves, the Mangani shot one of them. So they slew the Mangani, robbed them, and took the woman. The Llaneros fear the Mangani soldiers may come," Vicenti finished.

"It has been a very long time. How could they track us?" asked Huero Mundo from behind his dark, hooded eyes.

Moon Woman closed her eyes and began to rock back and forth, humming softly to herself. The others took no notice. They had seen her accept the trance before.

"I have talked to Gi-di, called Kit Carson by the Mangani," said Vicenti. "The Mangani are not like the *Nakaiyeh*. They are very persistent and very protective of their women. Their soldiers are not like *Nakaiyeh* soldiers. The Mangani know how to fight."

"I think this is so," said Chacon. "I have heard it said that when the Mangani army came the *Nakaiyeh* had a very strong position in the canyon to oppose them. The *Nakaiyeh* ran away without a fight. Later, that same winter in Taos, the *Nakaiyeh* opposed the Mangani, but the Mangani defeated them, brushing them aside like children. I think the Mangani are not *Nakaiyeh*. They can be dangerous in war."

"They are dangerous," said Huero Mundo, "as dangerous as an angry bear."

The humming stopped suddenly. Moon Woman stood. She extended her arms out in front of her, her palms flexed facing outward, turning slowly in a circle. Once, twice, and then she stopped facing the distant mountains and Rayado. Her palms were bright red. Power told her the direction the enemy would come from. Her hands felt warm when she turned them toward the enemy. How warm and how red depended on the size of the enemy force.

"The Mangani are coming," said Moon Woman. "They are near the mountains, but coming."

"I think there will not be a buffalo hunt this year," said Nighthawk. No one disagreed.

"Then perhaps it is time to return to our own valleys," said Chacon. Again, no one disagreed.

"How shall we depart without arousing the Llaneros to anger?" asked Vicenti. They talked long into the night without a decision. It did not seem right to leave their cousins, the Llanero, without the support of the Ollero. However, they had been misled. The Llanero had made war on a powerful enemy without asking the Ollero what they thought. Reaching a difficult decision might take many nights.

On November 8, Major Grier's newly reinforced battalion left Rayado. Kit and his friends rode ahead of the main body with the other scouts. On the morning of the ninth, Leroux discovered the White's noon camp in a little side canyon near Palo Blanco Creek. Papers and clothing were scattered about. Broken boxes and furniture lay on the ground. Near the fire pit was a tiny rocking chair.

Tough old Robert Fisher in greasy buckskins wept at the sight of the chair. Danny thought he heard Richens 'Uncle Dick' Wooton sniffle. All of the scouts were moved by the thought of the baby girl now in captivity and the dangers and hardships she must be enduring.

Rodado Verde rode up, looked at the tiny chair, and said, "That Ann White sure must have a skinny butt."

Danny turned and was about to say something harsh to Verde, but then he noticed him surreptitiously wiping a tear from his eye onto a leather cuff.

Kit found a lance stuck in the ground with a pair of moccasins hanging from it. "Danny, this is a Jicarilla sign."

Roque explained, "They set up a lance and moccasins like this when they want you to know who's been here, whose land this is, no? See the beadwork on the moccasins? See how the pattern is dark blue and light blue on a white background. That's what the Jicarilla prefer."

"This is the work of Acha and his friends," said Kit with finality.

Kit looked at what was left of the bloodstains on the ground. The site had been trampled by passersby and by the burial party. The bodies had been torn apart by wolves, crows, and coyotes. It had been two weeks and had snowed.

Kit said, "I think White's people killed one of the Jicarilla. The fight didn't last any time at all. The Jicarilla overwhelmed them."

Roque whispered to Danito, "I think the dead one might have been called Sonrisado. I think I recall him wearing those moccasins."

"I'm sure it was an ambush!" interjected chief scout Leroux. "They were overwhelmed quickly. Only an ambush could have done that. See the stones piled up? They're breastworks for the ambush."

Danny turned to Roque. "I don't see anything but trouble. Leroux is jealous of his position and his importance."

Kit looked concerned, but said nothing.

"Then they were tortured," Leroux went on. "See the signs of fire? They tied someone down close to it and let the flames slowly boil his brains."

This account was a new and different one of what had happened to White and his men, Danny thought.

Roque made a noise. It sounded to Danny like a strangled cough. He looked at his friend who nodded and smirked.

"Now comes the tough part," Leroux said to the gathered scouts. "There have been at least four parties per day traveling the Santa Fe Trail: forty-niners, trade caravans, *ciboleros*, and Pueblo Indians. It has been two weeks. We've got to find signs of riders headed toward the main Jicarilla encampment."

When he stopped talking, Kit added, "I've heard they headed toward the Canadian."

Leroux nodded, but he seemed annoyed. "So let's spread out and look in that direction. Look for pony tracks."

Leroux, thought Dan, was not pleased that Kit had assumed even a little of his, Leroux's, authority, but as lead scout he said nothing even as his face darkened visibly. Kit was usually sensitive to these things, but to Danny's mind, Kit had supplied the only useful bit of information. Everything else was obvious.

Among the trash, Danny found a crumpled paper lodged under the edge of a broken box. On it, he read words that would haunt him. Like Kit, he was starting to feel responsible for the unintended consequences his actions had caused. The paper read:

Certificate of Good Conduct

Hail, know all ye by these presents that the subject Pinacate, meaning Stink Bug, a Jicarilla, is a good Indian. He will not steal more than he can carry nor will he take anything that is securely fastened down or attached to anything heavier than he can lift. He is known to be lazy and indolent. A fair day's labor might be gotten out of him in a month provided one supervises him intently to the exclusion of all other tasks. Avoid him and all his clan, sort and tribe at all costs.

He showed the paper to his friend Roque but concealed it from others. "I wonder what role this piece of paper played in the tragedy."

Roque looked at his friend thoughtfully. "*Amigo*, it is best not to think too deeply on such things. It will make you *loco*."

Danny persisted. "You know what this means, don't you? I'm now as sure as Kit that Acha and his friends staged the attack. I gave that note to Pinacate. Did Mr. White read this and try to chase Acha and his party away? Did this note make them careless?"

"*Amigo*," said Roque calmly, "we gave the note to Pinacate, not you alone. Our joke doesn't seem so funny anymore."

Kit took the young men aside. Unbidden, Verde joined them. "I don't think we'll find a distinctive track from a horse to follow. Not after all this time."

Roque added, "There are lots of unshod *caballos* on the *llano*. Who can say which are ridden by Jicarilla? We won't find real tracks except where it's wet or sandy, but the Jicarilla will avoid such, but we might find branches on bushes broken and turned in the direction the riders went."

Kit nodded his approval, so Roque continued, "There might be scuffs on rock or hard ground. In summer, we'd see where the grass had been beaten down. In fall, the grass is all beaten down. What we really have to find is a camp."

Kit asked, "Do you know what we'll find in a camp, Danny?"

Danny thought a moment. "We might find fire pits and places where the grass was really compressed from people sleeping on it. We might find trash and rings of depressions from tepee poles."

"Good," Kit replied. "We'll find trash: old bones, baskets, and clothing thrown away."

"Their personal habits are clean," added Roque, meaning they took their toilet at a long distance from the camp, "but they'll drop anything that broke or that they're done with on the ground. The trash may tell us who we're following. We'll also find drag marks from travois."

Kit nodded again. His student had learned well and was better at putting his thoughts into words than he was. Kit added, "I know many of the places that they camp and the kind of places they like for camps. We'll check them."

Danny reflected that suddenly a vast plain had been reduced to a manageable number of discrete points. The Santa Fe Trail followed the most level terrain, ground good for wagons, from water to water. The Jicarilla did something similar. Amid the vast sea of grass, there were only a few islands, camping places that offered water, forage, and security. People moved from island to island. It didn't matter where they went in the sea between, when they checked the islands, sooner or later they would find the trail. It didn't matter that the older portions of the trail had been obliterated by weather and trampling feet, for once they found an island where the Jicarilla had camped, finding the next would be easier. Relieved, Danny realized they wouldn't be trying to discern pony tracks under inches of snow, even though that seemed to be what Leroux had in mind.

The next morning, November 10, Silva thought he'd found signs of where a large group heading east had turned and headed southwest toward the Canadian River. The movement of 600 people and their horses had ripped into the prairie in a way that even weather couldn't conceal. The earth would heal, but it would take time. Although snow stood on the ground, the disturbance had been great enough that some evidence still showed. Then the trail vanished.

"It's an old Apache trick," said Kit to his young friends. "If they think they're pursued, they scatter like quail to meet up later."

On November 11, Major Grier's scouts found signs of a camp, the first they had seen, near the Canadian. It may not have been obvious to the others, although Danny thought Leroux suspected, Kit had brought them to one of the places he knew the Jicarilla camped and then allowed Uncle Dick Wootton to "find" it. Richens Wootton was a former mountain man, braggert, comedian and a sometime friend of Kit Carson.

"Look closely," Kit said to Danny and Roque.

Once they knew where to look, they saw faint signs. Fire rings that had been buried and trampled over still showed. Uncle Dick found the remains of a basket. The herringbone pattern on the edge gave it away as Jicarilla. Danny found a scrap of beaded leather that had once been part of something. The bead pattern was dark blue, light blue, and white. Verde found a scrap of a woman's gingham dress hanging in a *chamisa*. *Chamisa* bends to the slightest touch; therefore, it wouldn't have torn off a piece of cloth.

"We must have an ally in the camp," Leroux told the scouts. "Mrs. White has left us this to guide us. She is letting us know she lives. Spread out and let's figure out which way they went."

The way they went was soon obvious. Leaving in small groups, they had departed in every direction from northeast to northwest. Trails soon disappeared as those who left them guided their ponies over rocks and into streams, picking ground where they wouldn't leave tracks, though snow and weathering probably would have obliterated tracks anyway.

"Scattering like quail," Danny mumbled. He was learning. The one direction they hadn't gone was north so the next camp would be between southeast and southwest. Still that was an awful lot of ground to cover.

Kit called Verde, Roque, and Danny to him. "We have a challenge. We have to follow an old trail. Those who made it were trying to conceal it. We have to move much faster than they to catch up."

"That means," Roque added, "that we can't track and backtrack or walk beside our horses searching out signs that aren't there. I think *Don Cristobal* has something else in mind."

About then, Leroux's scouts reported back to him. They had found at least sixteen trails leading away from the camp in different directions.

"In that case," said Leroux, "we must follow the most prominent one and one or two of the others." He gave them their assignments. At Kit's request, Leroux allowed the four friends, Kit, Verde, Roque and Danny, to work in the same general area.

Once they had set out, Kit told the three to dismount. He drew with a stick in the sand.

"It's an Apache trick," Kit said. "They agree where they will meet at the end of the day and then all go off by different routes. They lead you for miles, then backtrack and disappear. If you follow the trails all day, you'll see them converge. We haven't got time for that."

Knowing Kit didn't like to do a lot of detailed explanation, Roque picked up the narrative when Kit paused. "Granted they know fords and passes we don't, but we still know a lot about the country. They've gone to the Canadian because there are lots of places they can hide and places they can set up ambush. They hope to keep us confused in that maze of side canyons."

He went on when Kit nodded. "Warriors who don't mind killing their horses might make sixty or a hundred miles in a day, but we're following families dragging tepees. They could still make thirty miles in a day, but separating and coming back together they limit themselves to about fifteen miles. They will have to use some of the fords and gaps we know because by separating, they're using them all.

Roque looked to Kit for confirmation of the lessons Kit had so patiently taught him by example. Receiving it, he continued. "So, here we are. Where might they want to camp next within fifteen miles? What fords, springs, gaps, and descents to canyon floor and places they can get water do we know?" He drew them on the ground and Kit picking up a stick added a few more. "When we learn which paths they were taking, we'll know where they are headed for evening camp."

Kit spoke again, "Roque, you and Danito will be in the middle. Ride for this gap," he said pointing to his map on the ground. "Verde, you will be on the right and I'll be on the left. If we find anything, we stay put. If not, ride to the middle. Ride hard for your point. We should see each other in about two hours. Don't worry about checking the ground for sign until you get there."

Roque and Danny found sign in the place Kit had suggested. A large number of horses and travois had gone through the gap, one of the tributaries of the Canadian. Kit soon showed up, his search had been barren. Verde didn't, and they rode to meet him. He had found sign, too. From this evidence, Kit guessed the location of the camp the Jicarilla were heading to. They rode hard for that area and found sign of the Jicarilla coming together to make camp for the night. This was the second camp the Indians had made since changing their course near Point of Rocks. The place was hidden deep in the brakes where canyon walls towered above on all sides, seemingly even the downhill side where a clear stream rushed toward the river surrounded by oak, walnut, and cottonwood trees. The stream bent around, carrying the canyon walls with it like closing the gate of a fortress.

In this place of glowering cliffs, Danny shuddered. "I feel like I'm trapped in a well."

Roque nodded. "Perhaps not if you know the trails, and it is a hard place to find."

"It's a hard place to attack," said Kit without explanation, leaving Danny and Roque to figure out what he meant.

Roque thought a moment, and then said, "There is no place for riflemen to perch that is within range."

Danny had an idea. "This place can only be approached along the stream if you don't know the secret trails. It would be easy to set piquets to guard the camp."

Kit nodded.

Danny went on, "It's like a fortress on a hill in reverse. The walls are so high that guards aren't needed along them."

"Even if they stayed here a couple of days," said Verde, "we're still more than a week behind them."

After a quick search, the trio found a strip of cloth torn from a woman's garment hanging in a bush. There was no mistake; this was the Jicarilla camp. It had taken only four hours from when they left the first camp to find this second one. They set out the same way with plenty of daylight left to find the Apaches' third camp.

Sometime during that day's search, Danny realized that while the battalion moved its camp daily, the Jicarilla did not. They stayed for a few days, even a week, hunting and mending. War parties moved fast and light, but this was not a war party. The Jicarilla were on a hunting expedition, searching for buffalo so that they would have food for the winter.

As they rode, Danny thought about what they were doing and what Kit was teaching. The land looked big, but only a small portion had water and other things the Indians needed and wanted. In an effort to narrow the terrain to be searched, some men, who considered themselves great trackers, were slowly and methodically searching for tracks and other sign that for the most part were no longer there.

On the other hand, Kit and his group relied on their ability to see subtle changes in the ground that from experience told them stories of what had transpired on that spot. Kit can do that, just fine, Danny thought, but he's doing something much more intuitive and even scientific. Sure, Danny mused, he builds a theory of where they might have gone and then tests it. It was a lot faster than what the other trackers were doing, and they needed speed. More than that, Kit's method worked on a three-week-old trail, and the other method really didn't. Even more interesting to Danny's thinking was that men like Leroux really couldn't understand Kit's method. Some of the more ignorant even thought it some kind of witchcraft.

By late afternoon, Major Grier's scouts had located the third campsite deep in the brakes surrounded by canyon walls, lush vegetation, and a flowing stream. Like many of the spots the Jicarilla favored, it was a hidden place, a secure place, and a place of beauty. Verde found another piece of cloth. Roque was sent to bring in the scouts and the battalion. Leroux had wisely appointed a gathering place and Roque found them there. Leroux's scouts, Uncle Dick, Tom Tobin, Fisher and the rest were frustrated. They had lost the trail.

As they approached the campsite where Kit waited, one of the scouts called out, "How'd you do it, Kit? Witchcraft?"

Kit laughed.

To Dan, the man's joke sounded serious. He realized that people who didn't understand thought Kit's method was some dark art. They grew suspicious and jealous, even fearful.

Linking up with the scouts at dusk, the dragoons camped in a side canyon east of the Canadian River where the Jicarilla had stayed. It was November 12; they were in the Jicarilla's third camp since the Indians had captured Ann White. She'd been with them nineteen days. The Jicarilla had slept sixteen times since they left this place. The trail was still quite cold. Major Grier's battalion had come about forty-five miles from Point of Rocks.

The Canadian River flowed south out of the *Sangre de Cristo* from mountains near the Raton Pass. It was soon joined by the Cimarron and Rayado and descended into a deep canyon. It continued south for almost two hundred miles before turning east across the prairie. The river flowed within its deep canyon all that way.

"The trail," said Leroux the next morning, "descends into the brakes, the flat places along the canyon floor."

"We will live in fear of ambush," said Verde, "the whole way."

Rodado Verde talked about how the Jicarilla lived. "They move like a military camp. You've already seen how they confuse the trail by heading off in all directions when they break camp. They do that even if they don't think they're being followed. They set sentinels to watch around the camp, and sometimes they will leave some men behind to set an ambush. Our scouts will go out by ones and twos and never be heard from again. They'll just disappear.

"It looks like we're following the whole tribe. That means there are six or eight hundred of the creatures. Nobody knows for sure. I think there are about eight hundred meself. They'll have between one hundred fifty and two hundred warriors, outnumbering us two to one. Even with bows and arrows, they have the advantage in firepower. They can put a lot of arrows in the air while we reload. Look at how we're armed. The scouts have rifles good for long-range but slow to reload. The dragoons have pistols and sabers, and we don't need to count the musketoons. The volunteers have all sorts of things. Some have only a saber, a few have pistols, and some have only a lance. . ."

"Don't let him frighten you, Dan," said Kit. "If we take them by surprise and charge in with saber and pistol, we'll control the camp before they can react."

"True," replied Verde.

"And they don't want a pitched battle with us," said Roque. "If Major Grier loses a few men, he can recruit more from back east where there are many. If the Jicarilla lose a man, they lose a son, brother, father, or cousin. They cannot replace him. They will only stand and fight to protect the women and children."

"They might fight another way," said Verde. "If they realize we are following them, they might bring all of their warriors to an ambush. If two hundred warriors were waiting undetected along the sides of this canyon, Major Grier's whole command could disappear in less time than it takes to say it."

"The scouts will just have to make sure that doesn't happen," Kit said grimly.

He didn't deny that there was truth in what Verde said. For the next week, Dan, inexperienced with Indians and heir to lurid tales of Indian massacres, carried with him the mental image of the entire command riding down the bottom of the canyon in column of two. In his imagination, the air suddenly filled with arrows. Then there was silence except for a few low groans. The attack happened so fast in this fantasy that no one ever had time to return fire.

Sergeant O'Malley came over to Kit's campfire where the scout sat with Roque, Dan, and Verde. He'd regained much of his swagger. His men, he thought, and especially his friends were at his back. "Carson, the major wants you. Jump to it. He means now."

Kit got up. Roque, annoyed, started to rise as well.

"Not you, *chico*. The major don't want you," said O'Malley. He turned and disappeared into the dark before Roque had come to his feet.

"I don't like that *puerco cabron*," he mumbled. "Someday I will introduce him to my *cuchillo*. He is very sharp, I think. *El gordo* better not call me *chico* again."

When Kit returned, he told them, "Leroux thinks the Apache will have halted for a few days to hunt. He's probably right. One of the camps we find tomorrow should show that."

Verde added, "They will have stopped being cautious at some point. Four, five, six days at most, and they will think they have eluded pursuers. That will make our job easier."

On the morning of November 13, the camp was full of the sound of Sergeant O'Malley, who was full of himself, haranguing his troops. Danny noticed Major Grier frowning in the sergeant's direction, but the sergeant didn't seem to notice. The major went up a notch in Danny's estimation.

He mentioned his improved opinion of the major quietly to Roque who was watching the display. "Even the major seems to think O'Malley isn't much of a soldier." Roque nodded.

The sergeant thundered, "What are you? Are you a dirty son of a whore to keep your fine musketoon in such a filthy condition? And your uniform isn't much better. Nor you neither," he yelled at the next man. "Your musketoon is fouler than his. Does that mean your mother was a dirtier whore than his?"

"Sarge, you know the musketoon isn't much of a weapon," said one of his men. "We'll fight with pistol and saber, not musketoons."

"Nonsense," O'Malley replied. "The musketoon is a fine weapon, indeed and for sure. All it needs is training and practice. Why, I can pick the eye out of a charging buffalo at two hundred yards. If you hold still, I can shoot a fly off your nose at three hundred yards. I've done it many times. The musketoon is a dragoon's weapon, a fine weapon indeed," claimed Cillian O'Malley. "And you scum had better take good care of it."

Roque snorted, but a sergeant disciplining his men, even unjustly, was none of his affair or Danny's. Nonetheless, Danny wondered if they could trust *El Gordo*, this fat little popinjay, in a fight.

Leroux sent his scouts out to follow "the best trail,"

proceeding slowly to frequent dead ends. Then the scouts would start over. Kit and his followers continued to go from key point to key point as Kit had shown them, paying little attention to Leroux's instructions to follow the most obvious or best trail. If the Jicarilla had made a trail obvious, it was because they wanted pursuers to follow it. Such trails always led to a dead end. Antoine Leroux was a good and admirable man, but he was not half the tracker Kit was. He was irritated by Kit's constant success following the Jicarillas' trail.

In the late afternoon, Kit sent back word to Leroux of finding the fourth camp of the day. It was the seventh camp since Point of Rocks, so they had gained at least a week on the Indians in two days.

"This camp was occupied a long time," said Kit, "at least three days, I think."

There was more trash than before, and the ground cover was more beaten down. Danny thought that it looked like Kit was right. The Apache had stopped to hunt and stayed three or four days.

By Danny's reckoning, this camp was number seven since the Jicarilla left Point of Rocks, representing days seven through eleven that Ann White was their captive. She had been an Apache captive for twenty days. Major Grier and Kit had cut the Jicarilla's lead to nine days. Signs of them were fresher and easier to read. Danny and Roque had found bits of her clothing at most of the camps.

The soldiers rejoined the scouts a little before dusk, set up their tents, and lined up their packs and such as neatly as possible. Sergeant O'Malley set them about their business digging latrine pits and gathering firewood for what might be their last hot meal. As they gained ground on the foe, they would have to start being careful about noise and smoke. O'Malley remained in camp supervising, which it seemed to Danny was another way of doing nothing.

Verde, looking for some fun, wandered over to the soldiers' camp. There was a commotion.

"Get back to your own camp, heathen," O'Malley screamed, aiming a kick at Verde. "And don't come back!"

"What was that all about?" Danny asked.

"I saw O'Malley rummaging through the soldiers' packs and went to have a closer look," replied Verde. "Did you notice that fine silver cross about the sergeant's neck?" Danny nodded. "I made that, I did for Private Velarde. That thieving sergeant must have taken it, and the wee lad's too feared of his old sergeant to say aught about it."

Returning from council with Leroux and the officers Kit said to his friends. "We have a new worry. We're getting close, and the Jicarilla probably don't know they are pursued as yet. We don't want to let them know, so this is our last hot meal for a while."

Roque nodded. "Tomorrow we pack bread and jerky for eight days hard ride. We'll make cold camps until we come up on the Jicarilla."

At the end of November 13, Grier's battalion had come about ninety miles from Point of Rocks.

On the morning of November 14, the expected orders came. Roque's guess was right. They were to pack for eight days hard marching, eight days without fire. There would be no hunting. Military equipment was tied down tightly so as not to rattle. The entire force was ordered to minimize noise. The men were instructed that there would be no shouting or loud talking.

"We shall move," said Major Grier, "like the fog creeping across the land, silently, until we envelop the heathen."

Kit's party worked in the manner they had learned and practiced and by noon had gone through three camps.

"Look at this," Danny said to Kit. "It's just as you predicted. The Jicarilla are growing more careless. They're leaving fewer but wider trails, bigger parties, and they lead more directly from camp to camp."

"They are still headed south, generally," added Verde, "and still along the east side of the Canadian."

"They're staying together," said Kit, "because they're still planning a buffalo hunt even though the season is late.

That afternoon, Danny was working alone following a fresh trail that led west across the Canadian. At the ford, he found that many trails converged. Leaving the Canadian going west was the trail of many horses and travois. He followed the trail up a side canyon, Mora River, he thought, but wasn't sure.

Coming up on a gap through the cap rock to the plain above, he looked up to see an Indian watching him. Danny stopped. Foolish, he thought, if that Indian didn't realize I saw him, he knows for sure now. He carefully scanned the cap rock ahead and to his flanks. He saw, or thought he did, four, maybe five, more Jicarilla. If I can see this many, he reasoned, there must be more. His heart raced. There were too many to fight, and he didn't think he had a safe path back the way he'd come.

Kit rode into the gap from the plain above. "Careless weren't you, Danny, to ride into a trap like this?" He smiled. "Come on up."

They rode with the Jicarilla for several hours heading

west toward the *Sangre de Cristo* and came to a Jicarilla camp sheltered on low ground, making it difficult to see from any direction.

"They left warriors behind because they thought we might find their trail at the river," said Kit.

Kit and Danny were escorted to Chief Vicenti. Peregrino Rojo, his son, was with the chief.

Vicenti addressed himself to Kit, calling him Gi-di. He spoke at some length and with apparent sincerity. For Danny's benefit and to provide his father with time to consider any further remarks, Rojo translated. "My father wants you to know the Olleros had no part in what happened at Point of Rocks. We did not even know the woman had been taken for several days until we saw her in camp. The Llaneros hid her. It was their doing.

"My son, Rojo, spoke to her then and learned the story. She and her baby are well for now. But she was not prepared for our type of food or for walking to keep up with horses. It is hard on her body. She is getting skinny."

When Rojo paused, Chief Vicenti continued his account. "Lobo Blanco told the chiefs of the Olleros and perhaps the other Llanero chiefs as well that the Comanche were in the area in great numbers. It was decided that we must go south away from the Comanche. We were to hunt the buffalo further south. That was the plan. Then we learned we are running from Mangani soldiers. The Olleros want no more part of this. It will be a long, hard winter for us. Food will be scarce. We will not hunt the buffalo this year. We are returning to our homes.

"Will you let us return across the mountain in peace?" the chief asked.

Kit thought for a moment.

Rojo interjected, "The problem comes from Acha, as I once told you it would. He is out to prove himself a great war leader. He and his friends meant to scare those people into giving Acha and his warriors gifts, but the white people fired on them first. That is what Acha and his friends say. Those travelers fired on them first and killed one of Acha's friends. It is true his friend Sonrisado has been missing from the camp these past weeks."

"What of the servant girl?" Kit asked.

"Gi-di," Vicenti replied, "I do not know what has happened to the black, white woman. Comancheros came to trade in the camp before we left. I fear she has been given in trade."

Kit looked at Danny and spoke slowly but with intensity. "Danny, we must never tell anyone we have seen these people. I think we are the only ones who have seen their trail. If you say it is all right, we will let them go in peace."

Danny Trelawney looked at Kit and then at Rojo and his father. "We will let them go in peace," he agreed. Father and son nodded their understanding.

Rojo escorted them back to the Canadian. Impulsively, Danny grasped his friend. Rojo acted surprised. It was not the Apache way to be so demonstrative, nor had he realized that Danny had such friendly feelings for him.

Recognizing his error, Danny sputtered, "It's just that I felt uncertain when I would see you again in these troubled times."

Rojo grasped Danny's forearms and looked into his eyes. "We are *amigos*."

That same night the Ollero Jicarilla leaders planned

their move across the *Sangre de Cristo* Mountains. They knew secret trails that would take them between Truchas and Trampas. Once on the western slope of the mountains, they would disperse and go to their winter camps in the *Piedre Lumbre* and around Picuris and Abiquiu.

Chief Vicenti called Rojo to him. "Son, take some of your friends and ride south through the Galisteo Basin, south of Santa Fe where the Mexican *ricos* keep their sheep. Gather in the sheep of the *Nakaiyeh*. Bring them to us at our winter camps so we will have something to eat."

Even in the dark, Kit and Danny were able to pick up the trail left by eighty soldiers. In any event, they had the advantage of having a very good idea where Major Grier and his battalion were headed. The dragoons were camped where the Jicarilla had camped before them. The two riders arrived in camp long after dark.

"Just dead ends, I'm afraid," Danny told Verde and Roque, his comrades.

Kit confirmed this with a nod. "The Jicarilla are wily and prone to disappear. All the trails we followed turned to smoke. Long day and nothing to show for it." Kit shrugged as such things happened, even to him.

Verde and Roque looked suspicious but said nothing. Without fires, the camp was cold, dark, and quiet.

The battalion was at the Jicarilla's eleventh camp since leaving Point of Rocks. Signs said the Jicarilla had stayed at this camp at least two days hunting and resting. These would have been the sixteenth and seventeenth days that Ann White had been their captive. By the time the soldiers arrived at this camp, she had been a Jicarilla captive for twenty-one days. The signs were very fresh and easy to read.

"They left here four days ago," Kit informed his friends. He was reticent about saying much to the major in front of Leroux. "It's Leroux's turn to lead and be a hero," Kit told Danny.

"We've cut their lead to only four days," exulted Roque. "We'll catch them soon."

Verde brought in bits of Ann White's clothing to show the others. "She's still alive," he said, "or was four days ago. 'Spect she still is."

It was November 14, and the rescuers had covered one hundred and twenty miles since leaving Point of Rocks.

The soldier camp awoke on November 15 covered in frost. They ate a little bread and jerky and then set out as before following trail signs that were still fresh, searching for Jicarilla camps. Kit was quite concerned that the Jicarilla might have left a rear guard to watch for and ambush the soldiers. The canyon was so deep the sun shone only in the middle of the day. There were a thousand places where an unseen enemy could lie in wait in large numbers.

Danny watched Roque and Verde constantly scanning ledges above them, looking for movement or anything that didn't belong. Roque constantly looked over his shoulder. The hair stood up on the back of Danny's neck. He was uncertain about the rumbling in his stomach. It might have been fear or just the diet of dry bread and jerky. Kit was less obvious in his fretting, but it was clear he was concerned.

The day passed without incident. At day's end, the rescue party was one hundred fifty-miles from Point of Rocks. Ann White had been a Jicarilla captive for twenty-two days. The battalion was only a day or so behind the Jicarilla. Excitement filled the camp.

"Keep the noise down!" Major Grier ordered.

It was another camp without fires where they ate cold bread and jerky.

The camp arose to another cold morning on November 16 and ate cold bread and jerked meat. Roque shared some Chimayo apples that he kept hidden stowed in his pack. As the foursome was finishing breakfast, they saw Major Grier's top sergeant approaching.

"Major Grier wants you Carson, pronto," Sergeant O'Malley snorted at Kit. He spun and strode away. His musketoon was slung muzzle down over his shoulder. Kit didn't move. Roque stooped to pick something from the dust at O'Malley's heel.

O'Malley froze. "What you up to, *chico?*"

"Nothing, *Lambe Sargento,*" replied Roque with seemingly geniality.

"What'd you call me?" the sergeant growled.

"*Lambe Sargento.* Is like top sergeant, *no?*" said Roque innocently.

Lambe comes from the word to lick in Spanish. What is being licked is only implied. It's worse than boots, but bootlicker is probably the closest word in English.

"*Chico*, I don't like being called nothing I don't understand."

"*Si, Sargento Malo,*" said Roque calling him the devil.

"That's O'Malley. Oh-mail-lee. Understand you ignorant, dirty *mosco.*" It wasn't smart for the sergeant to call Roque a fly.

"*Si, Malo.* You don't like me; I don't like you." Roque grabbed two apples from his pack. "All the time you talk how good you are with musketoon. Tell you what. You put a *manzano* on your *cabeza;* I put one on mine. Maybe fifty paces. I use my *pistole.* You shoot musketoon. I give you first shot." He was laying on that thick Mexican accent to goad the sergeant who had made it clear he didn't like Mexicans.

"Roque, don't do it!" Danny yelped. "Kit, stop him."

"I can't. I've fought duels before. Besides, it's not really a duel. It's a test of skill," replied Kit.

"Is okay, Danito. He can't hit nothing with that musketoon. He's just makin' big talk," said Roque grinning.

"Go get him, Roque!" shouted Rodado Verde in his shiny green top hat. "Cillian O'Malley, indeed. Cillian, child of strife, and why not? He's probably an English Protestant!"

The scouts, Uncle Dick Wooten, Jesus Silva, Tom Tobin, and Bob Fisher, had noticed the commotion and had moved over to watch and laugh. They didn't care for O'Malley either.

O'Malley's men had overheard and egged him on. "Come on, Sarge. Show us how good you are."

The sergeant was cornered. He couldn't back down without looking the fool and a coward.

"What's the matter, Cillian O'Malley? No stones? No *cajones?* All show, no go, eh? Can I get you a white feather, boyo? Ain't you got no *huevos,* O'Malley?" continued Verde, watching O'Malley's eyes bulge and his face grow red. "You're stinkin' the place up. Set down the little, toy popgun and walk away while you can."

Danny scowled at Verde. "Damn it, man, you're pouring hot grease on a smoldering fire."

"Okay, Mex! Let's go," growled Cillian O'Malley, if not finding his courage, at least finding himself cornered. Besides, he had first shot, and he wouldn't be aiming for the apple.

Roque threw him an apple and turning counted out fifty paces with his back to the sergeant, disdainful of being shot from behind.

He turned and put the apple on his head. "*Malo*, now you shoot the *manzano* from my *cabeza!*"

Cillian O'Malley raised the musketoon to his shoulder, aimed carefully. To Danny, his aim looked low. O'Malley fired.

Crack went the cap. A tiny whoosh and a tinier flame came from the barrel of the sergeant's musketoon. It didn't sound right to Dan. It wasn't the bang of a gun being fired. It was more like a handful of black powder thrown on a fire. Everyone turned and looked. Roque was smiling and still standing.

"It is my turn, I think." He bent down and grabbed a little dust. Rising he released it in the breeze, testing direction and speed. Slowly he raised his pistol. Then he lowered it. "Maybe it's not fair. I didn't have my *tortillas y frijoles* this morning. Maybe I'm a little weak, and I aim low."

Sweat broke out on the sergeant's brow. He began to twist and fidget. Roque winked at him and then laughing, he raised his pistol again. "I'm laughing so hard, I can hardly aim." His muzzle danced as he aimed at O'Malley's apple.

O'Malley ran—right into Major Grier.

"O'Malley, didn't you hear me order silence and no fires?" asked Grier calmly.

O'Malley nodded dumbly.

"Do you suppose that was because we didn't want to alert the Apaches to our presence?" the major continued. O'Malley nodded again. "Then why have you fired a musketoon? We'll speak of this later.

"Mr. Carson, we'll head out in a few minutes, following your lead," the major finished and headed back to where the dragoons were preparing their horses.

Danny turned to his friend. "Roque, it was too dangerous. You could have been killed."

"It's not so easy to kill me, *mijo*," he held up something small and round. "I saw this and some black powder fall out of his barrel."

"Now that's cheating, Roque," said Verde. "Let me call him back and we'll start over." He offered his flask to Roque.

Danny shook his head. "I'd heard the ball was so loose in a musketoon that it could roll right out of the barrel, but I never thought I'd see it." Roque held the ball that had rolled from O'Malley's muzzle.

They chewed the last of their breakfast jerky as they tied down their gear tightly to their saddles. They were preparing for battle, not just another day of scouting.

Major Grier called the dragoons to mount up. The battalion set out without bugle calls or even a drumroll. Major Grier's rescuers were going as quietly as they could. The scouts were in the lead and spread well out to the flanks.

The camp crackled with excitement. This close to the Jicarilla, they could almost smell them. For the first time, the signs were fresh.

"We will find them today," Kit told his friends.

The foursome worked the trail as before, moving much faster with fresh clear sign before them all the time. In late morning, the trail veered suddenly toward the west and crossed the Canadian. A clear trail led from there toward the *Sangre de Cristo*. Leroux and all of his scouts except for Kit's party followed the trail the departing Olleros had left. The main body of dragoons followed behind them. Kit led Roque, Dan, and Verde south along the west bank of the Canadian, following a faint trail that became more pronounced as the day progressed. After fifteen miles, the trail crossed the Canadian going back to the east.

The Jicarilla had swung back toward the buffalo range on the Llano Estacado.

Kit sent Roque back to find Leroux. Having lost the trail to the *Sangre de Cristo*, Leroux had turned south and was not far behind.

"Kit is very close behind the *Indios, Señor* Leroux," Roque told him.

Leroux glowered and nodded. He would lead the party to Kit, but he was not happy. Kit had the trail when he had lost it. Although Kit was not in competition, Leroux seemed to think he was. He liked being chief scout, liked being important. Danny thought, I bet he hopes they'll write books about his exploits. Why not? He'd earned the acclaim.

They covered forty hard miles that day, coming close to Tucumcari Butte leaving Point of Rocks two hundred miles behind. It was late afternoon, two hours before sunset, when Major Grier called a halt near a grove of cottonwood trees.

As they dismounted, Kit spotted a large number of ravens flying up suddenly from the ground less than a mile from us. "The Jicarilla were camped there this morning," he said.

Chapter 12

A Cavalry Charge

Kit, Roque, Verde, and Danny along with the other scouts rode over to what had been the Jicarillas' camp. Wood still smoldered in the fire pits. Ravens flapped up from where they'd being fighting over bits of bone and other trash strewn about the camp.

Major Grier rode up with Captain José Valdez of the New Mexico Volunteers.

Leroux said, "I don't think they know we're here. They've been very careless, and they're not far ahead of us."

Grier asked, "What do you think, Kit?"

From near at hand, Danny Trelawney noticed Leroux's face darkened at Grier's question to Kit. Although Kit had consistently attempted to leave the credit to others, Grier, an intelligent officer, had long since realized that it was Kit Carson who had located camp after camp and made it possible for the major's force to get this close. Danny reflected that Kit had done everything he could to circumvent trouble, short of failing to provide the best service within his capabilities. He didn't show off or steal credit, Danny thought. Instead, he tried to stay low key, and most men respected him for it. It just wasn't in him to give less than his all. The major had created a bad situation by insisting that both top scouts accompany his battalion. He'd made it worse by going directly to Kit for advice.

Kit reflected for a moment. Silence was another aspect of Kit's personality Danny admired. Even if he knew the answer, he'd seem to think about it before responding. It made him seem thoughtful. Then Danny realized that Kit was also giving Leroux the opportunity to respond first as was his right as chief scout. Leroux, busy fuming, said nothing.

Confronted with a direct question, after hesitation, Kit responded, "We'll be in their camp by mid-morning tomorrow."

Major Grier asked, "How should we approach them?"

Leroux turned red and the veins in his neck bulged, but he said nothing. As chief scout, it was his place to answer these questions. If Kit had been asked, he'd have said Leroux was more than competent at least Kit's equal as a scout. He was honestly humble. At the same time, he'd have seen no conflict in keeping his own council about what was right. He'd have stepped aside in Leroux's favor. But Grier was asking direct questions, and Kit, Danny thought, felt compelled, duty bound, to answer.

Kit said, "As fast as we can manage. They will have sentries out. We want to be in the camp before they can react to the sentry's warning."

Major Grier continued, "How will they respond to us, Mr. Leroux?"

Thank the heavens, thought Dan, relieved. The major was finally directing his questions at the man he'd hired as his chief advisor. Perhaps Grier had realized how badly he'd offended Leroux's pride. The people of New Mexico thought highly of Grier. He was a good soldier and more, a worthy Indian fighter though he'd allowed conflict to develop between his scouts.

"Given time, the men will form on our side of the camp and fire on us as we come on," said Leroux. "If we're fast, many braves will be stranded in the camp fighting alone to protect their families. They'll be cut off and unable to offer organized resistance. That is, if we are upon them quickly enough." Given a chance to show off and lecture to Kit and the major, chief scout Antoine Leroux was making everything he could of the opportunity and stretching out his speech. "The boys will run for the pony herd, and together with women, children, and the old ones, they will try to get away. They will leave all the camp equipment behind." Leroux had been thrown a sop, and he took it with gusto. His chest swelled.

"Can we stop them from getting away with the pony herd?" queried the major. "Kit?"

Kit thought for a moment. Leroux's brows bunched and gathered. Kit's waiting for him to step in, Danny thought. Finally, Kit responded, "With luck, Major. With luck, if we send a detachment to circle round, they might get there in time."

"How do we ensure the hostages' safety?" Grier asked.

It was Leroux's chance to step in, but the scout was

fuming again. He should have been asked for this advice. He was so involved in his anger that he failed to notice the question that had been directed to both himself and Kit, who waited giving Leroux time to reply. At the same time, Kit was considering an answer.

Grier grew tense awaiting an answer. So like a white man, Danny thought, remembering what Kit had taught him about Indians. Unlike whites, they were willing to let silence stretch. It didn't need to be filled with empty, ill-considered words. Grier was growing visibly restive. Rescue, not retribution, was the purpose of the campaign. Finally, he spoke. "The hostages?"

Kit looked at Leroux who still reflected only angry brooding, and with little alternative, Kit answered. "We ride in as fast as we can before the Jicarilla have a chance to kill them. It will take them a few minutes for the *Indios* to respond to us, and the hostages will be the last thing on their minds in those few moments."

Inevitably, chief scout Leroux left with no other way to assert his authority, found reason to disagree, although only moments before he had been urging a swift attack.

Antoine Leroux stepped in to demonstrate his leadership. "I think we should negotiate with them. That seems the safer course. Once they can see we are here in strength, they'll want to negotiate. The *llano* here is flat and empty without cover. We will be seen a long distance off. The Jicarilla will have time to organize their defense and save their ponies. We cannot approach with enough stealth or be quick enough upon them."

Kit, concerned for hostage safety, spoke again. "We don't have enough men to surround them. They'll run, and as they run they'll deny us the prize by killing the hostages," said Kit flatly. "Our only advantage is speed."

"We must negotiate," demanded Leroux. "We cannot have enough speed."

"The Jicarilla can't negotiate now," said Kit. "They'd have to admit to what they've done. They'd rather conceal the murders and the hostages. It won't work."

Leroux became stiff-necked, insisting on his plan over Kit's. His eyes glared at Kit. He was chief scout.

Major Grier, Danny realized, was taken aback. Here were two diametrically opposed plans presented by two famous scouts of great knowledge and skill. Both plans sounded reasonable, the assumptions behind them equally plausible. Kit Carson's plan seemed to embody the greater risk, but also the greater chance for prodigious success. Grier looked thoughtful. Finally, thought Dan, he's thinking about the effect of his actions on these two men, thinking about why they are opposing each other. If he adopts Kit's plan, Danny hoped he throw a sop to Leroux to mollify him; otherwise, trouble was certain. Grier stood there awhile looking out at the horizon in the direction the Jicarilla had gone.

"Do we even know if Mrs. White is still alive?" the major asked finally.

"She was this morning," said Verde holding up a piece of cloth torn from a dress, the prize of the day found in the abandoned camp.

The major decided. "Gentlemen, I think we'll need to ride right in as Kit says." To Danny the major's decision seemed weakened by reference to Kit. He needed to present it as his own plan, not Kit's. Danny knew this would anger the chief scout.

"Sir," said Leroux, "it is safer for the hostage if we negotiate her release. If we ride right in, we could kill her by accident in the confusion."

"You have my decision, Mr. Leroux," the major said in a soft voice with no rebuke in it. "No fires tonight. We've got to remain quiet. We ride at sunup."

"The *llano* is very open and flat here, Major," Kit declared, "with little cover. We can be seen a long way off. In the morning, we need to put on all the speed we can."

Leroux should have been advising the major, Danny thought. This was bad. Danny realized it needed saying, just as Kit had, but Leroux should have been the one to say it.

"I defer to your judgment, Kit, we ride at the trot as we depart camp," responded Grier.

Leroux was a thundercloud ready to burst.

The Canadian River meandered to the east near Tucumcari Butte. Major Grier's battalion, which had crossed and recrossed the river, found itself on the west bank when the river made its great bend to the east and started out across the Llano Estacado en route to the Gulf of Mexico. What had been the west bank now became the south bank. Kit signaled that the trail led across the river to the north side. The brakes were behind them as they emerged from the canyons, and the cliffs stood behind them like a great palisade, and out before them were the featureless plains. Behind them now as well was the riverside growth of trees. They were entering a short grass prairie.

On November 16, the rescuers covered more than forty miles closing the gap between themselves and the Jicarilla. They had ridden almost two hundred miles in pursuit since leaving Point of Rocks. Every man in the party looked forward to releasing Ann White who had been a captive for twenty-three days. Her captivity was almost over. They had closed the gap to a few miles at most.

The morning of November 17, Danny awoke with frost covering his blanket. Although there were no fires and no coffee, excitement flowed through the camp like static electricity. The men were up long before daylight excited and ready for action.

"Here, Danito," whispered Roque, "have some jerky and my last apple."

Danny whispered back, "*Gracias, amigo.*"

Together they chewed jerked meat and hard bread. One of the dragoons dropped a musketoon, and the entire camp turned to glare at him. The weapon wasn't loaded, a precaution against accidental discharge ordered after O'Malley's little accident. The Jicarilla were close.

Rodado Verde sniffed the air, his nose up like a hound.

"What are you doing, Verde?" Danny asked.

"I can smell them," he replied. "We have no fires, but I smell wood smoke, roasting meat and with it horses . . . a lot of horses."

Leroux came by making sure no one lighted a pipe. He didn't want the Jicarilla to smell the battalion. "Anglo tobacco smells different than the wild stuff the *Indios* smoke," he said. "And be sure to lash down anything that might make noise." This should have been Major Grier's and his sergeant's job, but Leroux was asserting his dominance as chief of scouts, which wasn't a bad idea at all since the sergeant was a fool, Danny thought.

The men wrapped strips of cloth around metal fittings. Anything that would shine or reflect light was hidden away.

Major Grier walked over to Kit's circle. He wouldn't trust O'Malley again or deign to summon Kit Carson even though military leaders customarily summoned their subordinates to officers' call. Danny realized that Grier's respect for the legendary scout had grown.

At that moment, Danny also realized that his respect had grown too since his moment of disappointment in meeting a Kit Carson who wasn't seven feet tall and who was a bit quiet and shy. Danny Trelawney had come to appreciate qualities of determination and sense of duty to others that stood a good deal taller than Kit's contemporaries. If others had bragged about him, it was clear Kit was not the braggart. Leroux, Danny thought, was jealous that Pathfinder Fremont, in bragging about his own exploits, had also made Kit famous. Apparently, Leroux thought himself equally matched with Kit in skills, but Kit was the legend. Reflecting on the disparity of their legends and the fickle nature of fame, Danny concluded that it was more than a few books that had raised Kit from obscurity. His contemporaries already looked up to him and willingly chose him as a leader. More than that, they stayed with him as a leader. There were plenty of stories from the Mexican War, Danny knew, that told of officers popularly elected but who could not control their men. Men listened to Kit. Kit was so humble that he could sincerely tell others that Leroux was his equal as a scout. But Kit also kept his own council.

"Mr. Carson," the major asked, "How do you want to do this?"

Sought out, with Leroux not present, Kit was cornered. He responded. "I'll take the lead. Let the other scouts spread on a broad front a hundred yards behind me. Where do you want your big guns?"

The major responded, "I think the howitzer battery should be with the scouts so they can go into action immediately on contact and cover the advance."

Kit nodded his agreement. "Good. Then the dragoons and volunteers will follow one hundred yards behind the scouts who will be less noisy and less visible than the soldiers."

"I'll signal," said Kit, "as soon as I'm in sight of the camp. I'll lead at a trot from here because we're close. When I signal, I'm headed into their camp at the gallop looking for Mrs. White. The scouts will run through the camp and try for the pony herd."

"Good," agreed the major. "The dragoons and the rest of the volunteers will engage their warriors leaving the scouts free to move through the camp. I will order the battery to fire beyond the camp delaying any retreat in that direction, and delaying the pony herd with luck."

Kit thought for a moment. "Speed is everything. Don't let the dragoons get bogged down at the edge of camp fighting the Apache rear guard. Charge straight on behind me and ride hard into the heart of the camp looking for Ann White and her baby. That will confuse their defense. Braves will run to protect their families instead of the village."

The major called together his officers and explained the plan, then gave them time to pass the word to their men. Finally, he gathered the full battalion: scouts, artillery, New Mexicans, mountain men and *paisanos*, and 1st Dragoons.

He spoke. "Mr. Carson and Mr. Leroux have explained the prairie is, as you can see, very open and flat here with little cover. They think the enemy's sentinels will see us about the time we spot their camp. The enemy is very close.

I think we can afford to move at the trot this morning even though our mounts are worn. Our stock will not be too tired to gallop when we find the Indians' camp. Our best hope is to move fast and be upon them before they can react. With luck, the sentinels are tired and bored. Mr. Leroux thinks they may have grown careless and lazy. They have seen nothing behind them for a long time. In such circumstances, men grow careless. We must charge among them, slaying any who resist before they can organize a defense. We must be so horrible and swift that they think only of flight."

At dawn, the battalion moved out at the trot following Kit, who was looking, listening, and smelling the air. He looked for smoke for he knew the Apache had become careless with their cook fires. He looked for birds that would try to scavenge the fringes of the Jicarilla village. He sniffed for smoke and listened for the sound of children playing and women arguing. He followed their fresh tracks. He needed a little luck. Periodically, he adjusted his course. He rode at a steady canter. Roque and Danny with the scouts rode behind him using all of their senses as well. Alongside them, the battery's guns bounced over the open terrain. Moving apace, the dragoons and the remainder of the New Mexicans— mountain men and *paisano*—came last.

Kit stopped, like he'd hit a tree limb. He stood in the stirrups. He pointed ahead and then signaled, pointing to the scouts and then to their right to a hill half a mile away. Danny and Roque saw them at the same time, ponies, lots of them! Danny saw three Jicarilla close to Kit at the edge of a fold in the terrain running for cover. They were the sentinels, Danny realized, and they had seen Kit. All of the scouts showed signs of seeing the village now or at least seeing the smoke and the very top of the tepees less than a quarter of a mile ahead.

Kit signaled the battery to move to his left and indicated where he wanted fire. He turned in the saddle, signaled for the charge, and then galloped toward the camp.

Off to Kit's right, Danny and Roque galloped toward the pony herd. Verde followed. The three of them might stampede the ponies, thereby denying the Indians escape. Danny pondered something the major had said one evening at campfire: "No plan survives contact with the enemy." They hadn't planned to take the ponies this way, but the opportunity had presented itself.

The dragoons and the volunteers started their assault. They moved into a line, drew sabers and pistols, and started forward with speed steadily increasing from trot to gallop. The dragoon line remained dressed and as a solid mass, it would strike the camp a resounding blow. The New Mexicans were soon strung out but would be deadly once they closed with the Indians. The dragoons' guidon fluttered, urging the cavalry into battle. Sabers flashed. It was a fine, beautiful sight to see in the clearing mist of a November morn. The assualt was done in near silence except for the drumming hooves. Unable to resist the spectacle, Danny kept looking over his shoulder. He saw the major signal his bugler to hold back the call. It would come with more shock, Danny thought, if heard first unexpected on the edge of the camp.

The Jicarilla sentinels started firing at Kit. They had bows and arrows and old fusils. At least one was firing a rifle, a good plains rifle. From the sound and what Danny could see, it might have been an older flintlock, but it was still a rifle. They fired, reloaded, and fired again.

Kit was ahead of everyone, charging into danger alone as he had done countless times before. The scouts were right behind him and the dragoons behind them.

Admiring the fluttering guidon, Danny watched as the dragoon commander, Major Grier, flew from his horse. One moment, he was there charging forward the next his horse was charging alone having ridden out from under the major. Danny had never seen a man hit so solidly by a bullet and it took him a moment to realize what had happened. The bullet had stopped the major but not the horse.

The line faltered. Men looked back. Leroux sprang from his horse and was at the major's side. Major Grier rose from the ground clearly shaken, but apparently uninjured. Leroux called a halt, and the dragoons stopped in mid charge. At a nod from the major, the bugler sounded recall. Sergeant O'Malley rode after the scouts, signaling them to break off and pull back. On O'Malley's signal, another soldier rode out to stop the artillery battery.

Kit was almost on top of the sentinels charging completely alone, one man against a tribe. He sensed something had changed, was wrong. The beat of one hundred horse's hooves behind him had stopped. Kit turned in his saddle. Alarmed and disgusted, the scout rode back to where Major Grier stood with Leroux.

There was mayhem in the Jicarilla camp. People ran in all directions. Ann White searched for her child but could not find her. Order was being imposed on the camp. The men had begun to run in the same direction. Ann looked that way and saw a man on horseback galloping toward her. Even from a distance and atop a horse she could tell he was a small man. It wasn't Kit Carson, she supposed, come to save her, but she ran toward him anyway. He'd help her find the child who would be kept safe by the Jicarilla woman until Ann came for her. But her savior was alone she saw as he reined in his horse, turned and galloped back toward the mass of soldiers. She ran toward him anyway.

As Danny rode up, he heard the major saying, "We have been seen. We should negotiate."

It was plain to see he was shaken. Danny looked for a bloody wound and couldn't find it. The major's heavy gloves were tucked into his tunic.

Major Grier jerked the gloves out and rubbed his sore chest. "They saved my life!"

Leroux guessed what had happened. "Must have been a spent ball from a fusil. Probably misshapen. The Apache cut a piece of lead and chewed it into shape. By the time it got here, it didn't have enough power to go through the major."

It wasn't an aimed shot that had taken him off his horse, at least not aimed at him. The range was far too great. It was a spent round lacking energy. It had hit his chest upon the heavy rawhide gloves, which had stopped the bullet. For him, it had been like being hit in the chest with an axe handle, blunt but painful.

"Makes a man ponder his mortality," said Verde. It had done that to the major.

Roque looked at him. "I'd never call him a coward. In other circumstances, he has always been brave."

"Perhaps," said Danny, "On this day, in these moments, he was shaken, and his courage has departed him for a time." He was thinking darker thoughts. Had the major, Leroux, or O'Malley called off the charge? When an officer goes down, the next man in the chain of command is supposed to take over and continue the charge. Depending how one looked at it, the next in command was either Leroux or O'Malley. Both seemed to have agreed on a halt: Leroux because he said they should negotiate, O'Malley for more subtle personal reasons. Danny shook his head, thinking O'Malley's motivation was so that he could change his drawers. Leroux had signaled the halt, and O'Malley had assisted.

Kit galloped up sliding his horse to a stop and dismounting in one motion. "We must continue now. Mrs. White is in danger. We must take the camp before they run." As excited as he obviously was, Danny noticed Kit didn't raise his voice more than was needed to be heard.

"Look," said Leroux, "there goes the pony herd."

Danny saw it was true.

"The warriors are lining that hill," someone yelled. This too was true. It was too late.

"Take heart!" cried Kit. "We'll still ride over the top of them. We must do it for the woman and her child."

"They have seen us. They are taking action to defend their camp. We no longer have surprise on our side. We must negotiate," said Leroux flatly.

"We will negotiate," said a badly shaken Major Grier.

Hearing the Major's words, Verde rode up to the major and threw his saber and pistol on the ground in disgust.

And so the battalion stalled there on the prairie while the Apache camp emptied of women and children. The would-be rescuers watched as the ponies were herded away, and as the line of warriors facing them began to thin, the Jicarilla formed a new line on the far bank of the Canadian. The Indians retreated leaving their camp furnishings and equipment and equally important their winter supply of preserved food. They crossed over the Canadian River to the south bank. There the second line of defense commanded a broad field of fire that afforded the attacker neither cover nor concealment. If Major Grier had dared challenge this line, the best marksmen of bow and musket would have had ample opportunity to shoot at targets well within their range. It took only moments, but the Jicarilla camp had organized for war.

A few minutes before, the dragoons had been spotted by the Jicarilla camp. Warriors flew to action, ready to defend their families. They saw a single rider coming toward them and behind him a line of many soldiers.

Zapato Negro fired his fine rifle at the lone galloping rider. It was a flintlock taken from a traveler on the Santa Fe Trail who, thanks to Acha and Negro, would never reach his destination. It was an excellent weapon, accurate at many hundreds of paces. The rifle had been made by a skilled craftsman, and with it, he had taken a supply of molded lead ball ammunition and finally corned gunpowder. A ball of uniform weight and size propelled by powder that burned evenly would fly true. Negro had decorated the fine rifle with brass-tacks, fringe, and beads to lend it even more Power. Negro's shot missed the rider, passing close to the scout's head. The rider would have heard the shot, Negro thought, as it whistled by his ear. The shot was sure to land among the many soldiers following the scout. The pony soldiers were beginning their charge two hundred paces behind the lone rider. The Apache warrior smiled. Zapato Negro saw one of the riders fall. The Jicarilla's fine new rifle had Power.

Negro saw the white woman they had captured running toward the rider. Pinacate ran toward her.

"Let her go!" called Negro. "It is more important to defend the camp. Buy us time."

Negro shouted to the *N'deh* sentinels that he would return with help, and then he ran through the Jicarilla camp shouting to rouse the Apaches. Outside the tepee of Lobo Blanco, the chief was already armed and ready.

"Lobo Blanco," Zapato Negro cried, "we are attacked. There are more than fifty pony soldiers coming, perhaps one hundred."

Lobo Blanco took in the situation at a glance. Although it would have looked like bedlam to a stranger, Lobo saw the order underneath. Dogs barked and ran, women shouted, babies cried and screamed. The Apache, a warlike people, were always prepared for battle. From the sound of the first rifle shot and first shouts from Zapato Negro, men roused themselves rapidly, ready for battle as they came to their feet. Each knew his task. They fought as individuals, but there was underlying pattern. The young boys knew the ponies were their task. Seeing the direction of the attack, the boys gathered the herd and moved it out of reach of enemies. Women and girls gathered little children and the old along with whatever clothing and food they could. They ran toward the pony herd. Among the Jicarilla, women rode horses alongside their men. Men ran toward the fight to buy time for others.

The Jicarilla had many scattered, well-favored camps. Their people camped in places they had camped before. Since their grandfathers' grandfathers' time, they had known these camps. Long ago, they had worked out ways to defend each camp. They grew up knowing the plan of defense for each. It was taught to young men as children. Girls learned which trees and shrubs would bear fruit in which years and under what conditions of weather. Jicarilla children learned of concealed camps, hidden trails, and secret places where water and food could be found. All learned what to do if attacked.

Lobo Blanco repeated the outline of the plan for those nearest him. A young warrior ran to his chief, "Acha, gather the men to form a line of defense. Soon we will form a second line across the river by pulling men from the first line. Charge the enemy if you can. Force the Mangani to be wary of us. I will be there soon. Negro, gather the boys and send them to the pony herd. When the ponies are safe, come to me."

In the havoc of the camp, Lobo Blanco made sure all was going according to plan. He saw the ponies start across the river. He ran toward the fight.

As Lobo Blanco arrived at the front, Acha reported to his chief, "A small group has tried to attack us, but we have attacked them and run them off several times. The large group is afraid of us. They sit there out of bow shot and wait. Perhaps we can charge them and drive them off?"

Lobo Blanco turned to José Largo who had arrived moments before, "Will you take thirty warriors to the other bank of the river? I will send more soon." Largo nodded his agreement and began to collect warriors to take with him.

Saco Colorado joined Chief Blanco, "Why do they not charge? What holds them back?"

"I do not know," replied Blanco. "Perhaps Power is with us. Perhaps they see us and fear the Jicarilla as the *Nakaiyeh* do."

Leroux took his negotiating party forward three times.

Each time they were driven back. Each time they found fewer Jicarilla to fire on them. The last time Leroux went forward, he saw that most of the Jicarilla were already across the river.

Watching Leroux's attempts at negotiation Kit fumed, but he said nothing. Verde, Roque, and Danny stood beside their horses watching the spectacle.

"They've taken her with them. We'll catch up again and rescue her, maybe tomorrow," Danny told Verde and Roque. "They had time. They didn't need to kill her."

"*Mañana*, for sure," nodded Roque. His look was not encouraging.

Danny didn't think Roque Vigil believed what he was saying. The four companions knew beyond doubt that their best chance at rescue had been lost and could not be recovered. After weeks of campaigning, they had ridden hard for two days, hazarding all on catching the Jicarilla that morning.

"Our horses are spent," said Verde. "None of the stock will last much longer. The horses need to rest and feed. They need to be reshod."

Roque nodded. "We will not be able to do much more. Horses will start to die under us if we pushed them much harder."

Even Danny was despondent. "This was our one chance, and they muffed it."

Finally, Grier's battalion rode at a walk forward into the abandoned camp. The last of the Jicarilla rear guard was retreating to the far bank of the river. Soldiers fired on them. When shots came near, the Apache reeled as if stricken. A brave would fall only to disappear and crawl to another spot.

Danny saw a large man, maybe Acha, jerk as if hit in the head and go down. Riding to the spot where he'd had seen the big Indian, Danny found that there was no one there. Apache cat and mouse.

An arrow flew past Danny's head with a sound like a cat's hiss. Another and another flew from a bowman under the bank of the river. Fisher, one of the mountain man scouts, spurred his horse forward. The bowman turned splashing to swim his way across the river. Riding up beside the Apache, Fisher felled him with a single shot. As the fleeing enemy went down, Danny recognized Pinacate.

The Jicarilla camp was completely disordered. The Indians had been preparing breakfast. Pots were tipped over, their contents spilt on the ground. Fires still burned. Skins, robes, bags, and weapons were scattered about.

"Gather it all together," ordered Major Grier. His composure had returned and his color. "Leave the tepees. We'll burn them in place."

Thirty dwellings stood along the north bank of the river. The tops of the tepees were dark with soot and with the grease of cooking fires. They would burn well.

The men of Grier's battalion found a large supply of jerked meat, corn, and acorns. They'd captured not only Jicarilla tepees and winter robes but also the Indians' stored supply of food as well. Dressed meat was strung up to jerk, the result of a recent buffalo hunt.

Verde called, "I've found a pile of woman's clothing. Looks like a lady from the States was here."

They found other things that must have come from the White party, but there was more than could be accounted for from that source alone. Acha must have been raiding travelers for a while.

"Major Grier, we should pursue them," said Captain José Valdez of the New Mexico Volunteers. "At least, let me take the volunteers and maintain contact." It was only a few minutes since the Jicarilla had crossed the river. Valdez had sent riders to the far bank. They found no one there. It was already safe to cross.

"Go. Keep in contact with me. We will follow shortly," replied Grier.

Captain Valdez rode ahead with about thirty men of his unit and a few dragoons. Anyone who had a horse that wasn't blown went with him. After two days of hard riding and two weeks of hard campaigning, few of the horses were in good shape. The rest of the battalion had business to attend in camp.

A young sergeant, the company clerk of the Volunteers, found a small book and called it to Kit's attention. It was a paper volume of cheap construction of the kind called "dime novels."

"*Kit Carson: Prince of the Gold Hunters* by Charles Averill," read the young sergeant. He was one of the few volunteers who could read and write. "Do you know him, Mr. Carson?"

"Call me Kit, and I never heard of him. I've never hunted gold either much less been a prince," replied Kit.

"The book must have belonged to Mrs. White," the young sergeant proceeded to read aloud to the rescuers on the north bank of the Canadian.

He read, to Kit's great embarrassment, the story of how Kit had tracked Indians through blinding snowstorms and across trackless deserts. The assembled mountain men and soldiers listened enthralled to Kit's feats. They know him, thought Dan, but they still love hearing these tall tales, stories they must know are impossible. Kit fought off hundreds of hostile natives to rescue maidens in distress. On each page, Kit slew a dozen more Indians.

Verde snickered, "At the rate Kit's killin' Injuns the West will run out of natives long before it runs out of buffalo."

"And," added Danny, "just one man was doing all that killing. Imagine what would happen if he had help."

There was nothing the storybook Kit couldn't do. He was an incomparable hero, a mythical figure on the scale of a Greek god, Danny thought, but hollow, empty, a selfish murderer out only for himself. The storybook Kit rescued maidens because they swooned in his arms. The real man rescued maidens because, having the abilities he'd learned, he was able and felt obliged. Suddenly, the real Kit seemed to Danny so much more heroic than his counterpart.

Flames crackled around them in the Jicarilla camp as tepees burned. Before them, a mound of stolen goods, Jicarilla possessions and dried meat and corn blazed.

"Throw that book on the fire with the rest," urged Kit. "It's a pack of lies. I've never been near most of those places and never heard of them women much less rescued them. Please, throw it on the fire where it belongs."

Danny noticed Rodado Verde grinning and making faces. He's working himself up to cruel witticism, Danny thought, and then poked Verde hard in the ribs. For once, the little man remained silent.

"No," came a wail the like of which Danny hoped never to hear again, "*Madre de Dios!*" The roar of pure anguish came in Roque's voice. He was a little distance from the camp in the direction the attack had come from, near where

Kit had turned from his initial charge. Roque knelt in a screen of brush. The brush had concealed his discovery until now.

Men gathered around Roque where he knelt sobbing over the body of a woman struck by a single arrow. She had blonde hair and wore a white woman's clothing. They had found Ann White at last. The body was still warm.

"She must have seen me coming," cried Kit. "I charged, and she run toward me trying to escape them."

The others—mountain men and soldiers—understood, as well. She had been trying to escape toward her rescuers, toward Kit. She'd been shot in the back. The arrow had pierced her heart.

"If only we had continued the charge, we would have saved her," Kit lamented.

The young sergeant of Volunteers approached with the book still clutched in his hand. Kit saw it and looked stricken. He bowed forward, his arms wrapped about his stomach as he sorrowed. When he lifted his head, the gathered men could see his eyes were red. Kit rose and pointed, arm trembling, toward the book, *Prince of the Gold Hunters.* He seemed unable to find voice, so disturbed was he. Regaining his composure Kit looked at Ann White's body.

Ann White was a rag doll with half its stuffing missing. Her body was emaciated and badly bruised. Knees and elbows were torn. Her eyes were sunken, her cheeks hollow. Her shoeless feet were ripped and bleeding. Mrs. White had suffered exceedingly during her captivity. Whether she was tortured or not, none could honestly say. Danny Trelawney thought not and concluded others' hints at certain knowledge were born of bias. He had met the Jicarilla and they seemed likable folk. Ann White was beaten and forced to keep up on foot. Danny was certain of that judging from the condition of her feet. She hadn't been fed very well. She lay there in her ragged and filthy dress.

"She's been raped over and over by every man in the tribe," said Uncle Dick Wooton.

No one disputed him, though Danny was learning that many white and Mexican prejudices about Indians had no basis in fact. He had to allow that it was possible, but no evidence showed anything more than the woman, unaccustomed to hardship, had come by a hard trail in the hands of captors who showed little mercy.

"This poor lady was tortured," said Kit.

A little puzzled, Danny looked from the body to Kit and then understood that probably the undeserved guilt his friend felt was causing him to see more than was really there.

Uncle Dick spread his guesses as fact. "The braves took her as they wanted. They beat her into submission. They ravished her. The travails she has been through are too horrible to imagine."

"Look at the condition of her body," said Kit. "She is free from the horrors now. Perhaps it is for the best. Her heart and mind might never have recovered.

"She ran toward us. She was game to the end. If she read that book, she would have known I lived near. She would have expected me to come and save her. The book says that I always do. She saw Kit Carson coming and ran toward me. She expected me to save her. I was her hope, and I failed her." He fell silent, his head down in a posture reflecting defeat.

"Her baby and the negro nurse are still out there," said Roque.

Kit rose, going stiffly to his horse, a man in a nightmare. Suddenly his head jerked to the side as he caught sight of something from the corner of his eye. He charged toward a clump of bushes near at hand.

Danny looked and saw Acha rising dazed, tangled in the brush, blood oozing from a gash in his head. He had been hit. It was enough to stun him. The brush had concealed him. Then Kit was on Acha and knocking him back to the ground.

Kit was a fury. It was clear he intended to kill the warrior with his bare hands. Sitting astride the giant, Kit pummeled Acha's face. The Jicarilla's nose flattened under a fist, squirting blood. In moments, his eyes and lips were swollen and bleeding. The pain must have brought Acha back to full consciousness. The Apache's entire body convulsed as he threw Kit off him and sent Kit sailing.

Kit twisted in the air and landed on his feet ready to engage the giant again. Kit's face was unrecognizable, contorted with killing rage but with a light shining in his eyes that said he knew he was God's Sword of Justice about to execute a well-deserved judgment.

They cheered for Kit—the hard men of the mountains and the hard riding dragoons. Of course, they did, Danny thought. Acha had killed Americans. This Jicarilla was the source of much suffering and death. He was a bully who acted on his impulses without thought of consequence. This warrior was big enough to push anyone around. Acha probably had put the arrow in Ann White. Acha had earned retribution, and the Sword of Justice was going to make him pay.

Kit circled. He dropped low with a sweeping kick that caught Acha behind the knee. The Apache fell on his face, and as he rose Kit kicked him in the head and then the ribs. Acha started to rise again and Kit's kick caught him in the belly knocking the wind out of him. The Jicarilla was on his knees, doubled, gripping his stomach, biting the air. Kit grabbed Acha by the hair, pulling the Apache's head up in order to drive powerful blow after blow into Acha's face. Kit's knee came up and caught Acha alongside his jaw with a solid blow that snapped the Jicarilla's head back so far Danny thought his neck must break.

Danny didn't think Kit was aware of any of the men around him. He doubted Kit could hear their cheers. Acha, the bully, was the only thing in Kit's world. This man, Danny finally recognized, was the Kit of legend who slew Indians by the hundreds. This was a side of the gentle, soft spoken Kit that Danny had only glimpsed before and then only under tight control where anger fueled unexpected feats of strength and daring, things Kit often looked back on as having been acts of poor judgment. What Danny was seeing was part of the legend, too. For many, it was what made Kit a hero, a David who slew Goliaths. That look in Kit's eyes was close to a look of ecstasy. Was that how David looked when he killed the giant with a pebble? The rest of his face rivaled the wolf in ferocity.

Kit swung behind Acha who was still on his knees. Kneeling, Acha was as tall as Kit. Kit grasped Acha's head in the crook of his arm ready to break the neck.

Blam! Major Grier fired in the air, "Seize and bind that Apache. We'll take him to Taos to hang!"

No one moved. Kit looked up stunned by the sound of the shot awaking from a bad dream. He still held Acha's head. Roque ran to Kit and helped him release Acha. Dragoons scrambled forward and bound Acha hand and foot.

Major Grier's battalion buried Ann White there by the Canadian in the midst of the burning Jicarilla camp. They rode their horses over the top of the grave to conceal its location. Danny thought this action was unnecessary. Rojo had told him the Jicarilla had a dread of the bodies of the departed. No one would find the grave to disturb her deserved rest or to steal what little she had left. No one would disturb her dignity anymore. When the last trump sounds, thought Dan, she'll find herself alone and lonely with a long walk ahead of her. The battalion crossed the Canadian, and after a short while ran into Captain Valdez and his party returning.

"They easily outdistanced us, sir," Captain Valdez reported to Major Grier. "Their ponies were fresh. Our horses are spent. Then they broke into small parties like quail. There was no way to continue pursuit."

Major Grier nodded his understanding. Danny thought, even Kit knows the campaign is over.

Major Grier led his men along the banks of the Canadian all that day, November 17, and ordered camp pitched that night amidst cottonwood trees. The men, released from the need for concealment, made fires and were warm for the first time in days. They ate hot food and their bellies were full although their hearts were empty. Despite the meal, they were not happy. They did not sing. Despite the fires, they were cold inside.

Kit mumbled to Dan, "It will be hard on them." He nodded toward Leroux and the major. "They know they were wrong. They know she could have been saved if we'd just followed through with the attack. There she was, still warm and running towards us."

Danny Trelawney thought it was going harder with Kit

than with the other two, even though he'd been right. Being Kit, Danny knew, he would torture himself, thinking that there might have been one little thing he might have done better, for instance, Kit might have concealed his skill from Major Grier more effectively, allowing Laroux to shine a bit more in his commander's eyes.

Chapter 13

Desolation on the Plains

Peregrino Rojo went south with his friends into the Galisteo Basin. Finishing their sweep on November 18, they crossed the Rio Grande undetected between Cochiti and Santo Domingo. They disguised themselves as Navajo, which was not difficult, for they struck only at night. The shepherds expected the Navajo because the Navajo had always raided them. Rojo sought the herds of the *haciendados ricos* where he would find hirelings tending the sheep. They were the largest herds, easy to identify even in the dark. Shepherds slept without setting watch so it was easy to disappear with their sheep.

The Apache did not like to move about at night. They feared what might be out there, such as ghosts and other dark creatures that thrive on darkness. Fear of evil spirits did not stop Rojo and his friends. They turned the fear around

336 // Doug Hocking

and used it. The Apache companions thought of tricks to make the shepherds see ghosts and witches. Mexican sheep men were afraid of the dark, more so than the Apache. For them, the night held not only ghosts and witches, but also wolves, mountain lions and, most fearful of all, Apaches. The shepherds feared anything *cimarron*, wild, and the dark night was *cimarron*. The Jicarilla raiders made sounds like wolves to frighten the shepherds, but never did they use the cry of an owl. Owls were the bringers of death. The cry of the owl had death in it.

In a few nights' work, Rojo's raiders had gathered more than five hundred sheep. They headed west across the shallow Rio Grande toward the Rio Puerco that flowed out of the west from the land the Navajo called *Dinetah*, the Land of the People. When they were far enough west of the Rio Grande to make pursuers believe them Navajo, they turned north into the Jemez Mountains. Rojo and his friends worked their way along the Parajito Plateau toward Pedernal and the Piedre Lumbre.

The journey went well at first. The grass was not fresh, but it was plentiful and accessible to the sheep. They made the sheep run in the daytime and let them feed at night. The nights were cold, but nothing the raiders were not used to. Soon they would settle into their winter tepees.

On November 18, the day after the dragoons' "attack" on the Llanero village, Kit, Roque, and Danny headed west with the soldiers on the north bank of the Canadian. Leroux advised Major Grier to follow the river to its confluence with the Mora and then follow the Mora into Las Vegas. They rode slowly, dejected, on horses exhausted from the campaign. There was no need to push them now. They'd pushed them enough. To the last man, the battalion's only sense of urgency was to get home to a warm bed and a good meal.

The temperature dropped alarmingly during the day. The sky became completely overcast, dropping lower until it felt like a man could reach up and touch the roiling clouds. There were spirits in those clouds, evil spirits. It was like watching an angry mob overhead. Faces would appear screaming soundlessly for a moment and then disappear back into the mob, their place taken by others. The battalion was surrounded, hemmed in, and still the clouds came closer. The wind picked up, making the plains ever colder. That's when the voices began to call out from the sky. They murmured at first, and then grew louder. They whistled and shrieked. The wind spoke with as many voices as there were faces in the clouds. Each cloud canyon had its own windy voice. Where wind blew close between boulders and down ravines, new voices arose. Every tree and bush added a new tone. Even the grass spoke in that wind. The clouds glowered and accused. They reminded the soldiers of their failure.

The captive looked terrible. Acha's hands were bound to the saddle and his feet bound to the stirrups. He was a giant of a man and looked even larger atop a horse. It's hard to say how aware he was of his circumstances or even if he were really completely conscious. Both eyes were swollen shut. His nose was askew and his lips swollen so badly he couldn't eat, at least, he refused the food that was offered. Perhaps he feared what the soldiers might feed him. Even his ears were swollen. From the sound of his breathing, Danny thought Kit might have broken a few of Acha's ribs.

On November 18, as the dragoons struggled with the

approaching storm, Lobo Blanco and the other Llanero chiefs sent out riders to retrieve caches. The Llanero way was mobile. They couldn't carry everything with them when they moved, so they made caches and cysts, waterproofing them as best they could. These might be in a cave or rock shelter or in the banks of an *arroyo,* a dry streambed. They placed in storage food too bulky to be carried with the highly mobile tribe. Extra camp gear, old tepees nearly worn out with age, ammunition, and things they had traded for but couldn't sell right away went in as well. They were clever in preparing their storage, making it waterproof and difficult for rodents to invade.

These caches made it possible for raiders to travel light and fast. They didn't need slow moving wagons to follow them with food and tents and extra clothing. The Jicarilla didn't even need to lead pack animals. They would ride hard to a cache and then stop, eat, restock ammunition, and move on as fast as before.

The loss of the camp was a disaster, but caches would help. The *N'deh* would be cold and perhaps wet until they had gathered robes and bedding from storage. Then there wouldn't be enough to go around. Each tepee would be very crowded, which would be uncomfortable though warm. There wouldn't be enough food, but at least the people would not starve yet. February and March, the starving time, of the coming winter would be terrible unless fortunes changed dramatically.

Lobo Blanco thought about the ill-fortune of his people and about the starving time that would surely follow. He hoped there might still be a fall hunt. His people had their ponies and their weapons. There would have to be a hunt, or many would starve and many would freeze this winter. He looked to clouds that lowered and heard the wind growl. It would be very cold soon.

Saco Colorado joined Lobo. "We must find shelter soon. Old woman *Chíníí Hádiséí,* Dog that Sings (Coyote Woman), says it will snow and then be very cold. The cold will surpass anything we have seen in our lifetimes. The Power of Storm is with her. Dog that Sings is never wrong," declared Colorado.

Lobo Blanco nodded. Their luck had not changed yet. "Let us go to Rock Grows Overhead Screened by Many Trees. The rock shelter is large enough for all of us, and there is much fuel for fires," said Blanco.

"I will see what the others think," replied Colorado. "There may still be *piñon* nuts, acorns, and choke cherries to gather near there as well."

Power seemed to have deserted the Llaneros, Lobo Blanco thought. They should scatter in small bands. It would be easier for them to live. Nevertheless, they needed the buffalo hunt. They were on the Llano Estacado, the Staked Plains, where there was danger from the Comanche. They needed to stay together at least for a little while longer.

The Jicarilla woman walked clutching a white baby. She trembled with fear. The *Mangani* were fearsome, relentless enemies. Right now, she was cold, hungry, and tired. She would protect the white baby as long as she could, but she did not know how long that would be. The gray, swirling clouds looked ready to swallow her entire band taking the Indian woman and the small child away. She stooped and lowered the child to the ground. For a while, the two walked hand in hand, side by side.

Riding surrounded by soldiers, Acha didn't look any better the next day, November 19, as the battalion headed west across the plain toward the mountains. The skies were much as they had been the day before, dark and evil and roiling above them.

Kit rode up alongside Danny whose attention was on Acha.

"Yesterday, I could have beaten him to death," Kit said, "and felt fine about it. I don't feel good about taking him to be hung. He's caused some bad things to happen. He's a bully, but he's also a soldier like us."

Danny thought for a moment. "I understand. He was defending his village, sure, but someone murdered Ann White."

Kit nodded. "We don't know it was him."

"Someone should die for it." insisted Danny. "Might as well be him."

The rode silently side by side for a while, and then Kit spoke, "I used to think like that. I'm not so sure anymore. It's one thing to take a life in battle. It's another when you've time to think about the causes and consequences and see he's a lot like you, and you're taking something you can't give back."

He turned aside to ride alone, nearby but too far away for talk.

Roque who had been listening to the conversation saw Danny's puzzlement at Kit's remarks and said, "Things happen in the heat of battle. If we'd ridden into their camp at the charge, we would have killed some of them and might have killed some women and children who got in the way. But that's war. We would have saved that woman. Kit told you Acha made some bad things happen. He's a bully who chased ambition to be a war leader and made a lot of trouble."

"But Roque," Danito persisted, "Kit feels responsible, too. If Kit hadn't made Acha look the fool at Rayado, Acha wouldn't have picked the fight at Go Jii Ya. If Acha hadn't made Kit angry by being a bully, Kit might not have beaten him so badly. Then Acha might not have tried to kill us at Abiquiu and in the *Sangre de Cristo*. Intentionally or not, Kit foiled his plans over and over. He might have walked away from the White party if his leadership hadn't been in question."

"In the end," said Roque, "we are all responsible for our own actions, not those of others. Acha is responsible for what he did. Kit isn't.

"For all he did, though, Acha is still little more than an ambitious soldier looking out for his people," Roque said quietly. "Think about what we did. To teach the Apache a lesson, we burned their camp and stored food. They will have a very hard winter. Children and the old will die of cold and hunger. Are we so much better than Acha?"

Danny seemed startled at this thought. "Children will die? You're not saying we shouldn't have, are you?"

Certain of his position, Roque answered immediately. "Of course not. We had little choice. If we don't make them a lesson, they will feel they can take whatever they want, whenever they want. We cannot take their leaders to court and put them in jail, so they all suffer for the crimes of those who lead them. It is always so in war."

Danny thought about Roque's words for a few moments. "Are you sure what they did was a crime? The Jicarilla need to eat and travelers take their game. Acha went to collect a toll. That seems fair. Someone killed an Apache, and they responded in kind."

Roque was troubled by this thought. He was coming to the end of his ability to philosophize. The Mexican was big and brave, and no one could ask a truer friend. He had a deep feeling for right and wrong and knew what they had done was necessary. He said, "The response was out of proportion."

Danny replied, "We don't know that. James White killed one, Acha killed one, and the fight became general. At least, they spared the women and children. You said if we had charged, we might have killed women and children."

Roque spluttered. "We attacked to rescue *Señora* White! They made her a slave!"

"We keep slaves," Danny said quietly, "and we might have killed women and children."

Rodado Verde heard them talking and interrupted, "It happens. A whelp runs in your path, you'd like to turn, but if you do, that warrior ahead will bless you with an arrow. Or a woman grabs your arm to protect her man, and you have to shoot her or let him take you. It's battle. If you must make war, some will die, even the innocents."

"Kit would have beaten Acha to death yesterday," Danny said.

"That's war, too," said Verde. "When you let the creature out of its cage, sometimes it's hard to put it back. I doubt Kit knew Acha was past fighting back. He's glad now that we stopped him."

Roque nodded his agreement.

Verde continued, "And the most wonderful thing of all is that little book they found. Kit Carson feels an obligation to a woman he's never met because a writer he's never heard of writes a book that promises Kit would have come and saved her." He chuckled. "Now that beats all. Of all the saints of Ireland, not one ever felt such obligation. 'Tis a thing of glory to know such a man, an honor and a privilege." Verde, who seemingly respected no one, saw in Kit a saint and a hero.

Danny Trelawney was stunned but nodded his agreement.

"War is a puzzlement, boyo," Verde resumed. "Where two sides don't share the same idea of law and right, it becomes necessary to draw a wee line in the sand and say, 'You can come this far, but do further.'"

Major Grier rode back along the column and took a place beside Kit. The two leaders conferred for a few minutes and then Danny and Roque heard Kit say, "We should release Acha. He is a soldier like us protecting his family. He shouldn't be hung for it."

"I can't release him," responded the major. "He's all we've got to show for this campaign. The men would rebel. They want to see him hung. My superiors will want to offer him to the people."

"You know it isn't right," continued Kit. "We don't hang soldiers."

"I know," replied Major Grier.

The wind picked up making conversation impossible. All along the column men turned up their collars, but the wind still found openings. The temperature dropped alarmingly. Men brought out their blankets and wrapped them about themselves as they rode. Then the snow started to fall. It piled up fast on a plain already chilled by the wind. Soon, they were slogging through six inches of fresh powder with drifts much deeper in the low places and where anything impeded the wind. The snow hid holes, rocks, and low spots. Horses began to stumble over things unseen below the snow.

About midday, the clouds descended and brought the blizzard with them. It became impossible to see from rider to rider. The man ahead and the one to the side disappeared in a white haze. It was dark and the world swirled with white. At times, a man couldn't see his hand in front of his face. Most of the time, Danny could see his horse's ears, but nothing beyond that.

Kit rode back down the line. For a moment, his face was close to Danny's. "Danny," he said, "grab onto a strap on Roque's saddle or his horse's tail. Don't let it go. Keep hold on it no matter what. Verde will hold onto your horse and someone else to his. Stay together and don't go to sleep. If you fall asleep, you'll freeze."

When the wind allowed, Danny caught snatches of Kit's voice passing this message to others. Danny overheard another snatch of conversation. It was Kit telling the major that the battalion needed to head for the first available shelter.

The snow may have stopped falling. They were pushing through what to Danny seemed to be two feet of snow, with more in the drifts. He noticed it wasn't getting any deeper. It can't get really cold when there are clouds overhead. They act like a blanket and hold the earth's heat to the ground. Only when the earth is open to the stars can the cold really set in. The temperature dropped down below freezing and beyond frigid. It was the cold that turned metal and ears brittle and fingers and toes black. Danny knew about the warmth in clouds and unable to see the stars, sighed in relief even as his breath turned to frost. The wind continued to blow the snow.

The driven snow was still as thick as a snowstorm, though above, if Danny could have seen them, the icy stars were twinkling. His hand feeling frozen shut still grasped the tail of Roque's horse.

In such weather, feelings defy description. Danny was totally alone, isolated by snow and a screaming wind. He was cold to the marrow. Limbs and joints ached with it. His feet and hands cramped with excruciating pain that could only be relieved if the cold made them numb and dead. Breathing was difficult. The cold seared lungs with every breath, burning like he had swallowed a red-hot knife. Danny's breathing became shallow and slow as he inhaled through his nose, which burned and dripped with the effort until long frozen stalactites hung past his chin. His bones began to ache from the cold.

Roque was hunched forward on his horse. Both were white with frost and blown snow. His horse's tail seemed a frozen, solid pole extending from Danny's arm forward. Roque might have been frozen in place, a lump on the back of a slowly moving horse. Only puffs of fog emitted near his head to rise to freeze gave any indication of life.

Listening to the constant shriek of the wind was not hearing. The howling made hearing impossible. Looking at nothing but swirling snow was not seeing. Danny's eyes might have been frozen shut for all he could see. He wondered if he were still alive. How could he tell? In this frozen world, there was nothing to smell or taste. After while, his body numbed to the cold. There was no input from his senses, just his thoughts, and sometimes they were hard to tell from dreams. Kit had told Danny of the dangers of sleeping, but Danny didn't know if he was awake or asleep. The pain was gone. Death would come with sleep, and Danny could no longer tell waking from dreaming.

The riders knew when others were around them. Danny could sense Roque ahead of him. He clung to the tail of his friend's horse although he could no longer feel the hand that held it. He could sense Verde behind clinging to Danny's horse and life. Danny could sense none of the others around them, ahead or behind. There should have been a rider beside him, but Danny had no awareness of him. The snow and the shrieking wind foiled the usual senses.

Danny lived in nothingness for a very long time. It might have been hours. Finally, he spurred his horse up alongside Roque sliding his closed hand free of the horse's tail and feeling the tug of Verde being dragged along. Unable to use his hand, Danny nudged his friend with a shoulder and placed his face close to Roque's ear.

"Roque, who are you following?" he gasped.

"No one now. I was hanging onto Tobin's horse, but my horse and his stumbled, and we separated. I haven't been able to find him since," replied Roque in a voice barely recognizable and distorted by pain and cold.

"How long has it been?" Danny asked.

"A long time," Roque replied.

Struggling to make his numbed brain think, Danny asked, "Do you know where Kit wants us to go?"

"No, and I don't even know if we go straight or if we are making circles," said Roque. "I continue to move because if we do not, we will freeze."

Verde came up on Roque's other side. "I lost the one following me. He was there, then he was gone. It's been a while."

"It's okay," Danny said. "It's the three of us now." They rode on.

Danny felt like he was in a tunnel. He almost expected Jesus to appear at the other end. He'd be waving and inviting him to come home, to come into the light. Danny felt so calm and peaceful. When Death came, he didn't expect the face at the end of the tunnel to be angry, nor did he expect face to be attached to Kit Carson. The shouting face was followed by a mighty slap up 'side the head that dispelled the gathering clouds. Danny began to make out words.

"Wake up! Snap out of it!" Kit shouted. "You'll freeze. Can you hear me?"

Danny nodded. Beside him, he could see Verde and Roque nodding, too.

"Were you headed someplace special? Or would you like to join the rest of us? We're planning to make a fire and get in out of the wind," Kit continued.

"We'll go with you," Danny croaked.

As it turned out, they didn't have far to go, perhaps a mile, no more than that. Danny thought they'd have missed the spot without Kit's help. It was hidden. They'd arrived back at the canyons. That was where Kit was taking them. He gathered the soldier-command in a rock shelter under a lea wall. The wind didn't seem to blow there, but it was still cold.

Only about thirty members of the command had made it. The rest were still missing, still out there somewhere in the frozen abyss.

Kit conferred with the major and Leroux. Then he said to Verde, Roque, and Dan, "Take the saddles off your horses and rub them down as best you can. Then bring them into the shelter with the other horses. Hobble them. When that's done, start stacking up rocks to make a wall to block the wind. In groups, never alone, go out to gather firewood. Make the firewood part of the wall. Build bonfires inside the wall and keep them going. Come in for a while and heat up, then go out and gather wood. Keep moving. Don't sleep. Leroux and I will find the others."

Kit's friends circulated among the others showing them what to do. Soon they had fires going, and it began to get warmer in the rock shelter. It wasn't long before Kit brought in ten more nearly frozen soldiers. Tirelessly, he went back out looking for more.

As he worked, Danny moaned softly with the pain of returning feeling.

Verde overheard. "Reflect, boyo. Freezing may not be the most terrible way to die. Surviving nearly freezing is an experience from hell."

Danny replied. "Next time I will not be in such a hurry to tell Kit, 'I'll go with you.' I will at least consider that dying may be preferable."

Every extremity that was once numb screamed in pain as it returned to life. The experienced mountain men melted snow on the fires. While it was still cold enough to float ice on its surface, they had the others immerse hands and feet.

Plunging a hand in icy water, Danny yelped, "That burns like fire! Did you get the water boiling hot?"

"Aiee!" whined Roque. "It is like the stings of a thousand ants penetrating all the way to the bone."

Verde tried to chuckle, but pain held even his wicked sense of humor in check for a change. "Rub your hands, feet, noses and ears," he managed. "Don't get too close to the fire."

"*Viejo*," groaned Roque. "Do you think I could? The pain is too great." He opened his coat and shirt and held his cold hands in his armpits.

In time, they placed aching, frozen feet on each other's naked stomachs to warm them.

Cheeks and noses, any exposed skin, blistered as if burned and the skin fell away. Here and there, a man had a cheek, a nose, a finger, or a toe that had turned black. Frostbite killed the skin and the extremities, turning hide and limb black. What was black was dead. The Army doctor who travelled with the dragoons was busy removing the black flesh, toe, or finger before the rotting flesh spread poison through the whole body.

"We are fortunate," said the doctor cutting off a black toe. "I haven't had to remove any hands or feet, just the odd finger and toe."

Danny thought himself fortunate; he didn't lose anything, but the parts that had been most cold would trouble him for life. Hands and feet that once were not bothered by the cold would feel it ever after, a reminder of those hellish hours.

One man died. He was one of the company of volunteers and was so cold and so close to eternal sleep when Kit brought him in that his friends never succeeded in awakening him. They pulled him from his horse and set him near the fire. He huddled grasping his knees to his chest and shivered. After a while, the shivering stopped. The doctor checked him, shook his head, and then had them place him out beyond the circle of firelight to finish his long sleep.

Mountain man, settler, Mexican, and dragoon all eventually stripped to expose themselves fully to the fire. Warming, they rubbed their extremities to circulate the blood. When warm, they dressed again in cold clothes only partially dried. They made forays into the frigid night to gather more firewood and help to build their growing wall. Cottonwood, for that is what grew most profusely along the bottoms, burns quickly leaving few coals. After ten or fifteen minutes in the cold, they returned to the fires for a time. No one slept. Movement helped to keep them warm more than lying on the cold rock ever could. They made soup and coffee and fed great bonfires. They built a wall of fire, stone, and firewood against the terrible cold. They moved and kept moving though their bodies cried for rest, but at least their bellies were warmed by hot food. They had seen what happened when a man stopped moving and had no wish to join him in death. As the wind died, the temperature dropped still more.

Danny looked up as he pulled a dead limb from a spot above his head. "Roque, I can see the stars." Once the swirling snow subsided, the sky between the frigid stars was clear.

"Now it will get cold," his *amigo* replied.

In the clear night air, the fires reflecting from the cliff face became a beacon for those still on the plain. The entire cliff face glowed with reflected light.

Kit found some men still riding in great circles. In little groups of two, three, and five, he brought them in. Leroux brought some in, too, but after a while, he became too cold and had to quit. The chief scout, doing as any good man might, came in to stay near the fire. Kit continued to hunt for the battalion's lost men. A few found their way to the light of the fires on their own, though, Kit never quit looking until all were by the fire.

During the night, Danny saw Kit leading Acha's horse.

Acha miserable bound as he was had less freedom to move. A man less fit could not have survived, Danny thought. Perhaps Kit would untie the Indian, but untied, none of the soldiers would be safe near him. Danny was sure that if Acha didn't get circulation into hands and feet, he would get frostbite, and the Jicarilla's limbs would have to be cut off. Danny didn't dare cut him loose. Acha was a very powerful man. He might have killed many of the soldiers. He was certain that Acha was capable of treachery, and if freed and facing a frozen death, he might find pleasure in taking a soldier or two with him into the dark night that Apaches believed followed life. On a night like this with so much confusion, he might wreak havoc. The soldiers were weakened by the cold and their hard night. Danny knew it would be too dangerous to release him.

Later, at the edge of the firelight, where frozen night and death awaited, Danny saw Kit leading Acha away from the fire. The pair was headed away from camp. He had difficulty imagining why. Perhaps Kit intended to kill the Indian, ending his misery and saving him from the rope. It would make the camp safer as well. However, somehow Danny couldn't believe Kit would kill a bound man, no matter how good the excuse. A trick of swirling snow and flickering darkness, Danny concluded. It must have been his tired imagination, some trick of the night. Danny didn't see Acha again near the fire or elsewhere that night.

Before dawn, Kit brought in the last man. The exhausted men watched as Kit led in the horse and rider. Frost clung to the man in a way it had not clung to any of the others. The heat from a body melted snow and frost as it emerged through the clothes, which show a little color because of this rising heat. Dark, damp spots begin to appear. Ice and snow break away where limbs move and disturb it. This soldier was white with ice and frost which clung everywhere about him. Icicles hung below his chin clinging to nose and mustache. There were tiny icicles in his eyelashes. The rider's eyes were open but they did not move. They were flat, pale blue, and dead.

"*Madre de Dios!*" exclaimed Roque crossing himself. "It is a ghost riding."

Men edged away. They would not approach the dead rider.

Kit saw their fear. "Roque, Dan, help me with him."

They removed the dead man from his horse with the greatest difficulty. He was frozen to it and his limbs were stiff and unmovable. They carried him as gently as they could to where he could join the volunteer out beyond the circle of firelight.

In the morning, the major ordered that the frozen men be covered with rocks so wolves would not tear at the bodies. The ground was too frozen to dig graves and the men too stiff to fold over horses' backs.

Major Grier's battalion lost two men to the cold that night. Danny thought that perhaps three we gone, if they counted Acha. He and his horse were missing. No one was sure what had become of him. No one knew who was last to see Acha in the swirling snow. No one remembered who was leading and guarding him. So perhaps they lost three men that cold night.

No one stopped for long to think what might have happened to the Llaneros. That was war, and they had started it, bringing devastation on themselves and their families.

Verde noticed Danny staring off in the direction they'd

last seen the Jicarilla. "They had a hard night. Lot of 'em must have froze. It's hard, but that's how war is."

Danny nodded and then returned to work. He thought it might have been better if they'd killed a few braves and captured most of the rest of the village—better if they'd rescued Ann White. In that case, with Mrs. White alive and vengeance taken on a few warriors, the major might not have ordered the burning of the village.

As he worked preparing his horse for the day's ride, Danny continued his reverie. Kit had been right about a bold attack, and Kit had saved the command. Without Kit's help, not many of Major Grier's soldiers would have survived. Danny didn't know where Kit found the strength or endurance or how he kept himself from freezing, but his strength had saved them all. He looked around the camp and didn't see Acha anywhere. Strange, he thought, and wondered if in the darkness someone had taken revenge for Ann White. Perhaps it was Kit, Danny supposed, who hated bullies, but couldn't imagine the scout attacking a bound man. There were 100 men and horses in the camp. Acha was probably there somewhere.

On the day of the deep freeze, Lobo Blanco's people found shelter in a canyon under an overhanging rock shelter much like Kit had found for Grier's battalion. Having been warned of the storm's coming by old Coyote Woman, the *N'deh* were fortunate to get there before the storm broke. The shelter was in the lea of the wind. They too built up rocks and brush to help cut the wind, and built fires of brush and prairie wood, buffalo chips. The shelter was in more open and exposed terrain with no trees to provide fuel. Even buffalo chips soon disappeared under a blanket of snow.

They didn't have enough robes, blankets, or heavy clothing. There were only a few tepees. There was very little food. Supplies from their caches were coming in, but it would be days before a significant amount arrived.

Saco Colorado walked over to Blanco. "I worry about our young men who have gone to the caches," he said.

"They are clever and know how to take care of themselves. They will seek shelter from the storm," replied Lobo Blanco.

"I am sure they will, but some of them will never return," responded Colorado.

Saco Colorado's prophecy proved correct. Many young men were never seen again. The people of New Mexico never knew how many were lost. The Jicarilla did not speak the names of the dead for fear of calling back the spirits of the departed, for the spirits would bring death and sickness with them. The Jicarilla did not willingly touch the dead. Unlike the whites who keep mementos of the departed, the Jicarilla did not desire to have the favorite possessions of the dead around them. The Jicarilla killed a favorite horse when its rider died, not to give him a horse on the other side, but to keep the rider from returning for it. The *N'deh* did not let a man die within a tepee for fear his spirit would be trapped there.

If someone were to ask, "Where is Zapato Negro?" there would be no reply. He did not return, so his name was no longer spoken. Outsiders can only guess that he died alone and cold somewhere on the *llano*.

The Jicarilla were a modest people, but this night they stripped themselves of almost all their clothing. Some clothing went under them as insulation from the ground.

Most of it went over the top of what robes and blankets they had as additional covering. Underneath this thin and scanty pile, they huddled together, hugging each other for warmth knowing flesh on flesh would provide the most heat. From time to time, the men slipped out to gather the scant wood of low growing brush and add it to their fires.

The pony herd was tethered close to the fires. In cold like this, even the livestock was likely to freeze. The Llanero needed their ponies for the hunt. The buffalo would provide new robes, meat, and skins for tepees. The Llanero needed to kill many buffalo, or all of them were likely to die this winter.

They huddled under the pile of skins and blankets for a day and a half. At midday on November 20, several babies and small children together with two elderly persons, seven in all, were carried by the men a mile or so from camp. They had not survived the long cold night. They didn't have the health and strength of warriors or of their parents and elder siblings. They were laid to rest beneath the bank of an *arroyo*, which was collapsed over them to keep the wolves away. No one spoke their names, but perhaps the Jicarilla remembered them anyway, privately, and never admitting it to their fellows.

Virginia White had survived the night cradled in the warm arms of the Jicarilla woman who had adopted her. She felt the cold and whimpered constantly. The woman thought she looked weak and was sad. The weak were not apt to survive.

On November 19, Peregrino Rojo and his raiders found shelter for themselves and their stolen herd of sheep in Frijoles Canyon below the Parajito Plateau. The canyon was out of the bitter wind with water and grass. It was a good place to be in winter, and people had long recognized it as such. Rojo's friends were nervous. They did not like being surrounded by the ancient homes of dead Pueblo people. The Jicarilla had arrived the day prior and stayed in Frijoles Canyon throughout the storm. They found caves in the cliff wall and made fires to warm themselves, not realizing that these had been carved in the soft rock by ancient ones who had lived here. When the weather cleared a little, they continued their journey north to Abiquiu. Meanwhile a slaughtered sheep made them a hot meal. Soon, they would be able to share that meal with the rest of the Olleros.

On November 21, the little army of dragoons and volunteers started traveling again. The weather was still cold and the snow still deep in places, but it was clear, and they could see the mountains in the distance. Their path was again clear. Kit had travois made to carry the amputees. Long poles were suspended on either side of a horse dragging the ground behind. They were joined by a blanket or robe upon which the injured sat or lay. The invalids were wrapped in furs and blankets, but the cold penetrated anyway. The constant jolting was painful but not as hard as riding. The battalion could wait no longer; food was running out, and another winter storm might strike at any time. Not blessed with those who could foretell the weather, as the Jicarilla were, they lived in uncertainty of when the next storm would strike and how severe it would be. Major Grier's men needed to reach food and shelter.

Danny spurred his horse and rode up beside Kit. "Kit, I thought I saw you with Acha in the night leading him away from camp."

Kit glanced at him darkly. "Hush, don't say his name. He's a Jicarilla and he'll come back and haunt you."

"You didn't kill him, did you?" Danny demanded.

"Don't be silly," said Kit. "You heard me ask the major to release him. You know I felt he was a soldier doing his duty who didn't deserve to be hung."

Danny face forehead knit in consternation. "Did you release him?"

"Are you sure you saw us together?" asked Kit.

"No," said Dan. "There was snow. It was like a dream."

"Why not leave it at that?"

Danny was silent for long while. "Acha couldn't have escaped his bonds. He must have had help."

Kit frowned. "You know how I feel about duty. You know I couldn't have released him without orders. Let it go. The Jicarilla who was captured," said Kit avoiding Acha's name, "is with us no more."

Danny was confused. He didn't think Kit would lie, but his refusal to say the name indicated he was sure Acha was dead. No matter how hard he tried, Danny couldn't picture Kit executing a bound man.

Major Grier reined his horse in alongside them. With a tilt of his head, he urged Kit and Danny out away from the column so that they could speak privately. "Kit," the major said without preamble, "I'm sorry. You were right. We should have ridden straight into the camp. I thought you should know how I felt. I owe you much. You saved us all in the storm."

They rode on in silence for a time before the major could bring himself to speak again. "You were right about Acha, too. It wouldn't have been right to hang him, but the others don't understand."

"Don't say his name," Kit said.

The major rode back to the head of the column. Kit spoke. "Danny, a long time ago when I rode with Captain Fremont, he ordered me to do some things of which I'm no longer proud. I wouldn't do them again, even if ordered." With this enigmatic statement, Kit rode off leaving Danny to his thoughts.

The rest of the ride to Mora, where Kit and his friends parted company with the troops from Taos, was miserable, but uneventful. Anything, human or animal, with any sense had long since sought shelter. Roque, Kit, and Danny rode north toward Rayado. Verde had gone with the troops over the mountains to draw his pay in Taos.

Chapter 14

Home and Family

On November 18, while the Llaneros and the army were still suffering on the plains, Chief Vicenti's Olleros pitched their tepees in a sheltered valley on the western slope of the *Sangre de Cristo*, their home range. They broke up into small, family bands. Sensing the storm that was coming, they prepared for it moving their livestock to sheltered valleys and coves, bringing firewood near the tepees, and digging out their heaviest robes. They would not have to go far to get firewood or food. They would be safe and warm in their homes, sitting around the fire and telling stories to the children until the weather made it possible to move to their winter camps. The Olleros would not eat buffalo this winter, but the lamb and mutton Rojo was bringing would stave off hunger. The mountains of the *Rio Arriba* were crowded with Mexicans, Pueblos, and the newly arrived Mangani. Game had become scarce. Their only alternatives were to hunt the increasingly limited herds of buffalo or to rustle livestock from their neighbors.

On November 26, 1849, Encarnación Garcia rode up to Barclay's Fort at Mora. In the common room, he ordered a drink. Glancing around the room, he saw Alexander Barclay drinking with three men in military uniform. He walked over to them and bowed slightly saying, "*Don Alexandro*, a moment of your time."

Barclay stood, "*Don Encarnación*, I would like you to meet Captain Judd, Lieutenant Burnside, and Sergeant Swartout. Join us."

Garcia sat and said, "I have been on the plains looking for the Jicarilla. *Señor* Calhoun provided me with one thousand dollars to buy Mrs. White back from them. I have not been able to find them. I traveled all over their usual buffalo hunting grounds north and east of Point of Rocks, but there is no sign of them."

"They've been seen," said Captain Judd. "Major Grier passed through here a few days ago with his entire command. They found them, and they found Mrs. White dead."

"*Madre de Dios!*" exclaimed Garcia, "And what of her child and the nurse?"

"Still with the Indians, I guess," replied Captain Judd.

"I don't think they'll feel like trading for them, though," said Sergeant Swartout. "I took Lobo Blanco's daughter out to offer in exchange for Mrs. White. She went crazy and we had to kill her."

Garcia nodded. "That information I heard on the *llano* from *ciboleros* and *Indios*. The word has traveled fast. Lobo Blanco will know by now."

Weeks later and many miles distant in Santa Fe, Francis Aubry, the Skimmer of the Plains, sat in the smoky, low-ceilinged common room of the La Fonda. With him sat Colonel Munroe and Indian Agent Calhoun. Aubry would wait out the winter in Santa Fe before heading back to Independence, Missouri. He would take out a fresh caravan with the first sign of spring. It was mid-December, snow lay on the ground in the City of the Holy Faith.

"I have to admit," said Colonel Munroe, "these adobe houses are warm in winter. They're dirty and the roofs leak, but they are warm in winter."

The door opened, and an uncouth man in greasy, fringed buckskins entered the room. He looked around and then approached Aubry. He threw three scalps on the table. "I hear you'll pay a thousand dollars for information about where to find Mrs. Ann White and her baby."

Colonel Munroe wrinkled his nose at the stench that filled the room around the plainsman.

"You heard wrong," said Aubry calmly. "I'll pay one thousand dollars for her safe return."

The plainsman snorted. "Why I seen her and her baby the other day in a Jicarilla camp. That's where I took these scalps."

"Really?" asked Aubry earnestly. "When was that?"

"Three days ago," the greasy stranger replied. "Not far from here. I could take you there."

Aubry looked coldly at the man. "Mrs. White was killed by the Jicarilla over a month ago. How strange. Perhaps you saw someone else."

The man in buckskin retorted, "It was her. She matched the description perfectly. Maybe you heard wrong about her being killed."

Aubry looked at him without saying anything.

"These scalps should be worth something," the plainsman whined. "I took them at great personal risk."

"Are you sure they came from Indians?" asked Colonel Munroe. "Perhaps I should have you detained pending an inquest into wrongful death of three Mexicans who are missing from Las Vegas."

The greasy stranger exited the room in haste.

"Gentlemen, charge your glasses," said Colonel Munroe and paused. "To the scalp hunters, may they rot in hell."

"What of the baby and the nurse?" Aubry asked his companions. "What will become of them?"

Indian Agent Calhoun responded after careful thought, "We'll hear rumors for years. Someone will always be thinking they've seen her, especially if they think there is money in it. The Jicarilla will treat her well and raise her as one of their own, if she survives the life in the camp. It will be very hard this winter. Many of them will freeze and starve, especially the children. It may sound like a contradiction of what I've said about how they treat children, but they may trade her to another tribe. They'll do that to remove the guilt, so that we don't find them with her."

"Do you think they will kill her because we killed Lobo Blanco's daughter?" Colonel Munroe asked.

Calhoun thought for a minute. "I don't think so. The anger will be old and blunted. Her death was far off."

Peregrino Rojo returned to his father's tepee in the Piedre Lumbre. The night was cold. Something had disturbed the sheep. He went to check on it and found nothing. Perhaps a coyote had wandered near. He slid back under the buffalo robe and cuddled up to the naked, fat Pueblo girl. She would keep him warm for the winter.

In the spring, when she became too warm for his bed, perhaps he would take her back to her family at Jemez. To have used a Jicarilla girl this way would have caused problems in the tribe, but Peregrino Rojo was not ready to settle down with a woman yet. There was too much to see and do in the world. There was too much to learn and try. He would take her back in the spring, he thought, pulling her warm body closer.

He drifted off to sleep thinking about sheep. Lamb wasn't venison, but it had its advantages. Lamb stayed near the tepee until it was time for the slaughter.

Josepha and Teresina welcomed Kit, Roque and Danny back to Rayado like conquering heroes. They prepared a feast of *enchiladas*, *posole*, *calabacitas*, green *chili* stew, *refritos*, and so much more. They ate hungrily after the hard rations they had endured so long on the trail. Hot food has special savor after days of hunger and cold.

After dinner, the men sat by the fire and smoked their clay pipes. Kit was quiet. He was troubled. "I could have saved her if they had listened to me," was all he would say.

Danny pressed an old subject he should have avoided, but it served to distract Kit from his melancholy. "Kit, what became of Acha?"

"Don't say that name." Kit blew a ring of smoke. "I guess he got lost in the storm and froze to death."

"What if he didn't?" Danny continued. "What if he made it back to the Jicarilla? Will he raise a great war party and seek revenge on every settlement and ranch on the eastern slope of the *Sangre de Cristo*?"

Puffing on his pipe, blowing rings, and watching them disappear, Kit pondered this question for a while. "I think not. His time is done. He is discredited as a war leader. He has been shown to have no luck in war, or, as the Jicarilla would say, Power has left him. No one will follow him now. His closest followers are all dead, I think. He will hate loosing his status worse than death."

Josepha worried about Kit. Many times Danny caught her praying at the little shrine she'd made in the house, where he'd hear her mumble *"Cristobal."* Kit knew, and Danny thought it irritated him. Kit's still rejecting any kind of formal religion, he surmised. Danny and Kit came upon her praying, and Kit whispered to Dan, "The black robed ones are another kind of bully that likes to push people around and interfere with their lives."

Then he looked at Josepha and said, "But she's one of God's angels. He knows. He loves her and listens to her prayers. And He expects you and me to be strong and do what's right, no matter what." He smiled then. It was the first time Danny had seen him smile since they had found Mrs. White.

Roque and Danny decided they'd stay and help Kit through the winter. There wasn't really anywhere else to go. An unseasonable warm week permitted them to build their own simple adobe cabin nearby so as not to disturb the family, though neither of them seemed inclined to refuse Josepha's invitation to meals. They never had to cook for themselves. They did, however, get to cut a lot of firewood for the *horno*.

Settled in for the night in their cabin, Danny asked Roque about his plans for the spring.

"I don't know, Danito," Roque said. "Perhaps I will marry someday. Right now, I have no home or property.

How shall I acquire these? Without them, how can I support a wife? I know Mr. Maxwell would sell me some land. He would let me work for it."

Lucien Maxwell had a land grant that covered all of the Jicarilla lands from the *Sangre de Cristo* out onto the hunting grounds on the plains. Danny thought Maxwell was probably the largest landowner in the whole country. All of northeastern New Mexico was his. Lucien was a mountain man who had come to Taos and married the daughter of Carlos Beaubien. Lucien worked with his father-in-law acquiring land through the corrupt governor, Armijo. Maxwell held the deed to Kit's land.

"If you had the land, where would you get the cattle?" Danny asked. "A herd costs money."

Roque grinned. "Peregrino Rojo tells me he can get me a herd very cheap. Perhaps we should talk to him."

"We have a long winter to talk and smoke and think," Danny replied. "Two smart *hombres* like us ought to be able to come up with a plan to make ourselves rich."

"Roque," Danny said after they had smoked and thought deeply in silence, "I worry about Kit. He seems troubled."

"There is a story, Danito," said Roque, "about a general who dressed his army in the finest uniforms and provided them with the finest equipment. He drilled them and disciplined them until they obeyed his every command instantly. The enemy army was smaller than the general's and it was undisciplined and dressed in rags. This ragtag army only did what it was told in battle. At all other times, it was undisciplined drinking, looting, and fighting among themselves.

"The general set up his army on a big hill that blocked

the valley. The enemy had to come through this valley. The general thought this would force his enemy to attack him on ground he had prepared. He had his men dig trenches and checked their lines of fire. He set his artillery so that all the ground to his front was covered. He set out his skirmishers, as a general should. It was a classic defense. It was perfect. When the enemy marched into his front, surely they would all die. There would be no escape.

"The undisciplined enemy did not do as they were supposed to. They found a hidden route by which they passed in single file around to the general's flank and rear. When the enemy attacked, the general's highly disciplined army collapsed. Many died, and many were captured. Only a few, including the general, escaped by running away.

"The general reported back to his king about the wonderful campaign he had fought. He told the king of the best uniforms, equipment, and training. He told the king how ragged and undisciplined the enemy was. The general explained the perfection of his defenses, how every feature was designed to maximize the deaths of the enemy.

"The enemy, the general said, had not known discipline or how to fight correctly. If they had, the general would have defeated them utterly. It was a fluke, a mere chance, that the enemy had destroyed the general's perfect army.

"Kit is not like the general, *amigo*. We have seen Kit do many amazing and wonderful things. He discovered the Jicarilla's trail. No one else could have done that. He followed them for weeks without losing them or letting them know we were coming. Because of him, we never were ambushed in the canyons, the Brakes of the Canadian River. He led us to their camp and we had surprise on our side. If we had attacked then, all would have gone as Kit said.

"The decision not to attack was not Kit's. Others made that mistake.

"In the end, he saved the command from the storm and got most of us back alive. Think of his courage and stamina. Think how many times he went back into the storm looking for half frozen stragglers.

"Now he broods on the loss of Ann White's life because she may have expected him to come. He broods because he fought a bully too well and that may have led the bully to attack others. He feels his duty to others very keenly."

Danny nodded thoughtfully. "Roque, you're right. We are in the presence of a great man. From the moment I mistook you for Kit, I had not been sure how such a small man could be as great as the stories said. Now I see it."

Kit found plenty of work for them. Why not? They were living on his ranch and eating at his table, and they owed him their lives. It was late spring before Roque and Danny had time to get away and cross the mountain for some fun in Taos.

They found Rodado Verde set up in a corner of the plaza making silver and turquoise jewelry. Verde cackled. "Roque, Danny, I see you survived the winter. The very thought of it makes one doubt the existence of divine providence. In a just world, the cold would have taken you both."

Across the plaza, a noise caught Danny's attention. He looked and saw a ghost.

"Roque, look!" Danny blurted. "That looks like Acha."

"That is Acha! And he's very drunk," Roque replied.

Verde grinned. "Oh, he's been here for weeks now. He stays drunk. He pushes the Mexicans around. The Jicarilla who pass by won't even look at him. He is an outcast."

Acha was pushing Mexicans around for fun and laughing. He used his great size to slam the smaller people into walls. He grabbed a bottle of liquor from a Mexican. The Mexican protested and Acha hit the man with a backhand blow that knocked the Mexican to the ground. Acha tilted back his head and drank. The Mexican sat on the ground brooding.

Verde addressed the Mexican loudly across the plaza so all could hear. "What's the matter with you? Ain't you got no *huevos*? That big drunk stole your whiskey. Everybody saw it. Now everyone will know you haven't got any *cajones*. Everyone will feel free to push you around. That's your whiskey. Why don't you go and get it?"

"Verde, shut up," Danny pleaded. "Can't you see he feels bad enough? Don't make it worse."

Verde's words had already struck home. The Mexican leapt up and pulled his big knife. In one quick move, he cut Acha's belly open from side to side above his belt.

Acha cuffed the Mexican again, sending him reeling, and then roared in pain. Acha's intestines started to leak out. He dropped his bottle and grabbed his belly with both hands as blood and slippery intestine leaked between his fingers. The Mexican ran. Acha collapsed against the wall sitting, grasping at his innards, and, trying to push them back in.

Danny and Roque ran to him; Verde followed. The three of them watched as Acha tried to stuff his guts back into his belly. Of course, he couldn't. They were slippery and kept eluding him. Gradually, his efforts became more feeble. Finally, they stopped altogether.

~The End~

History Behind the Story

In 1849, Francis F.X. Aubry, the Skimmer of the Plains, made only one trip across the Santa Fe Trail, traveling in the early fall with James White, his wife Ann, their small child, and the child's negro nurse. She would not have been the first white woman in Santa Fe but one of very few. Mr. White grew anxious with the slow pace of the caravan drawn by oxen traveling in a dry land with poor grass and decided to hurry ahead to Santa Fe with his family and a few others. At Palo Blanco Creek in eastern New Mexico, a few miles from Point of Rocks, they met the Jicarilla. Exactly what transpired is uncertain. The Jicarilla who were the only survivors still won't talk about it. The men in the party were killed; the two women and the child were taken. Mexican buffalo hunters came along later and stripped and scalped the bodies and where then attacked by Jicarilla. All were killed except one boy.

The Jicarilla (hic-ah-ree-ya) ceremonials are accurately described. My guess as to where Go Jii Ya was celebrated in olden times turned out to be very close to what the Jicarilla tell me. Today, Go Jii Ya is celebrated in September at Stone Lake south of Dulce, New Mexico, and the two clans, the Ollero (oy-yehr-roh) the White Clan and the Llanero (yahn-nehr-roh) the Red Clan still compete to keep the world in balance. The Ollero lived west of the *Sangre de Cristo* and the Llanero to the east of the mountains at the edge of the Llano Estacado, Staked Plains. Lieutenant Ambrose Burnside, later a Union general, served in New Mexico and was wounded in the neck by a Jicarilla arrow. Lobo Blanco's daughter was held as a hostage, and the mail party took her to exchange for

Mrs. White. After singing her death song, the Indian maiden met her fate. Various rewards were offered, and a variety of schemes produced rumors and scalps for years to come. The maid and the baby were never recovered.

Colonel John Munroe, thought to be the ugliest man in the Army, was department commander and didn't like New Mexico. He was in favor of giving it back to anyone who would accept it: the Mexicans, the Indians, or the dust devils and scorpions. Colonel Munroe wasn't particular.

Major William Grier mounted an expedition at Taos with Antoine Leroux as chief scout and the other mountain men named as scouts. At Rayado, he recruited Kit Carson over the great scout's protests. Carson found and followed the three-week-old trail much to everyone's astonishment. Following a plan to charge in among the Indians to which Leroux had objected, Carson rode ahead of the main body as they approached the Jicarilla camp. As the charge began, Major Grier was struck by a spent round which impacted on his heavy gloves. He called a halt and decided to attempt negotiations. Carson found himself charging alone. The Jicarilla rebuffed the attempt to negotiate while they departed with their weapons and ponies. Ann White was found dead in the camp an arrow through her heart, her body still warm. A dime novel in which Kit was the protagonist was also found and upon its being read to him, he begged to have it burned. "Having read that and knowing that I lived nearby, she must surely have thought I was coming to her rescue."

The camp was burned. One Jicarilla was killed attempting to cross the river where the rest of the tribe had gone. In his autobiography, Kit notes that he is certain that those responsible for the failure to charge with him surely have come to regret their actions.

The next day the weather descended into the worst blizzard on record. One soldier froze to death, and an unknown number of Jicarilla died of exposure. The number is thought to be large and impacted most heavily on small children.

Jicarilla caused trouble off and on for another five years. Kit was recruited first to be Indian Agent and then to chase them down. The Jicarilla would be a long time finding a reservation. They lost all of their hunting grounds on the Llano Estacado. Finally, they signed a treaty for a reservation on the Piedre Lumbre near Abiquiu. The treaty promised training, farm equipment, and subsidies until the farms were producing. Congress, however, failed to act. The treaty was presented repeatedly, but Congress still did not act. Congress was unhappy with the provisions of the Constitution that required the government to deal by treaty with the Indians. The Senate had to ratify treaties, but the House controlled the budget. The House didn't like the idea that the Senate could commit funds without their approval.

The Abiquiu land was given to a Mexican with a dubious land grant. For a while, they were sent to live with their distant cousins the Mescalero far to the south and far from home. The two tribes did not get along. Finally, they were given a remote reservation west of the Jemez Mountains running north to the Colorado border adjoining the Ute reservation. They are still there today.

Kit Carson was called on by his country to serve in the Civil War. He fought against Confederates, Navajos, and Comanches and rose to the rank of general.

About the Author

Doug Hocking grew up on the Jicarilla Apache Reservation in the Rio Arriba (Northern New Mexico). He attended reservation schools, an Ivy League prep school, and graduated from high school in Santa Cruz, New Mexico, in the Penitente heartland among *paisonos* and *Indios*. Doug enlisted in Army Intelligence out of high school and worked in Taiwan, Thailand and at the Pentagon. Returning home he studied Social Anthropology (Ethnography) and then returned to the Army as an Armored Cavalry officer (scout) completing his career by instructing Military Intelligence lieutenants in intelligence analysis and the art of war.

He has earned a master's degree with honors in American History and completed field school in Historical Archaeology. Since retiring he has worked with allied officers and taught at Cochise College. He is now an independent scholar residing in southern Arizona near Tombstone with his wife, dogs, a feral cat and a friendly coyote. He is on the board of the Southern Chapter of the Arizona Historical Society and of Westerners International and is Sheriff of the Bisbee Corral of the Westerners.

Doug began writing a few years ago and has published in *Wild West*, *True West*, *Buckskin Bulletin* and *Roundup Magazine*. His photographs have appeared in the *Arizona Republic*, *Tucson Star* and *Sacramento Bee* as well as in numerous magazines. His short story "Marshal of Arizona" appears in La Frontera's *Outlaws and Lawmen* anthology, a second, "The Bounty," appears in *Dead or Alive,* a third, "Echo Amphitheater," in *Broken Promises.* His second novel, *Mystery of Chaco Canyon*, will be in print in 2014. He is working on a biography of *Tom Jeffords, Cochise's Friend.*

Historian Will Gorenfeld said: Very readable and informative. Your knowledge and description of Aubrey's train, the men, the countryside is, thus far, superb as is Grier's failed attempt to rescue Mrs. White.

Author Gerald Summers said: Doug Hocking has done himself proud. His writing flows smoothly, his historical references are spot on, and his action exciting. I recently read Kit Carson's autobiography and found it to be one of the most interesting historical presentations I've ever read. And that is saying something, for I have studied western history for many years. Doug has captured much of this famous man and his exploits and deserves much credit for bringing him and his other wonderful characters to life. I thoroughly enjoyed this book.

Jicarilla Apache teacher from Dulce, NM, on the Jicarilla Reservation said: Written by a resident of the community - interesting story line. Reading parts to my Middle and High School classes in hopes to spark their reading interests.

Shar Porier of the Sierra Vista Herald said: It [reveals] an historical view of the life and times in New Mexico in the 1840s and '50s in a novel story, written just as one produced by western authors of the past. It is hard to set the book aside.

Greg Coar: Just finished your book. Saved it for the trip home. Loved it. Hope there is more to come. Great to meet you and your wife in Tombstone. Keep the history coming.

Dac Crassley of the Old West Daily Reader: As you know, I have a considerable interest in Western History and enough knowledge to make me dangerous. And I read a lot because of my research for Old West Daily Reader. This book was comfortable, like worn in buckskins or one's favorite Levis. Everything felt right. The story unfolded in a coherent and, for me, personal fashion. I truly appreciated and enjoyed your obvious care in building the historical background of the tale. Characters were fleshed out, real, believable. I could picture the landscapes. The trail dust…Ok, I really liked the book! Great accomplishment and a fine telling!

Rahm E. Sandoux, *Desert Tracks* (OCTA) reviewer: Doug Hocking's *Massacre at Point of Rocks* is a fascinating story of historic events along the Santa Fe Trail in 1849. Setting the White massacre and captivity in context, Hocking reveals to readers the ethnic side of of the frontier, showing how Indians, Mexicans, and blacks were just as much a part of that historical tapestry as the white men were. He brings characters like Kit Carson, Grier, Comancheros, and the Jicarilla Apaches to life, revealing how tough life was on the frontier for all of its inhabitants. *Massacre at Point of Rocks* will definitely be of interest to readers who want to learn more about the history of New Mexico and the Santa Fe Trail.